The Shattered Throne

The Kronicles of Korthlundia

Book III

BY: JAMIE MARCHANT

BEWITCHING FABLES PRESS

Cover designed by Lou Harper

ISBN: print 978-0-9978624-9-2
PUBLISHED BY BEWITCHING FABLES PRESS
Printed in the United States of America

To Jim Elston,

The Best Friend a Writer Could Have

ACKNOWLEDGEMENTS

The author wishes to express her extreme gratitude to the members of the Robrek Steele Conspiracy Writers' Group: Jack Dickson, Jim Elston, Lexi Mitchell, and John O'Connor. (I wrote the names in alphabetical order, so don't go quibbling about order of importance.) I owe a special debt to Jim, who has been there for me since my first novel, *The Goddess's Choice*, and is still there for me today. He deserves a full paragraph acknowledgement, but he'll have to settle for sharing the same paragraph with the group and with Panera Bread who allows us to occupy a booth every Friday. I also thank my beta readers: Sherry Arnold, Angie McLaughlin Kipp, and Elliot C. Mendelson.

I wish to thank my husband Tim and son Jesse for their love and patience throughout this process. I also owe a debt to my oldest sister Jalane who introduced me to the wonders of storytelling as a child. She has supported and believed in me throughout the years

I am grateful to my sensei, Travis Page, who taught me everything I know about fighting and didn't look askance at me when I asked him the best way to kill someone with a staff.

Cheree Castellanos provided excellent editorial assistance. Lou Harper designed the beautiful cover.

CONTENTS

MAP OF KORTHLUNDIA

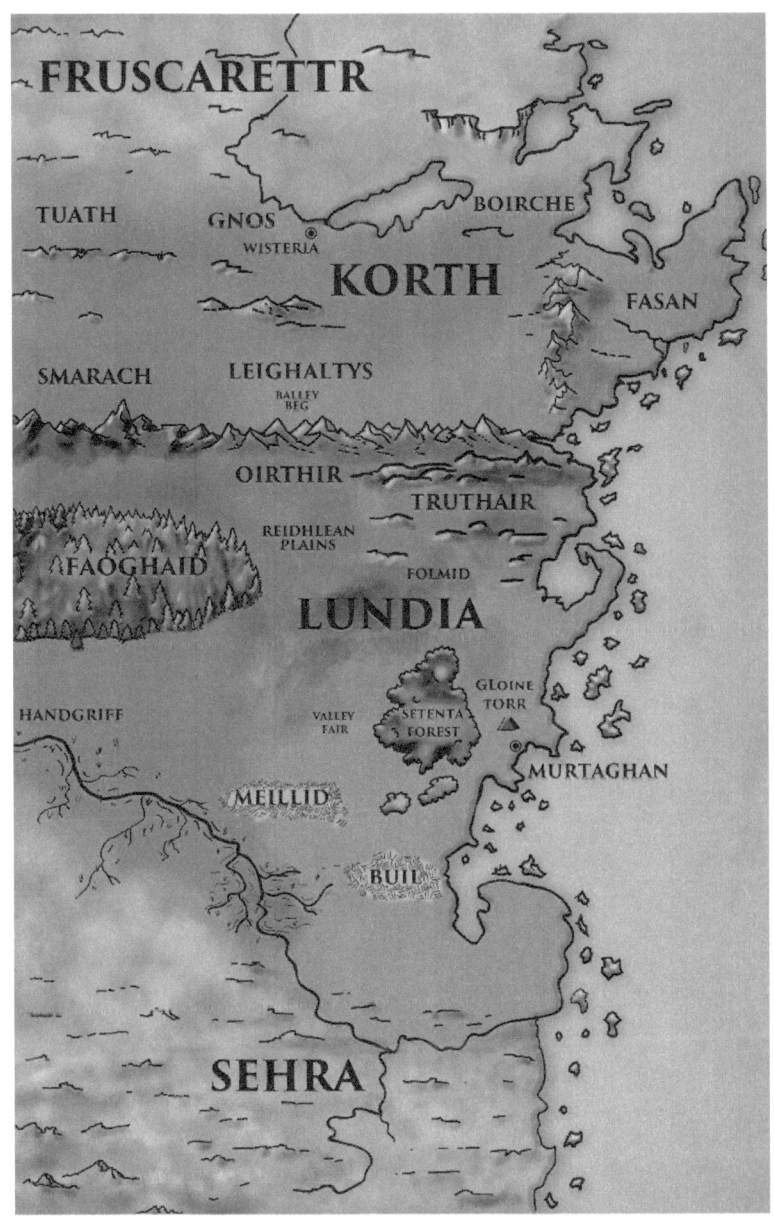

FRUSCARETTR

TUATH   GNOS   BOIRCHE
          WISTERIA
          KORTH   FASAN

SMARACH   LEIGHALTYS
          BALLEY
          BEG

          OIRTHIR
                    TRUTHAIR
          REIDHLEAN
          PLAINS
FAOGHAID   FOLMID

          LUNDIA

                    GLOINE
                    TORR
HANDGRIFF   VALLEY SETENTA
            FAIR   FOREST
                    MURTAGHAN

          MEILLID

            BUIL

          SEHRA

CAST OF CHARACTERS

Adalardo—Master of the Horse
Aislinn—Count Morfran's daughter; beloved of Lord Devyn
Altherr—Count Cadarn's university professor
Angus Camlinstamm—Robrek's father
Annagret—Hero of Svizran Revolution (deceased)
Arawn—Baron of Buil; Lundian
Ardra—Samantha's maid
Artan—Lundian novice
Barris—Mayor of Murtaghan
Bartle—Member of the Royal Guard
Bary—Member of Brianna's personal guard
Bearach—Member of Samantha's personal guard
Black Giant—Member of the Royal Guard
Blaine—Samantha's personal secretary
Brigitta—Darhour's wife
Brandon—Member of Brianna's personal guard
Brianna—Crown Princess of Korthlundia; Samantha's daughter
Cadarn—Count; member of the Royal Council
Calum—royal physician
Calvagh—Duke Sheen's steward
Cameron—Lundian priest
Cara—Angus's servant
Cece—Brianna's nurse; Ardra's sister
Cedric—Duke Sheen's second son
Conroy—Captain of Samantha's personal guard
Daray—Priest of the True Church of Sulis
Darhour, aka Sigurd—Former captain of Samantha's personal guard; Samantha's true father
Devyn—Duke Sheen's oldest son and heir
Donall—Baroness Eithne's footman
Donavan—Member of Brianna's personal guard
Donella—Robrek's mother; Angus's wife (deceased)
Drem—Robrek's personal servant
Dritan— Hero of Svizran Revolution (deceased)

Druce—Chief librarian
Duer—Samantha's spymaster
Dympna—Leigh's mother
Eadoin—Assistant to Father Faolan; later high priest of the True Church of Sulis
Edan—Member of the Royal Guard
Eghan—Baroness Eithne's footman
Eithne—Baroness; member of the Royal Council
Ennis—Servant of Leigh's father
Eolande—A Bard
Ewan—Member of Samantha's personal guard
Faolan---High priest of the True Church of Sulis
Fergal Taranstamm—Dealer in paipin leaves; Leigh's father
Fenella—Solar's third wife; mother of Samantha (deceased)
Fiacre—Duke Sheen's Master of the Horse
Flann Flannstamm—Murtaghan Baker
Floyd—A squire
Gael—Lord Duer's servant
Garran—Undersecretary in the palace library
Garrett—Undersecretary in the palace library
Gawladys—Vaughan's mother
Gerard—Lieutenant in the Royal Guard; later Captain of the Protectorate guard
Glynnis—Baroness; Baron Gwawl's wife
Golden Drop—A whore at the Jeweled Plum Tree
Guthrie—Member of Samantha's personal guard
Gwawl—Baron; Samantha's chancellor
Hafghan—High Priest of the Lundian church
Hawk—Captain of the Royal Guard
Henwas—Woodcarver of Nios Mo
Hueil—Weapons master of the squires
Iachus—Member of Brianna's personal guard
Irvine Keirstamm—Chief magistrate of Murtaghan
Jarlath—Member of the Royal Guard
Jennyfer—Stew maker of Nios Mo
Jodoc—Duke's Sheen's servant
Kelvin—Captain of Brianna's personal guard
Leigh Fergalstamm—Lundian priest
Maella—Neighbor of Vaughan's mother

Mack Mackstamm—Murtaghan blacksmith
Madam Plum—The proprietor of the Jeweled Plum Tree
Maeron—A squire
Maggie—Chief cook
Makan—Blacksmith in Korth
Malvina—Samantha's maid
Malvyn—Duke Sheen's marshal
Marcan—Member of Samantha's personal guard
Nara—Vaughan's sister
Neale Cedricstamm—Murtaghan weaver
Nealie—Vaughan's sister
Nealon—Count; Cadarn's father (deceased)
Nisse Hauptmann—Svizran mercenary captain
Oriana—Korthian novice
Ormande—Duke Sheen's Master of the Horse
Owen—Undersecretary in palace librarian; later chief librarian
Padrig—Son of Count Guto
Pandaran—Count of Fasan; member of the Royal Council
Pepper—Vaughan's Mule
Purple Leaf—Whore at the Jeweled Plum Tree
Quinn—Oriana's brother
Roberta—Samantha's horse
Robrek Angusstamm, aka Robbie—King of Korthlundia; Samantha's consort
Ronan—Robrek's cat
Rosvald—Count Cadarn's steward
Rhonda—Neighbor of Vaughan's mother
Ruadh—Member of the Protectorate guard
Samantha—Queen of Korthlundia
Sawyer—Peasant on Count Cadarn's estate
Sheen—Duke of Gnos; Korthian
Skye—Vaughan's sister
Slathek—Robrek's uncle
Solar—Former King of Korthlundia; father who raised Samantha as his own (deceased)
Teague—Baron of Smarach; member of the Royal Council
Tierney—Duke of Handgriff; member of the Royal Council
Tuathal—Blaine's assistant
Turi—Angus's servant

Ultan—Count of Folmid; member of the Royal Council
Varney—Member of the Royal Guard
Vaughan—Robrek's squire
Weylin—Count of Faoghaid; member of the Royal Council
Whiskers—Vaughan's horse
Wild Thing—Robrek's former horse
Wynne—Vaughan's brother
York—Priest of the True Church of Sulis
Zethar—Mayor of Nios Mo
Zinerva—Lady Aislinn's maid

CHAPTER 1

Exhausted from childbirth, Queen Samantha I of Korthlundia held her newborn daughter and heir in her arms and whispered, "Brianna, I'm your momma. Your momma loves you." But to call what she felt "love" was wholly inadequate. She'd felt love before but this intense desire to hold, nurture, and protect her daughter? This she couldn't even name. Tears streamed down her cheeks as she counted Brianna's fingers and toes. Her skin was lighter than her father's, more a chestnut compared to Robbie's walnut, but her eyes were a brilliant green that matched his. There was only the lightest of fuzz on her head, but Samantha thought it would be auburn like her own.

"She's perfect," she breathed.

Baroness Glynnis, a plump middle-aged woman, beamed down at the baby. The baroness had been her mother's best friend. "Fenella would be so proud of you. Now, her granddaughter can show the power of women as well." The baroness's words warmed Samantha's heart as she thought of the mother she'd never known. She glanced above the fireplace at the portrait of her parents that she'd had moved from the royal gallery. Her father was seated on the throne, his long white hair and beard flowing around his head. Next to the throne, stood her mother. As love for her own daughter filled Samantha's heart, she realized for the first time how deeply her parents had loved her.

Oriana, her hair braided into the hundreds of small braids favored by the Korthian priesstesshood, touched Brianna's arm. The fourteen-year-old novice had helped Samantha give birth. "I thought her magic was strong when she was still in the womb, but when I touch her now, it almost bursts inside of me. I still can't tell what form her magic will take, but it will be very, very powerful."

Scratching at the narrow nose that betrayed his half-Saloynan heritage, Father Leigh collapsed into a chair. A healer, like Oriana, he'd too helped in the delivery. They were two of the rare true healers in the joined kingdoms. "Even from this distance," he sighed, "the happiness of Her Highness's magic pulses inside me."

At that moment, colors erupted around the baby—a wild, dancing mixture that included all colors of the rainbow and lit up the queen's heart with joy and excitement. Samantha was an Aurora, gifted by the goddess to see the colorful auras that surround every human being and reveal their character. Seeing an aura was always accompanied by feelings or sensations that sometimes helped the queen understand the colors' meaning. All she could tell from her daughter's aura was it made her happy.

Samantha first began seeing auras when she began to bleed in the ways of a woman, but their appearance had been random and sporadic. The texts promised that once she'd born a child, she'd be able to call forth auras at will. She didn't yet know if that were true, but she'd never seen an aura quite like her daughter's. She gasped. "Her aura is brilliant and sparkling! She will bring back her father. You'll see." This was the one hope she'd clung to since Robbie had been so badly injured destroying the Soul Stone.

The two healers looked away. They had told her this was a vain hope, that the love of her life was no longer truly alive, despite the fact that he breathed and his heart beat. Even Glynnis shifted in her chair and became interested in the painting above the fireplace. But Brianna would show them all. She'd bring her father back to himself, and Samantha decided she wouldn't wait another moment to hear her name on Robbie's lips again.

She called Brianna's nurse forward and handed the baby to her. Then she swung her legs over the side of her bed. Oriana grabbed her arm. "Your Majesty, it's too early to get up. You must rest and recover."

Sure enough, her legs trembled, so Samantha put her hand on Oriana's shoulder to rise. "I'm taking Brianna to her father. Don't try to stop me."

Oriana opened her mouth to object, but Father Leigh held up a hand. "It's only a short distance to the king's quarters, and Her Majesty needs to see for herself before she'll believe us."

Oriana backed away, and Glynnis took her arm and said, "If you're going to insist, let me help you."

Samantha accepted the baroness's support in making the trip to Robbie's quarters. The nurse followed, carrying the most precious treasure in the world. Her guards surrounded them. When she reached Robbie's quarters, his guards bowed to her.

With a small squeeze of her arm, the baroness wished her well as the guards stood aside for her and the nurse carrying Brianna. When she entered her husband's reception room, his personal servant, Drem, bowed. "Your Majesty."

The love of her life sat on a sofa, staring at a blank spot on the wall. She carefully lowered herself next to him. As the heir to the throne, the one thing Samantha had thought she would never have in her marriage was love, but Robbie had filled her heart and soul with it. In moments, he would do so again.

She touched Robbie's shoulder gently. "Robbie, my love, I know you're in there. Please, look at me."

He continued to stare at nothing. Ronan, the gray-striped cat that had followed Robbie all the way from his father's farm, sat in Robbie's lap, but Robbie didn't pet it. The cat was just one of the many things Robbie seemed not to notice these days.

"Robbie, I've brought our daughter. Look at her." Robbie didn't even blink. Ignoring the horrible burn scars on his hand, she took it in hers. "You're a father now. I've brought her to meet you."

She reached for her daughter, and the nurse relinquished her. She gently pushed Ronan aside so she could place Brianna on Robbie's lap. The cat hissed as it jumped to the floor. After laying Brianna down, she placed Robbie's hand on their daughter's sweet head. Samantha almost cried at the contrast between Robbie's dark, rock-like skin and Brianna's smooth perfection. "Here she is. You feel her, don't you? You are the most powerful healer Korthlundia has seen in centuries. You felt her presence when she was nothing but a speck within me. You have to feel her now!"

Robbie continued to stare at nothing. Samantha put her hand on his chest and felt the steady thump of his heart. "You have to come back from wherever you are. The Holy Mother wouldn't take you from me! Not after everything we've been through!"

When he failed to make any response, she brushed the curly black hair back from his forehead. The right side of his face still held the exotic beauty that had drawn her to him that long-ago day at the horse fair. With trembling hand, she touched his chin and turned his face toward her. Even though she'd seen the damage many times, she let out a low moan. His hair grew only on the right side of his head. The left was bare, and the skin looked like boiling lava had pushed its way through his scalp and solidified. The damage flowed down the left side of his face and neck, then disappeared under his collar, concealed by his clothing. Gently, she touched the left side of his head where his ear should have been. The skin felt more like rubber than flesh, and an ornate eye patch hid his empty eye socket. She shuddered as she again imagined the agony he must have felt when the Soul Stone exploded. Her heart breaking, she whispered, "Holy Sulis, Robbie, was it the pain that drove you out of yourself?"

She turned the damaged side of his face away from her and placed his other hand on their daughter as well. "Sulis, Mother of us all," she said in a voice loud enough to ensure the goddess heard her Beyond the Far Mountain, "he destroyed the Ancient Evil that was sucking the life out of your land and your people. It isn't fair that his bravery should cost him his soul. Bring him back! You owe that to him! You owe that to me!"

But, as before, the goddess refused to acknowledge her demands, and her husband's eye remained blank. "No!" she shouted. "You are a father! You will know your daughter! You will know me!"

Brianna began to cry, but Robbie made no response. She put a soothing hand on Brianna, and again the baby's aura burst forth. Before Brianna's, Robbie's had been the most colorful, alive aura she'd ever seen. The brilliant bronze, silver, and gold dancing around him had drawn her to him. Fearing what she would find, she hesitated to try to call his aura forth.

She chided herself. *It will be there. It has to be.* She concentrated, but nothing happened. Not even a slight hint of color appeared.

No! No! Everyone has an aura. I must be doing it wrong. She looked at Robbie's servant and nearly wailed as the smallest exertion of her will caused color to bloom around Drem, a blue so bland it nearly put her to sleep. He was loyal but dull. She turned to Brianna's nurse. When the nurse erupted with bright purple and copper, a thick slime seemed to flow over Samantha, and she found herself unconsciously rubbing her fingers together as if she were caressing coins. *Holy Sulis, how did I ever allow this woman near my daughter!* The greedy wench could be bought. "Wait outside," she ordered the woman. She would see the woman tossed from the palace, but first she had to find Robbie.

When the nurse was gone, Samantha whirled back to her husband and tried again. But no matter how strongly she willed it, nothing happened. *Nothing? If he has no aura, Leigh and Oriana must be right. He's gone. He's truly gone. How can the goddess be this cruel?* With tears streaming down her face, she was forced to face the ultimate betrayal: Robbie had given everything for Sulis, and Sulis had taken him from himself. The goddess had allowed the love of her life to die.

Now she was truly alone. She was only twenty years old. She was queen of a kingdom plagued with problems from the church as well as from within the Royal Council itself. Duke Sheen had long opposed her, believing that women didn't have the mental capacity to lead. His disrespect grew worse when she married Robbie instead of his son, and she was now certain he was on the edge of outright rebellion. She had no one to help with either problem.

It wasn't fair! It wasn't right! But if the goddess thought Samantha would crumble, Sulis was about to find out how wrong she was. Samantha resolved that, except for Brianna, she would never let love touch her again. She'd take her love and pour it into her people instead. She'd show them all the queen Solar raised her to be. And damn to the seven hells anyone who challenged her, even if the challenger were Sulis herself!

* * *

Still raging at the goddess for what Sulis had taken from her, Samantha's entire body was rigid as she entered the nursery of her two-day old baby. But when she put her daughter to her breast and Brianna suckled from her, her body began to relax and she started to hum a lullaby she'd heard from the bard Eolande. She smoothed the tiny bits of hair on Brianna's otherwise bald head. "Holy Sulis, Brianna, you're all I have left. But I'll be the best mother to you the joined kingdoms have ever seen. I love you, sweetheart. Momma loves you."

Brianna let go, and Samantha brought the baby to her shoulder and patted her back. Brianna burped and fell asleep. This chance to feed her daughter was a precious gift, but she couldn't keep it up. A queen's schedule didn't allow her to be available at all the hours a newborn needed. She had Blaine, her personal secretary, organizing a search for a new wet nurse to replace the one she'd dismissed.

There was a knock on the door, and Ardra, her maid, entered. Ardra had served her for years and was closer to a friend than a servant. She was accompanied by a woman barely out of her teens with the same white blond hair, small stature, and round face. The younger woman was dressed in rags and looked weak and sickly. Her guards and Brianna's entered with the women.

Ardra and her relative curtsied. "Your Majesty, may I introduce my sister Cece?" Cece's eyes darted around the room, as if she were looking for a place to hide.

Samantha bit her lip. Ardra should know better than to bring a sick person into the presence of a vulnerable newborn. "Ardra, I'd love to meet your sister, but perhaps you should have Calum see to her. She doesn't look well." Calum was the royal physician.

Ardra put her arm around her sister. "Cece's not sick, Your Majesty. I wouldn't have brought her to see the little princess if she were. She's just weak since she gave birth two days ago, the same day Your Majesty did. Her poor baby was too small and only lived for half a day. She still has her milk, though, and I know you're looking for a wet nurse for the little one."

Samantha hugged Brianna closer, at the sudden fear that Sulis might try to take her daughter. If the goddess dared do that, she'd travel Beyond the Far Mountain herself and demand her daughter back. The thought of losing her child made Samantha want to hug the bereaved woman. With a slight exercise of will, Cece's aura immediately burst around her—pink and blue. Samantha felt almost as if she were a child again, cuddling the king on his lap, his comforting arm wrapped around her. Cece would give Brianna the same love and care she'd have given her own child, the love Solar had given her. "Would you like to nurse my daughter?" she asked.

Cece's eyes snapped to the baby and then down to the floor. "Your Majesty, I'd love to have a baby to care for." The way Cece had glanced at Brianna told her how much the young woman's heart was hurting. "But I know I'm not worthy of the honor. Ardra insisted on bringing me to you, but I'm sure Your Majesty will want someone better than a whore to feed the crown princess." Tears ran down Cece's cheeks. She wiped at them, but she couldn't stop them.

Ardra made a noise of disgust and squeezed her sister. "Don't talk that way about yourself. Your Majesty, my sister isn't a whore. She wasn't married to her baby's father—the cad left her as soon as he got her pregnant. But he's the only man she's been with. Our parents threw her out when she couldn't hide the pregnancy any longer. She came to Murtaghan looking for me, hoping I would help her. But she gave birth before she worked up the courage to send a note to me at the palace, and then her baby died. I've never asked you for anything, Your Majesty, and I haven't the right to ask for this but please, Your Majesty. Cece will take right good care of the little one, if you let her. She's a good girl."

As her maid's eyes pleaded with her, Samantha thought of all Ardra had done for her over the years. When Duke Argblutal had attempted to force Samantha into marriage, Ardra had taken her place in order to give Samantha time to escape the palace. She did so fully expecting the duke to kill her for the deception.

Samantha smiled at Cece and spoke softly. "I owe your sister a great debt. I'd be happy to have you care for my daughter." She turned to Ardra. "I've just fed Brianna, so it will be a little while before she needs to eat again. Get your sister a bath and something to eat. See that she's supplied with decent clothing and anything else she needs to get herself settled. The nurse's room is just through there." She pointed to a room at the back of the nursery

While Ardra burst into a smile, Cece fell to her knees. "Your Majesty, thank you, thank you. I promise I'll care for the little princess as if she were my own."

Samantha had no doubt she would.

* * *

When Iachus reported for duty, Captain Kelvin informed him and his partner Donovan that a new wet nurse had been found for the princess. "She's the sister of Her Majesty's maid, Ardra, and Her Majesty trusts her. Still, it wouldn't hurt us to be a bit cautious until we're sure of her."

"Yes, sir," Iachus said, and patted his sword hilt. He'd make sure no one touched the princess on his watch. He was still ecstatic he'd been chosen for the crown princess's personal guard. He had no idea how he'd earned the honor. He was good with his sword, but there were some better who hadn't been chosen. He couldn't have been chosen out of personal regard. Before being picked for the princess's guard, he'd hardly exchanged more than a dozen words with Her Majesty. Being the oldest of nine children, he was fond of little ones, but the queen surely didn't know that.

In fact, the queen's method of choosing the members of the princess's guard had been odd. She'd summoned them to the training arena, but she hadn't had them demonstrate their skills or asked them any questions. Holding the baby princess at her shoulder, she'd simply walked down the line and looked at each of them closely. Iachus couldn't imagine what she was looking for, but since Iachus was chosen, he couldn't fault her method.

What he hadn't anticipated was that, if no one attacked, being a guard didn't actually give one much to do. He couldn't stop thinking that a person he'd never met was alone with his charge. "I'm going to check on the princess," he told Donovan.

"The Captain came out of there just before you showed up."

Iachus ignored him and went in. A petite young woman sat in a rocker with the princess at her breast, and, Holy Sulis, were they admirable breasts. He'd never believed in love at first sight but one glance at the princess's nurse, and he was certain he was in love. She looked a lot like Ardra, with her pale blond hair and milky white skin, but there was a vulnerability in her eyes that roused the protector in him. She was so small she'd fit perfectly beneath his arm, and Iachus instantly wanted to spend the rest of his life holding her there and keeping her safe.

Turning a deep red, she made a small noise and scrambled to drape a blanket over herself and the baby.

Iachus turned his eyes away. "Sorry, I just wanted to introduce myself. I'm Iachus, one of Her Highness's personal guards."

"N-nice to me you. I'm Cece," she said in a voice so timid he could barely hear her. Her eyes flashed to his sword, and she fiddled with the blanket to make sure she was fully covered. "I'm feeding the baby." It was clear she wanted him out of the room.

"Ah, yes, we can get to know each other later."

"I'd like that," she said in a manner that told him she wished him to fall through the floor and into the depths of the seven hells.

What a way to make a first impression! He damned himself as he returned to his post outside the nursery.

* * *

Blaine, the queen's secretary, hurried toward the king's room, as he did every morning. He hoped against hope that he might have some good news to bring the queen this time. He stared at the papers in his hand. Since the queen had given birth only a week ago, it seemed wrong to bring her nothing but an endless list of duties she needed to attend to.

When he entered the king's room, Drem was reading aloud to the king. Blaine focused his attention on the servant, trying not to see the ruined shell of the king. The servant stopped reading and stood but didn't bow his head. The omission was a clear statement of Drem's belief he was Blaine's equal. While Drem was merely a body servant, he thought serving the king gave him special status. Blaine didn't have the time or the desire to play such silly games. He had a queen to serve and a kingdom to help her run. Despite his panic when the queen named him to this position, he hadn't let her down yet, and he didn't plan to fail her now. "How is the king this morning? Did he eat his breakfast?"

"He ate as he always does. Once I get him started with the spoon, he will continue eating until nothing is left on the plate. I was reading to him to help with his digestion."

"And does the king seem to enjoy your reading to him?"

Drem stiffened. "Are you questioning the way I perform my duties?"

Blaine rolled his eyes. Servants could be pricklier about status than nobles. "I was no more questioning your performance than I was questioning the clouds about how much rain they've been providing, so to speak. I am on my way to the queen, and I hoped to have something to report to Her Majesty."

Drem's shoulders relaxed, and a compassion Blaine had never witnessed before stole over the servant's face. "It was heartbreaking to see the king fail to respond to the baby princess." He glanced at the king, then he looked back at Blaine. "No, the king doesn't react to my reading or to anything else. I think the healers are right. He isn't truly alive anymore."

Blaine put his hand over his heart, as if the queen's loss were his own. The goddess could certainly be cruel at times.

* * *

When Blaine arrived at the queen's rooms, she was dressed and eating breakfast. The only signs of her recent childbirth were a few lines around her eyes. *Holy Sulis, she's quite a queen!* She even managed to give him a tired smile when he bowed to her. He'd fallen in love with that smile when he was only five years old and the queen three. He never imagined he'd get a chance to speak with her, let alone serve her as he did now.

"Good morning, Blaine. Have a seat and tell me what you have for me today." She gestured him into a chair where a mug of *bhat* was waiting for him. The hot drink made from roasted bhat beans and sweet cream had been the king's favorite. Even in her grief, the queen never forgot her courtesies.

Blaine took a sip before he turned to his list. "Considering Your Majesty has just given birth, I have canceled today's court session." The queen tapped a finger on the arm of her chair, and Blaine knew what she was thinking. "No one will blame Your Majesty for taking a single week off after the birth of a baby. Even among the lower classes, most women lie in for at least three weeks. If anyone has a petition that can't wait, they can bring it to Baron Gwawl. What's a chancellor for after all?"

The queen hesitated a second longer, then nodded. "You're right as usual. A single week to recover my strength isn't unreasonable."

Blaine opened his mouth to protest that she needed the rest but closed it as he realized he'd won the point and went back to his list. "The delegation you sent to Korth has returned. Baroness Eithne accompanied it and has requested an audience." The passes into Korth had remained clogged with snow far longer than usual this spring, but as soon as they'd cleared, the queen had sent a delegation to assess the needs of her people in wake of the damage the Soul Stone had caused. Although Blaine had been careful not to mention the stone, the queen's eyes sparked and her body tensed. *Sulis, Mother of us all, how could you take him from her?*

The queen seemed to force her body to relax. "I will, of course, grant her an audience."

"I knew Your Majesty would feel that way and have informed the baroness that you will see her within half an hour." Blaine looked at his list. "After the baroness, Lord Duer has a report for you." Blaine glanced at the queen. Lord Duer was the queen's spymaster, and not a very competent one at that. He was supposed to be ferreting out the hiding place of Father Faolan, leader of the so-called True Church of Sulis and condemned traitor. His followers rescued him from execution. They'd also tried to force Her Majesty to drink a potion that would have driven the spark of the baby's life from her. They'd failed in this, but the high priest had escaped and was still at large somewhere.

The queen was touchy about Duer's continued inability to find the rogue priest. Darhour, who'd been the queen's chief bodyguard and former spymaster, would have found the priest by now. But for reasons Blaine could never understand, Darhour had deserted the queen after slaughtering Duke Argblutal, the first man to threaten the queen's throne. The desertion was even more inexplicable given that Darhour had had an affair with the queen's mother long ago and was Her Majesty's true father. The queen took his desertion hard, but this morning she did nothing more than nod her acknowledgment. *Holy Sulis, what a woman!*

But that brought him to the last item on his list. Anticipating resistance, he let his words out in a rush. "Your Majesty has surely heard stories of the great festival King Solar threw to celebrate your birth. Along with Your Majesty, the people have endured loss, and they need a celebration of the birth of your heir as badly as a duck needs water, so to speak. It would also help cement the people's support behind you in the wake of the True Church of Sulis's opposition to your reign. Litha is just a month away. The summer solstice would be an excellent time for such a celebration, with the longest day of the year being linked to the brightness of the princess's healthy birth and the anticipation of Your Majesty's long reign."

The queen's lip quivered, but to Blaine's surprise, her only question was, "Can you put everything together in such a short time?"

Once, such a task would have sent Blaine into a hysterical panic but no longer, he'd successfully planned several such celebrations. "It might not be as easy as getting wet in a rainstorm, so to speak, but it can be done, Your Majesty."

"See that it is done. Father Hafghan should be asked to bless the princess when she is presented to the people." Unlike his rival, high priest Faolan, Hafghan was loyal to the crown and had proven useful in the past.

Blaine nodded. "Of course, Your Majesty."

"Brianna is a precious gift. Make sure the celebration reflects this." An expression of maternal tenderness lit the queen's face and nearly brought tears to Blaine's eyes. The king's tragedy hadn't completely crushed the queen's softer emotions. Her eyes cleared, and she gave a little laugh. "You've already been planning it for months now, haven't you?"

Blaine looked at his feet and then nodded. "I hope Your Majesty doesn't find me presumptuous, but I didn't want to bother you in your grief over the king's injuries."

Rather than seeming angry, the queen's eyes softened, and she reached across the table and squeezed his arm. "Thank you, Blaine. No queen could ask for a better secretary. I don't know how I could manage without you."

With a familiarity that Blaine would never have presumed earlier, he put his other hand over the queen's and gave their culture's most sacred oath. "Your Majesty, this I swear by the goddess and on my mother's grave, as long as there is breath in my body, you will never have to manage without me."

Neither of them moved for a few moments, but then they simultaneously broke apart. "Should I show the baroness in, Your Majesty? She will surely be waiting."

The queen nodded. "Please do."

* * *

Accompanied by Samantha's guards, a rather plainly dressed middle aged woman entered. Her hair was pulled back in a bun that didn't flatter her. The baroness bowed, and when she straightened, the queen noted how tall she was. Samantha would barely come to her chest. While Samantha was particularly short for a Korthlundian woman, Eithne was taller than most men, and in her late thirties, she looked fit enough to take most of them on in a fight. She was also one of the few women in the joined kingdoms who ruled a barony in her own right rather than through her husband. In addition, since Count Kayne had been executed two years ago, she'd been managing his estates for his nephew's sake. She'd spent little time at court, and Samantha didn't know her well. The Soul Stone had resided in the heart of Kayne's lands, and hers abutted them. Extending into Korth in all directions, the Stone had sucked all life from the land. Not even insects survived. Samantha was uncertain if the Dead Lands encroached upon Eithne's holdings, but they would have at least come close.

Samantha offered her a seat and refreshment. When the older woman was comfortably settled with a glass of wine, Samantha addressed her. "Baroness, I'm happy that you chose to accompany my delegation on its return to Murtaghan. I will, of course, hear their report, but perhaps you can give me your personal assessment on the needs of the people affected by the Ancient Evil."

The baroness's shoulders relaxed, as if a vast burden had just been removed. "Your Majesty, I have prayed long and hard to the goddess for relief. 'Bad' doesn't begin to cover the state of the people. As the Dead Lands spread, refugees fled from Leighaltys into Cailleachail. I fed them through the winter as best as I could, but my larder runs low. I won't have enough stock left to feed both my people and the refugees until a harvest is possible. Worse, the long winter lingering in the mountains kept me from seeking help from the crown before Spring planting. I had seed only to sow half of my fields and little enough to give to the refugees to return and plant their own farms. It is now too late in the season to sow more grain, and this year's harvest will be small.

"And it's not just grain. Most of these poor farmers lost all of their livestock to the Soul Stone. Most of my own flocks and herds were needed to feed everybody through the winter. Without the crown's assistance, starvation will be widespread in the coming winter."

Samantha's insides jolted at the word "starvation." While poverty had never been entirely absent from the joined kingdoms, under her father no one had ever starved, and no one would now. "Milady, this I will not allow. Please provide my secretary a list of your people's needs. We will not send you back into Korth empty handed."

The baroness beamed at her. "Your Majesty, Sulis has blessed this people in providing you to be your father's heir."

As the baroness left, Samantha wondered if the goddess had forgotten the people as thoroughly as she seemed to have forgotten her. Solar had always placed the needs of the people over the accumulation of royal wealth, so it was unlikely that the crown had enough resources to meet Korth's need. Worse, she didn't know if she could count on the Royal Council to support her. Many of the nobles lacked Solar's generosity of spirit. She heard again her father's words: "The needs of the people are a ruler's first responsibility, and she must always find a way to get the nobles to agree on this whether they like it or not. Often, they won't. No matter how much or how little people have, they always seem to want more." Her father had always been able to play the various nobles off against each other to ensure that the common people prospered. Holy Sulis bless that she could do the same.

But before she could think of strategies to deal with the Royal Council, Blaine announced Lord Duer.

After Duer was seated with a glass of wine, he cleared his throat. "I'm afraid I don't have anything to report concerning Father Faolan's whereabouts. His fanatics have hidden him well." Duer sipped more wine before continuing. "I have other disturbing news concerning the 'True Church.' Count Ultan has been seen entering the Shrine of the True Believer on at least two occasions." Samantha's nostrils flared at the thought of a member of the Royal Council consorting with the church that tried to kill her daughter. "Gael followed him there yesterday afternoon. The count was escorted into the back to speak with Father Eadoin." Eadoin was Father Faolan's chief assistant and had taken public control of the heretical congregation. "I'm afraid I haven't been able to learn what they discussed, but the count has always been something of a zealot himself."

"Have him watched more closely," Samantha commanded.

"I will, Your Majesty. There is one additional thing. A select group of worshipers from the True Church have been having Sulis's star tattooed on the back of their right hand. I have yet to determine the tattoo's significance."

Samantha gripped the arms of her chair more tightly but gave no other sign of her impatience. *Did Lord Duer not know anything of importance?*

* * *

With his novice Artan chopping herbs beside him, Father Leigh inventoried their potion making supplies. No matter how many times he counted them, no magical increase occurred. He'd sent a requisition to the Temple of the Mother's Love over two weeks ago, but his requisition had yet to be filled. Since Leigh's shrine was in one of the poorest sections of the city, he received little coin in offerings. When Father Hafghan had appointed Leigh to the position, the high priest had promised to support the shrine from the general church fund, but Leigh's every request was met with endless delays. To get what he needed, he'd have to go to the temple and again talk to the high priest.

It had been when His Majesty convinced Father Hafghan that having mixed blood was necessary for magical ability that the high priest had ordained Leigh. Because of the church's long-standing church doctrine on the importance of blood purity, some considered this heresy. Father Faolan had challenged Hafghan's right to the high priesthood. When Faolan lost, he'd split with the church, taking not quite half of the clergy with him. He formed The True Church of Sulis and laid claim to many of the temples and shrines in the city. Some of the clergy blamed Leigh for the schism.

Leigh sighed deeply, then scratched his narrow nose that proved he wasn't a pure blooded Korthlundian. He and Artan, the boy had an extremely large nose, were quite a pair, and neither of them was truly welcomed in the church. Leigh glanced at the potion boiling over the fire and nodded to Artan. "It's ready."

Artan got down from his chair and put his hand over the cauldron to add his magic to the mix, making it much more powerful than potions made with herbs alone. Whenever possible, Leigh had his novice add the magic. Although Artan was only ten years old, his magic was much stronger than Leigh's.

After Artan finished with the potion, Leigh gave him instructions on what to work on while he was gone. But before he could leave, he heard voices in the sanctuary. Leigh left the stillroom to see what his parishioners needed. When he entered the sanctuary, instead of parishioners, he found two priests. A relatively young one Leigh didn't know faced him. The man was huge, at least a head taller than Leigh, and he had Sulis's star tattooed on the back of his right hand. The second priest had his back to Leigh, examining the small stars on the wall that some of the children had made from wood scraps.

Something about the priests roused his healing senses, and his stomach quivered.

Fighting nausea, Leigh asked, "How may I help you?" The second priest turned, and Leigh gasped as he recognized Father Eadoin, Father Faolan's second in command from the True Church of Sulis. As Leigh looked at the priest's small beady eyes, he shivered. Leigh's voice turned frosty. "You're not welcome here."

Eadoin snorted and addressed the priest accompanying him. "Odd. I thought the sign out front claimed this shrine welcomed all of Sulis's children."

Leigh had made the sign himself to let the poverty-stricken know they wouldn't be turned away by their lack of ability to pay. Caught by his own words, Leigh folded his arms. "What do you want?"

Eadoin continued to address the other priest as if Leigh wasn't there. "So, this is Hafghan's pet, the *cothla* dog he claims proves his heresy that tainting the blood is necessary for Sulis's magic to manifest. He doesn't look like much."

Leigh stiffened at the use of the offensive slur for those with mixed blood. "Get out!" He pointed to the door.

Eadoin continued to avoid addressing Leigh directly. "Father York, ask the dog where his puppy is, so that we may examine it for His Holiness."

Not wanting the priests anywhere near Artan, Leigh said, "He isn't here. I sent him on an errand."

But as Leigh spoke, a crash came from the stillroom. Eadoin's lips curled. "One shouldn't be surprised when a dog lies. Fetch it for me." Eadoin nodded toward the stillroom.

Leigh hurriedly blocked the door with his body. "You will get near Artan over my dead body."

York looked toward Eadoin, who nodded. "Fetch the puppy."

As the huge priest took hold of Leigh's arm, Leigh shut his eyes and reached for his magic. The power to heal was also the power to harm. Leigh concentrated on sending heat into the man's hands.

Father York screamed and released him. As Leigh opened his eyes, York stumbled back, staring at his hands, which were covered with blisters.

Swaying with exhaustion, Leigh again pointed to the door. "Get out!"

Seeing his assistant's damaged hands, Father Eadoin actually hissed. "This demon's days are numbered." He whirled and left. With tears of pain streaming down his cheeks, York backed out the door.

The intruders gone, Leigh stumbled to the altar and prostrated himself before the goddess. He'd never used his magic to harm before, and doing so left him feeling filthy. He desperately wanted to bathe but was too exhausted to even lift his head. Using magic drained energy. He prayed to the Holy Mother to forgive him and even more strongly to help him to forgive. Robrek, who he'd known before he became king, had taught him the importance of not letting anger take root in one's soul. But it was hard not to hate the men who'd threatened the child under his protection.

The door from the stillroom creaked open, and a sobbing Artan rushed to him. "Father Leigh, did they hurt you?"

Leigh was so tired, he had trouble forming words. "No... hurt them."

Artan touched him, and Leigh felt the warmth of the boy's magic. Leigh wanted to do more to reassure the child, but darkness took him.

CHAPTER 2

With a glass of whiskey near his hand, Count Cadarn sat at his desk in the office of his manor house and drew yet another plan for taking the palace in Murtaghan. He'd drawn dozens upon dozens of battle plans since his father's death had forced him to return from Fribourg University and assume his duties as count. When Cadarn had left Svizra ten years before, he hadn't imagined it would take so long before he could put his plans into action. King Solar had continued to breathe far longer than any mortal had a right to. When the old king died, Cadarn had thought his moment had finally come. He'd briefly despaired when the young queen had married a powerful sorcerer, but the goddess had cleared that obstacle out of the way.

As he examined his newest plan, he sipped his whiskey, smiling as it burned its way down his throat and settled warmly in his stomach. Cadarn wanted to hate whiskey as he hated everything to do with his father, but that warmth burned courage into him as wine never could. His father had taken a technique used by the priests to make medicines and applied it to making a spirit stronger than wine or ale. The drink had caught on among certain nobles and wealthy young merchants, and his father had grown rich from its production.

But his father's profit from the barley distilled beverage was exactly why Cadarn shouldn't enjoy the stuff. Because of hunger for that profit, his father had insisted his peasants plant one of their three fields in barley every year and demanded the full production of that field as rent. And due to a near religious faith in the benefits of crop rotation, his father also demanded that one in three fields lie fallow. This left only a single field for the peasants to grow peas and beans, which made up the largest portion of their diet. In a year of bad harvest, peasants went hungry while his father continued to amass wealth.

Cadarn had changed that. He'd given his peasants freedom to grow whatever they wanted, lowered rents, and allowed them to be paid in a variety of ways. Soon he would do for his entire nation what he'd already done for his own estates. It would all begin just as soon as Nisse arrived.

Cadarn's eyes drifted to the shelves built into the walls of his office, where he had an immense collection of books on political philosophy, including a five-volume series by his favorite university professor, Master Altherr. He got up and fingered the books lovingly as he read over their titles: *A World History of Class Oppression; Svizran History, from Darkness into Light; Annagret, a Biography of Greatness; The Svizran Revolution and its Glorious Aftermath*. Cadarn removed the fifth volume from the shelf and brought it to his reading chair. He opened it to the title page and read aloud, *"The Intellectual Underpinnings of the Svizran Revolution* by Luca Matteo Altherr." Under his master's name, Altherr had inscribed, "May your goddess listen to your people's cries for relief, and may you also remember the justice of Annagret and beware of Dritan's brutality. If you do this, nothing will please me more than having educated the next revolutionary. — L. M. Altherr."

Cadarn smiled as he remembered the passion that lit his teacher's eyes when he lectured on the injustice of the class system. Cadarn's mother had been Svizran, and although she died when Cadarn was only seven, she had already, according to his father, "corrupted" her son and caused him to question why one person thought he deserved more than another. Cadarn flipped through the book, and it opened to his favorite passage, one that he'd read and reread a thousand times:

"The very idea that by birth, rather than by merit, some men are worth more than others and have a natural right to rule is an offense to reason and justice. All men are created equal and have the same unassailable rights. The government's purpose is merely to protect these rights and to prevent the strong from imposing upon the weak. Despite being born into nobility, Annagret the

Great understood this concept better than any man who'd lived before or since. Although the stories of the atrocities of the Revolution have been vastly overstated by those who benefited from the old order, Annagret was still saddened by the loss of life necessary to achieve Svizran freedom but knew in the end that freedom was well worth such fugacious afflictions."

Cadarn let the book fall closed. Some of the stories of the Revolution were indeed horrifying, including those of babies' brains being bashed out on the scaffolding where their parents hung. These tales had once caused Cadarn to question the wisdom of overturning the established order of his homeland. But Master Altherr had assured him that the worst of these stories were surely apocryphal.

Nisse had scoffed at what he called Altherr's "feel-good rewriting" of history, "If we overthrow your king, it will be bloody!" the friend of his heart had always insisted. "Very, very bloody! Revolutions always are!"

"Even if you are right, it will be worth it," Cadarn had told him as they spent countless hours at the taverns planning how to bring down Korthlundia's noble class and install a republic.

Cadarn remembered Nisse covering his hand in his own and meeting his eyes. "Know this, Liridona. However bloody, I will be there by your side through it all. I will be Dritan to your Annagret. When you are ready, send for me. This I swear on the Republic."

Liridona, meaning 'freedom lover," was a nickname Nisse had given him on the first Svizran Freedom Day they'd shared together, the day he realized what he felt for Nisse ran deeper than friendship. His friend accepted the existence of no gods, but he viewed a vow on his Republic as every bit as sacred as the one that Korthlundians swore "by the goddess and on their mother's grave." Cadarn had no doubt Nisse would keep his promise. He'd sent the letter summoning his friend on the first ship headed to Svizra in the spring. Nisse would arrive soon, and together they would let freedom ring!

He hugged Master Altherr's book to his chest.

Someone cleared his throat behind Cadarn, causing him to nearly jump out of his chair. "Don't sneak up on me like that," he yelled, as he turned to Rosvald, who stood in the doorway.

"I knocked, *Milord*," Rosvald said. Cadarn felt a slight chill at the overly deferential way his steward always said his title. Rosvald had been one of the most productive peasants when his father was count, so Cadarn had elevated him to steward when he took over and dismissed all of his father's men, who were nearly as monstrous as his father had been. Rosvald had served him well. It was largely due to Rosvald that the peasants prospered, so Cadarn had come to ignore his obsequious tone. Shortly after Cadarn appointed him steward, Rosvald had suggested Cadarn allow an enterprising peasant to copy his father's distillery on a smaller scale. He'd done so, and the peasants had begun making an inferior quality whiskey to sell to the common folk. Cadarn couldn't stomach the stuff himself, but the peasants didn't seem to mind its less robust flavor. His peasants made so much money from the whiskey that they'd grown fat. When Cadarn was a child, he'd never seen a fat peasant. It pleased him to see them on his estates now.

Cadarn put Altherr's book on his desk. "And what did you need?"

"A messenger has arrived from the capital. The queen has given birth, and a celebration has been scheduled to coincide with Litha."

Cadarn frowned. He'd hoped to avoid returning to the capital until Nisse's arrival, but as a member of the royal council, he was obligated to attend the celebration. "Tell my servants to prepare for travel on the morrow."

Rosvald nodded. "I already have, Milord."

Cadarn smiled that Rosvald had again anticipated his command. Having such a competent steward made running the estate much less of a burden. "Thank you. Send word to the stables to have horses ready in an hour. Although I'm sure you have everything in order, I'll be gone for some time, and I want to survey my estates before leaving."

* * *

When Cadarn arrived at the stables, the ever eager Rosvald was already mounted and waiting for him. Cadarn mounted, and they rode toward the nearest peasant fields.

Cadarn smiled, as field after field of thigh-high barley came into view. In the nearest field, a peasant crouched, examining the barley. As they approached, the man stood and bowed.

Cadarn dismounted. "Good afternoon, Sawyer. Looks like your barley's making a fine start."

Sawyer sighed deeply. "No, Milord, few tillers formed to begin with, and over half that formed have now died. You can see for yourself." He pointed to the stalk he'd been examining

Cadarn leaned down to take a closer look. The first stalk had only one tiller, the second none at all. Tillers were the part of the plant that formed the grain heads. They began to emerge two to three weeks after planting. For a good harvest, each stalk would have to produce about five tillers. No matter how good the plants looked now, without tillers, they'd produce no grain. Hoping the first plants he examined weren't typical, Cadarn walked down the field. When he got to the end of the row, he put his hand on his forehead. About half the plants had no tillers at all, and he'd seen only one with more than a single tiller.

Appearing to shrink into himself, Sawyer joined him. "The harvest will be poor, even worse than last year. I'm not sure I'll even have enough to pay rent, let alone buy food to feed my family through the winter."

"Your harvest last year was bad as well? Why wasn't I informed?" He looked pointedly at Rosvald.

Rosvald crossed his arms over his chest and jutted out his chin. "Milord, I told you some peasants had had a bad harvest. You told me to make sure they had enough to eat through the winter, and I did."

Shaking his head, Cadarn closed his eyes. He remembered the conversation now. Since so many unfortunate circumstances can lead to a bad harvest, he hadn't taken much note of it at the time. He opened his eyes, and although he already knew the answer, he asked Sawyer, "Have you been practicing crop rotation?"

Sawyer stepped next to Rosvald and mimicked his posture. "Milord, you said we could plant whatever we wanted! I make a lot more money from selling barley for whiskey than growing beans! And what's the point in not growing anything in an entire field?"

Cadarn rubbed at a burgeoning headache. "I also told you that without crop rotation the soil would get exhausted and not provide adequate nutrients." He let his hand drop to his side. "And without nutrients, no tillers form."

Sawyer put his hands on his hips. "When you became count, you'd said you'd make sure no one on your estates ever starved again!" Sawyer said, as if the grain's failure to produce tillers were Cadarn's fault.

In a way, he guessed it was. If he'd been paying proper attention, he'd have realized Sawyer had abandoned crop rotation and was exhausting his fields. There was only one remedy for it now. "Plow the grain under and let the field lie fallow for the rest of the season. I won't exact rent, and you and your family will be fed, but you'll have to do without any small luxuries you may have become accustomed to. Let this be a lesson to you!"

Sawyer flinched, and Cadarn stomped back to his horse. *Holy Sulis, I sounded just like my father!*

* * *

After completing the tour of his estates, Cadarn poured himself a glass of whiskey and slammed a fist down on his desk. He'd trusted Rosvald too much. The tiller problem he'd first seen in Sawyer's fields was widespread. Because of exhausted soil, he'd had to tell three quarters of his tenants to plow their nonproductive grain under. Only the handful of peasants that had eschewed the easy money of their neighbors and continued to rotate crops still maintained productive fields.

With his head hanging, Rosvald joined him. "They all seemed to be doing so well, Milord. Why should I have questioned their methods?"

Clenching the glass tightly, Cadarn picked up his whiskey and took a sip. He breathed, slowly quenching his desire to punch his steward. In order for that violence to be just, he'd have to punch himself as well. It was a good thing he was about to bring down the entire class system because, to feed his peasants until they could get a proper harvest, he'd need to beggar himself and sell nearly all the whiskey he had on hand, even that hadn't yet been properly aged. Cadarn sat down his glass and forced his hand to relax. "While I'm gone, make sure the peasants follow my orders about plowing the unproductive grain under. And give them some lessons on crop rotation, for Sulis's sake."

* * *

In the damp tunnels that lay underneath The Temple of the True Believer, Father Faolan examined the dull red stone in Father Daray's outstretched hands. Before taking the stone, Faolan put on gloves so it wouldn't touch his bare skin. Ignoring the oozing wound that marred Daray's right cheek, laying open his flesh from just under his eye to his chin, Faolan asked, "You're sure this is a piece of it?"

Daray nodded. "I followed your instructions precisely. As you promised, I found an entrance to the cave under the altar in the shrine at Balley Beg. The ladder climbing down seemed endless, as you said it would, but I found the cavern where the *cothla* demon king shattered the Soul Stone. Broken pieces of it littered the cave floor. This is one of them."

His heart beating rapidly, Faolan brought the stone to his nose, but it had no obvious scent. "Sulis is pleased with you. If you continue to serve the god this faithfully, you will surely earn a place at his right hand." As the young priest humbly bowed his head, Faolan touched his own cheek. "How were you injured?"

Daray fingered his wound gingerly. "When I tried to enter the shrine, I was attacked by a crazed novice from the heretic priestesshood."

Faolan lifted an eyebrow. "Are you sure? The girl at the palace is supposed to be the only one still alive."

Daray wrinkled his nose. "She reeked badly enough, but yes, she was one of them. She was dressed in ragged novice robes and wore her filthy hair in the hundreds of small braids they favor. She ordered me not to enter the shrine. When I ignored her and tried to enter it, she shrieked like an injured cat and pounced on my back. You wouldn't have thought someone as small as she would be any trouble, but she fought like a panther. She clawed at my face and opened my cheek with one of her filthy nails. I finally managed to throw her off, and I think she broke her leg in the fall. When she tried to rise, she couldn't. But she cursed me both as I entered the shrine and when I returned with the piece of the Stone. Her curse seems to have prevented the injury she gave me from healing."

"What did you do with her?"

"With a broken leg, she couldn't hinder me anymore, so I just left her where she'd fallen. Sulis probably will have seen to her end by now."

Faolan wrinkled his brow. This news of a second surviving member of the priesesthood was unwelcome, but he could see no way an injured mad girl could interfere with his plans. Daray was swaying on his feet and clearly needed his rest. But first, he'd demonstrate the power that Sulis had given him. "Come closer, my son, and let me lend Sulis's magic to speed your healing."

Daray knelt in front of him. After setting the stone fragment down, Faolan removed one glove and lay his hand over the wound. Blood pounded in his ears, as yet again he felt no warmth of Sulis's magic. As high priest of The True Church of Sulis, the power was his by right. But the heresy that Sulis was a woman had flourished for so long that even the god's most devoted followers were cut off from His power. When Faolan removed his hand from the wound, he promised, "It will heal rapidly now. But cleansing it with hot water and soap and some of my special salve will hurry the healing along. I put much of Sulis's power into that salve." He clenched his teeth on the knowledge that the *cothla* king, whose power had come from the seven hells rather than the god, had been the salve's true maker.

Daray bowed over Faolan's hand and kissed his ring. "Thank you, Father. It already feels much better."

After dismissing the young priest, Faolan put his glove back on and picked up the fragment. He carried it down a tunnel toward the hidden library he'd found when the bastard queen's persecution had forced him into hiding in these tunnels. When he reached the library, he smiled at the back of Father Eadoin's head. Eadoin, his most faithful follower, poured over books of magic that the great Father Shylah had hidden here. At first Faolan had ignorantly believed the blood magic they described to be evil. But he couldn't deny that the notes covering the margins of the books were written in Father Shylah's hand. Reading these notes, he'd discovered what Father Shylah had always known: nothing was evil when it served Sulis's will.

Eadoin was so intent on his studies he hadn't heard Faolan enter. Faolan cleared his throat, and Eadoin jumped to his feet and bowed deeply. "Your Holiness, forgive me. I didn't hear you." Eadoin's eyes had never quite seemed to focus, but that peculiarity was increasing the more he experimented with blood magic. Faolan wished he could spare his disciple, but Sulis could be a harsh master. From his use of the magic, Father Shylah had gone mad and taken his own life. From Shylah's marginal notes, Faolan discovered that Shylah had worried about what effects the magic would have on him. He'd torn those pages from the books before giving them to Eadoin.

Sulis needed Faolan's wisdom if His truth was to be restored, so Faolan had been unwilling to risk his own sanity. Eadoin, despite his devotion, was expendable.

Seeing the red stone Faolan carried, Eadoin rushed forward. "Is that...?" His eyes widened with awe.

Faolan bowed his head and drew Sulis's star. "Let Sulis be praised. Father Daray has succeeded in his mission. How soon will you be able to perform the ritual to return Sulis's power to us?"

Eadoin reached for the Stone. "May I hold it?" When Faolan placed it in Eadoin's ungloved hand, he rubbed it between his fingers. Picking up the book he'd been studying, he hugged both to his chest. "As soon as we have the requisite sacrifices. But..." He looked away.

"Speak, my son. Remember, nothing is evil when it serves Sulis's will."

When Eadoin turned back to face him, the madness in his eyes gleamed even brighter. "The ritual requires a lot of blood—a *lot* of blood. And unlike lesser spells, this blood must come from the heart. Those who give it won't survive doing so."

"Sulis's will must be done. He will provide the sacrifices."

CHAPTER 3

When Cadarn arrived at the palace in Murtaghan a week before Litha, court was in session. The queen was seated on her massive throne on the dais in the throne room. To Cadarn, the size of the throne had always been a symbol of how the noble class crushed the people beneath them. As he found a spot to observe "royal justice," a common workman jostled him. The man apologized profusely and disappeared into the crowd. Although it would be brazen for a pickpocket to operate right in the throne room itself, Cadarn felt for his purse. Not only did he find it, but there was a folded piece of paper in his pocket that hadn't been there before. Cadarn faded into the shadows and withdrew the paper. His heart skipped a beat when he read the single word on the outside: "Liridona."

With trembling hands, he unfolded the note. It was just a single sentence in Svizran. "I await your word where the wanderer may find rest."

After ten long years, Nisse was only a short distance away: at the Traveler's Haven, an inn favored by wealthy foreigners. He decided to head immediately to his friend's side.

But as he moved out of the shadows, Duke Tierney, a fellow member of the Royal Council, caught sight of him. The duke nodded to him, and Cadarn responded with a deeper bow. Protocol demanded all sorts of absurdities; the duke outranked him. For once in his life, Cadarn submitted to the protocol without resentment.

Nisse had arrived, and together they soon would bring an end to it all.

The duke cleared his throat. "I'm happy to see you have arrived in time for the council meeting tomorrow morning. We of Lundia must stand together against the Korthian attempt to rob us blind."

"I've just arrived, and I'm afraid I don't know what you are referring to."

"It's nothing more than highway robbery, I tell you. Baroness Eithne arrived three weeks ago with an absurd demand for assistance for the supposed victims of the Soul Stone. She claims there will be massive starvation without it."

Cadarn stiffened. Tierney had been gifted with Duke Argblutal's former estates when the duke had tried to usurp the crown. He wouldn't be short of resources to assist those in need. "The Ancient Evil caused untold destruction. It doesn't seem unreasonable that aid would be needed."

Tierney, who was half a foot taller, glowered down at him. "When Lundia is in danger of becoming a subject state to Korth, we can't get sentimental about peasants."

Cadarn was about to retort when Count Weylin, another Lundian council member, joined them. "Discussing the queen's demands, Your Grace, Milord?" The count gave Tierney the deeper bow required and nodded his head toward Cadarn. "I certainly wouldn't want to see people starve, but she can't be serious about the size of the need."

As Tierney and Weylin reassured each other that the queen was merely attempting a power grab, Cadarn suppressed his impatience. He had to stay, or he'd appear to be siding with the queen. How absurd it all was!

The queen's secretary announced the next case to be brought before the queen. "Flann Flannstamm, member of the baker's guild, verses Lord Padrig, the son of Count Guto." Lord Padrig was dressed in a red silk tunic covered with gold embroidery, and Flann wore a traditional baker's hat and apron, both clean but showing signs of wear at the edges. They both went down on one knee before the queen. Cadarn rolled his eyes at the farce being presented before him. As if there was any doubt who would prevail.

From her seat on her almighty throne, the queen looked down at the two men. "You may rise."

They both stood, but whereas the nobleman lifted his head and met the queen's eyes, the baker kept his eyes on the ground. He was trembling visibly.

To Cadarn's surprise, the queen addressed her first remarks to the baker. "You have no need to fear bringing your request for justice before me." Like Solar before her, the queen didn't use the royal "we." "Please state what you allege against this lord."

The baker hesitated, his eyes darting around the richly dressed crowd. Taking advantage of the baker's hesitation, the lord stepped slightly forward. "If I may, Your Majesty."

The queen turned toward him. "You will have your chance to be heard, but since Flann Flannstamm has brought the case, he will be heard first." As Cadarn choked back a surprised laugh, the queen turned back to the baker. "Truly, you may speak without fear."

The baker lifted his eyes to the queen and told a story that made Cadarn's blood boil. "Your Majesty, His Lordship contracted with me to provide bread and sweetmeats for a fete he held at Ostara. It was a large fete, Your Majesty. The biggest order I've ever had. I accepted a small down payment of only a single drachma with the agreement that the remaining nineteen drachma would be paid when I delivered the confections. A drachma wasn't even enough for me to purchase the supplies needed for such a large order. I had to contract a debt for five drachma to get everything required. I worked night and day for a week to prepare everything, but it became evident that I alone would be unable to complete the entire order on time, so I contracted with a couple of members of the baker's guild to help me. They insisted on payment in advance. Believing I was about to receive what to me would be a small fortune, I didn't hesitate in contracting more debt to give them two drachma each for their contribution."

After clearing his throat, the peasant continued. "I delivered everything on time, exactly as ordered to his kitchen on the morning of Ostara, but the servants who greeted me claimed that the lord was still abed and would send my money round when he woke. I had no reason to doubt their truthfulness, so I unloaded my breads and sweetmeats and returned home to await payment. The day passed without it being forthcoming, as did the next. At which time, I went again to His Lordship's dwelling to ask after the money owed me. I was again assured that His Lordship would send it around later that day. It will surprise Your Majesty to learn that he did not. I tried several more times to collect what was due me but was repeatedly put off with promises. Fearing the servants were not delivering my messages, I waited in front of his dwelling until His Lordship himself appeared in order to make the case directly to him. When I did confront him, he asked to see the signed contract stipulating our agreement. Your Majesty, I trusted to His Lordship's word, and I didn't get a signed contract. When I admitted as much, His Lordship claimed I had been paid in full and was now trying to cheat him. When I protested that this wasn't true, he had his retainers throw me off his property and told me that if I bothered His Lordship again, I would be charged with trespassing. Your Majesty, my creditor troubles me for repayment and is threatening to take my bakery, my only means of livelihood, if I do not repay him by Litha."

The queen looked intently at the baker as he concluded his story. "I tried to appeal to the municipal courts but was told that because His Lordship was noble, I would have to appeal directly to Your Majesty. I put my name on Your Majesty's list three weeks ago, but it has taken until today for my case to be heard. Your Majesty, I beg you, I must have the money due me or I, along with my wife and six children, will be thrown into the street in a week's time. I plead that if I cannot get the total sum owed me, that at least I receive enough to pay my debts. I throw myself on the mercy of the court." The baker went down on his knees before the queen.

The queen nodded to the baker and turned to Lord Padrig. "How do you respond to these allegations?"

The arrogant bastard snorted and glanced down at the kneeling baker. The queen watched him intently as he spoke. "Your Majesty, I admit that I did contract with this peasant to provide bread and sweetmeats for my fete at Ostara, but I assure Your Majesty that I paid my debt in full and this ingrate seeks to cheat me. For his imposition on me and on Your Majesty's time, I ask for a judgment of slander against him. Seeing his poverty, I will not be vindictive, but I seek five drachma damages for his besmirching of my good name."

The baker wailed. "Your Majesty, I beg you. Think of my wife and my young children. Your Majesty is a mother yourself."

The queen's ability to feign an expression of compassion was indeed impressive. "My good man, fear not the justice of this court." Her eyes narrowed as she turned to Lord Padrig, and Cadarn's mouth dropped open as she declared, "Your actions are reprehensible. A verbal agreement is binding in the joined kingdoms, and no nobleman worthy of the name would so grossly violate his given word. It is the judgment of this court that not only will you immediately pay this good baker the nineteen drachma you owe him, but you will pay an additional five to compensate him for the difficulty he has endured in collecting what is his due."

There was a collective gasp from those gathered in the throne room. *What game is the queen playing?*

Duke Tierney scoffed, "I see the queen is exacting her pound of flesh for Lady Briallen's affair with her husband." When Cadarn looked at the duke in confusion, the duke continued, "Lady Briallen is Lord Padrig's sister. The lady has breasts rather larger than Her Majesty's. The king dallied with them for a short while."

Cadarn shook his head. "That explains the decision." While he was certain the baker was in the right, it was petty of the queen to punish Lord Padrig for his sister's actions.

Lord Padrig threw up his hands. "Your Majesty can't be serious. This man has no evidence of any claim upon me. Is Your Majesty going to allow us to be robbed by every tradesman with a story to tell? This man is lying to the court. I will not endure such a gross insult!"

The queen's lips narrowed. "We both know who is lying here. My guards will escort you to a place where you may wait in comfort while you make arrangements for this man's money to be delivered to him."

Duke Tierney scoffed. "The queen's pettiness knows no bounds. Not only is she going to make Lord Padrig pay for his sister's actions, she'll hold him under arrest until he does so."

Count Weylin made a noise of disgust. "She didn't even call forth any witnesses before engaging in such travesty of justice. We all know where this will lead. Mark my words, we will all be besieged by tradesmen extorting money from us now."

Continuing to protest, Lord Padrig was taken away by the Royal Guard. As the grateful baker praised the queen, Cadarn wanted to punch something in frustration. Yes, justice had been done, but petty vengeance should be beneath the dignity of a ruler. Again, he patted the note in his pocket that signaled the beginning of the end for the short reign of Samantha I.

* * *

After court, Samantha sat in her reception room listening to Blaine's report. "Your Majesty, Count Cadarn was seen at court today. With his return, the entire Royal Council is back. At the council meeting tomorrow morning we can discuss the Korthian crisis."

"Any rumors on how they will respond?"

"There have been some murmurs of discontent among the Lundian council members, with the biggest complaints coming from Duke Tierney. He seems to be trying to stir up the beehive, so to speak."

Samantha frowned. Had she been wrong to give him Argblutal's lands and title? "He will have to be reminded what he owes the crown. Have him summoned to speak with me as soon as my schedule allows."

"I believe that would be wise, Your Majesty."

Samantha hid a smile. It always amused her when Blaine expressed approval of her actions, but she'd also learned to pay heed when he disapproved.

"The plans for the princess's celebration are proceeding…" Blaine trailed off as there was noise in the corridor, and a voice shouted loudly enough to be heard through the door. "I know she doesn't want to see me, but tell her that this time it isn't about my nephew."

The tortured accent could belong to none other than Slathek, Robbie's uncle. "Blaine, see what that's about," Samantha ordered.

Blaine went into the corridor and returned almost immediately. "Your Majesty, His Majesty's uncle insists he has news of importance. He promises on the Father and the Mother"—Blaine rolled his eyes slightly as he mentioned the foreigner's gods—"that this time he isn't here to persuade Your Majesty to allow him to take King Robrek away with him. I do believe he's telling the truth, Your Majesty."

Since Robbie's injury, Slathek had been trying to take his nephew to his home country of Mahngbhayo, where magic was stronger than in Korthlundia. He'd assured her that the healers there could accomplish what those here couldn't. She'd been so convinced Brianna would heal her father she'd refused to listen. Now she had to wonder if Slathek was Robbie's only chance of becoming whole again.

"I'll see him," Samantha said.

Blaine went to the door, and soon the foreign merchant entered, accompanied by her guards. As always, he was dressed in colors so bright they nearly hurt her eyes; this time his tunic was of an azure so radiant Samantha was certain it would shine in the darkness. It was fastened in front with huge gold clasps and his trousers were of a matching gold and fitted him so tightly that they revealed Slathek to be as fit as his nephew had been. He was wearing a floppy azure hat with three golden feathers at the back. But it wasn't his flashy colors that made the queen's breath catch in her throat. His skin was a shade darker than his nephew and his eyes were black instead of green, but his hair was the same wavy black and his face looked like a slightly older version of the man her love had been.

Slathek took off his hat and bowed elaborately. Staring at the resemblance to the love she'd lost, Samantha failed to invite Slathek to be seated or offer him refreshment.

Misinterpreting her lack of courtesy, Slathek closed his eyes briefly and shook his head. "Niece, my nephew loved you to the depth of his soul. For that reason alone, I won't take offense at the treatment I've received. I thought you'd like to know that someone in your court is about to stage a coup, but if the news doesn't interest you, I'll be on my way."

Robbie's uncle was given to dramatics, so she doubted he knew anything of value, but that didn't excuse her rudeness. "Forgive me. I was startled again by your resemblance to your nephew. Please, be seated." She indicated the chair across from her. "Would you care for some wine?"

His eyes softening, Slathek took possession of the chair as if the room were his own. "That would be delightful."

When Blaine poured him a glass, Samantha asked, "A coup, did you say?"

Slathek sipped his wine and then gestured flamboyantly. "Someone is bringing in Svizran mercenaries, and the cad has the audacity to stay at The Traveler's Haven." When in town, the king's uncle always stayed at the Traveler's Haven.

"The cad?"

"Yes, the captain of the mercenary company as well as his two lieutenants. They're here to scope out the situation. The remainder of their company will certainly arrive shortly."

Samantha looked askance at Slathek. "He told you this?"

Slathek scoffed. "He didn't have to tell me. He's Svizran. They're all mercenaries."

Samantha barely stifled a laugh. "All of them?"

Slathek shook his head. "I've never seen one who wasn't. The one staying at the Traveler's Haven has tried to disguise himself as a merchant, as if a merchant can't tell another merchant when he sees one. When a merchant walks into a room, he notices how richly others are dressed, the jewelry they wear, the type of wine on the table, the size of their purses, how many retainers they have. All the little signs that speak of wealth. When a man of violence surveys a room, he makes a threat assessment. This Svizran is a man of violence."

Slathek held up a hand as if she were about to interrupt. "But that's not all. This morning one of his officers almost saluted him." As if that settled the matter, he leaned back in his chair.

"Almost?"

Slathek's voice rose. "He started to raise his hand to do so but stopped when he saw I was watching. Do not doubt me, my niece. This man is a mercenary."

Samantha tapped her fingers on the arm of the chair. She'd worried about Sheen rebelling against her, but could he really be bringing in mercenaries to try to take her throne? The name of the country teased at her. Where else had she heard of it? "Didn't Count Cadarn go to university in Svizra?" she asked Blaine.

"I believe he did, Your Majesty," Blaine answered.

Cadarn had been recently added to the Royal Council. Samantha had never seen his aura. But she'd heard reports Cadarn had implemented reforms on his estates over the last ten years that indicated that, like her, he cared deeply for the people's wellbeing. He might be an important ally in getting Korth's needs met. She nodded to Robbie's uncle. "Thank you for bringing this news to me. I will look into it."

The merchant's eyes softened. "My nephew truly did love you, Your Majesty. I've never seen anyone so happy as he was on his wedding day. As my sister's son, he is as close a thing I've ever had to a son. I know a newborn must be protected against illness, so I understand your caution at confining your daughter to the nursery at present, but might I have leave to meet my grandniece? She is the only family I have left."

Samantha had to force her words beyond the lump in her throat. "You may. And after you have done so... how soon can you take her father home with you?"

Slathek froze, as if he didn't dare believe what he heard. "You will allow me to do so?" He glanced over at Blaine. "I did not break my word. She brought it up, not I."

Not trusting her voice to answer, Samantha merely nodded at Slathek.

A smile spread across the merchant's face. "I can sail with tomorrow's high tide. I know this breaks your heart, my niece, but it is the right thing to do. In Mahngbhayo, the homeland of his mother, he will get well again."

She stood. "Slathek of Mahngbhayo, I charge you with the life of a king. You will take him, and you will bring him back to me whole."

"If the gods will it, Your Majesty."

As Slathek bowed his way out, Samantha wished she hadn't left Robbie's fate in the hands of what now seemed to her capricious gods. "Summon Count Cadarn," she told Blaine. "Whatever is next on the schedule will have to wait."

* * *

Having at last freed himself from his fellow council members with the excuse that he needed to rest after his long journey, Count Cadarn retired to his quarters in the palace. He hugged Nisse's note to his chest. While waiting to ensure the coast was clear, he glanced above his mantle at the portraits of Annagret and Dritan. Master Altherr had given him the portraits to remind him of his ambition to free his own country from the bondage of class. Cadarn smiled at Dritan's portrait. The jaunty set of his hat and happy-go-lucky glint in his eyes had always reminded Cadarn that Dritan had enjoyed freeing his people from bondage.

Perhaps a little too much. Cadarn turned to the more sober mien of Annagret, his true hero, because Annagret didn't revel in the blood of the fallen.

Cadarn's cat, Snowflake, twined around his ankles. Although Cadarn's servants at the palace had taken good care of him, the cat had missed him. He picked the cat up and scratched between his ears. "What do you think, dear heart? Will my statue someday grace the city square as Annagret's and Dritan's do in Svizra? Will they call me Cadarn the Bold?" Snowflake purred and pressed his head into Cadarn's hand, demonstrating the cat's confidence in him. Eager to hold Nisse in his arms once again, he gave Snowflake a final scratch and set him down.

There came a knock on his door. He opened it to find a palace page. The boy bowed. "Milord, the queen requests your immediate presence."

"The queen?" Cadarn laughed but cut it off abruptly, fearing he might sound disrespectful. "What does she want with me?"

The page looked at him as if he were an idiot. "Her Majesty didn't tell me, Milord."

Shooing the child away as if he were an unwelcome dog, Cadarn slammed the door. Instead of going to Nisse, he had to attend the queen.

Cadarn went to his fireplace and clutched the mantle. "She can't know anything," he told his heroes. "It simply isn't possible." He tried to reassure himself that the queen simply wanted to talk about his fellow Lundians' reluctance to help the people of Korth. She must be aware of it.

Cadarn spent the long walk through the labyrinthine corridors of the palace breathing slowly and deeply. But when he rounded the corner and saw the monsters that were the queen's bodyguards, he shivered. He met the eyes of the taller of the two. This man had skewered Count Nola in the council chamber itself. Cadarn hadn't actually been in the room, but he'd heard the story many times. As a symbol of the queen's true tyrannical nature, Nola had been executed without even the semblance of a trial. Since the count's murder had created the empty council seat he now filled, Cadarn couldn't help but take it a tad personally and worry he might be next.

The two fierce men accompanied him into the queen's reception room. Although they made no aggressive moves, he felt them looming behind him.

Licking his lips, Cadarn bowed to the queen. "Your Majesty, you wished to see me?"

When the queen invited him to be seated, her brow furrowed as if she didn't know what to make of him. But whatever she felt quickly vanished from her face. He'd never met anyone better at hiding emotion. That alone was reason enough not to trust her. She smiled a court smile that conveyed no real friendliness and offered him refreshment. As he accepted a goblet of wine, he relaxed slightly; prisoners about to be interrogated wouldn't be so treated.

Her next words further eased his discomfort. "At tomorrow's council meeting, we will be discussing devastation caused by the Soul Stone and the needs of the Korthian people. Many will starve without relief, and the crown alone cannot meet this need. Can I count on your support in this matter?"

Cadarn was certain King Solar had hidden heaps of treasure somewhere. No monarch had ever lived as frugally as he'd pretended to. With access to that treasury now, the queen could easily address the problem on her own. Cadarn lamented the state of his own estates, which prevented him from demonstrating to the queen what proper concern for the people looked like. Complicating matters, he needed to do everything he could to make sure the queen had no reason to doubt his loyalty. Since he couldn't make a generous gift to the people of Korth, the only thing he could think to do was throw his fellow Lundians under her feet. For being willing to let their countrymen starve, they deserved it anyway.

"Your Majesty knows I have always put the needs of the people before my own. But the crops on my estates have been hit with a blight. I will need most of my resources to see my people through the winter. That said, I will give all that I can spare. But I fear not all my fellow Lundians feel the same. I was approached by Duke Tierney and Count Weylin at court today. They attempted to elicit my cooperation in uniting the Lundian members of the council against what Tierney called 'highway robbery.' I'd been about to request an audience with Your Majesty to report this when I received your summons."

The queen's brow creased. "This is troubling. How did you respond?"

"They caught me by surprise, Your Majesty, so I said little. I had planned on seeking Your Majesty's will on how to proceed."

The queen paused too long before replying, making him wonder if she believed him. Finally, she nodded. "Thanks for informing me. I will see to Tierney. But I would appreciate any effort on your part to bring the other Lundians to an understanding of their duty to the people."

"Your Majesty can depend on my every effort." No matter his feelings for the queen, he would never let his countrymen starve while he had means to prevent it. He couldn't count the times desperate people had begged at his father's gates, only to be turned away. *If my lands weren't so small, I wouldn't be having this problem.*

A slight quiver went across the queen's face. *Does it mean she doubts me? Sulis curse her, she's impossible to read.* Thinking he was dismissed, Cadarn rose. As he took a step toward the door, the queen asked, "If my memory serves me correctly, you went to university in Svizra, did you not?"

Holy Sulis, what does she know? As he turned toward the queen, Cadarn struggled to control his expression. "Yes, Your Majesty, my mother was Svizran, and my father thought the experience abroad would help to mold my character." He didn't tell the queen the true reason his father had attempted to get rid of him. Without being able to stop himself, he added, "What makes you ask, Your Majesty?"

The queen pursed her lips as if he were a book written in a language she didn't know well. Then a bland smile spread over her face. "I hear they have a most interesting system of government. Someday I would like to speak with you about it."

* * *

After the count left, Blaine said, "You asked little about the Svizrans, Your Majesty. Do you suspect the count?"

Samantha shook her head. "I don't know. His aura was strange." Bright orange and yellow had swirled around him in constant motion. Its happiness had almost made her want to get up and dance. But through the bright colors had snaked jagged black lines like those she'd seen long ago in Duke Argblutal's aura. Duke Argblutal had killed her father and tried to force her into marriage. What could such a stark contrast mean? The black lines had darkened more when she'd asked about Svizra. Auras didn't give her the ability to read people's minds, merely to discern their character. She'd thought once her ability became reliable, she would have no more difficulty knowing what those around her were up to. But that didn't seem to be the case. Since there hadn't been an aurora in Korthlundia in over a century, knowledge of their abilities was scarce. "It may be nothing, but tell Lord Duer to have him followed and search his rooms."

"Certainly, Your Majesty."

"And have your assistant Tuathal research all he can find out about auras. Tell him to be discrete in doing so." Only those she trusted absolutely knew of her ability, and she intended to keep it that way. "Then summon Duke Tierney. He needs to be reminded what he owes the crown."

As Blaine left to carry out her instructions, she tried to not to think that at this very moment, Drem was certainly packing Robbie's things to prepare for the journey. *Sulis bring him back to me, I beg you. I can stand a separation if he will return whole.*

* * *

After returning to his chambers, Cadarn drove his fist into the wall, then cried out and pulled his injured hand to his chest. That had certainly been stupid. Not only did such petty displays of emotion not solve anything, now his hand hurt.

Whatever the queen suspected, he had to be sure she found nothing to confirm it. He hurried to the locked chest beside his bed, took the key out from under his shirt, and opened it. About a quarter of the chest was filled with bundles of letters, tied together lovingly with bright ribbons. Each of the ten bundles represented a year of correspondence with the man he'd loved more than any other.

He gathered up the bundles and hurried to his fireplace. Hugging them to his chest, he dropped to the rug in front of the fire. He untied one of the bundles, but before consigning them to the flames as he knew he must, he opened the first letter in the stack. It had been written on Svizran Freedom Day five years earlier.

My dearest Liridona

My company was in Fribourg to celebrate Svizran Freedom Day this year. The fireworks were brilliant tonight. Since we last watched them together, some artisan has discovered how to give them color. But even though reds, greens, and blues exploded over my head, the lights didn't seem half as stirring as they did on the first night we watched them together. When I close my eyes, I can still see your face come alive in the bursting brilliance. Watching your wonder in seeing fireworks moved me deeper than anything had ever moved me in my life. I don't think I ever told you that was the night I fell in love with you. I stood by Annagret's statue tonight and touched his horse where you sat that long-ago day and proclaimed that you would someday make your nation as free as mine. It seemed empty without you there.

As I look over my soldiers, the thing that makes me happiest is that I have been able to grow my company large enough that I stand ready to fulfill my promise of being Dritan to your Annagret. I've trained them well, Liridona. Just send me word, and I will bring them to your side. I long to be there myself.

Lamenting that he hadn't taken these letters back to his estates, he untied the bundles one by one. As he burned each letter, he felt as if he were confining a piece of his soul to the inferno. But if the queen's spies ever found these letters, they'd be all the evidence she needed to condemn him for treason, if she even bothered to give him a trial.

When all the letters had been destroyed, he leaned back against the wall. Worse than the loss of the memories was the knowledge that Nisse was only a few miles away, and he couldn't go to him. In order to allay the queen's suspicions, he would have to spend time with his fellow council members, who he loathed. The question was how he would get them to do their duty. Count Weylin was a coward, so Cadarn was relatively certain what would work with him. He decided to try him first.

* * *

Waiting for Duke Tierney, the queen's jaw ached. Realizing how tightly she was clenching it, Samantha let out a long slow breath and tried to relax. She'd given Tierney Argblutal's lands and title for coming to her aid against Argblutal. She thought such generosity would ensure his loyalty for longer than a year and a half. How had her father kept the vipers from devouring the people for so long?

When Tierney arrived, he smiled broadly and bowed low over her hand to kiss it. While such a gesture was often considered common courtesy, as queen she'd discouraged it. Few men could do so without an air of condescension. Tierney wasn't one of them, and as he took the seat she offered, he looked at her as if she were a prized jewel he was considering adding to his collection. Samantha called forth his aura, a jagged mix of red and yellow. The yellow brought back a memory of the time he'd mistaken her for a stable groom.

He'd talked to her like something lower than the dust at his feet and, when she didn't immediately obey him, threatened to have her flogged. Later realizing who she was, he'd apologized and debased himself before her. She could have decreed any number of punishments for his disrespect, but she'd granted him mercy. She thought she'd taught him a lesson in respect and humility. She guessed she'd been wrong.

After he was seated with a glass of wine, she asked, "How are your estates prospering?"

The duke's smile broadened. "Excellently, Your Majesty, excellently."

Samantha returned a court smile. "I'm pleased. I have received reports of some resistance to caring for those devastated by the Soul Stone, but I'm certain I can count on your support."

Tierney sat his wine glass down and spread his arms wide as if to enfold her. "In light of what Your Majesty is offering, absolutely."

"Offering?" She stumbled over the word.

Tierney's laugh bounced hollowly off the walls. "I've spoiled it, haven't I? I know Your Majesty hasn't yet offered it, but we both know you were about to. But for form's sake, I'll just sit here as if I'm oblivious to your intentions and await your proposal."

"My proposal?"

Tierney shook his head. "There is no need to be coy, Your Majesty. My servants inform me that your consort's servants are packing to take him abroad. Of course, I'm the obvious choice. And as I said, I accept. To silence any discontent, I would recommend the marriage take place sooner rather than later."

Samantha glanced from Blaine to her guards, waiting for someone to tell her this was a joke, but they all gaped at her as if she or the duke had lost their mind. *Holy Sulis, Mother of us all, I don't need another enemy.*

She swallowed and composed her face. "Your Grace, I elevated you to duke and granted you estates worth many times your former ones. For this alone, I expect your support in addressing Korth's desperate need."

The yellow in the duke's aura flashed so brightly, she almost lifted a hand to shield her eyes. "If not me, who then do you intend to make consort?"

"I have a consort already. The king's uncle has taken him away for healing. He will return."

"What is this girlish foolishness? We both know that shell of a man will never be whole. The peasant was never fit to be king to begin with."

Clenching her jaw even more tightly than before, Samantha rose. "How dare you insult both me and your king! I am not some girl to be toyed with. King Robrek was chosen by the goddess herself to rule beside me. I made you duke, and I can unmake you as well!"

The duke stared at her as if his prize jewel had morphed into a serpent. "You are clearly overwrought. Childbirth can cause any woman to become overly emotional."

"Get out!"

Tierney stood, but made no move to leave. "Your Majesty, control yourself before you make a mistake you can't unmake."

Samantha glanced at Bearach, contemplating ordering him to run the duke through, an order her bodyguard would obey without question. Fortunately, before she could do so, Conroy, with his hand on his sword hilt, stepped between her and the duke. "Her Majesty told you to leave."

Bearach close beside him. "Out."

Both Conroy and Bearach were substantially taller than she, so they blocked Tierney's face, but his words sliced through the air. "You will regret this."

After her bodyguards escorted the duke out, Samantha fell back into her chair. She put a trembling hand to her face. *What have I done?* She couldn't remember the last time she let anger get the better of her, but the anger hadn't abated with the duke's departure. "How dare he presume so much! What am I going to do to put him back in his place?"

"Well, Your Majesty," Blaine's voice startled her. She'd forgotten he was still in the room. "I'm aware of no clear precedent for denobling a duke, as it were. The most common way to rid someone of his title has been to rid him of his head, so to speak."

Samantha stared at her secretary. "Are you out of your mind?"

All color fled Blaine's face. "Forgive me, Your Majesty. I don't know what I was thinking."

As Blaine seemed to collapse in on himself, shame flooded Samantha, taking her rage with it. He'd been growing in confidence over the last two years, but at the moment he seemed again the trembling junior undersecretary to the librarian he'd been when she'd promoted him to his position. "Forgive me. It's not you I'm angry with. No queen could ask for a better secretary."

Blaine immediately straightened and beamed. "Thank you, Your Majesty. I've tried my very best, and I've kept all the lists well organized." He pointed to a neat stack of paper on his desk. "I've even given my assistant work to do as you requested. I only want to serve Your Majesty. I—"

"Blaine."

"I'm babbling again, aren't I, Your Majesty? If Your Majesty wills it, I could research other ways that denobling has been done."

Samantha wasn't sure she wanted to strip Tierney of his title, but it might come to that. "Please do," she said. As Blaine left, she hoped Cadarn could rally the other Lundians to her side, but when she thought of the jagged black streaks in his aura, she doubted it. She would have to go to the council meeting prepared for battle.

* * *

As he knew he would, Cadarn found Weylin in the Hall of Games, playing Basset. Since he was smiling and laughing, Cadarn assumed he'd been winning. For reasons unknown, Weylin always had extraordinarily good luck at cards. Before approaching his fellow count, Cadarn watched him closely for half an hour, but like all those who previously tried to catch Weylin cheating, Cadarn couldn't see how Weylin was doing it. Still, nobody was that lucky.

Cadarn joined him at the Basset table. "Good afternoon, Milord," he greeted the count, as he was dealt thirteen cards face up on the table.

Weylin acknowledged him with a nod of the head and returned to examining his cards. Cadarn placed bets on two of his cards. But Weylin took so long looking at his that even the dealer seemed to be getting impatient, tapping his fingers on the table several times. He did it subtly so as not to give offense, but he was unable to stifle a yawn. Finally, Weylin placed bets on three cards. The dealer dealt a seven from the bottom of the deck. Weylin laughed. One of the cards he'd bet on was a seven. The dealer then flipped over a king and a deuce from the top of the deck. Weylin had bet on his king as well but not his two. Winning on two out of three cards was quite some luck. Cadarn lost on both of his. The losing cards were taken and replaced. Weylin chose to keep the king, but not the seven, in play. He surrendered the seven and turned up a corner of the king.

Cadarn quickly put bets on two of his cards, but then decided to place one on his kings as well. As Weylin studied his, Cadarn said, "Has the queen summoned you yet?"

Weylin's eyes whipped to him. "No, why would Her Majesty do that?"

Cadarn shrugged. "She summoned me after court. Maybe she's already made her decision about you."

"What decision?"

Cadarn nodded toward the dealer. "Ah, yes, of course, let's finish this round." Weylin went back to contemplating his cards, but he kept twisting his ring as he did so. As Weylin placed his bets, it dawned on Cadarn that the dealer's tapping might not be a sign of impatience but a signal. But if it were, Cadarn couldn't figure out how Weylin knew to place bets on the four cards he chose.

The dealer dealt a king from the bottom of the deck, causing them both to win, but since it was the second time Weylin had bet on his king, he won seven times his bet. He won on one other card but lost on two. Weylin hastily gathered his winnings and led Cadarn to a quiet area at the back of the room. "What is this about a summons from the queen?"

Cadarn decided to take a risk. "Rather clever of you to enlist the dealer to tell you which cards to bet on."

Weylin drew himself up. "Are you accusing me of cheating?"

Cadarn smiled. "The tapping pattern is rather complex. It took me watching for half an hour to figure it out." Weylin opened his mouth to protest, but Cadarn interrupted. "There's no use denying it, but we might be able to keep it our little secret."

Weylin leaned back in his chair and folded his arms. "How much do you want?"

"For me, nothing, but you might be able to help me out of a spot of trouble with the queen." Weylin merely glared at him, so Cadarn went on in what he hoped was a sufficiently agitated fashion. "The queen asked for my support in aiding Korth, and she wasn't so subtle in implying that failing to give it would be taken as an act of treason. The problem is, the crops on my estates have suffered a terrible blight. If I give anything to aid Korth, I won't have enough to feed my own people this winter. I told the queen this, but she didn't believe me." Cadarn dropped his voice. "You remember how she had Nola killed right in the council room. She more or less said I'd suffer the same fate if I didn't provide a better answer in the council meeting tomorrow morning. From the manner her guards looked at me, I wondered if she plans to make a clean slate of it and kill all of those who oppose her. She wouldn't be the first monarch to do so." He leaned in closer. "She summoned Tierney to meet with her after me. I think she knows about Lundia uniting against her."

Weylin paled. "She actually threatened to have you executed?"

"Not explicitly but her meaning was clear. That's where you come in. I need you to not only give your support to the queen tomorrow but also provide me enough supplies that I can contribute as well."

Weylin wrinkled his brow. "You're lying. Why would she summon you but not me?"

Cadarn shrugged. "Maybe she's planning to later, or…" He let his voice trail off.

"Or what?" Weylin practically shouted.

"Keep your voice down," Cadarn hissed. "Or maybe she's already decided your fate." Cadarn shrugged again. "But if you wholeheartedly support her plan, she'll have no excuse to go through with it, and if you supply me, she'll be well on her way to getting the Lundian support she needs. If we could get Baron Arawn or Count Ultan to go along with us, she might not find it necessary to kill anyone."

Weylin furrowed his brow. "I wouldn't suggest approaching Ultan. He's taken up the cause of the True Church of Sulis and has become completely irrational. But I think Arawn could be persuaded to join us."

Cadarn smiled. Whatever the queen suspected of him, this would surely convince her otherwise. But as he left the hall of games with Weylin, he was pretty sure he was being followed.

* * *

Cadarn returned to his rooms quite pleased with himself. With Weylin's assistance, he'd been able to convince Baron Arawn to support the queen's desires to bring relief to Korth. She shouldn't suspect him of anything now. After pouring himself a glass of whiskey, he collapsed in a chair and tried to figure out what he could do about Nisse.

A chill ran up his spine when he noticed that the pen box on his desk was slightly to the left of where he usually placed it and the desk's second drawer was just the smallest bit ajar. The more he looked around, the more objects seemed to have been disturbed. Several books on his bookshelf protruded more than the others; he was grateful he kept Master Altherr's books at his estates. When he concluded his inspection, he had no doubt that his rooms had been searched and thanked the goddess he'd destroyed Nisse's letters. Nothing else in the room could possibly incriminate him.

He picked up his whiskey glass and threw its contents to the back of his throat. *Sulis damn the queen! Just how am I supposed to meet with Nisse if she's watching my every move?* He could afford to alter nothing in his usual routine. In the normal course of events, about now he'd be on his way to The Jeweled Plum Tree, the most exclusive brothel in Murtaghan. While neither his heart nor his cock was in the mood, he decided he had to go. Besides, Purple Leaf always helped him to unburden his heart. He'd long ago told the whore about Nisse.

* * *

When Cadarn entered the brothel, Purple Leaf was giggling while some man Cadarn didn't know was jingling one of the small amethyst plums attached to the pasties covering her large, nicely shaped breasts. All the whores at The Jeweled Plum Tree took the names of some variety of plum. Purple Leaf was in her mid-twenties and had died her hair a lavender that matched the Purple Leaf plum tree in bloom. The only thing she was wearing in addition to the pasties was a lavender loin cloth. She was truly lovely.

When she caught sight of him, she squealed, pushed away the hand of the man playing with her breasts, and hurried toward him. Cadarn gave her a small smile. He was more than her favorite client. Cadarn had paid for Purple Leaf's younger sister's apprenticeship in the weaver's guild so she wouldn't have to follow Purple Leaf into the trade. The whore had vowed her eternal loyalty to him afterward. As she nearly skipped across the room, the small plums attached to the other rather larger plums bounced enticingly. Normally that bounce alone was enough to get his cock to stand up but not today.

The whore threw her arms around him and kissed him deeply. "My Lord Love," she whispered in that throaty voice of hers, "I'd heard of your return and was hoping you'd come today."

Somehow, she always knew when he was in town. Swearing the brothel had an even better spy network than the queen, he gave her tight bottom a small pat.

She kissed his neck in a way she knew drove him wild. "If you'd taken much longer to arrive, Madame Plum would have insisted I engage myself to someone else, and I would have missed out on all this." She grabbed his hand and led him toward the hallway. "I'm so glad you came. I've got a surprise for you. I've been waiting for weeks to show it to you."

Holding his hand, the whore skipped down the hallway. "You are going to love it, but you might want to tie me up first so I don't try to stop you." As she threw open the door to her room, she gave him a wicked wink.

At any other time Cadarn wouldn't have been able to stop himself from throwing Purple Leaf against the wall and grinding his cock against her. Today he merely followed her to the ornate chest at the foot of her bed where she kept her toys. She started to open the chest but abruptly let it slam shut and turned to face him. "You're not touching me." Her eyes flicked to his groin. "What's wrong?"

Cadarn laughed and hugged her. "You've always been able to read my mind, darling."

Purple Leaf shook her head and caressed his groin. "I wouldn't say I can read minds, but I do know *this* part of you intimately."

Despite his mood, his cock started to stir under her touch. He gently removed her hand and threw himself onto her bed. The whore curled up next to him and caressed his hair. "Tell me everything, and Purple Leaf will make it better."

Cadarn laughed without humor. "You know you have a special place in my heart, but my current problem isn't something you can help with." Still, he told her all about Nisse's note and the queen's summons.

"So, you need someone to get a message to your friend without arousing suspicion and arrange a way for you to meet him without anyone knowing about it?" A big grin spread across her face. "You should always have faith in Purple Leaf, Lord Love." She rolled off the bed. "Come on."

Curious, Cadarn followed her to her closet. She pushed her clothes aside, opened a door at the rear, and pointed to a staircase leading down. She lit a candle, and he followed her into an underground room, which had two passages leading from it.

He looked around, smiling. "What is this?"

"Your conspiring room." She pointed to the passageways. "The tunnels have entrances all over the city, at least four that I know of. I can easily use them to get a message to your friend and bring him here."

Cadarn laughed. "I'd heard that warrens like this existed under large parts of the city, but I considered them a myth. How many people know about them?"

Purple Leaf shrugged. "Hardly anyone. Smugglers use the tunnels near the docks, but they never come this far into the city. Madame Plum believes she is the only one who still uses them. She even has a map of them."

He laughed and swept Purple Leaf into his arms. "I always knew you were much more than a pretty face and admirable breasts."

"I'm a *lot* more," she purred, and this time when she kissed his neck, he swept her into his arms and carried her back upstairs.

CHAPTER 4

In the early morning light, Samantha watched through her window as Robbie's uncle helped him into the royal carriage. She hadn't been able to bear to see him again after he'd failed to acknowledge their daughter, and watching him now ripped the heart from her chest. Ronan jumped in the carriage after Robbie. His useless guardian was going with him. As the carriage, surrounded by Robbie's bodyguards, disappeared through the palace gates, tears flowed down her cheeks.

She was alone, absolutely and completely alone. *How dare you, Sulis! How dare you take him from me! If you expect me to fall apart now, you will be disappointed. I am Solar's daughter!*

Needing her daughter, she whirled and headed for the nursery.

When she entered, Cece was nursing the baby, and the Baronesses Glynnis and Eithne were cooing over her. They were all focused on the baby and hadn't heard her enter. "Isn't she just precious?" Eithne said.

Iachus, one of Brianna's bodyguards, cleared his throat. The three women looked up. "Your Majesty," Baroness Glynnis said, and they all started to rise.

Samantha hurried forward. "Stay seated," she said, and Eithne scooted over on the sofa to give Samantha room next to Brianna. She touched her daughter's head. Above all else, she'd keep Brianna safe.

"She's a hungry one, Your Majesty," Cece said.

Brianna let go of the breast, and Cece raised the baby to her shoulder and started patting her back. Samantha reached for her daughter. "Let me do that." Cece relinquished Brianna, and Samantha brought the most precious thing in the world to her shoulder. Brianna burped and snuggled against her.

As Cece excused herself to clean up, Baroness Glynnis patted Samantha's knee. It was a familiar gesture no one had ever used with her, but somehow it felt right. "I see Fenella's love for you in your face now. She didn't have long to love you, but she loved you deeply."

Samantha hugged the sweet warm weight of her daughter more closely,

On her other side, Baroness Eithne scooted closer, reaching out as if she wanted to touch Brianna. "I would have given almost anything to have had one myself." To reassure herself, Samantha called forth the baroness's aura. The older woman burst into colors—an array of blue and pink, yellow and silver—and Samantha felt nearly overwhelmed by sensations of power and wisdom, causing the queen to think about the open seat on the Royal Council.

Eithne beamed. "I wish Fenella could have lived to see this moment." She wiped away a tear.

"You knew my mother, too?"

"Oh my, yes!" Eithne grinned mischievously at Glynnis. "Perhaps not as closely as Glynnis here, but we got up to our share of mischief together."

Glynnis laughed, and the two women started reminiscing about a picnic they all attended when Fenella was only eleven. Fenella had had a servant mix maggots in the pie served to the latest suitor her father was trying to force her to marry. Eithne shook her head. "It certainly wasn't nice, but the duke was sixty-five."

Glynnis touched her friend's arm. "Remember how he stank as if he'd bathed in rotting cheese?" Glynnis's shuddered.

As the baronesses talked, Samantha held the now sleeping Brianna. Her mind drifted to the council chamber, where she imagined Baroness Eithne taking the seat beside her, but in her imagination, the woman sitting next to her quickly changed into her young mother as she appeared in the portrait over her fireplace. Her mother seemed to whisper, "I never truly left you, my daughter. I've always watched over you. My friends will do for you what I cannot."

Is Baroness Eithne the goddess's answer? Has the Holy Mother not forgotten me after all? Samantha so wanted a strong pillar that could support her when she had moments of weakness, a listening ear that could advise her when she was unsure, a bulwark against those who sought to undermine her rule.

Baroness Glynnis got up to leave. "I'm afraid I must run for the moment, but if Your Majesty needs the least thing, send for me. I'd love to care for you at this time, as Fenella would have wanted."

Baroness Eithne started to rise as well. "Could you stay a moment longer?" Samantha asked

"Certainly, if that is Your Majesty's wish." She settled back onto the sofa as Glynnis bowed out the door. "Glynnis said that I had to meet Fenella's granddaughter. I hope Your Majesty doesn't mind that I'm here."

"I'm happy to know another of my mother's friends. Besides, I need to speak with you about Korth's needs." She turned to Brianna's guards. "You may leave us."

They bowed and left Samantha alone with the baroness. A cloud paused over the older woman's face. "I gave the list of needs Your Majesty requested to your secretary. I'm afraid it is rather extensive."

"Yes, it is. They won't be easy to meet. We will discuss them in council this morning."

"Thank you, Your Majesty." The baroness beamed at Brianna. The baroness seemed unable to keep her hands in her lap, and Samantha realized what she wanted.

"Would you like to hold her?" she asked.

"I wouldn't want to impose," she said, reaching forward. "But if Your Majesty doesn't mind, just for a moment."

As she allowed the baroness to take Brianna's sweet warmth, Samantha felt as if she were giving a piece of herself away. Eithne brought Brianna to her shoulder and began rubbing her back. "Like Your Majesty, I married the love of my life when I was just nineteen. But my poor Perth took sick and died before he could get me with child." She wiped tears from her eyes. "Having known love, I couldn't bear to make a political alliance after his death." She paused for a moment, then went on in a rush of words, as if she had to make her opinion known before she lost courage. "It may not be my place, Your Majesty, but I feel I have to speak. Considering His Majesty's injuries, the Royal Council is bound to pressure you to marry again. But you too have known love. Don't let them bully you into a marriage you don't want. When you fill the seat vacated by Duke

Caedmon's death, fill it with someone who will support your wishes. Or at least put maggots in your suitors' meals when necessary."

The baroness's eyes twinkled, and they broke into simultaneous laughter, the first true laugh Samantha could remember in quite some time.

Samantha touched the baroness's leg. "If you didn't return immediately to Korth, is there someone you could trust to manage the emergency for a time?"

The baroness's brow furrowed. "There is quite a bit of work to see to. Why do you ask, Your Majesty?" Then understanding lit up the baroness's eyes. "But, Your Majesty, when I spoke of the council seating, I wasn't implying... I would never seek that level of power or influence. It's..." She looked around the room as if searching for the words to complete the sentence. "Has there ever been a woman on the Royal Council?"

Samantha shook her head. "Not that I know of. Baroness, I am only twenty years old. I have lost both my husband and my most important advisers. Factions you may be unaware of threaten the stability of the joined kingdom. I need someone I can trust to lend me wisdom."

"But Your Majesty barely knows me, and while you have my loyalty, I'm not sure how much wisdom I can offer."

Samantha looked again at the brilliant colors of baroness's aura. "You were my mother's friend. Do you know what Glynnis knows?"

Eithne looked down at her feet, then sideways at Samantha. "About the stable groom, you mean?"

Samantha nodded. "About the man who fathered me when King Solar could not. This makes me of mixed common and noble blood. Eithne, I am an aurora, and your aura tells me that you are precisely what I need. My only hesitation in naming you to the council is whether or not there is someone who can handle your responsibilities in Korth. With Kayne's estates on top of your own to manage, I worry you're needed there."

Eithne looked as if she still couldn't grasp the concept of sitting on the Royal Council. Her mouth snapped shut. "Truth be told, Your Majesty. I've never managed Kayne's estates. His sister Rowena has done a fine job on behalf of her son. After her brother's execution, she came to me wanting to name me protector for her son to prevent any man trying to act contrary to her son's interests. I was more than happy to oblige. So, yes, Your Majesty, between Lady Rowena and my steward, things can be handled without my constant presence. But Your Majesty, are you sure about this?"

* * *

When Samantha entered the council chamber with Baroness Eithne in tow, all were assembled save for Count Pandaran, who was always late. Everyone rose and bowed, but Tierney was noticeably slow in doing so.

She stood at the head of the table, but before she could speak, Count Pandaran stumbled in. He had, of course, taken the time to make sure his hair was curled just right. He bowed. "Forgive my lateness, Your Majesty. You know how servants can be. My valet is the fourth one I've had this year." He straightened the cuff of his sleeve.

Samantha sat and motioned for the others to be seated as well. "Before we discuss the Korthian famine, this council has been one member short for too long. It is time to fill the empty seat. Baroness Eithne, take your seat." She gestured toward the empty chair.

Sheen rose, and the air around him erupted in red, orange, and yellow in a violent, disorganized pattern. Samantha felt bombarded with waves of anger and hatred. He was even more dangerous to her than she'd realized and would stab her in the back the first chance he got. "You are not demeaning this august body by adding a woman to the Royal Council! King Solar may not have had a choice in his heir, but his coddling of you has filled your head with silly notions. First, you marry that *cothla* dog! And now, this! We will not stand for it!"

At the insult to her beloved, fire erupted in her blood, but before she could respond, Baron Teague stood. "How dare you speak to your queen in this manner! In Her Majesty's short rule, she has shown herself to be a woman of vision and honor. As for the king, he saved the joined kingdoms from almost certain annihilation. The Dead Lands grew almost to the borders of your own estates. You will take back your insult, or you will eat my sword." Grabbing a glove from his belt, he started to fling it at Sheen in challenge.

Teague's defense of both herself and her love cooled her own blood. She held up a hand. "Stop this at once! Right isn't determined by force of arms but by law." Conroy stepped beside her with his hand on his sword. She glared at Teague, who tucked his glove back into his belt with a bow. While she couldn't let Teague kill Sheen, the duke had forced her hand. If she showed weakness, the council would devour her. She turned icy eyes on Sheen. "That said, your disrespect will not be tolerated. You will get down on your knees and apologize for your behavior. While you are there, you will give your sacred vow of your loyalty to me as your queen and to King Robrek as my consort. You will do this in the goddess's holy name, or you will no longer be a member of this council."

Sheen practically spat his reply. "You cannot take my seat. The treaty that created the joined kingdoms stipulates that my house will always have a seat on the royal council."

"Your house, yes, but not you. If you do not do as I have commanded, the seat will be filled by Lord Devyn." Devyn was Sheen's oldest son, but Sheen had disowned him.

Sheen's face turned red, and the large vein in his temple throbbed. Bearach stepped up as well. Her guards flanked her as the entire council chamber waited in silence for Sheen's response. He hissed through his teeth. "I will rot in the seven hells before I pledge my loyalty to a peasant *cothla*!"

In a cold, clear voice, Samantha responded, "Your seat on this council is revoked, and you are banished from Lundia. You will return to your estates. If I ever lay eyes on you again, your head will rest on the executioner's block."

Sheen put his hand on his sword hilt but dropped it when Bearach drew his. Instead, he pointed a finger at the queen. "You will regret this day!" He swept out of the chamber.

Count Ultan clearing his throat broke the deadly silence that Sheen's departure had created. "Your Majesty, Duke Sheen's words were unconscionable, but I do wonder if you have thought things through. A woman on the royal council will increase opposition from the True Church of Sulis."

Although Lord Duer had warned her of Ultan's connection to the church, the baron's causal reference to the church that had tried to kill Brianna shocked her. She turned cold eyes on him. "This so-called Church is an abomination to all Sulis holds holy. Its founder is wanted for treason. It continues to exist only because the crown doesn't interfere in matters of religion. Nor, however, does the crown allow religion to interfere with matters of state."

Gwawl pounded a fist on the table. "Her Majesty is right. The Soul Stone broke free in the first place because of High Priest Shylah's persecution of the Korthian priestesses, which prevented them from preforming the ritual that held the Ancient Evil at bay for a thousand years. Faolan was Shylah's disciple. Calling his church an abomination is far too mild a term. The priest is soaked with the blood of all those whose lives were lost to the Stone!"

Ultan clenched his fists. Fearing another confrontation like the one with Sheen, Samantha cut him off. "Speaking of the Soul Stone, we must discuss preventing starvation in the wake of its destruction. Baroness Eithne made a list of the needs of the people of Korth. You have all been provided a copy."

Teague took up his copy of the list and shook his head. "The list is extensive, but I fear it may not represent all that is needed. The Dead Lands intruded at least ten miles into my lands, and my steward took in refugees in my absence. Relief is needed there as well."

Duke Tierney scoffed. "The need cannot be this great. Korth is trying to take advantage of Lundia yet again. And we Lundians will not stand for it." He looked to his fellow Lundians on the council as if expecting their immediate support.

Samantha couldn't allow Tierney to make this a personal issue. "This isn't a matter of pitting Lundia against Korth. We are the joined kingdoms, and the Soul Stone was an attack upon us all. No Korthlundian will starve while it is in my power to prevent it. Blaine, how many acres did the Dead Lands encompass?"

Blaine flipped through his papers. "Approximately two and a half million, Your Majesty."

Duke Tierney laughed. "That figure can't be accurate."

Blaine blushed but stood straighter. "I assure you it is, Your Grace. I have checked my calculations several times. The Dead Lands extended for fifty miles into Korth in all directions from their source at Balley Beg."

Baron Gwawl glared at Tierney. "If compassion doesn't sway you, there are practical matters to consider. Hungry people resort to desperate measures. Arawn and Weylin, your lands are just over the mountains from the affected areas. Do you want hordes of the starving descending on you?"

To Samantha's surprise, Cadarn stood. "Please, Her Majesty is right. We are the joined kingdoms, and we shouldn't let hardship divide us. We have been spoiled by over fifty years of peace among us that we forget what things were like before. Peace has made us all wealthy. Let us not forget how much the conflicts between Korth and Lundia cost both lands in lives as well as wealth."

Samantha blinked. Although Cadarn had said he would use his influence to support the cause, she hadn't expected such a passionate speech, and Duer had found nothing suspicious in his quarters. *What can those black jagged lines in his aura mean?* He continued, "I know this need seems daunting, but we should all take stock of our own resources."

Weylin looked hesitatingly between Tierney and Cadarn, but then he stood as well. "Lundia will not turn our backs on our brothers in need."

Baron Arawn didn't stand, but he nodded. "Indeed, we will not. I'm sure Korth will repay our generosity when the need has passed." He looked pointedly at the baroness.

Eithne smiled. "Certainly, Milord. Certainly."

* * *

Vaughan, the stable boy who'd become the king's squire, stomped his feet as he headed toward the queen's quarters. The rumors about the king's departure couldn't be true. They just couldn't. Vaughan had rescued the king from the cave where His Majesty had destroyed the Soul Stone. It hadn't been easy, either. All by himself he'd had to hoist the badly injured king up a nearly endless ladder. Vaughan's arms and back ached so badly by the time he'd gotten the king to the surface that he'd been reduced to tears. But he hadn't once thought of giving up. After that, he'd brought the injured king all the way back to Murtaghan. The queen had given him a medal of heroism. But if she'd sent the king off without him, the medal meant nothing. She probably blamed him for the king getting injured in the first place.

Just after passing the library, he saw the queen's secretary coming his way. Blaine would know if the rumors were true. He blocked Blaine's path. "It's not true, is it? The queen hasn't sent the king away without me, has she? A knight needs his squire!"

"Well... er..." he stuttered, but the way Blaine avoided looking at him told Vaughan everything he needed to know.

"So, it's true? The king is gone! Without me?"

"Well... er... Her Majesty does have a great many burdens that occupy her attention. Speaking of which, I do have duties to perform." Blaine tried to step around him, but Vaughan moved to block his path.

"Are you saying she forgot I exist? I carried the king's banner when he rode his horses up the side of Gloine Torr. I brought His Majesty back from Korth. It isn't my fault the king got hurt so badly. She thinks I should have died to protect him, doesn't she? I would have if he hadn't gone off without me. I told His Majesty I wouldn't let him go alone, but the king used his magic to make me fall asleep. It's not my fault!"

"Well... er..." But the queen's secretary couldn't seem to say anything else.

Vaughan whirled and ran. He ducked behind a statue so that no one would see him cry. What use was a squire without a knight?

* * *

Wondering if he should tell the queen about his encounter with the boy, Blaine frowned after Vaughan. She was quite fond of Vaughan, and she did owe him a lot. If she found out how he felt, she'd be upset she'd been insensitive to the boy's feelings. Right now, she hardly needed more things to worry about. After all, Vaughan was only a child. He'd get over it soon enough. He shrugged his shoulders and continued to the library to see to Her Majesty's business.

The first thing he saw when he entered the library was his assistant Tuathal standing in front of the library catalog with his hair in his hands as if he was trying to pull it out by the roots. Master Druce, the chief librarian, was sitting at his desk ignoring Tuathal. Druce met Blaine's eyes and then looked pointedly away.

Blaine shut the library door with some force, and Tuathal looked up. "Sir, thank the goddess you're here. I've been trying to do the research Her Majesty requested, but this catalog makes no sense, and that man"—he pointed a trembling hand at Druce— "is no help whatsoever."

With the knowledge that the queen believed him to be the "best secretary a queen could have," Blaine crossed the room and looked down at the man whose disorder had made the time he'd spent in the library a living hell. Druce continued to pretend not to notice him. "Is this true? Are you denying the queen your assistance?"

Druce's head snapped around, and he pointed a shaky finger at Tuathal. "That puffed up middle-aged crooked nosed churl is not the queen! That hedge-born fop had the nerve to question my ordering of the library!"

"But sir," Tuathal protested. "He shelves the books beginning with the nationality of the author! And then by their rank and then—"

Druce ignored Tuathal. "Why the queen ever chose such a fat-kidneyed clout for her secretary is beyond me."

"Your attitude is unacceptable!" Blaine surprised even himself with his tone. "You well know that Tuathal answers directly to me. He is performing important research on the queen's behalf. By refusing him assistance, you are undermining the throne itself. You will cease this petulance immediately and offer Tuathal all the help he requires."

"Petulance?" Druce spat the word back at him. "I will do nothing until he apologizes on his knees for insulting me."

Tuathal rolled his eyes and started sinking to his knees. Blaine grabbed his arm. While he appreciated Tuathal's willingness to humiliate himself to better serve the queen, Druce had gotten away with this behavior long enough. "He will not apologize for telling the truth. Because of your nonsense system, this library is about as orderly as a pile of leaves after a gale, so to speak."

"How dare—"

"I wasn't finished. You will not only offer Tuathal every assistance, but you will apologize for the insults *you* flung at *him*. After that, you will throw out this ridiculous catalog and reorder the library's contents by subject." Blaine had timidly made the same suggestion when he worked in the library, and Druce had come close to firing him for it.

Druce rose to his feet. "I have been in charge of the library longer than you and the queen combined have been alive, and I will not be dictated to by children. Get out of my library, and don't come back. If Her Majesty needs information, tell her to send someone else."

"The queen has been lenient with you, but you go too far. You may pack your things. I will arrange for a token of the queen's gratitude for your long service. But by this time tomorrow, you will have removed yourself from the palace."

Druce stared at him as if he were a filthy cur who'd stood on his hind legs and given a sermon. "Why, you little scrub-nosed loiter sack! I will not be spoken to in this manner!"

The twin undersecretaries Garran and Garrett scurried up to their master. "If Master Druce goes, we go," Garran said, while Garrett nodded.

During his time at the library, the twins, as Druce's favorites, had done their part to make Blaine's life miserable, so he smiled. "If that is how you want it, all three of you may pack your things."

Druce snorted. "You haven't the authority to fire me! If the queen wants me gone, she'll have to send the Royal Guard to drag me out and throw me in the street!"

"Fine." Blaine whirled, headed to the library door, and called the two guardsmen stationed nearby.

"Sir," one said as they both nodded to him.

"Escort Master Druce out of the palace. If he resists, drag him out and throw him in the street." To Blaine's surprise and pleasure, the guards didn't hesitate in obeying him.

Screaming curses at the top of his lungs, Druce was dragged from the library. When he and the twins were gone, the other library undersecretaries stood and gave a cheer. Blaine called to Owen, the oldest. "I don't have the authority to make a permanent appointment and the queen might have another preference. But for the time being, I'm appointing you chief librarian. Your first job is to help Tuathal with his research. Your second is reorganize the library so that it makes sense."

Owen smiled. "Thank you, Blaine. I mean, Master Blaine. You don't know how long I've wanted this."

"Good. Let's get to work."

* * *

Standing before his easel, Devyn stared at his painting of the royal wedding. Although the wedding had happened months ago, the painting still wasn't complete. The king and queen had been so busy dealing with the crisis of the Soul Stone that they hadn't had much time to sit. Now, if rumors were correct, King Robrek was gone. Devyn was going to have to finish it from memory. Something wasn't right about the king's face, but he couldn't quite put his finger on what.

The door of his room crashed open, and he whirled to find his father barreling toward him. Stupidly, he brandished his paint brush in defense. Although he managed to get brown paint on his father's tunic, Sheen threw him against the wall.

"Father, what—?"

"What did I do to be cursed with such a worthless son?" Sheen bellowed and slapped Devyn across the face so hard he tumbled to the ground.

This wasn't supposed happen anymore. Since the queen had made him court artist, his father officially had no more control over him. But at the moment, Sheen didn't seem to care. Although his father had beaten him viciously since he was a child, today Sheen looked as though he might kill him. "Father, please!" Devyn was ashamed of how pathetic he sounded. "I haven't done anything!"

"Haven't done anything?" Sheen loomed over him. "What have you been telling the bastard who thinks she can be queen?"

Devyn's eyes widened, wondering how his father could utter treason so openly. He'd always been careful before. "I haven't—"

Sheen drew his sword. "I should have smothered you the moment you came out of your mother's womb! It's time I rectified that mistake!"

Scrambling to get out of the way, Devyn grabbed a nearby painting of the Murtaghan harbor to defend himself. He barely got it up in time for his father's sword to crash down on it, breaking the frame and tearing the painting. "Father, please—"

As Sheen raised his sword again, two members of the Royal Guard burst through the door with swords drawn.

"Drop your weapon, and step away from your son, Your Grace," one of the guards ordered.

Sheen whirled on the guards and attacked. But his father was old and slow, and his sword soon flew across the room, tearing another of Devyn's paintings in the process. The two guards held their swords on his father. One of them flicked his sword toward the door, and said, "Allow us to escort Your Grace out of the palace! Your servants can pack your belongings and send them after you."

Sheen clenched his fists, and Devyn feared his father was going to make the guards kill him. "I will leave, but this isn't the end of it!" Followed by the guards, Sheen stalked out the door.

As soon as they were gone, Lady Aislinn ran in and grabbed Devyn in a crushing hug. "Devyn, my boy, I'm so glad I could get guards here in time. When I saw your father pounding toward your room, I feared the worst."

Mostly to reassure her he was unharmed, Devyn returned Aislinn's hug. "What happened? Why is he so angry?"

Aislinn buried her head in his chest. "I heard Her Majesty has removed Duke Sheen from the royal council and replaced him with you."

"With *me*?" Devyn laughed. "Her Majesty would never do that!" It was folly enough that she'd made him court artist.

Aislinn kissed his cheek. "Don't underestimate yourself, my boy. Her Majesty isn't as blind as your father. She can see your worth, as I always have."

* * *

Several hours after the council meeting, Blaine informed Samantha that Captain Hawk and two members of the Royal Guard were asking to see her. She took a sip of wine, prayed that they brought her no new problems, and told Blaine to show them in.

They entered with her personal guards, and they all bowed to her. As captain of the Royal Guard, Hawk led the closest thing the joined kingdoms had to an army. Since Korthlundia had been at peace for fifty years, it was neither large nor experienced in combat. Mostly, they dealt with palace security and bandit raids across their northern border. Hawk was only a few years older than she was. "Duke Sheen refused to leave quietly, Your Majesty," Hawk informed her. He asked the guards to report the incident.

The guard related Sheen's attack on Lord Devyn. "We hope we acted correctly, Your Majesty. We know His Grace is a duke, but his actions seemed dangerous."

I should have beheaded the bastard! She considered sending men to drag Sheen back for his own execution. But she remembered the first time she witnessed her father ordering someone executed. She'd only been five, but he'd sat her on his lap and explained why beheading the count was his only choice. The count had tried to annex portions of his neighbor's land, leading to the deaths of nearly one hundred men. Never treating her like a child, King Solar had always explained his decisions and he never seemed to tire of her endless, often childish questions. In addition to explaining the necessity of the count's execution, Solar had cautioned her about resorting to that particular form of justice too often. She could still hear his words: "Remember, my dear, executing someone isn't a mistake that can be undone. If the nobility fear for their life at the slightest offense, they have no reason to temper their actions. The more nobles you kill, the more you will have to kill to keep the peace, until you will rule over a kingdom soaked with blood and torn apart by warfare. This is something you must avoid.

"Keeping the joined kingdom at peace will be your most important job as queen. War not only hurts those directly involved in the battles, but its horrors spread to the common people. Hunger and starvation of the peasant class is almost always a byproduct of war. Not only that, war hardens the soldiers involved, deadening the natural concern for humanity Sulis implanted in all people. It rapidly becomes an endless cycle of barbarity until one wonders whether beasts have taken the place of humanity."

Solar had shuddered when speaking those words. He'd spent the first twenty-five years of his reign trying to end the wars his father had begun. When Solar had finally succeeded, he'd dedicated the rest of his long reign to maintaining peace. It was why he sometimes allowed the nobles' lesser abuses to continue unredressed. Again, she heard his words, "The wellbeing of the common people is a queen's responsibility, but you must always weigh the harm of the abuse against the harm of stopping it. The suffering of peasants under an abusive lord is small compared to their suffering during open warfare. I have seen both, and I know of what I speak."

Samantha was determined to be the queen Solar raised her to be. Duke Sheen would live for now.

The guards shifted their feet, still waiting for her answer. "I thank you for your quick action in saving Lord Devyn's life." She took a ring off each hand and handed them to the guards. "Take these with my gratitude."

One of the guards demurred. "Your Majesty, we were just doing our job." But they were both beaming with pride. Her father had also taught her to always show appreciation to underlings. Their loyalty was a powerful tool for a monarch.

CHAPTER 5

Having received a cryptic note from Purple Leaf, Cadarn headed to The Jeweled Plum Tree. He thought someone might be slipping through the shadows behind him but decided looking over his shoulder too often would make whoever it was more suspicious. Besides, an extra visit to the brothel wasn't out of the ordinary. *Sulis curse it! Just what does the queen know? And why wasn't I able to throw off her suspicions with my support of her?*

When he arrived, Purple Leaf wasn't in the main salon. Madame Plum saw him and bustled over. The proprietor of the brothel was a middle-aged woman as plump as her name suggested. However, she still showed signs of the beauty she must have held as a young woman. She even took an occasional client herself if a man interested her enough.

"Welcome, Milord." She spoke in an obviously fake Gallian accent; some referred to Gallia as the land of lovers. "Purple Leaf awaits you in her room. I know it is most irregular, but she claims she has a surprise for you. You know the way, of course."

Wondering what the whore was up to, Cadarn thanked the madam and hurried to Purple Leaf's room. He opened her door without knocking to find her on her bed kissing a naked man. A surge of jealousy shot through him. Did she honestly think that the sight of her kissing another would be something he'd enjoy? They broke apart, and Purple Leaf moved so that the man's face was visible. Cadarn froze. There was a wicked scar on his right cheek that hadn't been there before, but the same dirty blond hair fell into his eyes, the same close-cropped beard framed his smile, and the same rock-hard body rose gracefully to his feet.

"Liridona," the man said, "you took so long we almost started without you."

"Nisse!" Cadarn barreled across the room and crushed the friend of his heart in a hug, which Nisse returned with equal enthusiasm. "It is so good to see you, to hold you again!"

Nisse drew back to look at him, kissed him on both cheeks, and then gave him a more lingering kiss on the lips. "The same, my friend! I have missed you so."

Purple Leaf sat on the bed with her legs tucked under her, still wearing her pasties and loin cloth but nothing else. She beamed at them. "Do you like my surprise?"

Cadarn pulled Nisse close again. "Immensely, but I told you discretion was needed."

"I was very discrete. He—"

"It is an interesting story, but my cock is hard as a rock," Nisse interrupted. "Before we tell it, I thought we could share this beauty. Get your clothes off, and once we've sated ourselves, we can talk at our leisure."

Cadarn tore at his tunic's buttons.

* * *

Partially clothed and with a nice bottle of wine and a platter of delicacies on the table, Cadarn sat with Nisse in the "conspiring room." Cadarn couldn't stop smiling. "It's never as good when you aren't there." Now that they were alone, they spoke Svizran.

Nisse laughed around a mouthful of cheese. He'd always had a bad habit of talking with his mouth full. "I feel the same. I've even tried sharing a whore with other men, but the magic never happens."

Cadarn tried to tell himself it didn't matter who Nisse had slept with in the ten years they'd been apart, but he'd never considered sharing a whore with anyone other than Nisse. In fact, Nisse was the only man he'd ever been with. He wasn't sure why he'd assumed Nisse had been as faithful.

Nisse nodded toward the ceiling. "That little whore up there is something special. She brought me here through a deserted shrine near the docks. She wore a large hood and walked with a bent back. I thought she was an old woman until she disrobed to reveal that delicious body. You trust her?"

"Absolutely. I helped her sister out, and I pay her well."

While they ate, they reminisced about old times. Nisse had always been starving after sex, and that apparently hadn't changed. "Remember Blerina?" Nisse's eyes twinkled as he named their favorite whore in Fribourg. "She was a fiery one."

"How could I forget such beauty, especially after what happened the first time we shared her?" Cadarn groaned and shook his head.

Nisse raised an eyebrow, and then he burst into laughter as the memory dawned on him. "Master Altherr," the two friends said together.

He and Nisse had been carousing all night and had shared Blerina in the early morning hours. As the sun had started to rise, Cadarn realized they'd be late for class. He had thrown on his clothes and raced to the university. As he rounded the corner from the brothel to the main street, he'd run smack dab into Altherr, nearly knocking him over. As Cadarn apologized repeatedly, Master Altherr glared at him. The professor's words were still burned into Cadarn's memory. Imitating the master's voice, Cadarn repeated them now: "You think you own the streets here? Cadarn, isn't it? Son of some foreign duke?" Master Altherr had known perfectly well who he and his father were as well as the fact that his mother had been Svizran, but he'd played that game almost every time he spoke to him, as if to remind him that he didn't belong in a democracy.

Nisse had caught up to him in time to hear his response, which he repeated now. "My father's a count, not a duke, sir, but I assure you, sir, he doesn't like me."

Cadarn continued to imitate Master Altherr. "Not liked by your father? What a stirring recommendation for any son!" Cadarn groaned again. "Of all the people to run into, it would have had to be him! It took nearly three years before the master would think well of me."

Nisse caressed his arm. "But you became his favorite student in the end. If he'd lived, he would have been proud to see you now."

"No, he would have withheld his pride until I'd succeeded in making Korthlundia as free as Svizra."

Nisse squeezed his arm, then let go to pop the last shrimp in his mouth. "Which is why I'm here now. Why didn't you meet me at the

Traveler's Haven? I assure you I've been most careful to avoid arousing suspicion."

Cadarn shook his head. "The queen summoned me and asked me odd questions." He relayed what happened.

Nisse wrinkled his forehead. "Disturbing but not a definite indication she knows anything. Still, we should never be seen together. How far have you planned this revolution of yours?"

"The queen just gave birth. I thought if we kidnapped her baby, we could force her to abdicate."

"I like it. New mothers can be quite emotional about their offspring. Potential allies? The people I've talked to speak very highly of your queen. Who doesn't like her?"

"The most obvious is the True Church of Sulis." Cadarn explained the schism in the Lundian church.

Nisse turned up his nose in disgust. "Religious zealots! Anyone who thinks they have a god whispering in their ear isn't exactly sane. Still, they do have a lot of passion, and if you need someone to sacrifice themselves for your cause, no one's better than a zealot. Does this church have money?"

"Quite a lot."

"Good. Please don't think me mercenary." He paused, the obvious irony twinkling in his eyes. "For myself, your love and friendship are all I ask in return. But my men only fight for gold, and this undertaking won't be cheap. Who else?"

"As for the Royal Council, Duke Tierney has been already plotting to oppose her and won't be hard to bring to our side. And during today's council meeting, the queen made more allies for us. She had Duke Sheen thrown out of the palace and exiled to Korth. He's always hated her anyway. Then she called the True Church an abomination. Count Ultan is a zealot himself and closely tied to Father Faolan. He practically wants her burned at the stake for insulting the church. Count Weylin's a coward and will join whichever side is winning. To top things off, her secretary fired the chief librarian."

Nisse laughed, giving Cadarn a somewhat nauseating view of half chewed bread. "I'm not sure what use a librarian is to us, but we can definitely make use of the others." At least Cadarn was pretty sure that's what he said. Nisse swallowed, "I understand how these men can be turned against the queen, but will they then support the destruction of the system that gives them their power?"

"No, they'd have to be ignorant of our true goal and certainly will have to be dealt with once they learn of it."

Nisse poured himself a glass of wine and sipped it in silence for a few moments. "Liridona, with the addition of my mercenaries, we could succeed. But overthrowing a queen is no childhood game. Are you absolutely sure you want to do this?"

Cadarn straightened. "You know bringing democracy to my homeland has been my dream since our student days, and by using the queen's daughter against her, we can free my country without the bloody battles that freed yours."

Nisse leaned forward and squeezed his hand gently. "It is possible it may work out as you say, but I see many ways it could go wrong. At university when you spoke of your homeland, you made me believe it was a land of nightmares, its people crushed under an oppressive tyranny, being abused by every noble in sight. But my friend, I have witnessed plenty of tyranny, and this queen of yours doesn't seem so bad. Slavery is illegal here. Do you know how rare that is? And all children are taught to read and do simple sums, which is even rarer. It's a skill few of my men possess. The queen is loved by the common people."

Cadarn withdrew his hand from Nisse's and stood. "You are only seeing the surface. They *are* being crushed. No one should be allowed to act as my father did."

"I know you hated your father, but you would never tell me why."

"That's because I was ashamed of him. My father thought that being count entitled him to do anything he wanted. Do you know why he sent me halfway around the world to university? I walked in on him in the barn trying to rape one of the dairy maids. She struggled and pleaded with him not to ruin her. I pulled the bastard off her and broke his nose." Cadarn formed a fist. He could still hear the sickening crunch. "But my actions did no good. My father had me held down, and after beating the shit out of me, he forced me to watch as he raped the girl and had half a dozen of his men do likewise. Afterward, he'd loaded me on the first ship to Svizra, telling me that if I didn't respect noble privilege, I could go to my mother's homeland where there wasn't any and see how I liked it. I later heard the diary maid killed herself."

"Truly revolting." Nisse looked as nauseous as Cadarn had been when he realized his attempts to help the girl had only made it worse. "Your father was a repulsive human being and his actions terrible. But Liridona, revolutions always turn bloody. How far are you willing to go to bring down your queen?"

Cadarn slammed his hands on the table. "I'm willing to go as far as necessary! I will bring down this oppressive system, or I will die trying!"

Nisse stood and mimed drawing his sword. He dropped into a fighting stance and flourished the imaginary sword. "Then let us plot." Nisse went still, and a light shown in his eyes. "I have it! This is perfect!"

Cadarn leaned forward. "Out with it."

Nisse dropped into his chair and detailed his plan. Afterward, Cadarn grabbed his friend and hugged him. "You are the best friend a man could ever have."

Nisse returned the hug, leaned back, took Cadarn by the shoulders, and met his eyes. "The plan is brilliant if I do say so myself, but you still must know that few plans survive the first battle. Things could still go disastrously wrong and end up in a blood bath."

"You worry too much." Cadarn drew Nisse close and gave him a long lingering kiss. "I'll find Duke Sheen before he has a chance to leave Murtaghan."

* * *

While her older brother Quinn sat on her bed, Oriana looked through her wardrobe. Her hand trembled as she felt the hundreds of small braids, like those worn by every member of the Korthian priesthood. This morning each braid felt like one of her dead sisters. Over the last few months, she'd learned that every last one of them had died fighting the Soul Stone. She should have been there to die with them.

She jerked her hand away from her hair as if it had been burned and grabbed her cloak. "I'm sorry I have to hurry off, but I need to meet Father Leigh at city hall for our weekly clinic." The free clinic had been started by the king when he'd been well. Although neither she nor Father Leigh could manage the miraculous healing King Robrek had been capable of, they still helped a lot of people.

Quinn sighed. "I'm not stupid. The clinic is tomorrow, Sweet Thyme." He stood and glared down at her. "Oriana, you said you needed to stay in Murtaghan to see the queen safely through childbirth. You've done that. Both the queen and the baby princess are healthy. When are we going home?"

Oriana turned away from her brother and hung her cloak back in the wardrobe. When her healing gifts had started to manifest, her family had taken to calling her by the names of various herbs. That had once comforted her. Today she wanted to shove thyme down her brother's throat. "I'm not ever going home."

Quinn grabbed her shoulder and turned her to face him. "Oriana, you have to. The devastation caused by the Soul Stone is enormous, and you are all that remains of the Korthian priestesshood."

"Don't you think I know that? I'm not going back to be haunted by my sisters' ghosts!" She wiped viciously at her tears. She'd already cried enough over their loss.

Quinn hugged her to him. "Burdock root, I know it hurts, but you have responsibilities to the goddess and the people of Korth." He fingered her braids. "You are Sulis's servant."

Oriana pushed him away. "What I am is fourteen." She rushed to her dressing table and picked up a pair of scissors. "I can't restore the priesshood alone." With a trembling hand, she cut off a single braid. It felt like cutting off a piece of her soul, but if this was what she had to do to get her brother to leave her alone, she'd do it. She glared at her brother, daring him to object. He merely looked at her, so she clipped another and another, then grabbed a handful and hacked them off. Faster and faster she cut so that she couldn't change her mind. Quinn just watched her do it.

When she found no more to cut, he stared at her with eyes that didn't seem to see and then headed to the door. He paused before opening it. "Since you've decided to turn your back on the goddess, I guess this is goodbye."

After he left, she collapsed onto her bed, sobbing. *How dare he condemn me! Sulis, Mother of us all, you understand, don't you? I'm only fourteen!*

* * *

When Blaine entered the library, he gasped. Books were stacked all over the tables and piled high on the floor. Dozens of shelves stood empty. The library undersecretaries buzzed among the mess, adding books to stacks or taking them from stacks and putting them on the shelves. Although Tuathal had reported the reorganization of the library was in process, Blaine somehow hadn't expected such disorder. Putting a hand to his forehead, he assured himself that the mess was only a temporary necessity in making the library as orderly as he'd always dreamed it could be.

He sighted Tuathal nearly hidden behind stacks of books and headed toward him. Tuathal had been providing him regular reports on the results of his research into auras, but none of it had yet proven helpful to the queen. But last night Tuathal had indicated that, in reordering the library, the librarians had discovered several volumes about auras that hadn't been listed in the catalog. He hoped his assistant had learned something he could take to the queen who was growing impatient with the lack of progress.

As Blaine approached, Tuathal smiled widely. "Sir, I'm so glad you came. I have so much to report."

As Blaine sat next to his assistant, the weight that had been burdening him lightened. "The new books proved useful?"

"Yes, sir. Enormously." Tuathal looked down at several sheets of notes piled in front of him, covered with his rather cramped but neat handwriting. "The books have definitely confirmed that an aurora must be of mixed common and noble blood. I had been skeptical about that, but the new books leave no doubt." Tuathal looked up at him as if he were a puppy expecting a reward.

Blaine struggled to avoid rolling his eyes. The queen had, of course, known this from the beginning. But of course, Tuathal didn't know of the queen's power. He forced a smile. "Well done. What else?"

Tuathal looked down at his notes. "Auroras definitely must be female because the power comes from the womb, and it changes as the woman cycles through life, beginning when she starts to bleed, maturing with the birth of a child, and ending with the cessation of her monthly blood flow."

Blaine leaned forward. The only new piece of information was that someday the queen would lose her ability. That was hardly comforting and was certainly no use to her presently. Tuathal went through the rest of his notes, but there was nothing in them that was the slightest bit of use to the queen. His insides sank as he imagined seeing the queen's face as he again reported Tuathal's lack of progress.

Tuathal was still staring at him expectantly, and Blaine struggled to tamp down his own disappointment. One thing Her Majesty had taught him was that showing appreciation for an underling's efforts inspired him to put even greater energy into the task at hand. He patted Tuathal on the shoulder. "Well done. I'm certain Her Majesty will be pleased. I'm sure she'll want to send round a bottle of your favorite wine as a token of her appreciation. Carry on. Her Majesty is most interested in the colors an aurora sees."

Tuathal beamed. "There's an entire chapter on that in this book." He took one from the stack beside him. "I'll have more on that as quickly as I can."

* * *

Duke Sheen arrived at the Jeweled Plum Tree in answer to a rather presumptuous note he'd received from Count Cadarn. However, if it helped him get even with the queen, he could deal with the count's presumption later. When he entered, a whore with rather impressive breasts greeted him. "Come this way, Your Grace."

Sheen chuckled and grabbed one of the whore's breasts. "While I wouldn't mind playing with this, I have business with…"

The whore grabbed him and kissed him on the mouth. As she broke the kiss, she whispered, "Shush, Your Grace! The walls have ears. I'm to take you to him."

The whore took his hand, and he followed her to a room. After closing the door, she led him through a closet and pointed to a staircase leading down. "They are below, Your Grace."

Sheen hesitated; then voices rose from below. He recognized Count Cadarn's and Count Ultan's. Ultan was objecting to having been taken to a house of sin. *The self-righteous ass probably can't get it up anymore, even if he is fifteen years my junior.*

As Sheen descended, Cadarn sighed. "Here we can be safe from the queen's spies." He caught sight of Sheen and rose, as was appropriate. "Welcome, Your Grace. Thank you for joining us."

Ultan rose as well, as did a foreigner Sheen didn't know. Both Cadarn and Ultan bowed their heads to him, but the foreigner merely smirked. Sheen eyed Ultan. "Not worried about your reputation in coming to a brothel?"

Ultan glared, but it was Cadarn who answered. "I had him brought through an underground tunnel. Since he doesn't frequent whores, coming through the front door of my favorite brothel would have been suspicious.

Sheen snorted. A man who didn't appreciate beautiful women performing their proper function wasn't to be trusted. As was appropriate, the men waited for Sheen to choose a chair before retaking their own seats. At least, Cadarn and Ultan did. The foreigner seemed to have no sense of dignity, or perhaps he was of higher rank than he appeared. He'd seen some foreign nobles who dressed almost like peasants, and the king's uncle, who hadn't a drop of noble blood, dressed like an exotic bird.

When they'd taken their seats, Cadarn introduced the foreigner. "This is Nisse Hauptmann, my friend from university days."

Sheen snorted and addressed the upstart, "You think awfully highly of yourself for a man without a title."

The man rolled his eyes. "Forgive me, *Your Grace*. Is there some ridiculous rule of protocol I have neglected? Should I have bowed to your greatness, perhaps?"

"Please, Nisse," Cadarn admonished him. The foreigner shrugged, and Cadarn turned to Sheen. "Please forgive my friend's rough manners. I assure you he is necessary for our plans." He nodded to the overly pious Ultan. "I think we can all agree that Sulis never intended a woman to rule."

Ultan made a noise of disgust. "Especially one who has tainted herself by bedding a *cothla*."

Ultan could be extremely tiresome, but Cadarn had intrigued Sheen. "What is it you're implying?"

"The queen must go." Cadarn told them about the mercenary army the foreigner was bringing in. "For the plan to work, we'll have to lure the queen out of Lundia without her child. That's where you come in, Your Grace." He nodded toward Duke Sheen. "If you harbor Father Faolan at your estates, the queen will have no choice but to personally come to confront you. As soon as she crosses into Korth, we will grab the child, forcing the queen to come scurrying back. At which time, she will abdicate or die." He turned to Ultan. "Milord, you will bear the message to Father Faolan. I'm sure you know how to find him. We will also need funds to pay our mercenaries"

"The Holy Father's accommodations are less than comfortable. I'm sure he'd be in favor of the plan, especially since it would rid us forever of an abomination."

Thinking the high priest would be a rather tiresome guest, Sheen rubbed his beard. "I'm in favor of the bitch's death, but what do I get out of taking such a risk?"

Cadarn smiled. "You will become king of Korth." He nodded to Ultan. "And you of Lundia."

Taken aback, Sheen blinked. "You'd split the kingdoms?"

Cadarn nodded. "I see no choice. If I tried to make either of you king of the joined kingdoms, I'd divide our other support. Besides, the kingdoms were never meant to be joined."

Knowing he was the rightful king of both kingdoms, Sheen considered objecting, but decided he could be happy with Korth for now and take Lundia when the time was right.

Ultan touched the star of Sulis he wore around his neck. "Not all in the Royal Guard are loyal to the queen. Some among them would join our cause."

Cadarn grinned in a manner that told Sheen that this was a welcome surprise. "You're sure of this?"

Ultan nodded. "Lieutenant Gerard is a true servant of the god and has frequently expressed his unhappiness with the state of affairs to Father Faolan. He tells of others who share his discontent."

Cadarn exchanged looks with the foreigner, who nodded. "Excellent. If you are sure of his loyalty, you will have to bring this lieutenant to meet me."

Ultan said, "He is loyal. The priests of Sulis's true church have means to assure this."

Cadarn raised an eyebrow. "Please explain."

Ultan shook his head. "The means prevents me from saying more, but I assure you it is effective. But for the Holy Father to agree, he will need the assurance that Sulis's true word will be supported across both kingdoms."

"Since you will be king of Lundia, you can give him your personal assurance," Cadarn said. He turned to Sheen. "And Your Grace?'

Sheen wanted to throw the entire pious lot in a well, but that too could wait until the power that was rightfully his was in his hands. "Agreed." There was just one thing that didn't sit right. "And what do you get out of it?" he asked Cadarn.

"You will each give me a dukedom, as a reward."

Sheen nodded. "I can live with that." Believing the conversation completed, he started to rise.

Cadarn put out a hand. "One moment, Your Grace. For our plan's success, Tierney's forces and coin would be advantageous. I doubt Tierney will cooperate without being promised the throne. Only the three of us need know that it isn't a promise we intend to keep."

Sheen laughed. Tierney thought too highly of himself. He would enjoy the upstart duke getting what he deserved.

* * *

As Duke Sheen returned to the common room escorted by Count Cadarn's favorite whore, Lord Duer looked up from the delightful breasts he'd been nuzzling, which belonged to Golden Drop. Since his servant Gael had earlier seen Cadarn go to Purple Leaf's room and he hadn't yet returned, this was a development that would certainly interest the queen.

As Sheen gave Purple Leaf's admirable breasts a parting squeeze, the whore glanced in Duer's direction. To hide his interest in the duke, Duer lowered his head and flicked his tongue over Golden Drop's nipple. She moaned in a manner that went straight to his cock. Yes, the queen needed to know what he'd learned, but he didn't see why the news couldn't wait until after he'd fully sampled the plum in his arms.

* * *

When Purple Leaf returned from escorting Duke Sheen out of the brothel, she whispered in Cadarn's ear before leading Ultan back through the tunnels. After they left, Nisse picked up his glass of whiskey and leaned back in his chair. "By the republic, I hate nobles, such greedy little wenches, the lot of them." He downed the rest of his whiskey. "What did the slimy one mean when he said the priests could ensure loyalty?"

Cadarn frowned. "I don't know, but we may have a more immediate problem. Purple Leaf told me that Lord Duer asked her questions about me yesterday. I dismissed it as unimportant, but now she tells me that Duer is above and witnessed Duke Sheen leave."

Nisse sat his whiskey glass on the table. "Do you think this Duer spies for the queen?"

Cadarn nodded. "I'm concerned he may."

Nisse rose and hurried down a different side tunnel than the one Purple Leaf had used. He returned after about ten minutes. As he poured himself another glass of whiskey, he announced, "It's been taken care of."

Cadarn didn't ask, but he knew his friend had arranged for one of his men to kill the lord. Telling himself it was necessary, he tried to put it from his thoughts. "The meeting with Sheen and Ultan went well. Tierney will be even easier to bring on board."

"It did go well." Nisse leaned in and kissed him. "But since none of your co-conspirators have your idealism, you are playing a dangerous game."

Cadarn leaned away from him. "I'm getting tired of your naysaying."

Nisse pulled him closer. "Liridona, it is my job to point out potential problems. Don't be angry with me." Nisse grinned and batted his eyelashes.

Cadarn laughed. He'd never been able to stay angry with his friend.

* * *

"Just where are we going?" Duke Tierney demanded of the whore as she led him through a maze of underground tunnels. When he'd returned to his quarters, he'd found a note shoved under his door directing him to meet this woman at a derelict shrine near the docks if he wanted to get even with the queen. After a brief hesitation, he'd obeyed. The queen had been insufferable. He'd been briefly fooled into believing she was a woman, but she was nothing but a girl bent on having her own way no matter what it cost. Still, the farther he followed the old woman through the tunnel, the more he questioned the wisdom of agreeing.

"Just a bit farther," the woman said, which told him nothing at all.

Just as he was about to grab the whore and demand she take him back, he heard the laughter of two men ahead. The woman led him around the corner and into an underground room, where Count Cadarn and a strange foreigner waited.

They were seated at a table but got to their feet when he entered. Cadarn nodded toward him. "Your Grace, I apologize for asking you to meet in this manner. Thank you for coming." As the count gestured him toward the chair at the head of the table and offered him a very fine vintage, the whore scrambled up a staircase and disappeared.

Tierney glared at Cadarn. What he'd done in the council meeting had cost them all plenty, and it was unconscionable arrogance to summon him in this manner: the count was far below him on the social ladder. Still, since he was here, he might as well hear the man out. He sat stiffly.

Cadarn sat on one side of the table and the foreigner on the other. "Your Grace, this is Nisse Hauptmann, a friend from my days at Fribourg University. I've asked you to come because of your attempt to unite Lundia against the queen."

Tierney narrowed his eyes. "Which you undermined at the first opportunity."

Cadarn bent his head humbly. "I'm afraid I had to alleviate the queen's suspicions. I have only the best interests of the joined kingdoms in mind. I've long been concerned that the queen is far too young to rule alone."

At this statement of the obvious, Tierney sniffed. "She is a willful brat, spoiled by a too fond king gone soft in his dotage. She needs to be taken in hand. She summoned me before the council meeting, and I went with the full attention of accepting her offer of marriage in exchange for supporting her mad idea of aiding Korth, but the foolish girl rebuffed and insulted me. She claims to have no intention of replacing her consort."

Cadarn stood as if he were as shocked as Tierney had been. "I shouldn't be surprised, but I must admit I'm dismayed that she actually plans to rule alone. She must be forced to change her mind."

Tierney laughed hollowly. "And you think you have the charisma I lack to change it?"

"Oh, no, Your Grace." Cadarn took his seat and leaned toward the duke deferentially. "If she refused you, no mere charm could sway her." He leaned back and glanced at the stranger, who had so far said nothing. The foreigner nodded, and Cadarn went on, "I'm taking a great risk by trusting you, but I see no choice. The joined kingdoms needs you at its head if it is to survive, and I have a plan to put you there."

As Tierney listened, he scooted his chair closer to the count. He laughed when Cadarn concluded, "I'm afraid that in order to get Sheen's help, I may have told him untruths. I led him to believe that I intended to split the joined kingdoms and make him king of Korth. You are the only one I would trust as king of the joined kingdoms. The queen's forces will surely crush the duke, but in doing so, she will be greatly weakened. She'll have no choice but to accept your proposal, but you will be no mere consort, as King Robrek had been—you will rule. Please keep this our little secret for now, as I also may have indicated to Count Ultan that he will be king. But of course, that's absurd."

Tierney patted Cadarn's arm. "You acted wisely in keeping the truth from the others."

* * *

With the great Father Faolan and the ever-faithful Count Ultan seated at a table behind him, Father Eadoin knelt at the altar in the dank room far beneath the Temple of the True Believer. With *Blood Magic and the Faithful* on the altar before him, he poured wine into a chalice. That Father Faolan allowed him to perform the god's rites rather than doing so himself was the greatest of honors. Eadoin could now make the Potion of Secrets without referring to the book, but he'd found himself growing uncomfortable if separated from it for long.

Eadoin added a few simple herbs to the wine. After stirring the mixture with a silver knife, he lowered his head to implore Sulis's blessing. With the invocation complete, Eadoin brought the chalice to the table and offered the knife to Father Faolan. The great man made a shallow cut in his palm and squeezed his blood into the chalice. Count Ultan did the same. After adding his own blood to the wine, Eadoin returned the chalice to the altar and asked the god's blessing yet again.

When Eadoin had finished, the bright purple of the wine had dulled to a sickly blue. He brought the chalice back to the table and took the first sip himself, grimacing at the foul taste. When the others had partaken, Father Faolan greeted the count. "Now that secrecy is ensured, what brings you here, my son? Know it is dangerous to come too often."

Ultan bowed his head. "Yes, Your Holiness, but I have been approached with a plan that might be of assistance to Sulis's great work." The count told of Count Cadarn's plot to overthrow the queen. When he finished, the count bowed lower. "I would never think of taking the throne unless you assure me that it is for Sulis's glory and the restoration of his truth."

While Father Faolan questioned the count and elicited more details of the plot, Eadoin remained silent. At last, the great high priest put his hand on the count's head in blessing and bowed his head in prayer. After several minutes, Faolan raised his head. "Sulis decrees this plan is his will. While Sheen may have Korth to begin with, the god will shortly deliver both of the joined kingdoms into your hands."

While Ultan expressed his gratitude and his eagerness to serve the god's triumph, Eadoin blinked rapidly and looked away.

When the count left, the high priest said, "You are surprised, my son?"

Eadoin traced Sulis's star in the air and bowed his head. "I would never question the will of the god."

As Faolan patted his arm, Eadoin felt a shiver at his mentor's holiness. "Our original plan will go forward as Sulis has directed. But if it fails to provide us with all the necessary sacrifices, we will align ourselves with the forces of this world."

Eadoin touched the piece of the Soul Stone. He'd had it mounted on a gold star and wore it on a chain around his neck. "Forgive me for my lack of understanding, Father, but will not Sulis ensure our success as you have said he would?"

The high priest nodded. "In the end, he will, but Sulis sometimes tests our faith by allowing us to fail before granting us victory. Perhaps this Count Cadarn is the tool Sulis will use to bring his power back to his priesthood."

"But if you are to partake of the god's power, will Your Holiness not need to be nearby when I complete the ritual?"

Faolan shook his head. "No, my son. Sulis isn't so limited. His power will spread throughout the land." Faolan looked away in a manner that made Eadoin question if the great man feared being near the ritual. Immediately, Eadoin's chest tightened, and he found it difficult to breathe. Who was he to question Sulis's mouthpiece?

* * *

"Your Majesty?"

Feeling like she'd only just fallen asleep, Samantha awoke to the sound of Ardra's voice. Her maid stood over her, holding a candle. "I hate to wake you in the middle of the night, but Blaine is without, and he says it's important."

Since Blaine would never waken her without reason, she stifled a groan and freed herself from her bed covers. Ardra helped her into a robe, and she went out into the reception room to find Blaine pacing.

As she entered, he bowed. "Your Majesty, the city magistrates have just delivered Lord Duer's body to the palace. He was found floating in the river with a knife in his back. Since his purse strings were cut, the magistrates believe it was a simple robbery, but being who he is..."

Samantha sat and invited Blaine to do so as well. "You think he was murdered because he found something out? Do you think it was about the high priest?"

Blaine shrugged. "It's impossible to say, but it does smell like over ripe fish, so to speak."

"Send for his servant Gael. Perhaps he might give us some insight on what Duer was looking into."

"I already did so before waking Your Majesty. Gael is missing, and perhaps..."

"Perhaps he was killed with his master."

"Yes, and his body just floated out to sea like a limb fallen from an overhanging tree, so to speak."

Blaine's greater than normal use of metaphors told her he found the situation upsetting, and indeed, it was even if he had been murdered for his purse rather than for what he knew. "See what you can find out for me. And Blaine, I need a new spymaster. Has Tuathal made any more progress in his research?"

Blaine's wince told her everything she needed to know. "He is truly trying, Your Majesty. You can't fault his diligence. If any of the books in the library have the information you need, he will find it."

As Blaine left, Samantha didn't find his words comforting. With Lord Duer dead and Darhour still gone, she now had no spymaster at all. She went back into her bedroom and stared out at the palace grounds. "Just how worried should I be?" she asked the night sky.

But it held no answers.

CHAPTER 6

Early on the morning of Litha, Samantha sat at her dressing table while her maids arranged her hair. Blaine paced nearby, going over the list of the day's festivities for the hundredth time. She listened with only half an ear. Today the birth of her daughter would be celebrated. The people would learn to love her as Samantha did, but the day was marred by the absence of her husband. *Sulis, how dare you make him miss this day!*

Blaine heaved a great sigh. "Your Majesty, you aren't listening, are you?"

Samantha locked her anger in the hole in her heart. "I'm sorry, my mind was elsewhere."

Blaine tapped his fingers against the papers he held. "I said I believe that Your Majesty should invite Vaughan to ride in the carriage with Your Majesty and Her Highness when you go to the city square to bless the community garden."

At the sound of the boy's name, Samantha touched her throat and felt heat rise in her cheeks. Vaughan had saved her love, and it only now occurred to her that she hadn't seen him for some time. "Why?" she asked.

Blaine looked at the ceiling, as if he found an interesting spot. "It would be a nice gesture, Your Majesty. It would remind him that your gratitude is as deep as the ocean, so to speak. I didn't want to bother Your Majesty with it, but with the king's departure, the boy has lost his purpose, so to speak."

Her stomach roiled. She should have asked if Vaughan wanted to go with Robbie. Her lack of courtesy was unforgivable. "You're right, as usual."

Blaine's face brightened. "Excellent, You Majesty. You can put him in charge of returning the princess to the palace after the ceremony. Your Majesty is due at the Guild Hall for the performance in honor of Her Highness's birth. Your Majesty will notice I've limited Her Highness's public appearances, as Your Majesty desired. A move as wise as the ages, so to speak, considering Your Majesty's current lack of a spymaster."

At the reference to the murdered lord, Samantha thought again of the wisdom of taking Brianna from the palace at all, but her daughter would be well guarded.

Blaine rattled on more details. "After the performance at the Guild Hall, Your Majesty will return to the palace for the feast, which I allowed Maggie to plan without my interference." Blaine shuddered. Samantha knew Blaine had a hard time trusting anyone's competence, but Maggie had been planning royal feasts longer than both of them had been alive. "Of course, the Korthian emergency limited the elaborate nature of the feast and the number of commoners who could be invited to eat in the palace grounds, but the tickets have been distributed and entertainment fit for a humbler taste will, of course, be provided. Last, of course, is the Royal Ball, at which Her Highness will be presented to the court. Your Majesty opening the ball by dancing with Her Highness was a particularly good idea, I must say."

Samantha hid a smile. The idea had been Blaine's. By taking Brianna to the nursery after she danced with her daughter, Samantha could allow the ball to continue without her and would have to dance with none of the men.

There was a knock on the door, and Blaine answered it. Samantha heard the voice of a young palace page. "A message for Her Majesty from His Excellency, the High Priest Hafghan."

Blaine closed the door and handed her a folded piece of paper. She frowned as she read it.

"Is there anything wrong, Your Majesty?" Blaine asked.

Samantha shook her head. "Father Hafghan has come down ill. He will be sending someone else in his place. I hope it's nothing serious." Hafghan was an important ally. She couldn't afford to lose him.

* * *

Over his porridge in the squire's quarters, Vaughan glumly watched the other squires prepare their knights' armor for the Royal procession to the community garden for Litha.

Floyd, who had tormented Vaughan ever since he became the king's squire, spoke louder than the others. "Someone without a knight can't properly be called a squire. I don't think boys like that should be allowed to quarter with us, don't you agree?" he asked Maeron. "I think he should be made to return to the stables."

Vaughan clenched his fists. He wanted to argue he belonged here as much as the rest of them, but Floyd was right. A squire without a knight had no purpose. Besides that, he was worse than any of them with weapons. Maybe he should have never left the stables.

Floyd finished with his knight's armor, dished up his porridge, and sat directly across from Vaughan. "Got nothing to say for yourself, horse boy?"

Vaughan wanted to leap across the table and strangle Floyd, but Floyd had three inches and twenty pounds on him, and he was so much better at hand to hand combat he made Vaughan look like a toddler flailing about.

Before Floyd could get in another insult, a palace page carrying a necklace of flowers entered the squire's quarters. The boy came straight to Vaughan. He puffed out his chest and spoke in the pompous way the little jerks always did. "Squire Vaughan, in honor of your service, Her Majesty invites you to ride with Her Majesty and the princess to the city square." He held out the flower necklace. "She bids you don these flowers and wait upon her on the palace front steps in one hour."

Taking the flowers, Vaughan grinned across at Floyd, whose mouth was hanging open. "I guess I'll be riding in the royal carriage to the ceremony today. Where will you be riding? Oh, yeah, you won't be." Vaughan put the flowers around his neck and smirked at his tormentor.

* * *

Brigitta held out a necklace of flowers. "Sigurd, you have to wear one! Everyone is."

The name Darhour had hastily adopted when they first met seemed a love token when she spoke it, and while it wasn't quite true that everyone wore flowers, it was traditional on Litha.

Darhour scowled but lowered his head to allow Brigitta to put the flowers around his neck. He hadn't worn flowers since he was a young stable groom, but for Brigitta, there was little he wouldn't do. Brigitta got on her tiptoes and, despite being dressed as a boy, kissed him on one of his heavily scarred cheeks. He still had a hard time believing she'd agreed to marry him and that, even more miraculously, she didn't regret her decision. As she placed a flower necklace over her own neck, Darhour admired the red hair that was now tightly queued, worn like the warrior she'd become. When it was loose, it fell to her shoulders. He liked it better that way. When her hair flowed about her face, it made her softer, allowing him to forget for a moment how hard she'd become because of him.

They'd arrived in Murtaghan last night to discover that the birth of a granddaughter he hadn't known he had was to be celebrated today. He'd also learned the sorcerer he'd counted on to protect Samantha was as good as dead. He hadn't known Robrek well, but he knew Samantha would take his loss hard.

Brigitta took his hand and dragged him toward the city square. "Hurry, we need to secure a place where we can see the queen and the baby princess." It was traditional for the heir to bless the community garden on Litha.

When they reached the city square, Darhour put down the hood of his cloak. There were only two people in the world that his scowl didn't terrify: his wife and his daughter. Seeing him, bystanders quickly moved out of the way, allowing them through to a spot where Brigitta could see everything. When they were in place, he put his hood back up so he wouldn't be recognized by anyone in the royal procession. He didn't want Samantha to know he'd returned until he formally presented himself.

Through the crowd came an enterprising vendor carrying a large tray of pies. Brigitta signaled him over, then frowned as she noticed the flower petals in some of them. "You put flowers in your food?" she asked in her thick Massossinan accent.

The vendor laughed. "It's traditional on Litha." He leaned in closer and whispered loudly, "It's supposed to bring the blessing of fertility." Brigitta's lip quivered, and Darhour wanted to strangle the vendor. Brigitta had been taken as a slave and forced to become a whore. Her master had done things to her that rendered her infertile. Worse, she'd been forced to leave behind the two children she did have.

"If you prefer, I have some with seeds instead." The vendor pointed to the other side of the tray.

Brigitta looked at Darhour, and he shrugged. "The flowers are traditional. I'll have one, but you don't have to if you don't want to."

Brigitta turned back to the vendor. "Two of each."

"A tetra," the vendor said. Darhour was certain that if he lowered his hood, he could get the vendor to lower the price, but it was reasonable for the holiday, so he paid the man. The vendor handed the pies to Brigitta and hurried away.

"Are the flower ones good?" she asked in Massossinan. She'd become fairly proficient in Korthlundian but still found it awkward.

"Not really," he answered in the same language. "But it would hardly be Litha without them."

Brigitta handed him two pies and turned back to watch the crowd. As Darhour bit into the flower pie, he was reminded of his innocent childhood before his affair with the queen sent him into exile and made him a killer.

Voices at the edge of the square rang out, "Long live the queen! Long live the heir!"

Darhour turned. Leading the procession on horseback was Bearach. He smiled inwardly to see that his former subordinate was still keeping his daughter safe. Bearach had a smart mouth, but he was good with a sword, and Darhour had never met anyone better with a bow. Seeing him armed with both, Darhour nodded in approval. Instinctively, Darhour's eyes swept the crowd for danger. A nearby man had his arms folded and wasn't cheering. Like Darhour, the man was wearing a cloak that was too hot for the day. Darhour resolved to keep an eye on him.

He glanced back at the procession and sucked in a breath as an open carriage entered the square. It carried his daughter. She held his granddaughter on her lap. Samantha's auburn hair, which was the color his had been in his youth, flowed to her shoulders, and her head was topped with the royal crown. Unsurprisingly, she and the princess wore matching green gowns. Green had always been Samantha's favorite color, and she'd never looked more beautiful than she did now holding his granddaughter. A young man Darhour didn't recognize sat next to her. The young man fidgeted, and Darhour realized it was Vaughan. He laughed that he'd thought of his former stable boy as a young man. Conroy, another of his former subordinates, rode at the queen's side.

As the crowd cheered and continued to wish the queen and princess long lives, Samantha waved and smiled at the crowd. Although Darhour remained silent, Brigitta clapped and bounced on her feet. As the procession drew closer, Darhour stepped back both to make sure his hood completely hid his face and to keep the other non-cheering, cloaked man in view.

The queen's carriage stopped at the platform that held the community garden. Handing the baby to Vaughan, Samantha got out, then reclaimed her daughter. Vaughan trailing, the queen and the crown princess mounted the steps to the garden. A priest Darhour had never seen before accompanied the group. The queen stepped to the front and held up the infant princess for all to see. The crowd went wild, and Darhour felt his heart swell. If he'd done nothing else good in life, he'd blessed this people by fathering Samantha.

After the cheering began to die down, Samantha held the princess against her shoulder and put up her hand for silence. When the crowd quieted, she spoke in a voice that rang throughout the square. "My people, it is with great happiness I present to you my daughter and heir, Her Highness, the Princess Brianna." The crowd erupted in cheers again. The queen waited for them to quiet and then continued, "It is traditional for the heir to bless the community garden with the waters of life. Since I was a toddler, I have been privileged to do so. In a few years, Brianna will take my place, but today she still needs my help to accomplish the blessing." The crowd chuckled.

The unfamiliar priest stepped forward and lifted a jug that seemed too light to contain water. As he did so, the man Darhour had been watching reached under his cloak. Darhour was already moving when he saw a flash of metal in the priest's hand. The priest threw the jug at Conroy, the closest of the queen's guards, but a man Darhour didn't know shoved the queen behind him and took the knife that had been meant for her.

Darhour's target drew a bow, but before he could nock an arrow, Darhour tackled him. Without thinking, Darhour palmed one of his hidden knives and slit the man's throat. *How dare he attack my daughter!* He rolled to his feet to see another archer fall to one of Bearach's arrows.

The square was in pandemonium, and he could no longer see Samantha and the baby princess. Armed men were rushing the platform. Pushing anyone in his way aside, Darhour drew his sword and charged. He stabbed one man in the back. About five men, all armed with swords, turned to face him. He sliced one across the belly, and the square went silent as Darhour became focused only on the fight. He slashed and stabbed. The men he fought were amateurs. The only challenge was their numbers. Focusing only on getting to his daughter and granddaughter, Darhour struck out at anyone in his path. He had no idea how many he killed. At one point, he became aware of Brigitta fighting beside him.

He fought to the base of the stairs. As he grabbed one man off the stairs and stabbed him through the back, he came face to face with Bearach. His hood had fallen off in the fight, and Bearach's mouth dropped open, as did most of the other guards'. Darhour cleared the way as the guards surrounding the queen and the princess hurried them to the carriage. Surrounded as the queen was, he didn't think she saw him but Bearach would certainly tell her about his presence.

Alongside the queen's personal guards as well as members of the Royal Guard, Darhour helped escort the carriage to the palace gates. At some point, Brigitta appeared beside him, covered in blood. "Are you okay?" he asked.

She nodded. "It isn't mine. You?"

Darhour saw he too was blood soaked. "Also, not mine."

Once the queen's carriage was safely through the palace gates and the gates shut behind them, Darhour slammed his sword back into its scabbard and punched the wall. Someone would pay for what had happened today.

* * *

In the carriage, Samantha curled protectively around her screaming baby. "How dare they try to hurt you, my love! I will have them dead for this!"

The carriage stopped, and Conroy appeared beside her. "It's safe now, Your Majesty. We're inside the palace gates."

Samantha straightened and brought the crying baby to her shoulder. She rubbed Brianna's back to soothe her. The baby's cries were quickly reduced to whimpers. "Who were the attackers?" she asked.

Conroy answered, "They were from the True Church of Sulis. They had the star Lord Duer spoke of tattooed on their right hand."

"Causalities?"

Conroy shook his head. "Her Highness's guard Iachus took the knife meant for Your Majesty or Her Highness. I don't know how badly he was injured. Other than that, I don't yet know."

She realized Vaughan wasn't in the carriage with them. "Vaughan?"

"Again, Your Majesty, I don't know."

Her entire body shaking, Samantha said, "Keep me informed, and have Father Leigh and his novice summoned to help see to the wounded. Also, send someone for Father Hafghan. I will have answers."

Conroy bowed. "At once, Your Majesty."

Samantha heard a loud female shriek, and Cece appeared. "Her Highness! Is she hurt?"

Samantha hugged her daughter to her. "No, the princess is uninjured."

Sobbing, Cece fell to her knees. "Thank Sulis, Mother of us all. When I heard of the attack, I thought I'd die if anything had happened to that precious baby."

Brianna had stopped crying, and Samantha had duties to attend. She didn't want Brianna out of her sight, but her daughter would be safer in the nursery. "Take Her Highness to the nursery, please."

Cece jumped to her feet and reached for the baby. "At once, Your Majesty." Feeling as though she were surrendering one of her own limbs, Samantha handed Brianna to her nurse. Cece clutched her tightly. "Oh, my sweetness, thank Sulis, you're okay." In addition to the princess's uninjured guards, Samantha dispatched a dozen Royal Guardsmen to accompany Cece and the baby to the nursery.

As she got down from the carriage, Blaine prostrated himself at her feet. "Your Majesty, this is all my fault. After Lord Duer's murder, how could I have suggested bringing the baby princess to the public square? It was as stupid as charging a wild boar with your bare hands, so to speak. I don't deserve to live. Your Majesty, I—"

"Blaine, shut up!" As Samantha heard herself speak in a manner so unlike herself, Blaine's mouth dropped open. Struggling to control her desire to hurt someone, she put a hand on Blaine's shoulder. "Forgive me, but we both know who's really at fault here. Look over the planned events. The princess will not leave her nursery, but see what else might be salvaged and bring me a report in half an hour."

Blaine got to his feet. "Yes, Your Majesty. Of course, Your Majesty."

A cheer went up behind her, and Samantha turned to see Iachus being helped through the palace gate. His side wrapped in a bloody rag, Iachus was supported by Lord Edan, a Royal Guardsmen who had been a friend of Robbie. Samantha approached. "How is he?"

Iachus tried to throw off Edan's support but stumbled and had to be caught. Still, he insisted, "It's hardly a scratch, Your Majesty. I'll be back on duty in the morning."

She looked at Edan, who nodded grimly. "It's more than a scratch, Your Majesty. He's lost quite a bit of blood, but I think the knife missed anything vital."

She gave Iachus a royal nod. "I'm extremely grateful for your sacrifice and quick thinking. It will not be forgotten."

Iachus smiled through a grimace. "I was happy to do it, Your Majesty. No one will touch Her Highness on my watch. This I vowed by the goddess and on my mother's grave."

Samantha nodded and addressed Edan. "See that his wound is tended to by either Father Leigh or Oriana."

Edan bowed as well as he could while supporting Iachus. "I will, Your Majesty."

As Iachus was helped away, Conroy approached. "We should get you inside, Your Majesty."

Samantha didn't resist, but she stopped at the nearest reception room to be on hand to receive reports. She sat down, and a servant brought her a glass of wine. She sipped it to calm herself. In the doorway, Conroy and Bearach whispered furiously. Conroy raised his voice, "You need to tell Her Majesty right now!"

Imagining her favorite stable boy lying dead, she asked, "Tell me what?"

Both men turned to her and blushed. Bearach scratched at his beard. "I'm not sure now's the time, Your Majesty."

"Tell her! That's an order!" Conroy snapped.

Bearach shrugged. "The captain was in the city square, Your Majesty." Samantha felt her insides freeze. From the way Bearach said the word "captain," she knew he didn't mean Conroy or even Hawk. There was only one person Bearach would speak of with such respect. "He fought with us. I'm not sure we would have gotten Your Majesty and Her Highness off the platform without his assistance."

She breathed, "Are you sure it was him?"

"Yes, Your Majesty. I was shocked as the deepest of the seven hells to see the captain, but it was him, alright."

Samantha put a hand to her chest. *What was Darhour doing in the city square? Why is my father not at my side?* "Where is he?"

Bearach shook his head. "I lost track of him sometime during the retreat to the palace, Your Majesty."

"Find him!" she ordered, well knowing that if Darhour didn't want to be found, he wouldn't be. *Holy Sulis, has he been in Murtaghan all this time?*

* * *

Now that the square had gone quiet, Vaughan crawled out from under the large basket where he'd hidden during the fight. The dead and wounded littered the platform and the square. Most were the horrible people who'd tried to kill the queen and baby princess, but a few were of the Royal Guard. Some people milled around tending to the wounded or looting the bodies. Nearby, one of the wounded attackers groaned. Vaughan drew his sword and stabbed him through the heart. He kept stabbing until the man went still. Tears flowing down his cheeks, Vaughan fell to his knees and vomited. *Floyd's right. I'm not worthy to be anyone's squire. I hid and didn't even draw my sword until the fighting was over. Holy Sulis, what if the queen or the princess were hurt? It would be all my fault!*

He wiped furiously at his eyes. A coward like him didn't belong at the palace. He should just go home to his mother and become a blacksmith like his father. But Vaughan's mother didn't have money to pay for an apprenticeship. He should just run away or kill himself. But before he did either, he needed to make sure the queen and baby princess were all right, and he had to apologize to Her Highness. Though he could never face the queen to apologize to her.

* * *

With Brigitta in a tub beside his, Darhour scrubbed the blood from his body. It was something he'd done hundreds of times before. Brigitta had done it far less often. "Are you sure you're all right?" he asked again.

"I told you I'm unwounded. Do you want to check for yourself?" She leered at him suggestively.

Despite himself, Darhour felt himself hardening. He ignored it. "I wasn't talking about your body."

Brigitta looked at the ceiling. "I have killed men before, you know!"

Darhour reached across and touched her arm. "You've never been in a battle like today. Every life you take changes you. It hardens and darkens your soul. Sometimes I wonder if I should have taught you to fight."

Brigitta shot to her feet, sloshing water over the floor. "You think you should have left me as a helpless victim? I should be prey to whatever man wants to use me?" She grabbed a towel and wrapped it around herself. She jabbed a finger toward him. "I will be no man's plaything ever again, and I do not regret any life I've taken to be free." Before he could respond, she stomped out of the room.

Darhour sighed and picked up a brush. He knew he should follow her, but first he had to make sure all of the blood was gone. Brigitta was a bright light in his life, a gift and a blessing he'd thought he'd never have, but he often wondered if he'd been good for her. Then he cursed himself. Without him she'd still be a whore or worse. He didn't know the full extent of the abuse she'd suffered because she didn't like to talk about it. Of course, she was better off now. But having been tortured with guilt for years over the lives he'd taken, he hated to think he was leading the woman he loved down the same path.

Now wasn't the time to worry about the state of either of their souls. By now, Samantha would have heard about his presence in the square. He needed to apologize to his wife and then try to make peace with his daughter.

* * *

When Captain Hawk escorted Father Hafghan into Samantha's presence, the high priest was limping and had a bandage around his head. They both bowed, and Hawk said, "Your Majesty, my men found Father Hafghan tied to his bed with a wound on the back of his head. Several other priests in the Temple of the Mother's Love were similarly restrained and had various injuries."

Because he appeared to be having difficulty standing, Samantha invited the high priest to be seated. "What happened?"

As he sat, Hafghan wiped the sweat from his face. "It was rather horrible, Your Majesty. Not as horrible as the attack on Your Majesty and the little princess, of course. As I was preparing to attend the ceremony this morning, I heard a commotion outside my rooms. I opened my door to determine the cause and was struck from behind. I awoke tied to my bed."

Samantha passed the high priest the note she'd received that morning. "So, you didn't write this?"

Hafghan took the note and looked it over wide eyed. "No, Your Majesty, I assure you I did not."

She called forth his aura. He was telling the truth. Relieved he hadn't betrayed her, she turned back to Hawk. "Did any of the other priests see anything more?"

"Yes, Your Majesty, several reported having been attacked by a group of at least a dozen men. They all had Sulis's star tattooed on the back of their right hand, the same as those who attacked Your Majesty and the princess in the square."

Samantha dismissed the high priest. The True Church of Sulis had gone too far this time. She would eradicate it.

* * *

Accompanied by her chancellor Baron Gwawl and his wife Glynnis, Samantha sat at the head table in the palace banquet hall. Despite the attempt of her own and her daughter's life, the banquet hall was packed with nobles and the palace grounds overflowing with peasants celebrating the birth of her heir. Security was tight, and everyone who entered the palace grounds was checked for the tattoo that announced their adherence to the True Church of Sulis. Still, she wouldn't show weakness by giving zealots the power to control her actions. Brianna was safely in her nursery protected by an entire squadron of guards. Three members of the Royal Guard had been killed in the fight, and over a dozen injured. Worst of all, Vaughan still hadn't been heard from. She felt sick, imagining him dead. *I will wipe Faolan's church from the face of the earth!*

After opening the royal ball, Samantha went to check on her precious daughter in the nursery. When she entered, Cece jumped to her feet. She'd been sitting next to a cot that took up half the reception room. Iachus slept there, his hand resting on the drawn sword beside him. She turned to Kelvin, the captain of Brianna's guard. "Surely, he can be relieved of duty while he heals."

Kelvin bowed his head. "I know it is irregular, Your Majesty, but Iachus couldn't rest easily in the infirmary and begged to be brought here to protect the princess. Father Leigh said his wound wasn't life threatening, and he'd recover more quickly if his mind could be at ease concerning the princess's safety. I hope Your Majesty doesn't mind."

Samantha had to blink away tears at the depths Iachus's devotion. "He will be rewarded." She looked at Cece. "How is he?"

Cece glanced at the wounded man. "He's been asleep the entire time he's been here, Your Majesty, but I don't think he's feverish. The princess is asleep in her crib." Cece pointed to the other room.

She entered the room and gazed at the sleeping baby. She watched the rise and fall of her chest to ensure herself that her daughter still lived. Then she kissed Brianna's head once and left so as not to disturb her.

As she left Brianna's nursery, the full weight of the day descended on her. She'd been so busy exhibiting strength she'd given herself no time to be weak. Now she felt she barely had the strength to make it to her own quarters. The True Church of Sulis had made another attempt on her daughter's life. Vaughan was still missing. And Darhour…

As she entered the corridor where her quarters lay, a large shadow loomed outside her door. Her guards Ewan and Guthrie pushed her behind them. "Who goes there?"

The shadow straightened to reveal a man. He stepped forward into the light and lowered his hood. She gasped as she saw Darhour's scarred features. He bowed. "Your Majesty," he said, as if he'd just returned from some silly errand.

Both Guthrie and Ewan relaxed, but she felt every muscle in her body tightening. She didn't know if she wanted to run into his arms or draw her sword and run him through. She said and did nothing.

Darhour shifted his feet for a few uncomfortable moments. "Your Majesty, I'm sure you have heard of my presence during the fight in the city square. If you will hear me, I've come to explain myself."

When she spoke, her voice came out icy cold. "Have you been in Murtaghan all this time?"

He looked away, then answered. "No, I just returned last night. I've been in Saloyna. After slaughtering Duke Argblutal the way I did, it seemed right to return to the country where I became a killer."

Samantha saw again Argblutal's mutilated, headless corpse. His had truly been a brutal death. "I didn't ask you to kill Argblutal! I explicitly told you we would find another way!"

Darhour gave a small shrug. "The duke had to die, and I was the only one who could kill him. But I lost myself when I killed the duke. I thought I was a monster, irreparably tainted. I thought I'd taint you if I stayed. And it wasn't just the duke, either. After I'd once vowed never to kill again, I'd killed at least a dozen to get to him."

Samantha froze. "What vow?"

Darhour's eyes darted to her and then away again. "May we speak privately?"

She nodded toward the door to her quarters. Guthrie entered and made a sweep before standing aside for her to enter. Not trusting her voice, she gestured for Darhour to follow her.

Her maids were waiting for her. Ardra gaped at Darhour, and Malvina let out a small scream, but Samantha dismissed them without further comment and took a seat. She didn't invite Darhour to be seated. She asked again, "What vow?"

Darhour sighed. "I forgot I never told you. It was in Saloyna after I'd been King Frare's assassin for about ten years. I was soul sick from the blood on my hands. I found a small shrine to Sulis, knelt at her holy altar, and made a sacred vow to never take another life no matter the circumstances."

Samantha gripped the arms of her chair. "You lie! If you'd made such an oath, you'd never have agreed to become my bodyguard! You had to know that killing might be necessary to protect me."

Darhour looked at her as King Solar always had. "My daughter, I'd gladly go to the seven hells to keep you safe."

Her entire body began to shake. "Don't you dare make me feel guilty over your damnation! I never asked you to kill anyone! Never!"

Darhour stepped toward her, but she put up a hand to stop him. He stepped back. "The choice to kill was always my own. No one but I am to blame for the lives I've taken. I left here because I didn't want to darken the light within you, and I thought your consort's magic made him a stronger protector than I could ever hope to be. I didn't consider that he might be injured, and I never dreamed Duke Caedmon would betray you. But even if all that never happened, leaving you as I did was an act of cowardice." He went down on his knees before her. "I committed a terrible wrong against you. I don't deserve your forgiveness, but still I beg for it. Allow me to serve you once again."

"No... I can't... It's too..." She broke off, stifling a sob. She jabbed a finger toward him. "You said you were my father! But a true father would never leave as you did! King Solar lived until ninety for my sake, and he would have lived longer if he hadn't been murdered. I don't even know who you are. Are you my friend? My assassin? My father? My protector?"

"I've come to terms with my past. If you can forgive me, I'll devote myself to whatever you need of me without hesitation."

From his position on his knees, Darhour's eyes were level with her own. She remembered the dark days when King Solar's mind had been poisoned by Duke Argblutal. Darhour had been the shiny shield that had kept her safe. She doubted she'd still be alive today if it hadn't been for him. She wanted to fall on his chest, to feel his arms around her, to feel safe again. She missed him so much, needed him worse. Darhour's had been the first aura she'd ever seen. She called it forth now. His aura had always been a mixture of the green of health and life and darker more sinister colors. Now the green and the darkness seemed to have settled into an even balance. He was and always would be a killer, but he was her killer. Could she trust that he would remain so? She got up and went to her window to stare out at the darkness.

Darhour approached and put a hand on her shoulder. "Samantha, please forgive me."

She slapped his hand away. "They tried to kill my daughter today. My precious daughter is still alive because someone other than you took the knife meant for her. It is your fault they got so close to her.

If you'd been here, you'd have known what the True Church was planning. Father Faolan would have been found months ago."

Darhour deflated. "Your Majesty, this is—"

"Silence!" she shouted. "Do not say another word to me until you bring me the head of the man who tried to kill my daughter!"

Darhour bowed. "It will be—"

Samantha whirled on him. "Not one more word until I see Father Faolan's head!"

Darhour deepened his bow and left.

As the door closed behind him, Samantha dropped into a chair and curled in on herself. Her entire body trembled with the desire to run after him and beg him to stay. But she would not be weak.

* * *

Darhour left the palace the same way he'd entered it: through the sewer tunnels. He'd known Samantha would be angry with him, but somehow, he never doubted she would take him back. Maybe his leaving had cut too deeply to ever be forgiven. Even though the darkness of the night was sufficient to disguise him, he put up his hood as he made his way back to the inn where he'd left Brigitta.

She was pacing their room, and despite how he must have smelled after his trip through the sewers, she threw her arms around him when he entered.

"How did it go? Did she forgive you?" she asked.

Without answering, he stripped off his dirty clothes and collapsed onto the bed. He couldn't seem to find the words.

Brigitta sat beside him and put her hand on his thigh. "Oh, Sig, did she turn you away?"

Darhour cleared his throat. "My leaving hurt her terribly. She needed me more than she ever had. I'm not sure she'll ever trust me again." He told her what had taken place.

When he finished, she lay her head on his chest. "She might not have welcomed you the way you wished, but when we take care of this priest, surely, she'll forgive you."

Wanting to believe her, he ran his fingers through her hair. "You didn't see how angry she is. Holy Sulis, how could I have thought leaving was the right thing to do?" Darhour stared at the ceiling. The weight of her head on his chest reminded him that now more than one woman depended on him. Brigitta had left her homeland for him. If Samantha didn't take him back, what would they do?

Brigitta snuggled against him. "It will be all right," she repeated. "You'll see. How do we go about killing this priest?"

Hearing her matter-of-factness about murder, Darhour squeezed his eyes shut. If he tried to stop her from helping him, she'd tell him that her decisions were her own and he had no right to make them for her. Maybe she was right, but he'd do his best to make sure that this time all the blood was on his body. "First, we find him."

* * *

Vaughan crept through the quiet corridors of the palace. He'd waited until after midnight to avoid anyone seeing him. But the corridors were crowded with far more guards than usual, several of whom recognized him and told him that the queen had been looking for him. *Probably to take back the medal she gave me and condemn me as a coward.* He promised them that he was on his way to see her, so they wouldn't take him to her.

He been relieved to learn that the queen and princess hadn't been hurt, but it was no thanks to him. He'd decided that he would sign on with one of the ships in the harbor and sail away from Korthlundia, never to return. But he had to apologize first. He'd spent most of the day trying to write a note to the queen, but it was no use. He couldn't admit even on paper what he'd done. His apology to the princess would have to do, but even that was cowardly. Her Highness was an infant and wouldn't understand.

When he reached the corridor with the nursery, he saw a dozen guards hanging around. Usually, there were only two, but he guessed the queen was taking no chances. He almost turned around, but he couldn't stay in the palace another day, and he needed to see the princess before he left.

"Hello, Vaughan," Bary called out. "Have you seen the queen? She's been worried about you."

Vaughan froze and came up with a lie. "Yes, I let Her Majesty know I was all right, but I... I couldn't sleep... without..."

Bary nodded as if he understood. "You needed to see for yourself that Her Highness is unhurt?"

Vaughan nodded as if that was exactly what he'd been thinking. "I know everyone's asleep, but I'll be really quiet, and I wouldn't disturb anyone."

Bary looked at the other guards, who nodded. Brandon lit a candle for him.

But Vaughan shook his head. "I know the way."

"You sure? It's pitch black in there."

"I'll be okay." Vaughan stepped around Brandon and entered the nursery. He closed the door silently behind him and tip-toed toward the princess's bedroom. He cried out as his knee slammed into something that shouldn't have been there and he pitched forward on top of someone who let out an unearthly scream. The door to the nursery crashed open, and Bary and Brandon spilled in with swords drawn. Brandon also carried a torch. All the noise woke the princess, who started to scream.

Vaughan scrambled to his feet and saw that he'd landed on Iachus, who was now clutching his wounded side. "I'm sorry," Vaughan cried. "I'm sorry."

Bary chuckled. "Oh yeah, I forgot to warn you Iachus was in the way. You all right, Iachus?"

Iachus rolled onto his back, still clutching his side. He called Bary a few choice words that almost made Vaughan blush but in the end admitted, "I'll survive."

Grumbling, Brandon shoved his sword in its sheath. "About scared the life out of me." Brandon left and came back carrying the candle. He thrust it toward Vaughan. "Take it." Vaughan did.

With Bary continuing to chuckle, the guards left, as Cece, carrying a candle, burst out of her room. "How dare you wake the baby? I'd just gotten her to sleep." She pushed her way past them and entered the princess's room, slamming the door behind her.

Vaughan wished he could disappear or simply cease to exist. Iachus was the kind of hero he'd never be. "I'm sorry I fell on you," he mumbled.

Iachus waved him off. "It's all right. I won't pretend it didn't hurt like a demon. What are you doing coming in the nursery in the middle of the night?"

Vaughan looked around for a way to escape answering, but since Iachus was a real hero, he deserved to know the truth. "I just came to say good-bye to the princess," he said, barely loud enough to hear.

"What daft nonsense are you muttering?" Clutching his side, Iachus struggled to sit. "Where do you think you're going?"

"Anywhere but here!" Vaughan clenched his fists. "I panicked in the fight today. When you dived in front of the queen, I dived under a basket and hid until the fight was over! A worthless coward doesn't deserve to be at the palace!"

Iachus patted the bed beside him. "Have a seat. We need to talk." Vaughan considered bolting for the door, but Iachus seemed to read his mind. "You're not leaving this room until you sit and hear me out."

Knowing he was no match for even a wounded Iachus, let alone all the uninjured guards outside the nursery door, Vaughan shuffled to the bed and perched on the edge as far away from the princess's guard as the bed allowed.

"Let me tell you a secret. When I saw the knife in that fake priest's hands, I was so scared I nearly shit myself. It was instinct, not bravery, that made me jump in front of the queen and my charge. And after I was wounded, I was so sure I would die that I would have started blubbering like a baby, if I hadn't been afraid that I'd never hear the end of it from the other guards."

Clenching his fists, Vaughan jumped to his feet. "That's not true! Nobody but me was scared. I was the only one that hid. Lying won't make me feel any better. I'll never feel good ever again after what I did!"

"Sit down!" Iachus commanded, and Vaughan did as he was told. "You have no idea what you're talking about, kid! Every damned one of us was scared. The only man who isn't scared in a fight is one that wants to die. How old are you anyway? Twelve?"

"I'm fourteen!" Vaughan wanted to argue he was almost a man, but he'd proved otherwise today.

"Let me tell you about what I did when I was fifteen. My younger brother has a smart mouth. One day he said something to a group of young lordlings that they didn't appreciate, and they decided he needed a lesson. They attacked him five on one. They told me to stay out of it if I didn't want the same. Do you know what I did?"

Vaughan rolled his eyes and said in a sing-song voice, "You charged in to help your brother anyway!"

Iachus laughed hollowly. "I wish. No, I stood there and watched them beat him to a pulp." Vaughan's mouth dropped open. "I told myself there were too many of them so I couldn't save him and that he kind of deserved it anyway. I'd warned him about his smart mouth hundreds of times. But the truth was I was scared, and unlike yours today, my life wasn't being threatened. I was just scared of getting hurt, not of dying, so I stood there and watched while five lordlings beat my own brother nearly to death. They broke my brother's leg so badly that he walks with a limp to this day. If they're being honest, every damned man fighting in the square today could tell you a similar story."

Vaughan looked sideways at Iachus. "I don't believe you. If you were a coward then, how did you ever learn not to be afraid?"

"Haven't you been listening, you daft kid? You don't ever learn not to be afraid. Bravery isn't about not feeling fear. It's acting even though your mouth goes dry and your heart starts pounding so hard you think it's trying to burst through your chest. Fear isn't a bad thing. It can make you sharp, make you careful. But you have to learn to control it, not allow it to control you. That's a lesson every fighting man needs to learn, and you're lucky to be learning it young. What you did today was something every man has done at one time or another. But do you know what would truly be an act of cowardice? Running away now."

"But I have to go away! If there ever comes a time that the princess really needs me, how can I know I won't hide and let Her Highness die? Isn't it better to be a coward now than to fail Her Highness when she needs me?" He wiped at the tears coming down his cheeks, embarrassed that he was bawling like a baby.

"Unfortunately, you can never know for sure what you'll do in any situation until you're in it. But I'd bet any man a thousand drachma that if that time ever comes, you will control your fear and fight to the death to save her." Iachus pursed his lips, as if considering whether to tell Vaughan a secret. "There is one thing you can do to make controlling your fear easier, though."

"What?" Vaughan felt the first bubble of hope since the fight in the city square.

"You make an oath. I took an oath to the queen to defend the princess's life. When I saw that knife today, instead of shitting myself, I remembered the oath I had taken, and I pushed the queen and princess behind me." Iachus turned and shouted. "Cece, can you bring Her Highness out here?"

Carrying the princess, Cece came so quickly Vaughan thought she'd probably been listening.

Iachus pushed him gently. "Get up, kid, and go down on one knee before your princess."

Struggling to control his heartbeat, Vaughan did as he was told.

Iachus nodded his approval. "Now put your hand on her head and repeat after me."

Vaughan put his hand on Her Highness's head and repeated the oath as Iachus gave it to him: "I, Vaughan, vow this day to protect and defend Her Highness, Brianna, the crown princess of Korthlundia. By the goddess and on my mother's grave, I make this oath that I will fight to the death before I allow a single drop of her blood to be spilled." Vaughan felt the heaviness of the vow descend upon him and had no doubt that Sulis was bearing witness.

"Good." Iachus held out his dagger. "Now roll up your sleeve and make a small cut on your forearm. Bleed a few drops on the princess's forehead, and repeat these words. "With my blood I seal this oath.""

Vaughan took the dagger and rolled up his sleeve. Wincing, he cut himself, and Cece held the baby so he could bleed on her. The princess's scrunched up her face as the warm drops hit her, and Vaughan had never felt so much love in his life as he did when he repeated Iachus's words: "With my blood I seal this oath."

"Do you feel any differently now?" Iachus asked.

Vaughan got to his feet. "Yes. You were right. An oath is powerful. Next time the princess is in danger, I won't hide."

Iachus smiled. "I'd bet my life on that. Now get to bed. The princess and I need to get our rest."

"Yes! Yes! I will! Thank you, Iachus! I'll never forget what you did for me!" He hurried out the door, feeling like a vast weight he'd thought he'd carry for the rest of his life had been lifted.

* * *

With a grunt of discomfort, Iachus lay back down on his bed. Cece, in nothing but her nightdress, stood beside him with the princess. "That was kind. How much of what you told him was true?"

Iachus chuckled softly. "Almost none of it, but it was what he needed to hear."

Cece put a hand on his shoulder. She'd never touched him before. He hadn't said what he did to Vaughan in order to help his cause with the princess's nurse, but he certainly wouldn't object if it had. Holy Sulis, was she beautiful in the candlelight with a baby on her shoulder. "I was annoyed when I heard you asked to sleep in the nursery, but now I'm glad you did. I never would have known what to say to him."

Cece took the baby back to her crib, and Iachus fell asleep with a smile on his face.

CHAPTER 7

As Samantha ate breakfast, Blaine went over the schedule for the day. "In answer to your summons, Father Hafghan should arrive momentarily. After you speak with him, you will preside over the first of the trials. Baron Gwawl will be assisting, of course. I've provided him a list of defendants' names and professions." In the wake of the attack two days previously, Samantha had banned the True Church of Sulis and had everyone found with a star tattoo on their right hand arrested. The city magistrates and the Royal Guard were still tracking down suspected participants in the attack. Today she would determine the guilt of those already found. "Because of Your Majesty's ability, we should be able to run through those quickly. The guilty will be hanged this afternoon."

Since lies always shone purple in their auras, she would make no mistakes and condemn no innocents. Although that was comforting, Blaine's mention of auras brought up the question that continued to plague her. "Has Tuathal made any more progress on his research?"

Blaine looked down at his own notes, although he didn't appear to be reading them. "He has discovered one piece of information, but it's not good." Blaine briefly looked at her before his eyes again fell to his notes. "It seems that auroras were traditionally trained by other auroras. It was considered something of a heresy to reveal their secrets to outsiders."

Feeling an ache in her neck, Samantha rubbed at it. "So, what you're saying is that the information I need may never have been written down?"

Blaine nodded. "I'm afraid that is what it might mean."

She squeezed her eyes closed briefly, then let out a breath. "Have him carry on. Maybe some heretics defied the prescription. How are the people reacting to the ban and the arrests?"

Since Blaine didn't meet her eyes, she knew the answer wouldn't be good. "Not well, Your Majesty. There are those who believe the ban on the church goes too far. Your father established decades ago that the people were free to believe whatever they chose and that the state didn't interfere in the church affairs."

As she again saw the knife in the hands of the man who'd tried to murder her precious daughter, Samantha tightened her hand around her sword's hilt. As queen, she'd briefly stopped wearing a sword on all occasions, but the attack had changed that. The ice in her tone was so sharp her words alone would surely shred flesh. "Do you think my father wouldn't have changed this policy if the church had made an attempt on my life?"

Blaine quailed as if afraid of being struck. "Of course, he would have. I'm not saying I'm in agreement with the dissenters. I was merely reporting on the people's sentiments, as Your Majesty requested."

Samantha let out a slow breath. "Of course, you are. I apologize. Please continue."

Blaine's posture relaxed, and this time he did meet her eyes. "Others believe you don't go far enough in punishing only those who participated directly in the attack. All with the star tattoo are dangerous fanatics, so they think the non-participants are still as guilty as the man who holds the bandits' horses while the bandits commit robbery and mayhem, so to speak." Blaine's eyes expressed his agreement with this sentiment.

Two days ago, she might have agreed, but she'd had time to calm down. Her father taught her to rule by logic and justice, not emotion. "No one will be punished for merely belonging to the church. They will be tried for their actions, not their beliefs."

Blaine looked down at his notes. "Of course, Your Majesty is correct, as always." But his failure to meet her eyes told her he was unconvinced. Blaine's silent objection made her second guess herself.

She'd consulted with her chancellor, Baron Gwawl, before announcing her decision, and he'd agreed her approach was appropriate, but she had no advisers whose opinion she trusted absolutely. Was it possible she was going too far or not far enough?

Contemplation of this question was curtailed by Father Hafghan's arrival. Her guards escorted the high priest into her reception room. He bowed. "Your Majesty."

She invited him to be seated, and Blaine provided him with a glass of wine. "Father, since the True Church of Sulis is now banned, I would like you to install your own priests at all of their former temples and shrines."

Hafghan cleared his throat and shifted in his seat. "I'd be happy to do as Your Majesty asks, but many of the priests who presently occupy those temples won't simply leave. I fear they will react violently. Unlike the True Church of Sulis, I have no trained security force. I can't send servants of the goddess into such danger."

"Your concerns are justified. I will send a detachment of the Royal Guard to assist you in cleansing the temples."

The high priest smiled. "Thank you, Your Majesty. I will then be happy to do as you ask."

* * *

Count Cadarn observed the queen's demeanor as she sat on her throne in judgment. Although the queen had requested all members of the Royal Council be present for the trials, Cadarn would have been there anyway to bear witness to a miscarriage of justice. The queen had changed since the True Church of Sulis had tried to kill her and her heir. Although her anger was tightly controlled, he didn't believe he'd ever witnessed such a depth of fury, not even when his father beat him nearly to death for breaking his nose. The queen had actually banned the True Church of Sulis, rolling back over fifty years of complete religious freedom in the joined kingdoms. Cadarn wanted to beat Father Eadoin bloody himself. What had the priest been thinking in orchestrating the attack? They'd had a plan, and the priest preempting it could only hamper their ultimate success. Cadarn hadn't been able to do much to look for Eadoin himself, but he had set both Nisse and Purple Leaf to the task. He just hoped they found Eadoin before the queen did.

The trials were about to begin. If one could call this farce a trial, that is. The men would be allowed to present no witnesses; a judgment of guilty would be automatic.

Baron Gwawl banged a gavel on the desk he sat behind. When the room quieted, he said, "A terrible treason has been committed against our queen, Her Majesty, Samantha, the first of her name. The first of those accused will face justice today. Mack Mackstamm, blacksmith by trade, you will come forward."

Two guards forced a huge man forward. Mack Mackstamm was covered in chains and his arms bulged beneath his shirt. Even for a blacksmith, the man was large. Sealing his fate, the blacksmith glared at the queen and had to be forced to his knees. Cadarn heard weeping at the edge of the crowd, and a woman clutching two small children and hugely pregnant with a third fell to her knees also. Cadarn assumed they were the blacksmith's wife and children.

The queen's chancellor cleared his throat. "Mack Mackstamm, you have been charged with the attempted assassination of your queen and princess. How do you plead?"

"You can't call this justice. I have over a dozen witnesses who can testify I was elsewhere at the time, but since Her Majesty has refused to allow them to speak, get this farce of a trial over and hang me. Turn my wife into a beggar and let my children starve. I never thought a woman belonged on the throne anyway." The big man spat at the queen's feet.

The queen stared hard at the blacksmith. When she spoke, her voice was so cold that it sent chills down Cadarn's spine. "Mack Mackstamm, you have shown disrespect to your queen, but if you will now give your sacred oath of loyalty to your queen and pay a fine of five tetra for your insult, you are free to go."

There was a huge collective gasp throughout the room, and Cadarn could only stare. It wasn't even a large fine. The blacksmith looked around like he couldn't believe what was happening. He laughed and bowed low to the ground. "Your Majesty, I am truly sorry for my disrespect. I am truly innocent of this attack on Your Majesty and the young princess. I dishonored you by believing I wouldn't be treated fairly. I should have listened to my wife. I gladly give you my oath. By the goddess and on my mother's grave, I pledge my loyalty to Samantha I, the queen of Korthlundia."

She nodded with satisfaction and addressed the guards restraining the man. "Unchain him, and as soon as his fine is paid, release him."

The blacksmith's wife screamed, ran forward, and threw her arms around her husband. The children followed. Weeping, she reached into her purse and brought forth the coins. As her husband was being unchained, the woman went to the secretary's desk; he took the coins and recorded them.

The blacksmith swept his children into his arms, and then his wife wrapped her arms around him, and the four of them headed for the exit.

Cadarn scratched at his beard. *Why bring them to trial in the first place if she's just going to let them go?*

Before the blacksmith had left the throne room, Gwawl called another name. "Neale Cedricstamm, weaver by trade, you will come forward."

A scrawny little man, wearing chains only around his wrists, was brought forward. He dropped to his knees without the guards forcing him. Hope sparked in his eyes as he stared at the departing blacksmith. A nearby woman with children smiled at him and then at the queen.

Gwawl cleared his throat. "Neale Cedricstamm, you have been charged with the attempted assassination of your queen and princess. How do you plead?"

The weaver placed his forehead on the floor and then looked up at the queen. "I am innocent, Your Majesty. Like Mack Mackstamm, I thought I would have no hope of receiving justice, but I see you are a queen worthy of the name. I will gladly give you my oath of loyalty."

Again, the queen's cold eyes examined the kneeling man for only a moment. "Such an oath is not required of you. You are lying. Neale Cedricstamm, this court finds you guilty of treason and sentences you to death by hanging."

As his wife erupted into wailing, the weaver cried, "What? No! I'm as innocent as the blacksmith! I wasn't even there! Please, you have to believe me!"

The queen ignored his continued pleas as he was dragged from the room.

Cadarn frowned. *Just what is she playing at? Is she just going to sentence every other one? Does she think that letting half of them go will make her look just?*

But when the next five were found guilty, Cadarn decided she'd merely let the first go and was going to hang the rest. When a priest was called forward next, Cadarn was certain he would join the condemned. Gwawl said, "Father York, you have been charged with the attempted assassination of your queen and princess. How do you plead?"

The priest's nostrils flared as he glared at the queen. "I am innocent of the charges."

As had been her habit with all of the accused, the queen stared at him for a few moments before speaking, then she nodded. "This court finds you innocent of the charges. If you will now give your sacred oath of loyalty to your queen, you are free to go."

The priest's back went ramrod straight. He didn't draw Sulis's star, but he gave the words of the oath. "By the goddess and on my mother's grave, I pledge my loyalty to Samantha I, the queen of Korthlundia."

As the queen listened to the oath, her arrogance showed signs of cracking, and her hands fidgeted briefly on the arms of the throne. *Ah, she knows the priest forsworn himself. What will she do?* Cadarn leaned forward to make sure he heard every word.

But she said nothing, merely made some signal to her secretary Cadarn didn't understand and allowed the priest to walk free.

Another was called forward. He, too, was judged innocent and released upon his oath.

By the end of the trials, nineteen had been sentenced to death, and thirty-one released. Cadarn scratched at his beard. Whatever the queen's game was, Cadarn couldn't figure it out.

* * *

As Blaine explained the logistics of the afternoon's planned executions, Samantha stared at her reflection in the mirror. Interrupting a litany of details, Blaine paused. "Is something troubling Your Majesty? Surely your ability allowed you to separate the innocent from the guilty."

Samantha shook her head slowly. "Only two of those released were truly innocent. The rest blasphemed. They dared to use Sulis's most sacred words to swear a false oath. They didn't participate in the attack in the city square, but they aren't loyal to me and will likely betray me in the future." Samantha turned and met Blaine's eyes. "Was I wrong to let them go? To protect my daughter, should I have condemned them for the treason they are sure to commit in the future?"

Blaine straightened his papers. "Your Majesty knows my thoughts on the matter."

Samantha nodded slowly and turned back to her own reflection. Was Blaine right? Did extraordinary circumstances demand she take extraordinary actions? She couldn't have the false swearers publicly executed now that she had released them, but after Darhour killed Father Faolan, should she have him kill every one of the false swearers as well?

* * *

Samantha stood in the city square where a gallows containing five nooses had been erected. It was here that the True Church of Sulis had tried to kill her daughter. It was here it would begin to die.

The crowd jeered and threw rotten fruit and vegetables as the convicted men were brought in carts. One by one they were taken from the carts, brought onto the platform, and given a blessing from a priest. Some came quietly. Some fought with everything they had, and some wailed. But all were placed on barrels and had nooses put around their necks. Finally, the executioner kicked the barrels out from under the men's feet and they were hanged.

Samantha focused on keeping her breath slow and even, as the hanging men sometimes took up to fifteen minutes to go still. But Samantha didn't take her eyes off those who'd tried to harm her daughter. When the men ceased to struggle, their bodies were taken down and replaced with five more. The process continued until all nineteen had ceased to breathe. But there would be more trials and more executions. She wouldn't stop until all those responsible paid with their lives.

* * *

When Cadarn arrived at the Jeweled Plum Tree, Purple Leaf rushed forward, grabbed his hand, and hurried him to her room.

When she closed the door behind them, she nodded toward her closet. "Nisse found that high priest of yours. They're below, and please tell them to stop shouting at each other."

As Cadarn heaved a sigh of relief, the sound of raised voices came from below. He gave Purple Leaf a kiss on the forehead and hurried down the stairs.

When Cadarn reached the underground room, Nisse was cursing Father Eadoin in Svizran while holding a naked dagger and the priest was drawing the star of Sulis with his left hand in what looked like the beginning of an exorcism ritual. Cadarn interposed himself between them. "Quiet! Both of you! Are you mad? Do you want every whore in Murtaghan to know you're here?"

Nisse gestured toward Eadoin with his dagger and continued speaking in Svizran, although at a lower volume. "That son of a donkey's ass is the mad one!"

Cadarn answered in Svizran. "I'm as angry as you are, but we still need him, don't we?"

Nisse spluttered for a moment, then slammed his dagger back in its scabbard, plopped into a chair, and put his feet on the table.

Cadarn turned to the priest, but before he could speak, Eadoin drew Sulis's star with his right hand as if continuing the exorcism. "That demon possessed infidel dares to question the will of God."

Nisse snorted. "Your god is really that stupid?" Luckily, he said it in Svizran.

Cadarn glared at his friend as he struggled to restrain his own desire to punch the priest. "We had a plan, and if our plan wasn't Sulis's will, why did Father Faolan agree to it in the first place?"

Cadarn had noticed that Eadoin's eyes were often unfocused, but today they were even more so than usual. He appeared as if he were staring at something that wasn't there, but he abandoned the ritual. "Who are you to question His Excellency, the Sulis blessed? If the holy warriors had been successful in killing the queen and her demon spawn, we would have been spared the trouble of further conflict, but it was Sulis's will that our faith be tested before granting us victory. Therefore, we will now proceed as you outlined to His Holiness."

Cadarn raised his eyebrows and turned to Nisse, who snorted again and said in Svizran, "I told you he was mad."

Wiping a sweaty hand on his tunic, Cadarn turned to the priest and spoke in a calming tone appropriate for upset children. "Be that as it may, we must discuss how we are going to proceed from this failure to ultimate victory."

Without further word, Eadoin took a seat at the table. "Such is Sulis's will. However, I must ferret out the spy in my ranks."

Cadarn slowly lowered himself into his own seat. "Why do you think you have a spy?"

Eadoin touched his chest, revealing that he was wearing some kind of medallion underneath his robes. "It is the only explanation for the queen's judgments. All the holy warriors martyred by the queen's noose were among those who tried to rid Sulis's land of the demon spawn."

Cadarn stared. "Her Majesty didn't condemn one innocent?"

"On the contrary, they all were innocent. When holy warriors act on Sulis's will, all blood spilled is counted to their glory. But yes, they were all part of God's attempt to rid His land of evil. All of those released had been too cowardly to act that day, although most of them have since recommitted themselves to Sulis's cause."

Cadarn wasn't sure which shocked him more: the priest's final statement or that the queen condemned no innocent men. "You would have them violate the sacred oath they gave the queen?"

"Since they swore by the god*dess*, they made no sacred oath."

* * *

With Brigitta across from him, Darhour sat in a seedy tavern two hours' ride from Duke Sheen's estate. They had surveyed the estate and come here to plan. It'd been easier than he'd anticipated finding out where Father Faolan was hiding. The clues were obvious enough that it was almost as if Faolan wanted to be found. But Darhour hadn't anticipated the high priest being guarded by a small army. "Sneaking in will be difficult," he murmured. "We'll have to find a way to get them to let us in the front gate. Any ideas?"

They discussed and rejected a few until Brigitta asked, "We could pretend to be foreign nobles in need of shelter. Your goddess does command hospitality in such cases, does she not?"

Darhour scratched at the scars on his face. "I'm afraid that would depend on who you asked. Most believe that our goddess doesn't consider hospitality the sacred duty that the Saloynan and

Massossinan gods do. Besides. if we don't have a retinue of servants, Sheen would never fall for the ruse."

Brigitta pressed her lips together, thinking. "We had a carriage accident killing several of our servants. The rest are seeing to its repair."

Darhour shook his head. "That might work for you, but Sheen will be a lot more suspicious of a man. If they let us in at all, I'll be so closely watched that killing the high priest will be difficult. And before you suggest it, I'm not letting you go in there alone. It's too dangerous."

Brigitta scowled. "Then what *do* you suggest?"

He held up a hand. "Your plan is a good one. It just needs one refinement."

CHAPTER 8

Master Hueil, the squire weapons master, sneered when Vaughan showed up for weapons training, as he had every day since he made his vow to the baby princess. "Here again? You haven't missed in nearly a month now. Have all the hells turned cold?"

Vaughan flushed but kept his voice respectful. "I don't know, sir." Vaughan had taken a sacred oath, and not only did fulfilling it require bravery, it required skill. He wasn't about to tell Master Hueil anything about the oath or how he'd sealed it with his blood, but he'd make sure that if anyone ever came for Her Highness again, he'd be ready. Not only had he not missed a training session since he'd taken his oath, he spent every spare minute practicing on his own. It was working, too. When he held a wooden practice sword now, it didn't feel heavy anymore. Instead, it was starting to feel like an extension of his body.

Floyd still mocked him at every opportunity, but what was Floyd's mockery compared to swords of the queen's enemies? Master Hueil led them through the warm-up drills, and Vaughan was barely winded when they finished.

After warm-up, Master Hueil paired him against Floyd for the first time in a while. The last time they'd been paired together, Floyd had disarmed him repeatedly, forcing him to run around the room to retrieve his sword. The other boy smirked at him. "Get ready to play fetch, horse boy."

Vaughan merely assumed a fighting stance, ignoring Floyd's smirk.

As Floyd came at him, he swaggered, showing that he didn't see Vaughan as a serious opponent. Vaughan easily parried the first few thrusts. Then Vaughan felt his mind let go and his body take over. He'd heard fighters achieved this state, but he'd never been able to do so himself. Before he even thought to do it, he performed a move the king had taught him that he'd been practicing the day before: he not only parried Floyd's thrust but moved his blade under his opponent and gave a quick upward thrust. The other squire's practice sword went sailing across the room and hit the weapons master in the forehead. Vaughan put the tip of his sword at Floyd's throat. "You're dead."

The room went quiet, and Vaughan glanced around. Everybody had stopped training and was staring at him, including Master Hueil. Floyd was looking at his hand like he couldn't believe it was empty.

Master Hueil snarled at Floyd. "Fetch your sword, and try to keep your hands on it this time. The rest of you stop standing around like a bunch of nincompoops."

When Floyd returned from picking up his sword, he glared at Vaughan. "You got lucky. It won't happen again."

Floyd was right about that. For the rest of their match, Vaughan didn't get close to scoring on Floyd, and the boy hit him hard enough that he'd end up with some significant bruises. But Vaughan forced the other boy to actually work at defeating him, and his own sword remained in his hand the entire time.

When Vaughan was so exhausted he could hardly stand, Master Hueil finally called a halt and dismissed them for the day. As the other boys were filing out, Master Hueil called Vaughan over. Wondering what he could have possibly done wrong this time, Vaughan dragged his feet.

"Where did you learn that disarming technique? It's more advanced than anything we've done."

Vaughan met Master Hueil's eyes. "The king taught me."

Master Hueil looked Vaughan up and down, then nodded thoughtfully. "You were with the queen and princess at the city square when they were attacked, weren't you?"

Did Master Hueil know he'd hidden instead of fought? Vaughan flushed and looked away. "Yes, sir."

Master Hueil patted him on the shoulder, something he did only when he thought a boy had done a particularly good job. "Carry on."

* * *

Samantha sat in the Royal Gallery in front of the wedding portrait of her and Robbie. Devyn had just finished the painting, and Samantha wanted to like it, but Robbie's face wasn't quite right. Two-month-old Brianna sat on her lap. Her eyes were even greener than they'd been at birth, and a small amount of auburn fuzz covered her head. She was big for her age and growing rapidly, and she was unquestionably the most beautiful baby to ever live.

"Yes, that's your daddy," Samantha said, pointing at Robbie and wishing it looked more like him. "He's just gone for a little while, but he's coming back to us soon."

Eolande, the Bard, finished singing "The Ballad of Gloine Torr," which told of Robbie's victory over the glass mountain, their betrothal, and marriage. Still strumming her lute, Eolande asked, "Shall I go on, Your Majesty?" Samantha nodded, and the Eolande launched into "The Ballad of the Soul Stone," which told of Robbie's destruction of the Ancient Evil. Even though Brianna was still far too young to understand them, she needed to hear these songs so she'd know what a hero her father was.

When Eolande finished, she lowered her lute. "Your Majesty, I have a favor to ask."

Samantha patted the bench beside her. "Sit. Whatever it is, I'm sure you've earned it." At great personal risk, Eolande had helped distract the Bard Witch Alvabane while Robbie destroyed the Ancient Evil.

Eolande sat and reached for Brianna. "May I hold the little one?" Samantha released her, and the bard took the precious child in her arms.

After smiling at her daughter, Samantha met Eolande's eyes. "And what favor can I grant you?"

"Your Majesty, I'd like your leave to depart."

Samantha's stomach tightened. "I thought you were happy here. You said you'd tired of the life of a wandering bard."

"I have been, and I had. But now, I'm growing restless. It seems the road is in my blood. I've always dreamed of visiting my mother's homeland and finding someone who can teach me exactly what it means to be a Bard. There are no true Bards in Korthlundia, and I can learn nothing more from books. If I'm going to progress further in my magic, I need a teacher. It had once seemed an impossible dream, but thanks to Your Majesty's generosity, I now have the resources to do so. There are plenty of others who can sing to this little one of her father." She kissed the top of Brianna's head. "But there's an entire world out there that is finally within my reach." Eolande's eyes sparkled, and a dreamy smile spread over her face.

Although she had to choke out the words, Samantha made herself say what she knew to be right. "I would never try to keep you if your heart is elsewhere. When you find what you are searching for, I hope you will return. Know that there will always be a place for you here."

"You don't know how much that means to me, Your Majesty." Eolande pulled her into a hug, a surprising familiarity. Few dared even touch the queen. Brianna protested being squished between them. Eolande laughed and released Samantha. "I will return some day, Your Majesty. Korthlundia is my home, but for now the road calls to me again."

"When will you leave?"

"I've learned of a ship leaving for my mother's country tomorrow morning. I plan to be on it. Who knows how long it will be before there is another?"

"I will miss you. Is there anything you need?"

Eolande lightly touched Samantha's arm. "I have need of nothing, and I will miss you too, and especially this little one who will probably be all grown up when I return." She picked Brianna up, kissed her cheek, and handed the baby back to Samantha. Eolande started to get up but hesitated. "I know life has been hard for Your Majesty, but happiness is waiting for you down life's road. I'm sure of it." Since bards weren't known for their prophetic powers, Samantha took little comfort in Eolande's words.

As she was leaving, Baron Gwawl, her chancellor, entered the gallery. The expression on the baron's face did not bode good news. Samantha called Brianna's nurse forward to take the child. Cece left trailed by Brianna's guards.

"What is it?" she asked, signaling the baron into a seat.

As he sat, the baron sighed. "Another secret meeting place of the True Church of Sulis has been discovered. The city magistrates raided it during a worship service this morning. They estimated that at least one hundred were in attendance. I'm afraid that the worshipers reacted violently to being told to disperse. Two magistrates were killed before they sent for reinforcements from the Royal Guard. With the Guard's assistance, they were able to quell the violence and close the temple. In doing so, seven worshipers were killed, thirty arrested. The remainder managed to flee. Your Majesty, I don't have to tell you the crowds at these illegal services are growing larger and more violent."

Samantha's jaw clenched. Crowds at the executions of the attackers had also grown less supportive and more unruly. Her attempts to eradicate the heretic church only seemed to make it grow stronger and more popular. "What do you advise?"

Gwawl seemed taken aback by the question. "If you lift the ban on the church, you will look weak, but continued efforts to try to suppress it are likely to backfire."

She waited for him to continue, but that seemed to be all he had to say. Samantha wanted to slap Gwawl for merely saying she was damned either way. She'd needed an adviser with more wisdom.

She sent for Baroness Eithne and asked for her advice. The baroness squeezed her shoulder. "They tried to kill your daughter. You have to stay the course."

Samantha nodded, but she wondered if Eithne was correct. Trying to suppress the cult only seemed to be making it grow stronger. She cursed Duke Caedmon for betraying her. He would have known what to do. She cursed Tuathal for his continued failure to find anything useful about her ability. And she cursed herself for sending Darhour away. *No, I don't need him. He deserted me. I can never need him again.*

* * *

While grunting and rolling his eyes, Darhour scanned the area around Duke Sheen's gate. With as many troops as Duke Sheen had, he and Brigitta would have to leave before anyone realized Faolan was dead. The two men they'd hired as guards flanked them. Brigitta's hair was done up in an elaborate style, and she was dressed in a pink silk dress embroidered with gold thread. It was the only dress elaborate enough to be found on a moment's notice. It fit her well, but the pink clashed badly with her red hair and had put her in a foul mood.

"I hate pink," she muttered. "And I hate riding side saddle." Before she could complain anymore, a man who looked a lot like

Lord Devyn appeared at the top of the wall. Darhour assumed he was Sheen's other son.

"I am Prince Cedric," he said. "My men have informed my father, the king, that you seek refuge."

At the use of titles they had no right to, Darhour's eyes widened and his hand itched to palm a knife, but he pressed his lips together and grunted more. Brigitta presented herself as a traveling Massossinan noblewoman and her idiot brother, giving the duke's son a highly theatrical rendition of their supposed carriage accident, and asking for lodging until the carriage could be repaired.

As the gate started to rise, Darhour felt cold sweat on his forehead. He wanted to grab Brigitta's arm and demand a change in plan. But the goddess seemed to have decreed that he involve himself only with strong-willed women. Besides, it was too late to retreat without causing suspicion. They would never have another chance to enter so easily. He breathed deeply to calm himself before the sweat could ruin his facial cosmetics.

Before riding through the gates, Brigitta paid their guards. "We are safe now. Return to help with the carriage."

Darhour hissed in her ear, "Find out about the titles."

Lord Cedric hurried down from the top of the wall, and Brigitta allowed him to help her dismount. "Did you call yourself Prince Cedric? I wasn't aware Korthlundia had a prince."

Cedric cleared his throat. "The joined kingdoms are no more. Korth has split from Lundia, and my father Sheen is now the king of Korth. I am his heir."

Brigitta glanced briefly at Darhour for direction, but he could say little to help without blowing his cover. He sat on his horse and grunted toward the walls, hoping she'd get his meaning.

"Oh dear, from the forces on your walls, I gather you expect trouble. I hadn't meant to involve myself or my brother in foreign disputes. Perhaps we should leave."

Cedric took her hand and patted it between his. "I understand your caution, but trouble is at least two weeks away, and there is nowhere fit nearby for a lady of your status to stay. Let His Majesty, my father, shelter you in your difficulties. I promise I will see you on your way before trouble arrives."

Darhour gave her the smallest of nods. She glanced over her shoulder at the closing gates as if thinking of leaving but then smiled at Cedric. "I guess there can be no harm in that, can there?"

Cedric looked toward Darhour. "Does your brother need help dismounting?"

Brigitta blushed. "No, I'm sorry he's an idiot and has to be told what to do." She pulled on Darhour's leg. "Come along, Raynor," she said in Massossinan. After dismounting, Darhour tried to head in the direction of the stable, but Brigitta grabbed his arm and directed him inside.

Cedric looked at them curiously but said nothing. As Darhour had hoped, he didn't have Darhour searched for weapons before leading them into the great hall, which had been re-purposed as a throne room. Sheen sat on a throne. In order to avoid a murderous glare that no idiot would use, Darhour wandered away from Brigitta and grunted at the wall coverings. Brigitta curtsied low to Sheen. "Your Majesty, thank you for your hospitality." She looked toward Darhour who wandered down the length of the hall. "Please forgive my brother. He is an idiot and has no notion of proper protocol." She hurried to Darhour, took his arm, and led him back to the king. "Bow, Raynor," she said in Massossinan. While Darhour bobbed up and down at the waist, Brigitta sighed wearily. "I'm afraid he doesn't understand Korthlundian either. In fact, he only understands a few simple commands in our own language."

Sheen looked at Darhour as if he'd just allowed a filthy beast into his boudoir. "I see. We were about to dine. Would you care to join us and tell us what you're doing in this part of the country?"

Before Brigitta could respond, Darhour squealed loudly and pointed toward a corridor. "Shush!" Brigitta slapped Darhour on the arm. "Your Majesty, I am famished and would love to dine with you. However, my brother has always been my trial. He cannot stand still for more than a moment, and you do not want to see him eat. I'm afraid his minder was killed in the accident." She looked uncertainly between Darhour and the duke. "I know this is an unusual request, but do you perhaps have a servant you could lend me as a minder until I can employ a new one?"

"Yes, of course." Sheen looked around and spotted a servant. "You there." He called the servant forward. "You will be at this lady's service."

The servant bowed. "Jodoc, Milady. How may I be of service?"

"Take my brother to our rooms," Brigitta commanded in the haughty tone of a noblewoman.

The servant took Darhour's arm and tried to direct him, but Darhour squealed like a pig and pulled in the opposite direction.

Brigitta put her hand to her forehead and rolled her eyes. "Just let him wander as he pleases."

Sheen lifted his eyebrows. "As he pleases?"

Brigitta's lower lip trembled as she met the duke's eyes with tears in her own. She was becoming a fabulous actor. "I must beg this indulgence, Your Majesty. It's truly the only way to quiet him. He won't hurt anything, and your servant can make sure he doesn't go anywhere he shouldn't."

"Yes, of course." Sheen waved the servant away impatiently, then rose from the throne and offered Brigitta an arm. "Can I escort you to the dining room, Milady?"

* * *

Followed by Jodoc and doing a lot of grunting, Darhour did a thorough survey of Sheen's castle. Curiously, almost none of the rooms were locked. Apparently, Sheen had great faith in the army guarding the walls.

However, when Darhour put his hand on one door, Jodoc scurried forward and grabbed his arm. "Not in there, Milord. The duke's mistress won't want you among her things." Jodoc tried to direct him further along the corridor.

Darhour hid his reaction to hearing Jodoc refer to Sheen as "the duke" by clenching his fists and letting out an ear-piercing shriek. Jodoc put a hand over Darhour's mouth. "Stop that!" Darhour bit the servant's hand, and when Jodoc swore and pulled it away, he continued to shriek. "Shut up!" Jodoc yelled, cradling his injured hand. "Be quiet!" When Darhour continued to shriek, Jodoc threw the door to the room open. "Don't touch anything, or it will be my head!"

Darhour quieted immediately and wandered into the room. The curtains were drawn, so it was fairly dark, but that was no hindrance. When Darhour had been the chief assassin of the Saloynan king, his eyes had been magically enhanced, allowing him to pierce any shadow. He could even see in the complete darkness of a cave.

If this was Sheen's mistress's room, he wasn't that fond of her. It was a single room rather than a suite, and the room itself was rather small and cramped. The furniture was constructed from simple pine that grew abundantly in Korth, and the bed covering wasn't even silk but simple cotton.

Darhour grunted again and left the room. Jodoc didn't try to stop him again until they came to a door guarded by two men. Darhour was careful to drool and snort as they approached. Looking at him with disgust, one of the guards stepped in front of him. "Who are you? What are you doing here?"

Jodoc sighed loudly and rolled his eyes. "He's the idiot brother of some Massossinan noblewoman that's dining with the duke. He likes to wander and makes animal noises. He doesn't talk."

"Get him out of here," the guard commanded, but he didn't correct Jodoc referring to Sheen as the duke.

Jodoc grabbed Darhour's arm, so he resumed shrieking.

"Holy Sulis, Mother of us all, what is wrong with him?" the other guard roared over the noise.

"He doesn't like it when you stop him from going somewhere."

"We're not letting him in His Grace's rooms. Move him." The guard too seemed not to accept Sheen's royalty.

Jodoc tried to pull him along, but Darhour held his ground and continued to shriek. Jodoc swore. "He won't budge."

One of the guards drew his sword. "I'll shut him up!"

Darhour tensed in case he needed to defend himself, but Jodoc stepped in front of him. "You can't kill His Grace's guest! He'd have both our heads! Can't you just let him look around? It's the only way to shut him up. He never touches anything."

The guard with the drawn sword looked uncertain, but the other one threw open the door. Darhour abruptly stopped shrieking and stepped around the guard with the sword, who made no move to stop him.

After looking around long enough to justify the fit he'd thrown, Darhour left Sheen's quarters and continued down the corridor, opening rooms and looking around. Jodoc made no move to interfere.

Finally, Darhour found what had to be Father Faolan's rooms. The reception room was dominated with a huge altar covered with a fine silk cloth embroidered with a gold star surrounded with baskets of fruit and roses of the deepest scarlet. Darhour recognized the cloth as having belonged to Father Shylah. Faolan had been the child-murdering high priest's chief assistant.

Grunting, he examined the door. It had no bar, and he'd have no problem with the locks. But the room was in sight of Sheen's guards. They'd have to be dealt with.

After checking the escape route from Faolan's room to the castle courtyard, Darhour headed for the servant's section of the castle, since it was often easier to escape that way. He kept up his grunting and rambling gait. All Jodoc did was sigh loudly and follow him.

When he entered the kitchens, servants backed away from him. Since they didn't ask Jodoc who he was, word must have spread. He grabbed a turkey leg from a platter and ate it noisily, letting scraps fall to the ground.

One of the cooks turned up her nose. "Holy Sulis, I don't care if he is noble born. Idiots like that should be locked up so decent folk don't have to see them."

Jodoc nodded vigorously. "I've about had it with him. If I didn't already want to kill him for being a traitor, I'd like to skewer His Grace for assigning me this duty."

"Shush! Shush!" The cook put her finger to her lips. "You don't know who might overhear. And remember to refer to him as His Majesty, Sulis curse you."

"I don't care who hears," Jodoc persisted. "He's a Sulis-cursed traitor, he is. How dare he call himself king? Queen Samantha I is the only monarch I acknowledge. After King Robrek stopped the Dead Lands from spreading not more than twenty miles to the south of here, his dukeness gives shelter to the man who tried to kill His Majesty's unborn child! I should gut that priest myself, I should."

The cook grabbed Jodoc's arm and whispered, "You know I'm on your side. I lost my sister's family to the Ancient Evil. But there's some hereabouts that feel different, and His Majesty has hired himself a small army."

Jodoc grunted. "Small army? Half those boys on the wall have about two weeks' training, and most of them are refugees from the Dead Lands."

The cook glared at him. "We can't be sure how many of them are with us, and we don't want to tip our hand before Her Majesty shows up to deal with him. When she shows, we'll help her out just like the palace servants did when Duke Argblutal tried to usurp the throne."

* * *

After he'd bathed off the stink of weapons' training, Vaughan put his hands in his pockets and walked down the palace corridor, kicking noisily at the flag stone floor. He wasn't trying to attract attention, and the fact that this happened to be the corridor where Oriana had her rooms was just a coincidence. He never saw her hanging around in the palace anymore. He passed her door, but it remained closed. He turned around and went back the other direction kicking even harder, but still, no one peeked out. He glanced around the corridor, trying to figure out how to attract her attention without actually knocking on the door.

Before he could come up with a plan, the door opened behind him, and Oriana stepped out. "Vaughan, what are you doing here?"

All Vaughan could do was stare. The hundreds of small braids Oriana usually wore were gone, her hair cropped short. "Why did you cut off your hair?"

Oriana put her hand to her hair. "Because I got tired of the braids. Do you like it?"

"No! You look like a boy!"

"Well, you do, too!" She stomped back into her room and slammed the door in his face.

"Of course, I like look a boy. I *am* a boy! Why are girls so weird?"

He'd ask Cece. Maybe she could explain how girls thought.

* * *

Oriana leaned against the door she'd slammed in Vaughan's face. *How dare he tell me I look like a boy! I hate boys! How can he not understand that I lost my entire sisterhood? How can I be the only one left? What right did I have to survive while the rest of them died?*

Oriana waited a few minutes, then peeked out to make sure Vaughan was gone. She needed to make potions for tomorrow's clinic. She hated going to the stillroom. Master Calum, the royal physician, always glared at her and made sarcastic remarks. He had no healing magic, and he didn't like it that she could make more powerful potions than he could.

When she reached the stillroom, she was surprised to find a priest leaning over a cauldron with a novice beside him. Calum was nowhere in sight. The priest turned as she entered. "Father Leigh!" She almost clapped. "What are you doing here?" The novice was Artan. Together the three of them had helped Eolande distract the bard witch so the king could destroy the Soul Stone.

The priest smiled at her. "I thought we could all make potions for tomorrow's clinic together today. I know how you hate to come here alone."

Sunshine peeked through the dark clouds that had filled her since the death of her sisters. *Why can't that stupid boy be as thoughtful as Father Leigh?*

The priest sighed. "I also don't have much in the way of supplies. They keep being diverted to other shrines because the priest in charge of supplies doesn't like me. He refuses to admit one has to be mixed blood to have magic."

"Men are so stupid! None of them has the sense Sulis gave a bull frog." *How dare that stupid boy think my hair's ugly.* Father Leigh stopped what he was doing and stared at her. She blushed. "I didn't mean you, Father Leigh. Or you, Artan."

Father Leigh put a hand on her shoulder. "Have you had a fight with Vaughan?"

She shrugged off his hand. "Why would I care what that loser thinks?"

Father Leigh raised an eyebrow, but fortunately, he didn't say anything else about the stupid boy.

* * *

When Iachus entered the princess's nursery, Cece sat in a rocking chair with the baby on her lap. "Back again so soon?" she asked.

Holy Sulis, she's beautiful. The progress he'd thought he made when he'd spoken with Vaughan hadn't lasted. "I need to survey the grounds from the princess's window." Although it was entirely unnecessary, he crossed the room to do so. The nursery was high in the palace, and the palace walls were too sheer to be climbed. When he thought he'd looked long enough, he turned to Cece. "And how is Her Highness?"

Cece hugged the child. "She's growing so fast."

"That's interesting." *You blundering idiot, why can't you ever think of something witty to say to her?* Iachus frequently thought of witty things to say when he lay awake thinking of her, but they all disappeared the moment he was in her presence.

The door opened, and the king's squire entered. The princess began to bounce in Cece's arms. "Vau, Vau, Vau." She reached out to Vaughan.

"Hello, Little Squirt." Vaughan took the baby, and the princess began laughing and patting his face. It seemed odd she able to do such things at her age.

"Well." Iachus cleared his throat. "It seems like you have everything under control in here." Cursing himself, he left the room.

* * *

After Iachus left, Cece sighed. She knew why he really came in here all the time, and it wasn't because he was afraid of someone climbing the palace walls. Iachus seemed like a nice guy, but that's what she'd thought about Allen when they'd first met. Allen had been lovely to her right up until the moment she'd let him have his way with her. The very next day he'd started getting nasty, and when she'd told him she was pregnant, he'd called her a slut, claimed the baby wasn't his, and walked out.

When her tiny baby had died hours after its birth, she'd wanted to die, too. Ardra had saved her, as she'd always saved her when they were children from whatever harebrained situation she'd gotten herself into. She smiled at Brianna, who was poking a finger into Vaughan's nose. The little princess had given her a reason to go on again.

"How's a boy supposed to know how girls think?" Vaughan asked, startling her out of her reverie.

She stared at him. Had he somehow known what she was thinking?

He turned bright red. "I'm not asking for myself," he stammered. "My friend has this girl he likes, and he said something that made her mad. He wants to apologize, but he doesn't know how. I thought maybe you'd know what to do, you know, to help my friend out."

Cece pursed her lips. "What did you say to Oriana?"

She'd thought he couldn't turn any redder, but he somehow managed it. "I wasn't talking about Oriana. I was asking for my friend," he snapped. He sat down on the carpet and put Brianna on the floor next to him. He pulled at the rug for a moment, then looked up at Cece. "She cut her hair really short. I told her she looked like a boy. I didn't mean it, though. She's really pretty. I was just surprised by her hair, you know?"

Cece nodded and thought of what Ardra had told her of the young girl's loss. "Get her a ribbon or metal band to wear in her hair, a nice one. Tell her how pretty it makes her look."

Vaughan wrinkled his forehead. "How can I tell what girls think is nice?"

"Spend a couple of tetra on it, and it will be nice enough."

* * *

After learning all he could from the gossip in the kitchen, Darhour wandered out into the entrance hall with Jodoc still following him. The duke's party, including Brigitta and the high priest, was coming out of the dining room. He gave her a small nod.

Brigitta nodded to Sheen. "And there is my brother. Thank you so much for your hospitality, Your Majesty. Hopefully, my servants will be able to fix the carriage and arrive here some time tomorrow."

The traitor patted her on the shoulder, letting his hand linger in a manner that made Darhour want to remove it from his body. "There's no need to rush. A beautiful lady is always welcome to stay with us. Isn't that right, Cedric?"

"It is our pleasure, Milady." The duke's son bowed his head to her in a simple gesture of courtesy.

His eyes roaming Brigitta's body, Father Faolan stepped forward and took her hand. "I hope you'll join us for some music."

Glad that he'd soon be slitting the lecher's throat, Darhour watched Brigitta shiver as she freed her hand. As he thought of the licentious attention she must have endured throughout the meal, his hands itched to palm one of his hidden knives and slit the priest's throat now.

Stifling a yawn, Brigitta smiled. "I thank you for generosity. But now I'm quite exhausted. If your servant shows me and my brother to our rooms, I would be most appreciative." She nodded toward Jodoc.

"I'll show you myself." Cedric offered his arm. "You may be off." He told Jodoc who sped off quickly, seemingly so the lord couldn't change his mind.

The priest stepped between them. "No need to trouble yourself. Now that I think about it, I'm rather tired myself. You gave the lady the rooms next to my own, did you not?" His smile showed that sleep wasn't the first thing on his mind.

Cedric cleared his throat. "You have so enjoyed Bard Airic's music, and he promised to have something special for Your Excellency this evening. Surely, you can listen for a few moments. Besides, I'd like to make sure the lady has everything she needs." The young man smiled down at the shorter priest, but his eyes held a deadly spark. Darhour's opinion of the duke's second son increased measurably.

Brigitta stepped around the priest and took Cedric's arm. She turned back to Darhour. "Come along, brother," she ordered in Massossinan.

The priest glaring after them, Darhour grunted and followed them up the staircase. As soon as they were out of earshot, Cedric said, "I apologize that a lady such as yourself has had to endure such boorishness. My father refuses to curb the priest's appetites. I have had to assign only male servants to attend to him because he can't keep his hands off the women."

"And your goddess approves of this in her priests?" Brigitta asked.

Cedric stiffened. "Absolutely not. But my father insists Father Faolan is an important man." When they reached the door next to the high priest's, Cedric opened it and escorted them inside a sizable sitting room. Candles spaced around the room provided plenty of light. "There is a bedroom for your brother." He gestured to one on the right. "One for yourself. A maid will be here momentarily to help you undress. Is there anything else you have need of?"

When Brigitta assured him she had no need of a maid, Cedric bowed his head. "My father's guards are just down the corridor. I shall instruct them to make sure you receive no unwanted attention during the night."

When the door closed behind the lord, Darhour enfolded Brigitta in his arms. She held herself stiffly and didn't melt into him as she usually did. "Why are men like that? They sat me next to that horrible priest, and he wouldn't keep his hands off me. If we weren't already going to kill him for betraying your daughter, I'd say we should kill him for the way he treats women."

He held her tightly and kissed the top of her head. *Please, Sulis, don't let her become me.*

* * *

Just before dawn Darhour watched through a crack in the door as Brigitta approached the guards in front of Sheen's door with a tray containing glasses of wine and mugs of cold *bhat*. All contained *keimai*, a subtle Saloynan drug that would render them quickly unconscious. He hated involving her, but she was right that he wouldn't be able to get them to drink, and using drugged darts was riskier.

"Can I offer you some early morning refreshment to thank you for watching my door last night?" Brigitta asked.

Darhour couldn't hear the guards' answer, but they both picked up a drink. Moments after they'd taken their first sip, the men's eyes rolled back into their heads and they collapsed with a resounding clank of their armor. Darhour stepped out into the corridor and listened carefully to make sure the noise hadn't attracted attention. When he was certain no one was coming, he bent down to pick the lock on Faolan's door. When the lock clicked open, he whispered to Brigitta, "I won't be long."

He silently stepped inside the high priest's rooms and made his way through the reception room and into his bedroom. Darhour's ability to see in the dark made it a simple matter to do so silently.

The high priest was snoring on his bed, and to make matters even easier, he slept on his back. Thinking of the attack on his daughter and granddaughter instead of the act he was about to perform, he moved to the head of the bed, positioned himself to avoid the inevitable blood spray, and drew his dagger. In one quick movement, he grabbed Faolan's hair, tipped his head back, and drew his blade across the priest's throat, severing the windpipe and the large arteries on the sides of his neck. As blood sprayed across the bed, Faolan's eyes shot open and he clawed at his neck. He opened his mouth as if trying to scream, but the severed windpipe assured he made no noise but a bloody gurgle. Within moments, the uncanny stillness of death crept over him.

Darhour waited until the worst of the bleeding had stopped. Then he drew his sword and finished severing the head. From a canvas bag at his belt, he got out a piece of cheesecloth, carefully wrapped the head, and then placed the wrapped head in the canvas bag. He wiped his weapons and hands on the priest's bedclothes.

When he rejoined Brigitta in the corridor, he held up the bag containing the priest's head. "It's done."

While Brigitta inspected him for blood, he expected to feel the guilt that had threatened to choke him for over a decade, but it failed to come. In fact, he felt nothing more than a mild satisfaction in a job well done. What did it mean when taking a life elicited so little emotion?

When Brigitta pronounced him clean, they headed for the stables.

* * *

As they left Duke Sheen's fortress behind, Darhour hoped bringing justice to the high priest would be enough to earn his daughter's forgiveness.

The rest of the plan had gone like clockwork. He and Brigitta had walked to the stables, and she claimed she was taking her brother for an early morning ride so he didn't disturb the other inhabitants of the castle. She claimed the bag held provisions for an early breakfast. The guards at the gate hadn't looked twice at them when they opened the gates and let them ride free.

Darhour glanced back at the site of his latest murder, but still, no guilt surfaced. Brigitta insisted he wasn't a monster, but could someone other than a monster feel so little about the death of another?

He looked over at his wife. "How do you feel?"

"We need to ditch these horses and clothes before the high priest's body is found. We can worry about feelings later."

Brigitta's causal dismissal of emotion unleashed the guilt that killing Faolan hadn't.

* * *

Holding *Blood Magic and the Faithful* next to his heart, Father Eadoin wandered through the underground tunnels to the room under the house of sin. Not that he needed the book with him, but the book felt uncomfortable if he wasn't nearby. The spy in his ranks still eluded discovery. Perhaps he had no spy, and demons from the seven hells had whispered in the queen's ear. When he reached the meeting place, Count Ultan and Lieutenant Gerard were kneeling at the altar Eadoin had insisted be constructed. They immediately rose and bowed to him, as was appropriate.

Eadoin went straight to the altar and poured wine into the chalice and began preparing the Potion of Secrets. After mixing the other ingredients into the wine, he lowered himself to his knees to implore Sulis's blessing. As he prayed, he heard someone arrive.

Eadoin opened his eyes and brought the chalice to the table. Duke Tierney had joined them. The door above them opened, and Count Cadarn and his infidel friend clamored down the stairs, laughing. Their shirts were half unbuttoned and their hair disheveled. Eadoin's lips tightened. *How dare they appear before me not even bothering to disguise their indulgence in the sins of the flesh!* Cadarn might be necessary for the god to regain his power. But when Sulis's magic again flowed in the veins of his priesthood, he would deal with the worldly.

"My honored co-conspirators." Cadarn again used that ridiculous word

Eadoin placed the chalice on the table and handed the count the silver dagger he'd used to stir the mixture. After Cadarn had cut himself and bled into the chalice, he passed the dagger to Count Ultan, who did the same. The chalice made its way around the table, Eadoin adding his blood last.

After invoking the god's blessing again, he took the first sip himself. The chalice again made its way around the table until it came to the infidel.

After emptying the goblet, the infidel smacked his lips. "Delicious."

"Serving Sulis isn't supposed to be pleasant," Eadoin reproved.

The infidel rolled his eyes. "Then perhaps you need a god with a better temperament."

Eadoin whirled on Cadarn. "Your friend's blasphemy endangers us all! We cannot expect Sulis's blessing on our endeavor if we consort with infidels!"

Nisse threw back his head and laughed. While the count offered no verbal reproof of his friend's heresy, he did glare. The infidel sobered, but further mocked the god through miming locking his lips with a key and throwing the key over his shoulder.

Cadarn sighed. "This infidel is providing the soldiers we will need for our plans to succeed. Surely Sulis will understand since we do this for his benefit."

Father Eadoin leaned toward the count. "Sulis isn't a patient or forgiving god. Beware of how far you push him."

To begin the meeting, the infidel gave a report on the arrival of his troops. They were trickling in on different ships so as not to arouse suspicion. "Within a week they will have all arrived. We should act soon after, or they will get restless. My men aren't the type you want getting restless."

They went over plans for the attack on the palace and the roles they each would play.

CHAPTER 9

Darhour smiled as he watched Brigitta arranging Faolan's head on a piece of brilliant crimson silk. She wore gloves to avoid touching the rotting flesh. It had taken them nearly a month to travel to Sheen's estates and back again, but now they were in an inn only a short distance from the palace.

When Brigitta was satisfied the dead eyes were facing upward, she surrounded the head with white and green flowers, wrinkling her nose while she worked. "Randgrid, it's rank."

"That it is." Darhour put a handkerchief to his nose and sat on a chair beside her. "I told you the way I had it was fine. You needn't have touched it." He pointed to the plain wooden box sitting beside the ornate silver casket Brigitta had insisted they buy.

Brigitta shot him a glare. "You don't give a queen a gift in a wooden box." When all the flowers she'd purchased were inside the casket, she spent still more endless minutes rearranging them before she pronounced the gift acceptable. At long last, she firmly attached the silver lid. Fortunately, the lid fit tightly and did much to reduce the stench.

Brigitta spent several moments staring at the casket, then abruptly cried, "The dress! She said it would be ready by noon." She rushed for the door without saying goodbye. Darhour decided not to follow. He'd spent more than enough time yesterday sitting around the dressmakers as Brigitta picked out a dress and was measured to have it altered to fit her. Despite the delay it had caused and the expense they couldn't really afford, Darhour hadn't objected to the purchase. Brigitta wanted to be sure she created the right impression. He knew how his wife dressed wouldn't matter. It was his reception that was in question, not hers. But it was a small thing to help relieve his wife's nervousness.

* * *

After a while, Darhour regretted letting Brigitta go alone. He twirled his knives in his hands and threw them at the wall. Obviously, the dress hadn't been ready, and if she took much longer, he might have to pay for a new wall. The sun was starting to set, meaning it would now be tomorrow before they could go to the palace and report their success. He hissed at the delay, and then chided himself. Brigitta deserved the dress.

He retrieved his knives and threw again. They'd hit exactly where he'd intended. They always did and had ever since he'd been a mere boy of nineteen and the long dead Phelix had taught him to throw.

Finally, he heard footsteps in the corridor, and Brigitta burst in carrying the gorgeous blue silk dress. Embroidered red and yellow flowers decorated the bottom of the skirt and the bodice. Delicate lace embellished the sleeves. "Isn't it fine? I've never had anything so beautiful."

Feeling a warm glow from seeing his wife smile, Darhour laughed. "Put it on, and let me see."

She hurriedly stripped and pulled the dress over her head. As he stood behind her, fastening the many buttons, he admired the way the dress clung to her figure. The dressmaker had done a good job with the alterations. It fit perfectly. "You look fabulous," he told her.

Rather than being pleased with the compliment, Brigitta's face fell. "Is it really fine enough to meet a queen? What if she doesn't like it?"

Darhour put his arms around her. "Stop worrying." He kissed her neck. "The dress is glorious."

"It is, isn't it?" She detached herself and sat at the dressing table. "How should I do my hair?"

He sat back on the bed. "You'll look beautiful no matter how you do it."

She rolled her eyes at him. "Sig, why won't you take this seriously? How do ladies do their hair here? How does your daughter?"

"I think she mostly wore it in a braid."

She let out a huff of impatience. "Think harder. That can't be how a queen wears her hair."

He thought more, and then shook his head. "I never paid much attention."

Brigitta stood and glared at him. "Within five seconds of walking into any room, you've noticed how every person is armed, assessed their strengths as a fighter, located all possible hiding places and escape routes, and planned how you might kill every one of them, but you never noticed how your daughter did her hair?" When he could think of no better answer to give her, she whirled back to the mirror, muttering "Men" under her breath.

She stared at herself in silence for a moment, then got up and removed the dress. To his utter shock, she burst into tears. "What's wrong?"

"I don't know what I was thinking in coming here. I'm an orphan peasant girl and former whore. No dress can ever make me into a lady. Your daughter will see right through me."

Running out of patience, Darhour clenched his fists. "Samantha isn't like that."

She grabbed her boy clothes and pulled them on. "You don't understand women!"

Darhour leaned against the wall. "What man can?" he breathed, wondering if they were going to fight. Part of him wanted to. Anything to ease his tension at facing his daughter again.

"I thought you did."

Before Darhour could think of a response, she fled the room. Darhour started to go after her, but stopped, knowing he'd say something in his present mood he'd later regret. Once she'd calmed down and started thinking reasonably again, she'd come back.

* * *

When Brigitta didn't return after several hours, Darhour started to worry. She didn't know the city, and she couldn't have had more than a few coins on her. He grabbed his cloak and went out into the night. Certain she wouldn't have gone far, he searched in a methodical pattern spiraling out from their inn. But when the taverns started to close and he still hadn't found her, he remembered rumors of young women kidnapped from the streets of Murtaghan and forced into whoredom. He tried to remember if Brigitta had taken her sword when she fled the inn. He was pretty sure she hadn't. *Holy Sulis, have I failed my wife as badly as I failed my daughter? Was it wrong of me to think I could marry and have any small measure of happiness after the things I've done? Please, Holy Mother, don't make Brigitta pay for my mistakes!*

When his search ranged farther and farther from their inn, the more convinced he became she wouldn't have gone that far on her own. Burning to kill those who'd taken her, he headed for the docks. His old underground contacts would know who trafficked in women. Near the docks several of the seedier taverns still had light and noise pouring out of their doors. He paused outside one of them, and laughter floated outside. A woman's laughter rose above the rest: Brigitta's laughter. Thanking Sulis that he hadn't yet failed her, he stepped into the tavern.

As often happened when he entered a place, the tavern went instantly silent. When he was a young man, he'd tried to cultivate a menacing look, but now he didn't know how to present any other. Brigitta was sitting at a corner table with five sailors and was drunker than she should have been able to afford. He noted with approval that her back was to the wall; she had a good view of the entrance, and she hadn't allowed the sailors to block her in.

"Sigurd!" she called out, trying to get to her feet and falling back on the bench. "Come join us! I'm a warrior, not a lady! Aren't I, boys?"

As he approached the table, Brigitta looked from him to her companions, who'd gone white. "Hey!" She slapped the shoulder of the one next to her. "He's not here to kill you. He's looking for me. That's my husband!"

At the word "husband," the five men jumped to their feet and began backing away. Four of them drew daggers, but the fifth put out his hands. "Whoa, buddy! All we did is buy her drinks. We didn't know she was yours!"

Brigitta slammed her hand on the table. "I am *not* his! I am *mine*! Aren't I, Sig?"

Darhour didn't answer but allowed his eyes to narrow and addressed the sailors. "Out!"

Within seconds he and Brigitta were alone. Even the tavern keeper had disappeared. He sat across from his wife. "It's late."

Brigitta shook her head, and tears started running down her cheeks. "Please don't be angry with me, Sig. But I just can't be a lady."

He reached across the table and squeezed her hand. "As long as you're with me, you can be whatever you want."

"But your daughter won't want me if I'm not a lady."

He wiped the tears from her cheek. "You don't need to worry about my daughter." *I do.*

* * *

As she listened to Baron Gwawl detail the state of the treasury as a result of the Korthian famine, she tapped her fingers on the arm of her chair. Resources were low, but no one in Korth would starve. "You don't look as happy as I expected, Your Majesty," he said.

Samantha forced a smile. "I'm overjoyed." Yes, she was happy, but she was missing something, and she knew it. Getting the nobles to help out had been far too easy. Despite their initial resistance, the members of the Royal Council had all turned out to be generous. She'd had to make few concessions, grant few favors, make no threats. Count Cadarn had been true to his word about using his influence on the Lundians, but she couldn't explain his success. He was probably the least wealthy and powerful member of the council. What could he have offered them to cause them to change their minds? And the problems with the heretical church were growing.

She regretted sending Darhour away. She needed his wisdom.

Anger erupted within her at the thought of the man who'd fathered her and then deserted her when she needed him most. She wanted to hit something. She had been lax on her training lately anyway. She summoned her maids to help her change and then headed for the training arena. The king had insisted she learn how to use a sword as soon as she was old enough to hold one. More than once those skills had saved her life.

* * *

As she rode with her husband to the palace, Brigitta's head pounded and she fought against vomiting. Last night had been foolish, and even though Sigurd hadn't berated her, he had to be furious. He'd hardly said a word all morning. Even when she put on her leather armor instead of the beautiful dress that had cost most of their remaining coin, he'd merely nodded, as if indifferent to her apparel. Or perhaps to her.

Not knowing if she could face both his anger and meeting the queen at the same time, she glanced at him to see if she dared ask his forgiveness. His hands clenched the reins tightly, but since he wore a large hood to hide his facial scars, she couldn't see his face. Still, Brigitta was almost sure his hands actually shook, and the nearer they got to the palace, the slower he rode.

Randgrid curse me! He's not angry with me! He's terrified of the queen!

She remembered when she'd called him a coward for leaving his homeland. Her words rang in her ears: "Your life means little to you, but you won't risk your heart." If his daughter rejected him, his heart would be crushed. Today he was being braver than she'd ever seen him. Shame flooded her as she realized how selfish she'd been. *He* was the one who would be devastated if the queen rejected them.

She reached across and squeezed his arm. When he turned to her, she whispered, "I love you. I'm right beside you."

Although he said nothing, he gave her a slight smile, and some of the tension went out of his shoulders.

When they approached the palace gates, Sigurd lowered his hood. The guards came to attention and their mouths dropped open. They stared as if they were looking at a ghost. Nobody spoke for an uncomfortably long time.

Sigurd broke the silence. "Please inform Her Majesty's secretary of my arrival."

One of them finally saluted him. "Captain." He ran off, and the others stood aside to allow them to ride into the palace courtyard. She clutched at her stomach. *Dear Randgrid, don't let me vomit now.*

They dismounted, and stable grooms came forward to take their horses. Sigurd thanked them by name. Even though she knew he'd served at the palace, his familiarity with everyone made her feel as if she'd entered a bard's tale. While they waited, Sigurd tried to talk to the guards, but they looked at him as if they were going to piss themselves and gave him short answers until he asked, "How is the crown princess?"

At the mention of the royal baby, the guards broke into grins, and one of them answered, "Her Highness is a lovely, happy child. The queen is a wonderful mother."

A shock traveled down Brigitta's spine. Although she'd seen the infant with the queen in the city square, she'd somehow never thought of the queen as a mother. Her stomach unclenched. She wasn't going to meet a distant, disapproving queen, but a mother like herself.

Everything would be fine.

* * *

Samantha sparred vigorously with Guthrie, the youngest of her personal guards. She'd never beaten one of her guards, but she was determined to this time. She'd been holding her own, but she was tiring, and Guthrie still seemed fresh. If she didn't end it soon, she would lose. Using a trick Darhour had taught her, she sidestepped Guthrie's next attack and tripped him as he passed. Before he could roll to his feet, she stepped on his sword and put hers at his throat. "You are dead!" She smiled fiercely.

The room erupted in applause, and she stepped back. She hadn't realized so many people were watching.

"Well done, Your Majesty," Guthrie said. Grinning, he got to his feet. "I wasn't expecting that. I will be next time."

"Bravo!" Bearach cried. He and Conroy had joined Guthrie and Marcan, who were presently on duty. "I remember when the Captain taught you that trick." He was practically bouncing on his feet.

Conroy hit him lightly on the shoulder and grinned. Samantha scrunched her eyebrows. While Bearach was occasionally boyish, Conroy wasn't. "A word, Your Majesty," Conroy called her aside and spoke in a low tone. "A present has been left for you in your reception room."

Could it be? Slamming her practice sword back onto the wall, she hurried from the room with Bearach and Conroy following her.

When she reached her reception room, an ornate silver casket rested on the sideboard. Her heart sank. Such a container wouldn't be from Darhour. But when she opened the box, a horrible stench emerged, and Father Faolan's dead eyes stared back at her. His head was surrounded by white roses and green chrysanthemums.

The man who'd tried to kill her daughter had paid for it. Still, her hand trembled as she closed the lid. Something was off. Darhour would never have included flowers with the severed head.

Holding her hands behind her back to hide their shaking, she turned to Bearach and Conroy. "Where is he?"

"He is in his old quarters awaiting Your Majesty's pleasure." Conroy grinned and again hit Bearach playfully on the shoulder.

What is going on with my men? "Send for him, and then leave us."

She sat in her chair and forced herself to remain seated as Darhour entered. He bowed. "Your Majesty, I have brought you the priest's head, as you commanded." He gestured toward the casket.

"So, I see."

Shining with unguarded love, his eyes met hers. Like the flowers and the silver casket, his open expression was out of character. She gripped the arms of her chair. *Who is this man?* He got down on one knee and held out a hand to her. "Samantha, I beg you, let me take on some of the burden you bear. I don't ask for my former position of captain of your personal guard. I wouldn't displace Conroy, who stood by you when I didn't. You don't even have to forgive me for leaving. All I ask is to serve you in some capacity."

Fighting the urge to run to him, she got up and went to her window seat. "You've been gone so long, and I've been all alone. If I take you back, I'll never be able to bear losing you again."

"My daughter, I'll never leave you again. This I swear by the goddess and on my mother's grave."

Staring out at the palace grounds, yet seeing nothing, she shook her head. *Do I dare trust him again? But how can I not? I'm so alone.*

Despite all her efforts to repress them, sobs tore from her throat.

She heard Darhour get to his feet. He approached and put a hand on her shoulder. The warmth and gentleness of his touch both burned and soothed. "I've lost Robbie. Sulis took him from me. Even if you didn't leave willingly again, she'll take you from me, too. I couldn't bear it."

"My poor daughter, you've suffered much loss in your young life, and I'm a poor substitute for your love, but let me come back. Let me fill at least a little of your emptiness."

She turned and fell against his chest. Making soothing noises, he caressed her hair. He kissed the top of her head, much in the manner that she so frequently kissed Brianna's.

Remembering the head surrounded with flowers, she pulled away from Darhour and again became the queen. Her voice sounded cold again when she asked, "Where have you been? I expected you back much sooner."

Darhour took a step back but nodded as if the coldness wasn't only expected but deserved. "I had to travel farther than anticipated. Faolan was hiding in Korth. At Duke Sheen's estate. The duke has proclaimed himself King of Korth, and his estate is guarded by a small army." Darhour described the fortification.

Samantha walked to the sideboard and slammed her hand down on it. Naturally, the goddess wouldn't return something to her without tearing something else away. "He's in open rebellion against me?"

"Yes, but many inside aren't loyal to him." He told her what he'd learned in the kitchen.

"Sheen's rebellion cannot go unchallenged. I'll have Blaine call a meeting of the Royal Council. You will repeat for them what you told me."

"Yes, of course," Darhour said. "But first, would it be possible for me to present my assistant?" Although he didn't smile, his eyes brightened.

"When have you ever used an assistant? Who is he?"

"I met her"—he paused at the word—"in Saloyna."

Samantha gaped at her father. "By all means, present her then," she said. While Darhour left to fetch the woman, Samantha collapsed into a chair. Darhour and a woman? What could it mean?

Darhour returned with a fierce-looking woman dressed in leather armor and wearing a sword. Her brilliant red hair was tightly braided. She wasn't exactly pretty, but there was something striking about her. As the woman bowed, Samantha called forth her aura. It was a mixture of the same green of Darhour's aura mixed with pink. But there was also a dark edge to the aura. Like Darhour, she was dangerous. Darhour cleared his throat. "Your Majesty, may I present Brigitta, my wife?"

Samantha's mouth dropped open. If Darhour was truly back, then she shouldn't have to share him with another. "She's Massossinan. You hate Massossinans!" It was the only thing she could think of to say.

Darhour actually blushed. "That was once true, Your Majesty. But you once said the right woman would look beyond my scars. Brigitta has. She was the one who made me see how wrong I was to ever leave." He put an arm around the woman.

There was something strange about his expression, and then Samantha realized the truth. *Darhour is in love.*

The room whirled around her. *Darhour is in love.* She'd never really believed what she'd told him about the "right woman." She stared at the stranger, then shook herself out of it. Sheen had declared himself the king of Korth. She had neither the time nor the leisure to sort out her own emotions. She asked, "Does she know?"

Darhour nodded.

Samantha stood, but she nearly had to force herself to reach out both her hands to her father's wife. "Then welcome, stepmother."

As Brigitta took her hands, she felt the callouses that matched her own. Of course, Darhour's wife would know how to use a sword. "I do not mean to intrude where I do not belong." Her Korthlundian was understandable, but heavily accented. "I am nothing more than a peasant. But Sigurd, I mean, Darhour, he said you wouldn't mind." Brigitta glanced at Darhour as if she doubted this.

"Of course, you're welcome. But a fuller welcome will have to wait until after the Royal Council has been informed of Sheen's rebellion."

Darhour nodded. "Of course, Your Majesty, but while the councilors are gathering, is it possible to meet my granddaughter?"

Samantha agreed, and after instructing Blaine to call the meeting, she led him into the corridor.

* * *

As he followed his daughter the short distance to the nursery, Darhour briefly clutched Brigitta's hand. Samantha's stiff back told him he wasn't forgiven yet, but at least she'd accepted him and Brigitta and was taking him to meet his granddaughter. He scratched the facial scars that had sent far more than one child running and screaming from him as a monster. In fact, nearly everyone he met was afraid of him. Samantha, at fourteen years of age, had been one of the few who hadn't been. It seemed too much to hope that his granddaughter would accept him as readily as his young daughter had. As if she knew what he was thinking, Brigitta squeezed his hand in reassurance.

As they approached the nursery, two guards tensed, hands on their swords. Their eyes widened, recognizing him. Staring at him, they bowed to Samantha. "Your Majesty." They stepped aside, still staring.

Old habit dictated he never allow Samantha to enter a room he hadn't confirmed as safe, so he stepped in front of her and entered the nursery. A young woman who looked familiar snatched Brianna from the rug and backed to the edge of the room, her eyes darting around as if seeking escape.

He stood aside for Samantha to enter. The queen gestured the woman forward. "Cece, I'd like you to meet Darhour, the former captain of my guard. He has my complete trust. Darhour, this is Brianna's nurse, Cece. She is Ardra's sister." He nodded at her, now seeing her resemblance to her sister.

Still clutching the child tightly, Cece bobbed her head. "Pleased to meet you."

Brianna reached out to Samantha. "Momma! Momma!" Darhour was certain he hadn't heard correctly. The child was certainly too young to form words.

As Samantha took his granddaughter in her arms, he also noticed that she was too big for her age. She was closer to the size of a baby at six months than at two. Samantha kissed the top of Brianna's head, and Darhour forgot her unusual size. He'd had never seen anything more beautiful.

Samantha told Cece, "You may leave us." After the nurse left, Samantha kissed the child's cheek. "How are you today, sweetheart?"

Brianna laughed and caught hold of Samantha's nose. She didn't yet have much hair, but what there was of it was the same auburn color as her mother and as his had been in his youth. She had her father's emerald green eyes and a hint of Robrek's darker skin. *Ah, my poor daughter, she must be a constant reminder of the one you have lost.*

He hadn't known Robrek well, but he still felt a weight in his chest as he thought of his daughter's beloved. He leaned down to the child but not too closely for fear of scaring her. "Hello, Brianna, I'm your grandpa."

Making happy babbling sounds, Brianna reached for him. He held out his arms, and she willingly came into them. "P... p... p... p," she said, grabbing his nose in one hand and running her fingers all over his scarred features with the other. He laughed. The goddess had taken much from him, but his girls had both instantly known him.

Brianna bounced in his arms. "She's a strong one. And big."

Samantha drew close and put her hand on Brianna's head. "She's perfect, isn't she?"

Darhour drew back as Brianna put a finger up his nose and decided to say nothing more at present about Brianna's size. "That she is, Your Majesty."

Brigitta stepped beside him. "Ah, my love, she is a precious jewel." Brigitta smiled at the baby, but she quickly wiped away a tear. Surely, she was thinking of her own lost children.

Brianna bounced more vigorously in his arms and continued babbling, "P… p… p… p… papa."

No, I certainly couldn't have heard that correctly.

But Samantha must have heard it as well. She leaned toward her daughter. "What did you say, sweetheart?"

"P… p… p… p," Brianna said as she returned to tracing his scars.

Blaine knocked and entered. "Your Majesty, the councilors are assembling."

Darhour drew Brianna close and kissed her forehead. "I've got to go, little one, but we'll see each other again soon." He turned to Brigitta. "I've duties to attend to."

"Yes, of course. Might I stay with the child?"

He looked to Samantha, who after calling in Brianna's guards, agreed. Telling himself that Samantha's caution concerning Brigitta was only natural, he handed his granddaughter to his wife.

As Darhour and the queen exited the room, he nearly ran into Vaughan, whose mouth dropped open. "Captain Darhour! You're back!" Belatedly, the boy remembered to bow to the queen.

Darhour smiled at his former stable hand. "That I am. We'll talk later. We are due in the council chamber."

* * *

Vaughan stared after Captain Darhour. *He's back! When did that happen?* Vaughan put his hand on his sword, as if to convey to the backs of both the queen and Darhour that his skills were improving. Then he entered the nursery. A strange, foreign-looking woman held the little princess he'd vowed to protect. He wanted to rush forward and snatch Brianna out of the woman's arms, but the queen and

Captain Darhour wouldn't have left her with the princess if they thought she'd harm Brianna, and the guards didn't seem alarmed. "Who are you?" he demanded.

Before the woman could answer, Brianna reached for him, saying, "Vau… vau… vau." Despite how young she was, she was trying to say his name. The magic the healers all claimed Brianna had within her had made her smarter than a normal baby. He held out his arms for the princess, and the woman relinquished Brianna to him. He took a couple of steps back, feeling better now that he held the crown princess.

"My name is Brigitta," the strange woman said with an accent so strong he could barely understand her. "I marry your Captain Darhour."

Vaughan's mouth dropped open. "The Captain can't have a wife. He's too old."

The woman laughed, as did Brianna's guard, Iachus. "He's not so very old," the woman insisted.

Iachus nodded. "I'm sure the captain is still quite vigorous." The princess's guard looked at Brigitta in a manner that made Vaughan turn a deep red.

He blurted out. "But you're a Massossinan. The captain hates Massossinans."

The woman threw up her hands. "Why does everyone say that? I not give him his scars."

CHAPTER 10

With a palace page following them carrying the casket that contained Faolan's head, Samantha and Darhour neared the council chamber. Samantha put a hand on her stomach to calm it and glanced at Darhour. Everyone they passed gasped when they saw him, many of them blanching or hurriedly drawing Sulis's star. As the signs of others' fear of Darhour multiplied, Samantha felt weight being released from her shoulders. She was safe now, and she'd be able to do what King Solar raised her to do no matter how many obstacles the goddess threw in her path.

Conroy and Bearach jostled each other more than once as they passed through the corridors.

When they reached the council chamber, Darhour preceded her into the room. The collective gasp was loud enough to be heard in the corridor, and Duke Tierney's voice rang out. "Holy Sulis, what are you doing here?"

Yes, he's back! Do you dare to fight me now? Her back straight and her head held high, Samantha entered, and the councilors all scrambled to their feet and bowed to her, but they didn't take their eyes off Darhour. They were all assembled, even Pandaran. "As you all see," she said, "the former captain of my personal guard has returned. He has my complete trust. He also has news."

Duke Tierney stared at her as if she were mad. "But, Your Majesty, isn't this the man who butchered Duke Argblutal's corpse? I mean, the duke certainly deserved to die for his attempt to usurp the throne, but this man cut…" At a glance from Darhour, Tierney went silent. In fact, all on the Royal Council, with the exception of Baroness Eithne, blanched or trembled visibly. Even Baron Gwawl cleared his throat and didn't seem to be able to look Darhour in the face. From the moment she'd met him, Darhour had always been her close friend. She'd never before appreciated just how frightening others found him.

She signaled to the page to put the casket in the middle of the table and dismissed him. She sat and bid the councilors be seated. Although they did so, their eyes remained on Darhour.

Moments later, Captain Hawk entered. On seeing Darhour, a smile spread across his face and he grasped Darhour by the arm as men do in greeting each other. "When I saw a corridor full of green guards shitting themselves, I should have known you were back."

Samantha called the council to order. "As you are all aware, Father Faolan escaped from his just punishment for treason and an attempt on the life of my heir and has been in hiding for some months. I sent Captain Darhour to locate him, and I am happy to report that justice has now been done."

Ultan put a trembling hand against his chest. "Surely you don't mean he has murdered Father Faolan?"

Darhour gestured toward the casket. "His head lies within."

Staring at the casket as if it contained a relic, both holy and dangerous, Ultan's lips quivered. "Your Majesty, what have you done? Many considered the high priest Sulis's chosen."

Count Cadarn touched his arm. "As Her Majesty said, Father Faolan was guilty of treason. Justice has been done."

Ultan jerked his arm away and opened his mouth, but when he met Cadarn's eyes, he closed it without speaking. *What is going on between them? What strange power does Cadarn possess?* As Darhour reported where he'd found the renegade priest and Sheen's declaration of himself as king of Korth, she called forth Cadarn's aura. The colors danced more fiercely around the count, but she still didn't know what to make of them, and his face showed nothing. *Sulis curse Tuathal, why hasn't he been able to find anything useful?*

Lord Devyn had gone white. "Holy Sulis, Your Majesty, I never thought my father would go this far. I am no son of a traitor. He must be dealt with."

Devyn's words jerked her out of her concentration on Cadarn's aura. To her relief, all of the councilors except Ultan nodded agreement.

Baron Gwawl said, "Your Majesty, an army should be sent at once to unseat Sheen and install Lord Devyn as duke."

Devyn turned even whiter, but his voice was steady when he announced, "Your Majesty, I am ready to do my part."

Gwawl continued, "Considering the extent of the duke's treason and the importance of his position, I suggest Your Majesty lead the forces yourself."

"Your presence will send a powerful message, Your Majesty," Baroness Eithne agreed.

Samantha squeezed the arms of her chair. At no time in her life or even in several decades before her birth had Solar led an army. She turned to Captain Hawk. "How many men from the Royal Guard can be spared?"

Hawk bowed. "There are only two hundred in Murtaghan at this time, Your Majesty. The city magistrates can take up some of the slack, but I wouldn't want to leave the palace guarded by fewer than a hundred. Messages could be sent to some of our closer outposts. Perhaps another hundred men can join you on the road."

"Sheen has at least three hundred," Darhour said. "They have a fortress to protect them, but most aren't well trained, and we have no idea how many are loyal to him. The servants spoke of helping Her Majesty take the castle."

Samantha looked at her councilors. "How many men can each of you contribute to the cause?"

"Your Majesty," Baron Gwawl said. "Since you're leaving, I should probably stay to manage things here. But I will send word to my estates, and my men will meet the Royal Guard as they near Sheen's. I don't have a large force, only about 100 men, but they have bloodied themselves fighting bandits. They will be useful."

Eithne spoke next. "I will send a message to my seneschal to release all men that can be spared to join Your Majesty. My household guard isn't large, but I believe that would add about fifty men. And meaning no disrespect to Captain Hawk, but no member of the Royal Guard has the combat experience of Captain Darhour; perhaps it would be wise if he led the force. Captain Hawk could remain in charge of the forces here in Murtaghan."

Samantha looked to Hawk first. He'd served her well, and she didn't want to insult him. To her relief, he nodded. "I agree," Hawk said, and she smiled. If she left him here, surely he could handle any problems that might arise in her absence. He would keep Brianna safe.

Teague said, "I can send a message to my estate for one hundred men. Also, so that this is not seen as an act of Lundia against Korth, I think it would be wise if I went as well and that no Lundian member of the council do so."

No one objected, and without hesitation, the rest of the council, including Ultan and Tierney, committed an additional five hundred men. Cadarn promised fifty himself, which, considering the size of his estate, was quite generous.

* * *

When Darhour returned to his rooms. Brigitta wasn't there, so he went to Brianna's nursery to look for her.

When he opened the nursery door, Brigitta had her back to him. She was sitting on the floor playing some kind of game with Brianna's toes. She was talking to the baby in her own language, saying something about pigs as she grabbed each toe in turn. Brianna broke into giggles when Brigitta reached the littlest toe. *Holy Sulis, I love them!* He didn't deserve such happiness; a part of him was certain it would soon be taken from him. Perhaps that was why he felt uneasy. Since the long-ago day when he was caught making love to the young queen, Samantha's mother, nothing in his life had been smooth or easy.

As his wife and granddaughter continued their game, he sat down on the floor next to Brigitta and rubbed his face against her back, breathing in her scent.

She leaned into him. "The little princess likes this game as much as my Elva did." Her voice was thick with unshed tears.

He hugged her close. "I wish I could give you another child."

"After what the Saloynans did to me, I won't ever be able to conceive another."

"We could try." He moved her hair aside and kissed the back of her neck; somehow it didn't bother him that both Brianna's bodyguards and nurse were watching.

Brigitta said nothing but got to her feet and reached to help him up. He took her hand and marveled at her strength as she pulled him upright. Holding hands, they left the nursery.

When they got to his quarters, they slowly undressed each other. As she ran her fingers over his scars and kissed the worst of them, his manhood stiffened. He lay her on the bed and took her nipple in his mouth.

"Yes," she whispered. "Make me feel alive."

He took his time. Who knew when they'd have the privacy to do so again? As he slipped himself inside of her and her hips rose to meet his, he worried whether a goddess could be trusted who was capricious enough to lead him to Brigitta, while taking his daughter's love.

* * *

When Cadarn reached The Jeweled Plum Tree, Purple Leaf ran to meet him. "Thank Sulis you're here." As they made their way to her room, she kept looking over her shoulder.

"Is everything all right?" he asked.

Her face was pale, and her lips quivered as she answered. "There are people waiting for you below, and they're angry. I don't think you should see them alone. Let me send one of the girls for Nisse."

"Who's waiting?"

"Count Ultan and Father Eadoin, and they brought a half dozen underlings."

"How dare they! Nobody but the co-conspirators themselves are supposed to know about the room! I'll have words with them, I tell you that!" He hurried his step, but Purple Leaf caught his arm.

"I think they mean to kill you. Please don't go down there alone." She was trembling in an adorable fashion.

He opened his arms for her, and she fell against his chest. "It's sweet of you to worry, my dear, but I didn't kill their high priest." He frowned as he kissed the top of her head. *Do they blame me for Faolan's death? Fanatics are so unpredictable.*

But he wasn't about to send a whore running for help, as if he were a little boy who needed his daddy. He broke the hug, took Purple Leaf's hand to comfort her, and continued to her room. She tried to stop him again at the top of the staircase, but he patted her hand. "I'll be fine." Besides, he needed to take them to task for revealing the secret tunnel complex. The queen hadn't left yet.

He prepared his lecture on the way down the stairs, but before he had a chance to deliver it, two young priests grabbed him and slammed him against the wall. Father Eadoin, his eyes seeming to focus nowhere, put a knife to his throat. "Because of you, the oracle of the holy word is dead. Say your prayers, and prepare to join him!"

Cadarn swallowed. "You can't blame me for his death. I made sure he had an army to protect him. Nobody should have been able to penetrate Sheen's fortress. How could I have known the queen's pet assassin had returned? Don't you want to see the high priest properly avenged? Sulis's power restored?" Cadarn had qualms about Darhour's return, but since the killer planned to accompany the queen, he would have no effect on their plans.

The high priest lowered his knife. "The great Father Faolan *will* be avenged. Sulis will rise to see to it." Eadoin nodded to the two priests holding Cadarn to release him, but his eyes still refused to focus. The effect was most disconcerting. *Will I truly be able to control him after the queen is removed?*

But then he saw the poor milk maid as she was repeatedly raped by his father and his father's men. *One problem at a time. First, we end the evils of class. Then we'll worry about the church.*

* * *

Devyn hurried from the bed, grabbed the chamber pot, and vomited as if he were trying to expel his entire stomach. Aislinn rolled over and put her hand on his back. "Was it really that bad?" she laughed.

Devyn shook her hand off and stood. "You know it's not that. It's..."

Aislinn sat on the bed, wrapping the sheet around herself. "I know, it's your father."

"Yes, it's my father!" Thinking he'd feel more in control of himself if he weren't naked, Devyn grabbed his trousers and pulled them on. He sat on the bed, still turned away from Aislinn. "I have to help arrest him. And maybe my brother, too."

"You don't have to be afraid of him. You'll have Her Majesty and an army with you." Aislinn kissed his back, scarred from the repeated application of his father's whip. Aislinn ran her tongue over the worst of the scars.

Devyn arched his back. "I don't think you've grasped the situation, my love. If both my father and brother are imprisoned or worse, I will have to be duke whether I like it or not." Devyn shot to his feet and began pacing. "My father was right about me, you know. I can't manage a dukedom. I thought I was through with all of that when Her Majesty made me the court artist."

"If you were duke, no one could stop us from marrying."

He hurried to the bed and took both of her hands. "Our wedding day will be the happiest day of my life, but don't you see, Aislinn? I'm not worthy—"

"Stop this nonsense!" Aislinn's eyes narrowed. "You've been spouting such rubbish since we were ten. You believe this only because your father knocked you around while telling you how worthless you were. If duke is indeed what you become, you will rise to the occasion."

Devyn turned away. Aislinn had always had too much faith in him. He'd disappoint her someday. Hadn't he betrayed the queen when she'd put her trust in him?

Aislinn grabbed his shoulder and turned him to face her. Even though he'd just sated himself, the fire in her eyes went straight to his groin. "Stop thinking about the night of Her Majesty's betrothal." Somehow, she always seemed to know what he was thinking. "Yes, you made a mistake, but it all turned out okay. You won't make a mistake like that again."

Devyn laughed without humor. "Wouldn't I?" He caressed the side of her face. "If another man threatened to rape you in front of me, you don't think I'd do the same thing again? I'm not strong enough to choose my queen over you, my love. I'll never be strong enough for that."

Aislinn's eyes glistened with tears. "You'll be as strong as you need to be. Come back to bed with me. We must make the most of the time we have before we're separated."

Devyn tore his trousers off and did as she ordered.

* * *

As Vaughan entered the arena, Samantha paused in her training. At Blaine's urging, she had invited him to accompany the army north and assigned him to Lord Edan, who didn't have a squire of his own. *How can I keep forgetting the boy who brought back my love?*

Vaughan bowed. "Your Majesty, I appreciate the honor, but I can't go to Korth with you."

Cocking an eyebrow, she held her hand out for a cloth to wipe her sweat. "Master Hueil reports you are making great progress. Lord Edan was a good friend of the king."

Vaughan bowed his head. "Respectfully, Your Majesty, my skills are for one purpose: to keep the crown princess safe. On Litha, I made a sacred vow to Her Highness. I will stay and protect her."

"You made a vow? Why do I know nothing about this?"

He raised his head and met her eyes. It surprised her that his eyes were now level with her own. He seemed to have grown a foot in the last year. More surprising, when she looked within them, she no longer saw the eyes of a child. "Because it was a vow I made after my cowardly response during the attack." He told her for the first time how he'd hidden. "That will never happen again. Next time I will defend the princess to the death."

Understanding what the admission had cost the young man, Samantha put her hand on his shoulder. "Very well. Keep Brianna safe for me."

* * *

Upon leaving the queen, Vaughan fetched a box from the squire's quarters and headed toward Oriana's. He peaked in the box at the headband it had taken him five trips to the market to choose. It was silver with roses and Sulis's stars engraved on it. It cost way more than the couple of tetra Cece had recommended, but Vaughan didn't want Oriana to be angry at him anymore, especially since she'd now be leaving with the queen. He'd been trying to think of the perfect way to give it to her, so that she'd have to forgive him, but he'd run out of time. As he neared her corridor, he worried that the box was just plain wood. Maybe he should have decorated it somehow, but there wasn't time now. He closed his eyes, drew Sulis's star, and sent up a little prayer to the goddess that Oriana would like his gift.

He cried out as he rammed into one of the stupid decorative tables that lined the corridors. The huge silver candelabra on it wobbled, and before he could catch it, it fell to the floor with a clatter. "Holy Sulis, damn everyone to the seven hells!"

As he bent down to pick up the candelabra, he rubbed at his hip where he'd smashed into the table. The door across from him flew open. Oriana stood there with her mouth hanging open. She frowned and crossed her arms. "Watch your mouth! There's no need to talk like you grew up in a sewer pit."

The blood rushed to his face. *Of all the people to hear me swear, why did it have to be her?* "Sorry. I... er... smashed my hip against the table."

Her brow unfurrowed, and she stepped toward him. "Are you all right? I don't know why someone put in a table that blocks half the corridor. People are always running into it."

"I'm fine," Vaughan said. The dress Oriana wore was a bit tighter than the novice robes he was used to seeing her in. He couldn't help noticing that her shape was becoming more womanly. He tore his eyes away and thought furiously for some way to bring up his gift. "It's a nice day, isn't it?"

Oriana glanced out the nearby arrow slit. "I guess if you like pouring rain, it is."

"Er... It used to be a nice day." *Stupid! Stupid! Stupid! How was a boy supposed to know what to say to a pretty girl?*

"Yes, it was sunny this morning." She glanced at a painting on the wall. "It's such a pretty painting, isn't it?"

Vaughan looked at the painting of some long dead princess or queen or something. "I guess it's pretty. But not as pretty as you. I got you something." Heat rising in his cheeks, he held out the box to her.

She took it. "Why would you do that? It's not my name day or anything."

Not knowing how to answer, Vaughan stuttered. "Well... I... I shouldn't have said that about your hair... I wanted to... I mean it looks pretty... I don't... I mean... I figured you'd be going with the queen... and... I just wanted to. That's all." Before he could embarrass himself further, he fled.

However, as he turned the corner, he paused and glanced back. Oriana still stood in the corridor holding the box. She opened it slowly, and a smile spread across her face, but tears started flowing down her cheeks. *Holy Sulis, does that mean she likes it or not? Why are girls so confusing?* She picked up the band and put it her hair. Still not knowing how she felt, Vaughan hurried away before she realized he'd been watching.

* * *

While packing his meager belongings, Father Leigh instructed his novice Artan about taking care of things in his absence. Because he was one of the few true healers in the joined kingdoms, the queen had asked him to accompany her army north. He'd never seen a battlefield, but the stories he'd heard made him adamant about not subjecting his young novice to them.

"Yes, yes, you told me that already," Artan said, and Leigh realized he'd been repeating himself. Despite the earlier visit from Father Eadoin, Artan didn't seem uneasy about being left alone. Since the True Church of Sulis had been banned, they didn't operate as openly as before, so perhaps he needn't worry.

He patted Artan's shoulder. "If you do need anything and the church won't provide it, or if you feel you're in any danger, go to my father."

"But you said..."

"Yes, I know what my father does harms the goddess's children, but despite that, he still loves me, and in an emergency, he will provide for you if you ask in my name." Leigh's father was a dealer in the illegal herb paipin leaves. It had led to a rupture between them, but still his father had protected Leigh from Duke Argblutal, and he would help the boy, if necessary. Artan nodded.

"There's one last thing." Leigh opened a cabinet and brought out a small locked chest. He took the key out from under his robes and unlocked it. Inside was a thick sealed letter. He got it out and showed it to the boy. "On the night King Robrek left to fight the Soul Stone, he wrote this to his unborn daughter. Fearing that he wouldn't return alive, he entrusted me with this letter to give the crown princess when she's old enough to understand it. Since the Soul Stone did destroy the king, these are the only words the princess will ever have from her father.

"When Robrek handed this letter to me, the depths of his sorrow at leaving those he loved lined his face, but his willingness to sacrifice his life to protect the joined kingdoms glowed in his eyes. I can only imagine the power of a father's last words to a daughter he will never meet."

"Since I will almost certainly return, this precaution is probably unnecessary." He put the letter back in the chest and locked it. Then he held out the key to Artan. "But anything is possible. While I'm gone, I'd like you to wear this key, and if something does happen to me, you must deliver the king's letter when it is time."

Artan swallowed, took the key, and hung it around his neck. "I owe the king my life. I'll protect this to my last breath."

Leigh hid a smile at the boy's melodrama, but then he realized it might not be melodrama. The king had rescued the boy from the Temple of the Mother's Love, where he was being badly mistreated. Father Faolan had been in charge of the novices and he'd treated brutally those like Artan with mixed blood. Many hadn't survived.

Tears formed in the boy's eyes. "Why didn't the goddess save the king?"

Leigh put a hand on Artan's shoulder. "Only the goddess can answer that. I cannot."

CHAPTER 11

Samantha held Brianna tightly. She would be leaving in less than an hour. "Sweetheart," she whispered, "how can I bear to leave you? But it won't be safe for you where Momma is."

Brianna struggled against the tight hold, and Samantha loosened it. Brianna put one of her sweet small hands on Samantha's cheek. "Momma, Momma!"

Brianna's guards watched her. She'd summoned all of them to meet her this morning. The brothers, Bary and Brandon, who were assigned night duty, were fighting yawns. Cece was present as well.

She forced her face into a smile but still her voice quivered. "You have all taken a vow to protect my daughter."

Kelvin, the captain of the princess's guard, stepped forward. "You can depend upon us to do so, Your Majesty." The other five nodded, beaming at Brianna as if she were their daughter as well. *They'll keep her safe. I needn't worry.*

"As a queen, I trust your oaths. As a mother who has never been parted from her child, I hope you will indulge me in repeating them here today."

Without hesitation, Kelvin went down on one knee before her, and Samantha held the baby out so he could put his hand on her head. "By the goddess and my mother's grave, I, Kelvin, swear my loyalty to the goddess and my princess. I will sacrifice my life and honor in the eyes of the world to her protection." He dropped his hand and met Samantha's eyes. "And I do so without regret, Your Majesty."

Iachus dropped to his knee next, put his hand on Brianna's head, and repeated Kelvin's oath. Brianna grabbed his fingers and tried to bring them to her mouth to suck. Iachus laughed and allowed her to do so. "I love the little one, Your Majesty."

The rest followed. She nodded regally to each, but the thought of relinquishing Brianna to Cece tore at her heart.

"I'll take right good care of her, Your Majesty," Cece promised.

Samantha knew if she didn't leave now, she'd do something unqueenly, so she kissed her daughter one more time. "I love you," she whispered, handed the baby to Cece, and hurried out.

* * *

As she stood in the palace courtyard, Brigitta tried not to fidget with her sword belt or cloak, part of the uniform of the Royal Guard that the queen had provided her. These foreigners were all so tall, and surely, every member of the Royal Guard was better than she with a sword. They clearly didn't think much of her, their eyes passing quickly over her as if she weren't there.

Sig had been called away to check on something. She wasn't sure what. As she waited by their horses, she found herself tapping her fingers against her sword hilt and willed herself to stop.

Half a dozen more guardsmen joined those already assembled. One of new ones smiled when he noticed her. He sauntered over to her. "I haven't seen you around before. My name's Varney. I'm always willing to show a new man, or a new woman I should say, the ropes."

Before she could respond, one of the other guards grabbed Varney's shoulder. "Are you daft, man? She's the Captain's."

Varney paled and bent low. "Forgive me, Mistress. I meant no disrespect." He hurriedly retreated.

She nearly laughed. *They're ignoring me because they're afraid of Sig. Randgrid curse them all! He's not that scary!*

But she caught a glimpse of her husband making his way toward her, his mouth held in its habitual scowl, and remembered her own terror the first time she'd seen his face. Sigurd rarely showed his soft side to others. Besides the queen, did anyone other than she know how loving he could be? And even though she'd killed by his side, did she truly appreciate how dangerous he was?

172

As soon as Sig joined her, the men around them started going down on one knee, and she turned to see the queen approaching. Brigitta sank to a knee and lowered her eyes.

After indicating they should stand, the queen asked Sigurd, "Is everything in readiness?"

Sig bowed. "Yes, Your Majesty."

"Then let's be off," she said, and a stable groom brought the queen a magnificent white mare. The queen mounted, and Brigitta saw her blink tears out of her eyes as she glanced at the palace. Mounting, Brigitta felt her heart clench. *She's leaving her little one for the first time.* She wanted to reach out to comfort the queen, but it probably wasn't proper, and besides, she didn't know how.

* * *

Because Sigurd rode next to the queen, Brigitta found herself getting crowded further and further back in the procession. What was worse, none of the men would even look at her, let alone talk to her. Did she have a place in Sigurd's world, or would she always be seen as nothing more than an extension of her husband? Trying not to feel sorry for herself, Brigitta looked around. She spotted a young girl in the procession wiping a few tears from her eyes. *Others have it much worse. For most of your life, you had it much worse.*

She rode toward the girl. "Hello, I'm Brigitta."

The girl's eyes widened. "You're Darhour's wife," she said, as if this were an awe-inspiring thing. "I'm Oriana."

"Glad to meet you, Oriana." Figuring the girl was probably homesick already, she asked, "Is this your first time away from home? Did you miss your mother?"

The girl's eyes teared up further. "My mother's dead. I have no home. The Ancient Evil destroyed it."

"I'm so sorry," Brigitta said, which seemed completely inadequate, but she could think of nothing else to say about such a loss. The girl touched a silver band in her hair. "That's very pretty."

To Brigitta's complete surprise, Oriana burst into sobs. Her own maternal feelings stirred by the motherless girl, Brigitta touched the girl's arm. "Tell me what's wrong. Perhaps I can help."

"I don't know why he gave it to me," the girl wailed. Brigitta didn't completely follow the girl's story. Not only did the girl's sobs make the words difficult to interpret, but there were cultural references Brigitta didn't understand. From what she gathered, the pretty headband was a gift from a boy named Vaughan that Oriana favored. But since it contained Sulis's stars, she wasn't sure whether the gift was a mark of affection or if the boy were trying to criticize her for her abandonment of the priestesshood, evidenced by her short hair. The boy, Vaughan, had said it made her look like a boy.

While some of the details didn't make sense to Brigitta, she did know men. "Men not that subtle. That's expensive band for boy to give girl. He bought to apologize and tell he likes you."

Oriana wiped her eyes and sniffled. "You think so? My brother said I had a responsibility to the goddess because I am the last remaining member of the priestesshood."

"I not know your goddess or duty you owe her. But boy gave you that present"—she pointed to the headband—"not concerning himself with religion. No, that Vaughan likes you just fine."

Oriana gave her a small smile and touched the band in her hair. "It is very pretty, isn't it?"

Brigitta nodded. "It is. I'm certain he spend long time picking it out."

Oriana's face brightened, and Brigitta felt her own self-pity vanish.

* * *

His entire body glowing with contentment, Nisse listened to the friend of his heart reporting on the queen's departure. As the candlelight sparkled in his friend's eyes, Nisse thought of the exercise they'd shared above before descending for this meeting. His Liridona had aged since they'd been university boys together, but the years had only sharpened his beauty and improved his stamina. While Nisse had built a fine life for himself, he'd never found anyone who could fill the hole left by Liridona's return to his country.

After Liridona finished speaking, one of the three men his friend had promised the throne asked, "When do we act?" Duke Tierney's eyes turned to Nisse, as did those of the rest of the men at the table.

"My men are ready," he reported.

Liridona cleared his throat, directing the men's attention back to him. "We give the queen two weeks to travel a sufficient distance into Korth. Until then secrecy is of the utmost importance. The princess's guards can't be alerted. Our success depends on taking her."

It was a bold plan, a beautiful plan. And it might work. It really might. But even as his blood stirred, his stomach tightened at the thought of how many things could go wrong. For himself, the plan's success or failure was of no consequence; the bigger the fight, the more he relished it. But despite the outward changes, his Liridona was still the naive boy he'd known at university.

His friend had never killed a man and was far too innocent to truly understand what he was about to unleash. Nisse scratched at his beard. If this thing became a bloodbath, what would it do to him?

* * *

Iachus leaned over Cece's embroidery and feigned interest. "Stunningly beautiful. You're very skillful." Vaughan was playing with the crown princess, her laughter covering his conversation.

Cece jabbed the needle into the cloth. "No more skilled than most."

He didn't need anyone to tell him that his pursuit of the princess's nurse wasn't going well. He just wasn't sure why. He'd never had this much trouble with women in the past. "And what will it be when you're finished?"

Before Cece could answer, the door opened, and Captain Kelvin entered. Iachus straightened and saluted. "A word." Kelvin gestured him toward the corridor.

Guts twisting, Iachus followed the captain out. Donovan was standing guard. Kelvin led him out of Donovan's earshot, then turned to him with nostrils flaring. "I've had just about enough of this. When you guard the crown princess, you cannot allow yourself to be distracted."

Iachus tried to look confused. "But sir—"

"You know exactly what I'm talking about. Everyone has seen how you look at Her Highness's nurse, especially when she's feeding the baby."

The heat rose in Iachus's cheeks. "With all due respect, sir, I resent the accusation that my attraction to Cece is in any way interfering with my duty to the heir."

Kelvin hooked his thumbs in his sword belt. "And I resent finding you unnecessarily within the nursery. I know you saved the princess's life at Litha, and that does entitle you to some consideration, but if the queen hadn't specifically forbidden me to make any changes to the princess's guard without her approval, I'd be sorely tempted to dismiss you on the spot. From now on, you do not enter the nursery without cause. You do not address the princess's nurse. You keep your mind on your duty, not your cock—"

"But—"

"—or I will have a serious discussion about your service with the queen when she returns. Am I understood?"

Iachus hunched his shoulders and bent his head. "Yes, sir."

"Carry on." Kelvin walked away, and Iachus slumped back to Donovan.

Donovan lowered his eyebrows. "She isn't even interested in you."

Iachus just glared at him. He didn't need reminding.

* * *

Angus watched his son's wife ride by at the front of the Royal Guard. She smiled and waved at the crowd, but somehow, she seemed an ocean away. Her eyes moved in his direction, but there was no reason the queen would recognize him. They'd never met. He searched the procession for any sign of his granddaughter, but she wasn't among them.

Angus took a deep breath that seemed to tear his lungs and squeezed his eyes closed. When Robrek had been on his way to destroy the Soul Stone, he'd stopped at Angus's farm, and they'd reconciled. He'd promised his son that the granddaughter then growing in the queen's womb would know her grandfather. At the time, he'd meant to keep that promise.

But when Robrek had returned, horribly damaged, Angus hadn't known how to make good on his pledge. The queen knew nothing of that final conversation with his son. She'd known him only as an abusive, uncaring father who hadn't even accepted the invitation to his son's wedding. She hadn't sent him word about Robrek's injuries. He learned of them the same way the rest of the population of Korthlundia had, and he didn't know any more than the next man which stories were true and which were merely rumors.

Was Robrek even at the palace anymore? Some rumors said he'd been taken abroad by Donella's brother. Some even claimed he was dead. If he tried to see his son, would the queen allow it? And after the way he'd treated his own son, why would she ever let him near the little princess? He'd gone to Murtaghan several times with the intention of at least presenting himself at the palace. A couple of times he'd even ridden up to the palace gates, but his resolve failed before he identified himself.

No, Her Highness Brianna was better off without him. Besides, he was already damned for his failures as a father, so how could breaking a sacred promise damn him any further?

He turned his back on the procession and mounted his horse.

CHAPTER 12

As the queen and her army reached the Reidlhean Plains, she saw the herd of Horsetads in the distance and ordered a halt. Before Robbie and Wild Thing, this was as close as she'd ever come to a Horsetad. The wild horses avoided humans and couldn't be tamed. Her husband had been the only one outside of legend known to have ridden one. As she continued forward, one of the Horsetads detached itself from the herd and came racing toward them. Even more surprising, it was followed by a young foal.

When the Horsetad came nearer, she recognized the mare. "Wild Thing!" she cried, and quickly dismounted. "You're alive!" Samantha threw her arms around the horse's neck and buried her face in the great horse's coat. "When Vaughan didn't find you with Robbie, I was sure you'd died." Seeing the mare alive and seemingly well made it seem almost as if a piece of the man she loved had returned to her.

"The rest are coming, Your Majesty," Darhour said.

Samantha glanced up, and the herd of Horsetads was indeed approaching in what seemed like military order. Horsetads could be quite dangerous if they believed one of their own was threatened. Wild Thing looked over her shoulder, and Samantha could've sworn the mare rolled her eyes.

* * *

Wild Thing trumpeted at Autumn Storm, the bossy stallion who always thought he could tell her what to do. :*Go away. This Apple Lady. Apple Lady no hurt Wild Thing.*:

Autumn Storm didn't go away, but he did stop the herd where they were. Only Smart Mouth continued forward, which was all right with her. Smart Mouth was almost always all right with her. He didn't let Autumn Storm boss him around, either. She turned back to Apple Lady. She could see neither Robbie nor a small one, but maybe Apple Lady's foal was hiding in the back of the group, as foals hid behind the herd. But where was Robbie? She sniffed the breeze but could catch no scent of him.

When the herd felt the destruction of the evil thing and Unrelenting Valor didn't return, Autumn Storm had sent Smart Mouth and a couple of others in search of him. Despite the bossy stallion telling her not to, Wild Thing had gone with them. They'd found Valor chomping on flowers, but the stallion hadn't been able to tell her anything about Robbie. The stupid horse just kept saying how good the flowers tasted. They'd brought the stallion back to the herd, but Valor still wasn't right and talked about flowers all the time. Autumn Storm had insisted that, since Valor was damaged, Robbie must have died destroying the evil. Wild Thing had told the bossy horse that Robbie wasn't dead. Robbie would come back for Wild Thing. Only Smart Mouth believed her, and only Smart Mouth was there for her when the doubts started creeping in. Now that Apple Lady was here, surely she could learn the truth. *:Apple Lady, where Robbie? Where your foal?:*

Apple Lady's face was wet. Wild Thing remembered that humans did that when they were sad. *Why is Apple Lady sad to see Wild Thing?* She tried to ask about Robbie and her foal again, but Apple Lady muttered nonsense. Robbie was the only human whose words made sense.

Wild Thing called to Babbling Brook and nudged her foal forward with her nose. *:Babbling most beautiful foal. Babbling make Apple Lady happy.:*

Apple Lady cried out. Who knew what she meant by that? She put her hand forward as if to pet Babbling, but she stopped and looked at Wild Thing. Wild Thing nodded. *:Yes, pet Babbling Brook. Babbling most beautiful foal.:*

Apple Lady petted Babbling Brook, who babbled like she always did, and Wild Thing could hear how much she liked her head scratched. But Apple Lady's face got even more wet. *:How come most beautiful foal not make you happy?:*

A horrible thought struck Wild Thing. It was so terrible she tried to push it away. But if Apple Lady wasn't happy petting most beautiful foal, it was the only thing that made sense. Apple Lady had lost both her foal and her mate. Autumn Storm had been right. Robbie was dead.

Wild Thing let out a squeal of pain. Babbling retreated behind her. She hadn't meant to scare her foal, but Robbie was dead, and his foal hadn't survived. No part of Robbie lived on as he'd promised. She turned and galloped away. If she couldn't see Apple Lady's wet face, maybe Robbie wouldn't be dead.

* * *

Samantha cried out in wonder as she ran her hand over the head of what had to be Wild Thing's foal. Wild Thing had made a life for herself without Robbie, and her baby was beautiful. She wanted to be happy for Wild Thing, but seeing the mare tore at her heart. All the grief she'd kept carefully locked away inside of herself broke free, and she couldn't stop the tears from flooding her cheeks.

Suddenly, Wild Thing let out a great wail of pain, and her foal retreated behind her. She met the mare's eyes. The Horsetad wailed again and then sped off. "No, Wild Thing," she called out. "He's not dead. He will be back. I know he will." But she had no way to make the mare understand, and she was having a hard time making herself believe Robbie wasn't lost to her forever.

You are queen. You can't let them see weakness in you. But it was no use. She couldn't hide her pain any longer. She collapsed into the grass and wailed out her grief.

Quickly, an arm surrounded her. "Your Majesty, I'm so sorry for your loss." Brigitta enfolded her in a hug, and she collapsed against the other woman's chest.

The kindness of the other woman's touch caused her tears to flow faster. She wanted to allow herself to be cared for and comforted. She wanted to sob without restraint and let out everything she felt. But she heard the men fidgeting, reminding her that she wasn't acting like a queen. Besides, if the goddess thought taking everyone she loved from her was going to turn her into a sniveling coward, Sulis had another thing coming.

With a supreme effort of will, she took the handkerchief Brigitta held out for her and wiped her eyes. She handed it back and accepted

Darhour's hand to help her to her feet. As if nothing unusual had happened, she walked to Roberta and mounted, and they headed north toward the mountain pass through which they would cross from Lundia into Korth.

* * *

Brigitta sat in the tent while Sigurd talked strategy with the queen and other important people. He was standing over a table that held a diagram of Sheen's castle with the layout of his forces as they had been when she and Sigurd had killed the high priest. He pointed to a spot on the drawing. "Sheen's gate is strong, and his walls high. Breaching them will be difficult."

The queen nodded, as if she knew all about castles and walls. She seemed so young to know so much. When Brigitta had been the queen's age, she'd barely known how to cook a meal and manage a garden. But then again, the queen probably didn't know how to do those things either. The queen said, "We can't afford the time to lay siege. That can take weeks or even months."

Sigurd nodded. "It's entirely possible those loyal to you inside the fortification will open the gates for you. They view your consort as a hero of legend. If they don't, I'll find a way to sneak in."

Sigurd's daughter touched the diagram. "Do you really think you could? I can't afford to lose you."

Lord Devyn leaned forward, and his voice trembled. Brigitta wondered why he always seemed so timid. "Your Majesty, there's a small tunnel we used to use as children to sneak in and out. The entrance is just about here." He pointed to a spot on the diagram.

Sigurd smiled a smile Brigitta had come to associated with plans to kill. "Excellent. So, if Sheen won't surrender, I'll lead a small party through the tunnel."

"I beg your pardon, General, but the tunnel was one for children. Some places are quite narrow. You wouldn't be able to fit through. It would take a boy."

At last having something to contribute, Brigitta brightened. "Or a woman, perhaps."

Sigurd glared at her like the overly protective father he sometimes acted like. "No! You aren't going in there without me."

Brigitta stood and matched him nose to nose. "That isn't for you to say."

Sigurd switched to Massossinan and started to argue, but she told him in no uncertain terms he would never control her. Sigurd opened his mouth to respond, but the queen held up a hand and interrupted. "Enough! We can discuss who will go in through the tunnel as we get closer."

Before Brigitta sat back down, she told her husband one final thing in her own language. "You know it makes sense for me to do it. Nobody pays attention to women during a battle."

A glare from the queen stopped her husband from saying any more about it now, but his eyes told her that they weren't finished. *Randgrid, I love him! But he can be such an ass.*

Sigurd and the others continued to discuss options, but they spoke so rapidly she had a hard time following. Finally, she'd had enough and left the tent. When she emerged, the men around the fire still refused to look at her, and she didn't see Oriana. She found a large rock out of the fire light and sat on it. Other fires sprinkled the plains around them; she ignored them and looked up at the moon and the stars. The stars were the only familiar things about this new land. An unexpected wave of homesickness clutched at her gut. *Why would I miss that place? Massossina was never good to me.* Still, she wondered if she'd ever feel at home in this land of her husband's. She snorted. She wouldn't if Sigurd didn't stop treating her like a child. She stared at the constellation of The Great Wagon and imagined rolling away in it.

She jumped as a voice spoke behind her. "Thinking of taking up farming?"

She turned to see a member of the Royal Guard she didn't remember seeing before.

"I'm Edan. Lord Edan, if you want to be technical, but I never saw being the youngest son of a count much to my advantage. I know your name, of course." He gestured to the rock next to her. "Mind if I join you?"

Brigitta scooted over to allow him more room. "Please yourself." As he seated himself, she found her hand going to her sword. *Randgrid, woman, he's not going to rape you.*

Edan scooted farther away. "I didn't mean to make you nervous, lass. No one with an ounce of concern for his own life would mess with the captain's woman."

Grinding her teeth, Brigitta snapped, "Randgrid curse it! I am not my husband's possession. I am my own person."

Edan held up his hands. "Forgive me, I didn't mean to give offense."

Lifting her hands and then letting them fall, she looked away from Edan and back at the sky.

Thinking of nothing to say to this strange man, Brigitta picked at her cloak while he hummed a tune. Finally, Edan blew out a breath. "I guess it never struck me how insulting that could be. Why not tell me about your interest in farming?"

Brigitta wrinkled her forehead. "I do not understand what you mean."

"You were contemplating The Plow." He gestured up at the night sky.

"Oh," she laughed. "My people call these stars the Great Wagon."

"So, it's a journey you're interested in, then? Not happy in this land of ours?"

"No, I mean, yes, I'm happy. I love Sigurd, I mean Darhour, my husband, in all my heart."

Edan chuckled. "When I see the two of you look at each other, it's stranger than anything I've ever imagined. I almost pissed myself once when he gave me one of his looks. How were you not afraid of him?"

"At first I was, but that fierceness is just at the outside. At the inside, he's the kindest man I've ever known." *Even if sometimes he's the most stupid.*

Edan raised his eyebrows. "Far be it for me to argue." He looked at her sword. "How good are you with that sword you thought about skewering me with?"

Brigitta drew back. "You not think woman can use weapons?"

Edan laughed. "Anyone who's seen Her Majesty in the training arena would never think that. The queen could best at least half the men out here." He gestured back toward the camp. "I've never sparred with Her Majesty, but I'm pretty sure she could beat me. Could you?"

She searched his face for any sign he was making fun of her. She didn't find any, so she looked back up at the sky. "I not know how good. Sigurd says I am good student, but before I met him, I never touch a sword. These men have been training all of their lives."

Edan shook his head. "Actually, some of them have been training less than six months. Life's been hard on the Royal Guard recently, and we have quite a few new recruits." He stood and drew his own sword. "Show me what you've got." He assumed a fighting stance and gestured for her to join him.

"Why not?" She rose, drew her sword, and attacked immediately. Sigurd taught her that most men will wait a moment before attacking, and if you make your move immediately, you can often catch them off guard.

Edan jumped back, barely parrying her blow. "Wicked." He nodded in approval, then counterattacked. She parried, and the fight was on. It took every bit of skill Sigurd had taught her to keep his sword at bay. She shut out all distractions and saw only her opponent.

They traded blows, and Brigitta could find no way past his guard, but he didn't get past hers, either. She made a particularly difficult parry, and a cheer went up behind her. The noise startled her, and her eyes darted briefly away. Edan used her inattention to come at her. She managed to parry, but badly.

"Don't take your eyes off your opponent even for a second. The king taught me that. He taught me a lot, actually."

* * *

When the meeting broke up, Darhour went looking for Brigitta, needing her to understand he wouldn't allow her to walk into such danger. He was told she was sparring with Lord Edan and headed toward the gathering. When he reached the circle, he kept to the shadows. If he interrupted the match to argue with her, she'd be even less reasonable. Edan wasn't the most skilled member of the guard, but he wasn't bad, and Brigitta was holding her own against him. As Darhour watched, he couldn't help contrasting her skill now with her helplessness when he'd rescued her from the two men in that alley. If she'd known then what she knew now, she wouldn't have needed his help. A certain coldness came into Brigitta's eyes as she concentrated on the match, and he couldn't help wondering. *Just what is Brigitta becoming? I can't let her go in there alone.*

By now, she was breathing heavily, and sweat ran into her eyes. Darhour winced as she made the same error in parrying a thrust toward her heart that she always made when tired. Edan took advantage of her mistake, catching the edge of her sword and twisting it out of her grasp. When Edan put his sword at her throat, Darhour had to fight an instinct to rush forward and save her.

Lowering his sword and stepping back. Edan grinned. "Thank Sulis, I got you. I was afraid I was going to lose there for a minute."

Brigitta clutched at her side, panting. Her hair was disheveled from the fight and clung about her head in a sweaty mess, but she laughed, seeming in a much better mood than when she left the tent. "Next time you will."

Edan turned to Black Giant, a huge soldier with a black mole covering one side of his face. "Pay up now."

Getting out his purse, Black Giant grumbled. "I'm not betting on anything ever again."

The gathered soldiers laughed and ribbed him, making it apparent Black Giant regularly made this claim. Brigitta wiped the sweaty hair out of her face and stared at the huge man. "You bet on me?"

Edan smirked and wiggled his eyebrows. "No, that oaf bet your sword was just for show and you had no more skill with it than a newborn kitten. I told him the captain would never have a woman carry a sword without teaching her how to use it."

Black Giant and Edan weren't the only ones who exchanged coin. Count Feoras, who'd joined them with a large number of men earlier in the day, stepped forward. He hit Edan lightly on the shoulder. "What sorry swordsmanship. Without those lessons from the king, the lass would have beaten you." Feoras bowed to Brigitta and introduced himself. Darhour knew nothing of the men's relationship with his daughter's consort, but they talked like they'd been friends.

As he sheathed his sword, Edan said, "As the loser of the match, it is traditional that you buy a drink for the winner!"

"He's lying," someone shouted. "There's no such rule."

Brigitta's face glowed. "I don't mind, but where would I buy drink here?"

Edan nodded toward the fire. "There's an ale keg back near the fire. It's free, of course, but if you draw it for me, we can pretend you paid for it and call it even."

Brigitta laughed as they went back toward the fire. Deciding now wasn't a good time for an argument, Darhour went to their tent alone.

* * *

Feeling an inner warmth, Brigitta filled a mug with ale and brought it to Edan with a bow. "At your service."

Edan winked and took it from her. He took a sip. "Get your own and have a seat." He patted a log near him.

As the other men joined them around the fire, she smiled and did so. The huge one with the mole on his face was still grumbling about losing his bet. "I've lost every Sulis-cursed bet since I disrespected the king. I thought I might get rid of my losing curse if I saved the king's life someday, but I failed to be there when he needed it, and now it's too late." There were actually tears in his eyes.

Brigitta wondered just what sort of man this very young king had been. "How did you disrespect the king?"

A large vein at Black Giant's temple pulsed. "The king was a great man." He glared at her, as if daring her to dispute it.

Brigitta leaned away from the huge man. "So I have heard."

A man across the fire smiled at him. "What was it you told the king's squire? That His Majesty ought to be shoveling shit?"

Black Giant's lip curled. "Bartle, it's unnecessary to remind me how I ran my Sulis-cursed stupid mouth off." He glared around the fire, and when met with nothing but nods, he relaxed. "A king can have you killed for speaking like that. He could have at least dismissed me or even thrown into the dungeon. But instead, he proved to me how wrong I was about him by challenging me and four others to fight him. Five against one, if you can believe it."

The man sitting beside Bartle shook his head. "And he beat us, too." He nodded toward Brigitta. "I'm Jarlath. I was one of the four the huge oaf tricked into fighting with him, as was Bartle here." He gestured toward his friend.

Bartle nodded. "The king was small, short." He stood and used his hand to indicate someone that barely topped his shoulder. "But Holy Sulis could he fight! He moved as if he were made of magic. Not to brag but I'm fast. But the king made me look like a snail. He nearly severed my sword hand, too." Bartle held up his right arm, but since there was no scar, Brigitta figured he was lying. "I thought I'd never hold a sword again."

Jarlath threw back his head and laughed. "His Majesty smashed Black Giant twice in his oversized balls, broke Ormande's leg, and nearly caved in Gerard's head. I was the only one sensible to yield before being injured." He darkened. "He was truly Sulis's chosen. Fighting against him as we did was the worst kind of blasphemy."

All around the fire men raised their hands to their heart and drew Sulis's star, causing Brigitta to break out in goosebumps. As he too drew the star, Black Giant wept. "There has never been any greater man than King Robrek. When I offered him my life or my sword to pay for my disrespect, he took my sword, and I pledged it to him with my entire heart and soul."

"We all did," Jarlath agreed.

Bartle shook his head. "Not Gerard. He hated the king for besting the five of us. He still does. He told me that someday he's going to get even with His Majesty."

Black Giant's mouth tightened as if he'd just tasted something rotten. "Gerard always was a fool. As if any of us could stand against Sulis's chosen! Far worse is going to come to him than losing every bet. The king was the only man that could be worthy of our great queen."

Bartle nodded in agreement. "And his healing power could only exist in legend." Bartle held up his sword hand again. "He nearly cut off my hand. It was hanging on by barely a thread. But he touched me with his power and the goddess's holy magic entered me, reattaching my hand and closing the wound. He didn't even leave a scar to prove I'd been wounded." He twisted his hand as if still amazed he still had it. "It's never troubled me since."

Brigitta stared at his unscarred wrist. *Can the story actually be true? Is anyone that powerful?* Not a person around the fire questioned the story.

Black Giant snorted. "A truly great man. Despite his power, he never killed except in self-defense." Black Giant glared across the fire at Brigitta. "A true man faces his enemy. He doesn't slit his throat while he sleeps."

Knowing the man was referring to Sigurd, she opened her mouth, but Edan spoke first, turning cold eyes onto the giant. "Until you have to make the decision to kill or not to kill, I'd be careful how you judge others."

Black Giant stood, looming over everyone. "There *is* a right way and a wrong way to kill someone."

Brigitta wanted to build a wall between the man she loved and this criticism. "But if a man has harmed others and you know he will do so again, how is it not right to end his life before any more can suffer?"

A man whose name Brigitta didn't remember called from across the fire, "If the man deserves to die, why in the seven hells should you give him an equal chance to kill you? How would dying while the queen's enemy lived serve the queen's interests?"

What followed was an all-out shouting match, with the men around the fire taking sides on when killing was justified. Since they talked over each other and spoke rapidly, Brigitta had difficulty following or knowing who was taking which position. Finally, she stood. "Enough, please!" She surprised herself by her forcefulness and was even more surprised when everyone stopped talking and turned their attention on her. She walked over and stood in front of Black Giant, her head coming only to the middle of his chest. "Yes, my husband slit Father Faolan's throat while he slept. Would you have had my husband wake the priest up and give him a sword before killing him? If he had done that, the priest would have surely yelled for help. My husband would have still killed him, but we would have never made it out of Duke Sheen's estate alive, and my husband would not be here now to lead Her Majesty's armies. Are you saying that would have been better? Should I and my husband have died? Should Her Majesty be left without her best protector to satisfy some stupid masculine idea of honor?"

The huge man seemed to be struck dumb by her questions. She jabbed a finger at his chest. "My husband is a good man, and dead is dead. If a man deserves to die, how can you say that one way of killing him is better than another?" Not giving Black Giant a chance to respond, Brigitta whirled away from the fire and went in search of Sigurd. She'd let him know how much his continued breathing meant to her.

As she walked away, Edan swore, "Black Giant, you shit-for-brains moron, what a way to piss her off before we got to hear the story of how she married the captain?"

CHAPTER 13

It was early afternoon when Samantha and her army descended into Korth. Men sent by Baroness Eithne and Count Teague met them on the other side of the pass. Even though far fewer men than promised by the Lundian lords had arrived, they still had a sizable army.

Darhour nodded as he looked over the gathering. "We will have significantly more men than Sheen."

Brigitta snorted. "Those men won't do much good if we can't get inside."

Samantha breathed deeply. Those two were still bickering over Brigitta going through the hidden tunnel into Sheen's castle. On the road, she'd come to respect her mother-in-law. She'd never heard anyone other than herself dare stand up to Darhour. But she'd grown weary of their bickering. She put her hand to her forehead. She'd lost her love. How could she allow Darhour's love to endanger herself?

Blaine rode up to her. "Your Majesty, a delegation from Nios Mo is requesting the privilege of speaking to you."

"Escort them to me," she said. She dismounted, and someone took Roberta to care for her. There was a time when Samantha cared for her own horse, but being queen rarely allowed her to do so.

Blaine soon returned accompanied by a man in his fifties carrying a bronze bowl. He was accompanied by a woman of about the same age and a couple of younger men. They all went down on one knee before her.

She told them to rise and gave them her best queenly smile. "What can I do for you?"

The older man answered for the group. "Your Majesty, my name is Zethar, and I'm the mayor of Nios Mo. Last winter as the Dead Lands spread unchecked, the entire Korthian priesshood lost their lives fighting it, and we had come to believe the goddess had deserted us and the Ancient Evil would soon destroy us all. As we were about to give up hope and die, a hero out of legend appeared astride a Horsetad. Your Majesty will, of course, know him as your esteemed consort."

As Samantha took a quick intake of breath, Zethar continued, "He honored us with his presence and ate stew with us out of this very bowl." Zethar held up the bowl in his hands, then caressed it lovingly. "We had it bronzed in his honor. He told us of his love for Your Majesty and the child growing inside you. The next morning he rode on, and soon the Dead Lands burst into life again, signaling that His Majesty had succeeded in destroying the Ancient Evil."

Samantha struggled to keep her voice steady. "I thank you for sharing this with me."

"We wish to share more, Your Majesty. We of Nios Mo know that things might seem dark for you now, what with your consort's injuries and the duke's rebellion. We would like to invite you to share a meal with us this evening. Eat our simple stew from this very bowl, as His Majesty once did." He lifted the bowl again. "And as we eat, the people of Nios Mo wish to share with Your Majesty what His Majesty meant to us. By sharing our stories and songs we have composed in his honor, we hope to convey to Your Majesty our faith in the goddess and in yourself. Sulis will ever strengthen the rightful queen."

The man's final words nearly caused Samantha to burst into sobs, but she managed to blink back the tears. "I would be honored to dine with you." She ordered her men to set up camp.

* * *

As the mayor of Nios Mo spoke with the queen, Oriana rode behind Brigitta. Although she doubted the mayor would recognize her, she'd seen him many times when he brought offerings to the temple in Balley Beg. When he spoke of her dead sisters, Oriana raised a trembling hand to the headband Vaughan had given her. She traced one of Sulis's stars with her finger. She'd believed Darhour's wife when she'd insisted Vaughan hadn't been trying to censor her for deserting the priestesshood, but when the mayor declared the death of the entire priestesshood, she couldn't help feeling her sisters' ghosts rising and shaking their heads in disappointment.

She turned her horse and galloped away.

* * *

As the queen spoke with a delegation about something Brigitta didn't understand, she heard a sob behind her. She turned to see Oriana riding away. *That poor girl. She needs a mother.*

Brigitta rode after her and found her behind some rocks, curled into a ball and sobbing. Brigitta dismounted, tethered her horse, and went to her. She placed the young girl's head in her lap and put her arms around her. Knowing that sometimes a person just needed to cry, she didn't ask the girl any questions. She just rocked her and sang her a lullaby she used to sing to her own children.

Elva had only been two and little Vigi still a babe in the cradle when Brigitta had been taken by Saloynan soldiers. When she'd returned with Sigurd two years later to claim them, they hadn't recognized her and had hid behind the woman who'd taken her place. Her husband had told the children nothing of her, and Laila was the only mother they'd ever known. Sigurd had offered to take her children with them, but she loved them too much to take them from everything they knew into an uncertain future. Since she could no longer show her children her love, she now poured that love into the poor motherless girl who sobbed on her lap.

Brigitta sang lullaby after lullaby as Oriana sobbed. After the girl ran out of tears and hiccupped in her lap, Brigitta brushed the hair back from her forehead. "Tell me what's wrong. Let it out."

Oriana touched the headband the boy she favored had given her and traced one of the stars. "If the Holy Mother truly loves us, why did she allow all my sisters to die? What kind of goddess would do that?"

Caressing the girl's hair, Brigitta said, "When the gods fight among themselves, humans often suffer." When Oriana stared up at her in confusion, Brigitta went on. "We mortals are of little concern to the gods. In my youth and young motherhood, I devoted myself to Frigg, the goddess of motherhood. She is supposed to know the future, yet she did nothing to aid me when Saloynan soldiers raped me in front of my children and stole me from them. In the two years I was held as a slave, Frigg did nothing for me. It was your Darhour that freed me. When I watched him fight the men abusing me, I knew I had chosen the wrong goddess. I changed my loyalty to the Valkyrie Randgrid, who believes women should learn to fight to protect themselves." She touched her sword. "Darhour bought me this and taught me how to use it. Although I still send up prayers to her, I don't know if Randgrid has ever helped me or if I prospered merely because Darhour taught me how to fight."

Oriana looked at her with such horror Brigitta realized she'd been indulging her own emotions rather than caring for the suffering child. "But enough of my gods. Perhaps your Sulis is different from the gods of my homeland. Perhaps your Sulis truly loves humans like her children."

Oriana nodded. "She does. I know she does. I have felt her love."

"Then perhaps the Ancient Evil was so strong only the deaths of your sisters would save your people from it."

Oriana was silent for a while. "My sisters sacrificed their lives for the goddess. Even though I'm only fourteen, do you think Sulis expects me to come back to Korth and rebuild her priesthood?"

Brigitta thought what the gods expected mattered little and humans owed them nothing, but this wasn't what the child needed to hear. Again, she brushed Oriana's hair back. "I can't tell you what your duty is to your goddess, and neither can anyone else. The answers to your questions can only be found in your own heart." She placed her hand over the child's heart. "Listen to your heart, then you know."

The child seemed to turn her eyes inward. Again, she was silent for some time, and Brigitta merely held her without intruding on her thoughts. Finally, she sat up. "Thank you. I don't know the answer yet, but at least I now know where to look for it." She took Brigitta's hand. "Since I've lost my mother and you've lost your children, would you mind so much if I called you 'mother'?"

"I'd like that very much." Tears leaked from Brigitta's eyes, as the motherhood she thought lost to her forever was given back to her. *Maybe my husband's goddess really is the Mother of us all.*

* * *

When Samantha arrived in the village, accompanied by her guards, the people went down on one knee before her. They numbered about two hundred. Logs were set around a fire pit, along with one large carved wooden chair. Upon the chair was a velvet cushion. Over the fire, a huge pot of stew bubbled.

"Rise, my people," she said. "Thank you for the opportunity to dine with you."

The people stood, and Zethar approached. "Please excuse the simplicity of the setting, Your Majesty. When His Majesty visited us, we'd been forced out of our homes by the Evil and had lost nearly everything. But we had a fire, a stew pot, and simple logs to sit upon. We celebrate this way in his memory."

Zethar led her to the chair. "This chair was made from the log upon which His Majesty sat and was carved by Henwas, our most skilled wood carver."

Zethar gestured toward the woman who stood next to the chair. She bowed to Samantha. "I'd be honored, Your Majesty, if you would sit upon it. I had to carve His Majesty from memory. I hope I did him justice."

Now that Samantha was closer, she could see the carvings. They were scenes from what must have been Robbie's visit to these people: arriving on a Horsetad, praying with the people, sitting on a log with a bowl of stew in his hands. At the top in the middle was an image of Robbie's face. It was almost a perfect likeness, far better than the one hanging in the Royal Gallery. She gasped and touched it. "Robbie, my love," she whispered. She turned to the wood carver. "You have captured my love's likeness almost as if he were here with us. I'd be honored to sit here."

Tension draining out of the woman's shoulders, she beamed and smoothed the velvet seat for the queen.

As Samantha sat, a woman came forward holding the bronze bowl. It was full of steaming stew and encased in a knit covering. It would certainly be too hot to hold without the covering.

The woman bowed, and Zethar introduced her. "Your Majesty, this is Jennyfer, the chief cook in charge of this night's stew."

The woman handed her the bowl. "I'd be honored, Your Majesty, if you'd eat of my stew. Your Majesty may want to let it cool a bit."

Samantha thanked her and took the bowl. She could feel its heat through the covering.

"With Your Majesty's approval," Zethar continued, "the children would like to perform a dance they created for the festival of Urachad, the Day of Renewal. That is what we call the day we celebrate His Majesty's visit, the day when life was returned to us. The Ancient Evil was especially deadly to little ones, and these children are the only ones who survived. They are most precious to us."

"I would be honored by such a performance."

Zethar and Jennyfer moved to the side but remained close. In the space in front of her, a group of six children—four girls and two boys, ranging in age from about six to twelve, took their places. *Only six children.* Samantha had known the losses from the Ancient Evil had been terrible, but until today, they'd never been completely real to her. Upon seeing these few remaining young ones, she pressed her hand over the heart that ached within her. *Why didn't the goddess prevent this? Why did my love have to sacrifice himself instead?* The children crouched down and covered their heads with their arms. A lone drum began a slow beat. The children began the dance hesitantly, glancing up one at time and then hurriedly covering their heads again. The drumbeat picked up, and a fiddle joined in. The children raised their heads as one and looked toward the musicians. Their eyes widened, and they rose to their feet and danced with short, furtive movements. A flute joined in, and the pace of the music increased. The children clapped their hands and let out a cry of joy. They told a story through their movements that even Samantha could read: their eating at the campfire with the king, the king's departure to destroy the evil, and their delight when life returned around them. At that point, their faces beamed, and the music and dance became one of pure jubilation. As Samantha watched, she realized the children's dancing represented emotions they actually experienced when Robbie returned their young lives to them. Tears began to flow down her cheeks. For once, she didn't try to stop them. As the children brought the dance to a close, four women holding infants and another three in various stages of pregnancy joined them. These were the new lives made possible by Robbie's destruction of The Soul Stone.

As the dance ended, she brought her hand to her mouth. "That was the most beautiful thing I've ever seen!"

During the dance, the stew as well as bread had been served to the others. One by one the people came forward and shared their memories of the dark time and of Robbie's arrival. The man she loved had truly become a legend whose name would be remembered for a thousand years, as Armunn's had been.

Tears continued down her cheeks, but she found herself smiling and laughing through them. They had suffered so much. For Robbie's sake and her own, she would be the queen her people needed, and Sulis be damned.

* * *

As she returned to her army's camp, she glanced at Darhour and Brigitta's tent. It seemed a horrible thing to do, but her people needed her. She'd intended to wait until morning, but when she saw Darhour leaning against a tree, she knew waiting would make things no easier.

She joined him. "Having trouble sleeping?"

He nodded toward the tent. "She's angry with me. She won't listen to reason."

Samantha cocked her head. "Is it reason she won't listen to? Does she lack the skill to complete the mission?"

Darhour went deadly still. "Even the best can fail. Don't ask this of me, I beg you."

She glanced up at the night sky to avoid her father's eyes. "I forbade Robbie to go after the Soul Stone alone. When he did so anyway, I wanted to execute Father Leigh since he knew of Robbie's plans and did nothing to stop him. Robbie as good as died on that mission, and my heart bleeds without him. But as much as I hate it, he was right to go. No one else could have done as he did, and he saved thousands of lives, if not tens of thousands."

Darhour's words sounded as if they'd been forced through glass. "Samantha, how is this—"

She lowered her eyes to his. "I am your queen, as well as your daughter. If Sheen's rebellion isn't quickly put down, how many lives will be lost? This isn't a battle I can afford to lose. If someone other than Brigitta can complete this mission, tell me who. If there is no other, stop fighting with your wife and help her prepare to complete it successfully so that your heart won't bleed as mine does." She walked away without giving Darhour a chance to respond.

* * *

After the goblet had made its way around the table in the underground room, Cadarn announced, "The queen has been gone long enough, she should have passed into Korth. There's no need to wait any longer. Tomorrow we act."

Grinning, Nisse got to his feet and unrolled a map of the capital city on the table. "Let's review the plan. My men will be responsible for taking the city walls, subduing the city magistrates, and sealing up the gates so that no one can leave. Once that is done, those who can be spared will join the attack on the palace itself."

Tierney snapped, "Yes, we've gone over this over a dozen times."

"Indulge me," Nisse said, and Cadarn was surprised at how much threat his friend's voice carried.

Tierney sighed. "Mine will take the palace front gate and secure the walls."

Each of the men around the table repeated the part they would play in the attack. When Gerard recited his task of securing the crown princess, Cadarn leaned across the table and touched his arm. "Yours is the most important task. The princess cannot be allowed to escape the palace."

Gerard smiled fiercely. "There's no chance of that happening."

After they reviewed the plans, Nisse told everyone to get a good meal and a good night's sleep.

The others left, and soon Cadarn was alone with Nisse. Cadarn rubbed at an ache in the back of his neck. "This will work, won't it?"

"Undoubtedly. But Liridona, you realize that taking the capital tomorrow will be the easy part? Destroying is easy. Building is much more difficult."

Cadarn's lips tightened. "You keep talking to me as if I were a child. I know we aren't planning a picnic. People will die, but those deaths will lead to something great."

Nisse searched his face, for what Cadarn didn't know, but he guessed Nisse found it because he nodded. "And speaking of people who will die, two of your co-conspirators think you mean to make them king. It would be fortunate if they fell in tomorrow's battle."

Knowing what Nisse was suggesting, Cadarn stared at the ceiling. He saw no chance that either Ultan or Tierney would go along with his plans to abolish the nobility. They would have to be taken care of eventually, and if they died in the battle, the high priest wouldn't be able to blame him. Without meeting his friend's eyes, he said. "Yes, that would be most fortunate."

He tasted bile as he remembered when he'd heard his father say similar words. It had been a dry year, and in order to protect his own lands from overgrazing, his father had started grazing his cattle in a meadow that was by rights a peasants' common. Though still a boy, Cadarn had known what his father was doing was wrong. Without being able to graze on that land, the peasants' few cows and goats would either starve or have to be slaughtered, and the peasants needed the milk from those animals to make it through the winter.

The peasants appealed to the king's magistrate. The night before the magistrate was due to arrive, Cadarn had eavesdropped on his father and Cerball, the captain of his father's guard, who was also one of the men who later raped the dairy maid.

"Gwenhael has a reputation for honesty," Cerball had told his father. "I wouldn't try to bribe him."

His father had scowled into the fire. "If I proposed a hunt for the morning of his arrival on the pretext of throwing a feast for the peasants to smooth things over, would he agree to it?"

"It would be rude not to." Cerball's voice held a note of glee Cadarn hadn't understood.

"I thought as much. It would be fortunate if the magistrate met with an accident while hunting."

Knowing how unlikely that was, Cadarn had had to cover his mouth so his laughter didn't reveal his hiding place. He was happy his father was finally going to get what was coming to him. But the next morning on the hunt, Cadarn had seen Cerball push the king's magistrate in the path of a charging boar. As the boar trampled and gutted the poor man, Cadarn realized his father had ordered him killed.

Gwenhael's replacement had been more amenable to bribes. The peasants lost their commons, their livestock, and several of them their lives, as starvation hit the village that winter. Cadarn had told his father they were starving. He'd even tried to smuggle bread to them himself, but he had been caught and punished for it. Cadarn clenched his fists remembering his powerlessness to get his father to do the right thing.

But he was powerless no longer. Having Tierney and Ultan killed in the battle might be underhanded, but unlike his father, who'd done it to enrich himself, Cadarn was doing it so that the evil his father committed would never be repeated.

A little underhandedness in pursuit of so worthy a goal couldn't be wrong.

CHAPTER 14

Pounding his right fist into his left hand, Iachus walked across the palace lawn. He'd stopped going into the nursery unnecessarily, but he wasn't happy about it. How dare the captain suggest his interest in Cece was causing him to neglect his duty to the crown princess? Hadn't he proven at Litha he'd never allow anything to endanger the sweet little baby? But whether or not it was fair, he had to admit he was endangering his position over a woman who cared nothing for him.

He heard a shout. When he looked in the direction of the palace gates, it took him a moment to process what he was seeing. Two guards tumbled from the palace walls filled with arrows. One of the guards at the gate dropped to the ground, as an unknown ruffian pulled a bloody sword out of his heart.

The palace was under attack! "The princess!" he cried and ran for the nursery.

When he burst through the palace side door, he was met with chaos. Guards and men dressed as servants, but not fighting like servants, clashed in a confused melee, making it impossible to know friend from enemy. But at a moment like this, anyone who stood between him and the princess had to be considered an enemy.

Iachus drew his sword and barreled ahead, striking aside any who impeded his passage. Thanks to a staircase hidden behind the tapestries that few knew about, he avoided the main staircase to the royal residences which was teeming with men. When he burst out from behind a unicorn tapestry across from the nursery, he found his fellow guards in a pitched battle before the nursery door. He bellowed and ran toward the fray, sinking his sword into the back of a man fighting Kelvin. He cut another one down and then another. When a fourth fell before him, he saw that Bary and Donovan were down and not breathing. The other three were all wounded, Kelvin bleeding heavily from a wound in his thigh. "We have to get the princess to safety," Kelvin said.

"The entire palace is in chaos," Iachus said. "I'm not sure the four of us can get a baby safely through."

Vaughan appeared at the door with a drawn sword, Cece holding the crying princess behind him. "The tunnel in the queen's rooms! Follow me," Vaughan cried and took off down the corridor.

Kelvin shrugged. "Unless anyone has a better idea, follow the lad." Taking a last look at his fallen brother, Brandon, accompanied by Marcan, did just that, with Cece and the princess between them. Iachus brought up the rear. Kelvin tried to keep up, but the wound was slowing him. There was a shout behind them, and men came from the staircase after them. Kelvin shoved him ahead. "I'll slow them. Get the princess safe! I'll see you Beyond the Far Mountain."

Knowing his duty, Iachus ran on, leaving Kelvin to die. When he reached the queen's rooms, Brandon and Marcan were moving a heavy table aside. Holding a lit torch, Vaughan snatched up the carpet, revealing a trap door. The boy yanked it open and preceded the group onto the staircase. Cece followed with Brianna, then came Brandon and Marcan. Iachus was about to follow when armed men burst through the door. He slammed the trap door shut, stood on top of it, and faced the attackers. There were five of them. He prayed he could buy the others enough time before he joined Kelvin at the goddess's side.

* * *

Cece's heart skipped a beat when the trapdoor slammed shut behind them and she realized what Iachus had done. She clutched Brianna, who continued to scream at the top of her lungs. *He's dying, and I never even gave him a proper smile.* But now she had to get the princess to safety; she ran through the tunnel after Vaughan.

As they neared a staircase heading back up, Marcan yelled, "Hurry, I can hear pursuit."

The pursuit meant that Iachus must now be dead. She sent out a prayer to Sulis that she'd be able to honor his sacrifice. She followed Vaughan up the staircase.

He opened the trap door at the top, and she found herself in an underground room with a ladder. Vaughan scrambled up the ladder and reached back for Brianna so that Cece could scramble up after him. When she reclaimed the now quiet baby—she had no idea how Vaughan had managed to soothe the princess—she was surprised to find herself in the office of the Master of the Horse. As Marcan and Brandon followed them up the ladder, Adalardo, the Master of the Horse, burst into the room armed with a pitchfork. He gasped when he saw the crown princess.

Vaughan grabbed his arm. "They're after the princess. You have to make sure they can't open that door so we can get her to safety."

"Thank the goddess she's still alive." Adalardo called for help, and as their small group crept out the back door of the stables, Adalardo and the stable grooms were busy piling every heavy thing nearby on top of the trap door.

* * *

As Vaughan looked out the door at the rear of the stables, Marcan pushed past him with drawn sword. The grounds were relatively quiet here, as the attack had converged on the palace itself. Surely, they could get the little princess to the small side gate, which was now completely unguarded.

They crept toward it, and they might have made it all right if Brianna would have stayed quiet, but Vaughan tripped over something in the grass. When he fell, the little princess must have thought he was hurt because she let out an ear-shattering cry. Vaughan nearly screamed himself when he met the dead eyes of the guard he'd tripped over. He scrambled to his feet, but Brianna's cries caught the attention of some of the attackers, who sent up an alarm.

As Marcan ran through the side gate, dozens of men were running to stop them. Marcan grabbed Vaughan's arm. "We'll give you all the time we can. It's up to the two of you to see the princess to safety."

As the two remaining members of Brianna's guard turned to face the attackers, Brandon yelled, "I'll join you soon, my brother. For the princess!"

The narrowness of the opening would prevent too many from attacking at once, but they couldn't hold them off for long. Trembling at the thought that his sword would soon be the last one left to protect the princess, Vaughan drew it and led Cece away from the palace. If the attackers found them, no matter how hard he'd been training lately, he wasn't anywhere good enough to hold them off.

As they ran over the cobblestone street, Cece let out a cry. He whirled too late to stop her from falling. She managed to twist her body to take the impact and protect Brianna, but the baby let out a squall. He hurriedly sheathed his sword to help Cece to her feet, but the nurse cried out when she tried to put weight on her foot.

"It's no good," she cried. "I've twisted my ankle. Take her, Vaughan. Keep her safe." She held out the crying princess.

Vaughan's mouth went dry, but he could hear voices calling and the clang of armor from around the corner. He grabbed the princess and ran.

He turned a corner and heard more clanging coming from the street ahead. Soldiers were closing from both directions. No one had seen him yet, but he was trapped. He glanced around for a place to hide. He saw nothing but a rubbish bin that would never be enough to conceal him and the princess, but the clean alleyway offered nothing else, so he tried to crouch behind it. To his surprise, the rubbish bin had been blocking a crack large enough for him to squeeze through in a building's foundation. Unfortunately, Brianna's continued crying would give them away. He clutched the baby tightly to his chest. "Please, Your Highness, you have to stop crying. If they hear you, we're both dead."

To his utter relief, Brianna quieted immediately. He shoved Brianna through the crack and wriggled after her. It was a tight fit, but he made it. He grabbed whatever debris he could get his hands on to hide the crack.

He laid his hand on top of Brianna and whispered, "You have to stay quiet. Please, don't cry." He closed his eyes and prayed. *Holy Sulis, Mother of us all. Keep the princess quiet.*

Running footsteps and the clang of armor came from the street. "No sign of the abomination?" one voice asked, and Vaughan touched his sword, wishing he could skewer the man who'd dare refer to sweet little Brianna that way. He kept rubbing the princess's stomach and praying she stayed quiet.

"No," a voice answered.

"She can't be far. Check all the doors."

Vaughan heard pounding and doors being broken in. People protested and were dragged into the street. He whispered again, "Please, Your Highness, no crying."

* * *

Vaughan lay still in his hiding place. It had grown quiet outside as the search had moved on. He was safe for the moment, and Brianna had fallen asleep, snoring softly with his hand still on her chest.

He felt the silk of the princess's dress. It was stupid to dress a baby in silk even if she were a princess. Babies were always barfing and pooping over everything.

As he touched his sword again, a cold sweat broke out. Iachus and the others were so much better than he could even pretend to be, and they were all dead now. Knowing he was the only one the princess had left, he wanted to curl into a ball and forget the world existed, but the crawl space was too small. He tried to slow his breathing, telling himself he didn't have to do anything right now. He would wait for dark to leave his hiding place, and then… *Holy Sulis, what will I do then? How can I get Brianna to the queen? How will I even get her out of the city?*

Vaughan's stomach growled. He was always hungry these days. Luckily, he'd started carrying food with him. He reached for the roll and cheese in his pocket, but as he brought it to his mouth, he froze. *Sulis curse it! When Brianna wakes up, she'll be hungry.* And when Brianna was hungry, she screamed her head off. Despite how big she'd grown, she had few teeth, so he didn't think she could chew it. His mother used to chew up food to feed his younger brothers and sisters. *That is so gross, but how else will I keep the princess quiet until nightfall?*

Remembering his mother gave him the glimmer of an idea. She and his six younger siblings lived on the other side of the city. Somehow, he'd get Brianna to her.

Brianna began stirring beside him. "Momma, Ce," she whimpered in the darkness.

"It's okay, Your Highness. I'm here," he whispered while caressing her chest and putting his head next to hers.

"Vau." She grabbed his nose. Her whimpering grew louder and would soon escalate to a full scale crying fit if he didn't feed her soon.

"Shush!" he whispered and got out the roll. "We have to be quiet. If the bad guys find us, they'll kill us."

As if she actually understood him, Brianna let out a small cry and buried her face in his chest. His stomach heaving at the thought, he bit off a piece of the roll and began to chew. His stomach growled again, but he told it to be quiet. When he thought he'd chewed the bread well enough, he spit out into his hands. "Sorry, Your Highness, I know this is gross."

He put his hand up to Brianna's mouth and fed her the bread. She gobbled it and didn't seem to think it was gross at all. He did the same with the rest of the roll and started on the cheese. She only ate about half the cheese before she started turning her head away. Vaughan was so hungry that, trying not to think about it, he put the half-chewed cheese back in his mouth and swallowed.

Brianna began making happy noises and grabbing his nose and lips. He didn't know why babies always wanted to put their fingers up your nose. He hoped he hadn't done that when he was a baby.

"Shush!" he whispered. "We have to stay quiet." But even if Brianna wasn't hungry, she rarely stayed quiet for long. He shifted some of the debris aside so that he could see out into the alley. It seemed deserted at the moment, but he knew the sounds of a baby coming from under a building would draw attention. It would be at least another two hours before it would be dark enough for them to leave their hiding spot. *Holy Sulis, help me keep her quiet.*

He remembered Cece was always singing to the princess. As quietly as he could, he started singing a lullaby his mother had always sung.

* * *

More tired than he'd ever been in his life, Cadarn leaned against the wall, just outside the palace's main entrance. There were bodies scattered across the palace lawn and on the pathways. His own body ached. He scratched at his face, and he nearly heaved as it came away bloody. He had further trouble controlling his stomach when he realized he was standing in a blood puddle. In fact, he was covered in blood. He hadn't intended to become personally involved in the killing, but the Royal Guard had fought like fiends, and even the palace servants had picked up makeshift weapons or stolen swords from the dead.

In an insane burst of courage, the stable hands, armed with pitchforks and scythes, had charged his position before the palace's front door. He'd had to draw his sword to help fend them off. Among the bodies near him were several he'd personally killed. He'd never killed anyone before, and he had to clutch the wall for support as he heard again the sound his sword made as it penetrated the body of a stable groom whose expertise with horses had always impressed him. As the groom's dead eyes stared at him now, he realized he'd never asked the man's name. Didn't that suggest the height of hypocrisy? He'd preached equality, but some part of him must have thought himself so far above the dead young man at his feet that knowing his name was unnecessary. He kicked the body over so the dead eyes wouldn't accuse him any longer.

Why had the stable hands done something so hopeless? If they'd just waited to learn what he brought to Korthlundia, surely they would have embraced his cause. But what was done was done. The palace was now his, and no one could restore life to the dead.

A smile crept unto his face. He'd done it! He'd taken the first step toward freeing his people, and surely, it wouldn't be long before the queen surrendered to him.

Nisse joined him. "Glorious, wasn't it?" Though Cadarn had thought himself bloody, Nisse looked as if he'd bathed in blood. "There's nothing like a fight for his life to make a man feel truly alive! How I do wish your little Purple Leaf were here now, so I could plow her a new one." He thrust his hips suggestively.

Cadarn stared at his friend as if he were a stranger. Sex was the last thing on Cadarn's mind.

Nisse clapped him on the shoulder. "No need to worry. As we agreed, your co-conspirators have been taken care of. I skewered that pious little count myself. The chicken-livered cunt was hiding in his quarters. When he opened the door to me, he claimed he'd been praying to Sulis for success. Boy, was he surprised when my sword pierced his guts! I love to see the shock in the eyes of a man who hadn't expected to die!"

Cadarn opened his mouth to speak, but he couldn't figure out what to say to this madman who'd taken the place of his more-than-brother. But as Nisse smiled at the scene of slaughter, Cadarn reminded himself that this was hardly Nisse's first battle, and Nisse had done it out of love for him. Besides, Nisse probably didn't mean he'd actually enjoyed killing. He'd read that men frequently boasted after battle in order to avoid confronting the horror they truly felt.

Cadarn patted Nisse's shoulder. "Thank you."

When Nisse turned to him, his eyes softened. "For you, Liridona, anything." Looking into those eyes, Cadarn understood how Nisse could think of sex at a time like this.

Lieutenant Gerard rounded the corner of the palace followed by several of his men. One was carrying a bound woman over his shoulder. "Milord," Gerard said, and his man dropped the woman at his feet. Looking more like a girl than a woman, the princess's nurse darted her eyes around and then squeezed them shut, as if by not seeing the armed men surrounding her, she could make them go away. "We found her outside the palace side gate. She's injured her ankle and can't walk. Milord, there was a tunnel leading from the queen's room to the stables we knew nothing about."

"What are you saying?"

Gerard kicked the terrified young woman. "This whore and a few of the princess's guards were able to get Her Highness out through the tunnel. We found all of the guards' bodies, but she won't say who has the princess now."

A wave of dizziness passed over Cadarn. "How could you have allowed this to happen?"

"I apologize, Milord, and take full responsibility for the failure."

But taking responsibility did nothing to help recover the princess. Cadarn squatted by the princess's nurse and took her chin in his hand. "There's no need to be afraid," he said, trying to make his voice as gentle as possible. The nurse opened her eyes. "Cut her bonds," Cadarn ordered, and one of the soldiers did so. "I know they may have treated you a little roughly, but if you just tell us where the princess is, I promise no one will hurt you. I'll even get someone to look at that ankle for you." Her ankle was so swollen it was certainly broken.

Closing her eyes again, Cece hugged herself tightly. "I'll tell you nothing."

Cadarn smoothed the nurse's hair back from her forehead. "I vow to you on the goddess and my mother's grave I have no intention of harming the princess. Just tell me where she is, and you could earn more money in that moment than you've ever seen in your life."

Cece opened her eyes. "I love Her Highness as if she were my own child! Here's what you can do with your money!" She spat in his face.

Wiping off the spittle, Cadarn stood. "Damn you to the seven hells, you silly little girl."

Gerard shifted his feet. "I can make her tell."

Cadarn swallowed bile. "Torture is the tool of a tyrant. It has no place in the world we're bringing about."

Nisse put a hand on his shoulder. "There is no need to use such an ugly word for a small bit of persuasion. Without the princess, there will be no statue of Cadarn the Bold in Murtaghan's square."

Remembering the coolness of the marble of Annagret's statue, Cadarn looked away. He'd waited so long, planned so carefully. But how could he authorize the torture of this small woman? He just stood there, saying nothing.

"I understand, Liridona. Don't worry yourself."

Praying the goddess would forgive this sin, Cadarn said nothing, as Nisse addressed Gerard. "We need that baby. Do what is necessary. And keep the princess's escape quiet."

* * *

Vaughan crept through the alleys and back streets of Murtaghan. Brianna was bouncing in his arms as if excited to be out so late. She didn't care that she'd wet herself all over him. Babies were so gross. Miraculously, she'd stayed quiet all afternoon. It was almost as if she understood their situation. He'd glimpsed soldiers patrolling the main streets a time or two, but so far he hadn't been seen, and he'd nearly reached his mother's house. She'd always given him plenty of advice he hadn't needed or wanted. She'd better give him some useful advice now.

He passed the back of the blacksmith shop his mother had been forced to sell when his father died. He'd only been eight at the time, and his mother wouldn't talk about the accident that killed him. She always said the same stupid thing about Sulis calling him to the Far Mountain. Although they'd lived all right off the money from the sale of the shop and the sewing his mother had been able to take in for a couple years, Vaughan hated to think of what would have become of them all if he hadn't gotten his position in the palace stables.

He reached the back door and silently slipped inside. Everything was dark and quiet. He guessed everyone was asleep, but as he crept from the kitchen into the main room, he saw a shadow looking out the front window. "Mum," he whispered.

At the sound of his voice, she let out a cry and damned near suffocated him with a hug. "You're alive! Praise be to Sulis! I was so worried when I heard what happened at the palace."

Brianna loudly objected to being squashed, and his mother broke away. "Who have you got with you, Vaughan?" She fumbled around and lit a candle. His mother stared at Brianna's rich gown and green eyes. "Holy Sulis, that's not..." She backed away as if he were holding a demon. "Why would you bring her here? Soldiers will be searching everywhere for her. What do you think they'll do to us if she's found here? How many people know you have her?"

"No one knows!" he snapped. *Why is she asking questions instead of helping me?* "Well, Cece knows, but she'd never tell anyone." He told her briefly about their escape from the palace and the nurse's injury.

"Of course, she'll talk! I hate to think what they're doing to her. You better hope she's held out this long."

Bile burned the back of Vaughan's throat. *Holy Sulis, did I leave her behind to be tortured? What else could I have done?*

"Children, up!" his mother shouted. "Get dressed and pack a bundle of your things. Nara and Nealie, help the little ones."

"What's going on, Mum?" his oldest brother Wynne asked, yawning.

"Soldiers will be here looking for your brother any minute now. We're going to your uncle's."

Vaughan's jaw dropped. His mother hated her brother so badly that Vaughan had never even met him.

"What's Vaughan done?" Wynne rubbed at his eyes.

"No time for questions," his mother snapped. "Every second's delay could be the second that gets us caught." His brothers and sisters erupted into activity.

"But what about me, mum?" Vaughan asked, as his mother began shoving food into a bag.

"I suggest you leave the baby here and come with us."

Vaughan set his jaw and glared at his mother. "I've given the princess my holy vow."

She grabbed a smaller bag and began stuffing more food in it. "As much as it breaks my heart, if you won't leave that wretched child behind, you're on your own. I have six little ones I have to think of." She shoved the smaller bag into his hand. "If you won't listen to sense, I suggest you change into one of my dresses and bonnets. A woman with a baby will attract less attention than a boy. And get rid of the princess's fancy dress. You both reek of piss. You need to clean that baby, or she'll get a rash. Wynne can take you to the drainage ditch he uses to go under the city wall." She went to the chest at the foot of her bed, got some clothing out for him, and then began packing a bundle for herself.

"But mum, where am I supposed to go? What should I do?"

She stopped and looked at him with tears in her eyes. "I don't know, child. I'll pray to the goddess to keep you safe."

Vaughan felt as if the room were spinning around him. He sat on his mother's bed to keep from falling. Brianna made a small noise and touched his face. "Don't worry, Your Highness. I'll keep you safe."

"Don't call her that, child," his mother snapped. "You don't want to tell all of the joined kingdoms who you've got there." She lay a long scarf next to the dress she'd got out for him. "You can tie the baby to your back with that." She went to another chest and drew out some baby clothes. After laying the clothes beside him, she started to help his siblings. "Hurry, children, we have no time to waste."

With shaking hands, he lay Brianna on the bed. He grabbed the dress and crushed the fabric in his hand. If Cece could face torture for the princess's sake, he could do this. Besides, his own clothes had baby piss all over them. He changed his own and Brianna's clothes as quickly as his trembling hands allowed. He used the shawl to put Brianna on his back and grabbed the provision bag which was all the help his mother would give him.

As soon as he was ready, his mother shoved him toward the alley entrance. "I'm sorry I can't give you any coin. I need it for the little ones." Her eyes teared over, and she grabbed him into a hug. "Stay safe, lad." She released him and turned to his brother. "Wynne, take your brother to the ditch and wait for the rest of us. We won't be long."

The world still spinning, Vaughan followed his brother through the alleyways. When they got a little way from their house, Wynne grinned at him, "Why'd Mum make you dress like a *girl?* What you done that gots her in an uproar?"

"I saved the crown princess," Vaughan said.

"Crown princess is pretty important, but you're wearing a skirt." He giggled.

Vaughan gaped at his brother. *How can he not realize how important this is?* Vaughan would do much worse than humiliate himself to save her.

When Vaughan didn't react to the teasing, Wynne shrugged. They'd reached the city walls. Wynne hopped down in a drainage ditch and pushed some brushes aside revealing a hole under the city wall. "Well, here's your way. Where are you heading?"

Vaughan stared blankly at the hole. "I don't know."

"Don't she have a grandpa that's a peasant or something?"

Vaughan nodded. He shivered as he remembered meeting the king's father; the disgusting drunk surely couldn't be of any help. But disgusting or not, he did have a horse and he did have money. Besides, Vaughan didn't have any other idea what to do.

He said goodbye to his brother and squeezed under the wall.

CHAPTER 15

All Cece knew was pain. She'd revealed nothing about the little princess, but she wasn't sure how much longer she could hold out. Her torturer, who hadn't told her his name, had his back to her now, looking over the things on the table, no doubt deciding how to hurt her next. He wore a dagger at his waist. If she could just get a hold of it, she could end this. She tugged against the manacles holding her hands above her head. Her hands were smaller than the manacles were designed for and sweat coated her arms. She could slip the manacles past her wrist, but her knuckles caught. *Holy Sulis, please help me. Please welcome me Beyond the Far Mountain and keep the little princess safe.*

As she ended her prayer, she tugged with all her remaining strength on her right arm. The manacles pinched and scraped her hand, but at last it popped free. Wasting no time, she reached forward and grabbed her torturer's dagger. He whirled and laughed as she pointed it at him. He leaned back on the counter with his arms folded, just out of reach.

"Just what do you plan to do with that, lass? You know I can easily disarm you before you could touch me."

"I know," Cece rasped in a voice that didn't sound like her own. She quickly flipped the dagger around and plunged into her own heart. "Holy Mother, take me!" she cried out, as her life's blood flowed out and the pain ended.

* * *

How could I have failed Sulis like this? Father Eadoin wanted the abomination dead, but Gerard couldn't kill what he didn't have. Gerard stomped up the stairs from the dungeon. He desperately wanted to kill somebody. To shove his sword into someone's gut and twist when they screamed. *You had one job, you pathetic fop! Secure the crown princess! You haven't been able to do anything right since the king made a laughingstock of us all! It's all his fault.*

When he emerged from the dungeon, a palace footman was lounging against the wall. Many of the palace servants had fought back when they'd taken the palace. Hoping this one would give him an excuse to kill him, Gerard put his hand on his sword.

Glancing at Gerard's sword, the footman licked his lips. "I hear you're looking for the crown princess."

Gerard drew his dagger, slammed the footman against the wall, and held his dagger to his throat. "No one is supposed to know about the princess. Who told you?"

"I-I-I don't remember. The gossip is all over the palace, but for the right price, I could help you find her."

Gerard moved his dagger under the footman's right eye. "You should be willing to tell for Sulis's glory and nothing more, but I offer you an eye. You tell me what you know, and you get to keep it."

"Okay, okay, I don't know where Her Highness is, but if anyone has her, it's Vaughan."

Gerard drew the blade back slightly. "The king's squire?"

"Yes, he almost always visits her in the morning, so he was certainly in the nursery at the time of the attack."

Gerard lowered the knife. "And where would he take her?"

"I don't know, but his mother lives near the blacksmith guild hall."

Gerard released him and threw him a tetra. "Take me to it, and if the princess is there, I'll up that to a drachma."

The man crossed his arms. "Five drachma."

Gerard shrugged. "Five if she's there. An eye if she isn't."

Gerard wrote a note to Cadarn and tried to find a page to deliver it. No one answered his ring, and there wasn't one to be seen in the corridors. He had one of his men take the message instead.

* * *

Eating breakfast with Nisse, Cadarn kept seeing the dead eyes of the stable groom he'd killed staring back from his plate. The rest of the blood spilled yesterday was also on his hands. *If I free my people, those deaths will have been worth it, but can we win without the crown princess?* Nisse had tried to comfort him but had given up and was carving his bloody steak. Cadarn couldn't imagine how he could eat it after yesterday's slaughter.

A soldier arrived with a note. As Cadarn read it, hope bubbled in his chest.

"Good news?" Nisse asked.

"The greatest news. Sulis is watching over us after all. Gerard has learned where the crown princess is. He's gone to fetch her."

"Fantastic. I told you it would all work out."

Cadarn squeezed his friend's arm. "And I should have trusted you. We'll go ahead with the throne burning ceremony this afternoon as we originally planned."

At that moment he heard a meow, and something rubbed against his leg. He looked down, and the cat jumped into his lap. "Snowflake!" He scratched the cat between the ears. "I've been worried about you." He hadn't seen the cat since yesterday's attack and had been concerned it had been harmed. Taking Snowflake's return as a good omen, Cadarn attacked his breakfast with new appetite.

Nisse again talked with his mouth full, but Cadarn grasped his gist. "A throne in flames is something Annagret would have delighted to see." He paused, and then gestured with his knife. "You should put a heavy guard on the nursery."

"When Gerard returns with the princess, I'll have him see to it."

Nisse shook his head. "No, put the guard there now. No one needs know the crown princess isn't inside."

Seeing the wisdom of Nisse's suggestion, Cadarn gave the orders. Afterward, he lifted his wine goblet, proposing a toast. "To our great victory."

Nisse lifted his own. "To the heirs of Annagret and Dritan." They touched goblets and downed the contents. Then they set about planning the council meeting to be held in an hour.

* * *

Chewing on her fist, Aislinn looked out her window at the sun sinking behind the horizon. When the palace was taken yesterday, soldiers with blood on their uniforms had searched her rooms and told her not to leave them until it was safe to do so. Slowly, she realized she was a prisoner. She'd blocked out her fears by painting a picture of kittens and puppies, fluffy clouds and flowers. Her creation was so sweet it gave even her indigestion.

Her maid Zinerva ran into the room from the servants' corridors, grabbed her hand, and started pulling her toward the door. "Hurry, Milady, this way!"

Aislinn resisted. "What's going on?"

Zinerva pulled harder. "There's no time to explain. If you value your life, come now."

Aislinn stopped resisting and followed her maid into the servants' corridors. As she closed the door, she heard knocking on her door that led to the main palace corridors. Zinerva dragged her around a corner and into what appeared to be a linen closet and handed her one of her own dresses. "Change now!"

Since Zinerva seemed to have rescued her just in time from whatever danger there was, Aislinn turned so Zinerva could unbutton her dress. As she stripped, Zinerva hid her fine clothes beneath piles of sheets. When she was dressed in the maids' clothes, which were slightly too small for her and pinched uncomfortably in numerous places, Zinerva held out her hand. "Your jewelry."

Aislinn removed her bracelet, necklace, and earrings. Zinerva took them, hiked up her own skirt, and put them in a pouch hidden underneath. Then she commanded Aislinn to sit on a step stool. Aislinn did so, and Zinerva quickly undid the hairdo she had painstakingly fashioned only an hour earlier and instead fixed her hair into a simple braid. She handed her a bulky cap, and Aislinn put it on.

Zinerva then examined her. She grabbed a sheet and wiped the makeup from Aislinn's face. When the maid was satisfied, she handed her a pile of linens. "Keep your head down and don't say anything. You speak like a lady." Zinerva grabbed some linens herself and opened the closet door.

As Aislinn followed her down the corridor, she heard a crash and a woman's scream coming from the room of one of the other minor ladies at court. Zinerva whispered, "Head down. Don't speak."

They turned a corner, and two guards blocked their path. One of them asked, "Where are you off to?"

Aislinn kept her head down and allowed her maid to do the talking. Zinerva emphasized her lower-class accent. "We be taking these linens to the surgery to help make bandages for the wounded."

The guards grunted, and they searched through the linens to make sure they hid no weapons. Then they stood aside. "All right. Move along."

They passed three more sets of guards before they made it to the stairs leading down into the cellars. With her heart thumping in her chest, Aislinn followed her maid down the steep, narrow steps. When they entered the fruit cellar, they found it packed with palace servants. Figuring they were safe for the moment, Aislinn asked, "What's going on?"

Zinerva shook her head. "The guards are gathering up all the nobles. It can't be for anything good. We'll hide here until it's our turn to sneak out through the sewer tunnel." She pointed to a hole in the floor a footman was descending into. "None of us want to serve a traitor, but we have to sneak out only a few at a time, so we don't attract attention."

Aislinn nodded and sank on to a barrel that probably contained apples. Only then did she start shaking. She'd thought Devyn was going to be the one to face danger. She'd never dreamed she might not be safe herself.

* * *

With Nisse and a group of his mercenaries behind him, Cadarn made his way to the council room.

When he entered, Father Eadoin, who alone occupied the room, jumped to his feet. "I've heard rumors you allowed the abomination to escape. How could you have let this happen? And where is Count Ultan?"

Cadarn settled himself in the chair at the head of the table. "Father, do you have to refer to the crown princess in that manner? And while it's true she temporarily eluded us, she has been found and returned to her nursery." Cadarn assumed what he hoped was a more sober expression. "But I'm afraid both Duke Tierney and Count Ultan were killed in the taking of the palace. It is a tragedy, but the count hadn't anticipated the servants joining in the fight and turned his back on several palace footmen."

Eadoin paled and sank into his seat. "This is horrible news. Who then will be king?"

Cadarn shook his head, as if the count's death were indeed a terrible setback. "When the other members of the former queen's council arrive, we'll discuss it."

The door opened, and Baron Arawn and Counts Weylin and Pandaran entered under guard. They were followed by the queen's chancellor and Baroness Eithne, both of whom had had to be bound and gagged.

Baron Arawn sneered at him. "So, you've taken the palace and the capital. Do you really think the queen can't take it back from you? Do you think the people will bow to you as king?"

"The queen will surrender to save her daughter's life, but I don't intend to make myself king. I have no right to the title, nor does anyone else. In the city square this afternoon, I will announce the dissolution of the monarchy, burn the ancient throne, and allow its ashes to scatter in the wind. Too long has this people suffered under the tyranny of class. A man's worth will no longer be determined by birth but by merit, and the people themselves will choose their own rulers."

Baron Arawn stepped back. "Are you insane? You want to turn sovereignty over to an ignorant mob?"

Nisse leaned across the table. "I assure you, my *former* lord baron, the mob isn't as ignorant as you believe. 'The mob' rules well in my country."

Arawn ignored Nisse. "Your father was a fool to send you abroad for an education! That university has filled your head with treason and heresy. We live as Sulis intended." Arawn turned to Father Eadoin. "You can't support this blasphemy against the goddess."

Cadarn hurried to speak before the priest could. "The *god*, you mean. The blasphemy of divine power in the body of a woman has ended as well."

Eadoin relaxed back in his chair. "The church doesn't interfere in the affairs of the state."

Baron pounded his fist on the table. "Your peers will fight this ridiculous notion to their last drop of blood."

Unflinching, Cadarn met Arawn's eyes. "Some bloodshed is unavoidable, but I do hope most will come to see why the feudal system crushes the human spirit. True power and authority can only come with the consent of the governed. You in this room have a choice to make. After the throne burning ceremony, you can renounce your titles and pledge your loyalty to the new order." Cadarn paused for dramatic effect. "Or, you can lose your heads. Captain Nisse's men are rounding up all nobles in the city, and they will be given the same options."

Arawn laughed. "You intend to take our titles. What about our lands?"

Allowing his eyes to turn cold, Cadarn explained the new order as he and Nisse had designed it. "Nobles were given land based on the fiction that their duty was to protect the people. Since they have oppressed them instead, half of their land is immediately forfeit and will be redistributed to the peasants who occupy their estates. The other half will belong to the governors of what we will now call provinces. Any noble who willingly renounces his title and pledges his loyalty to the new order will be made temporary governor over his province, a title he will retain for a period of five years, after which the people will have the opportunity to choose to keep him as governor or select someone else."

Count Weylin jumped to his feet. "You *are* mad! If given a choice, my peasants will never choose me. Do you intend to leave me penniless?"

"My dear Weylin, you can amend your ways and govern so that your peasants *will* choose you as their governor, or yes, you can be penniless. If neither of those is appealing, you can lose your head this afternoon."

Weylin sank into his chair. "You can't do this."

Nisse laughed. "I have five hundred mercenaries that say he can."

"But   "

"No more discussion," Cadarn snapped. "I will have your decisions. Will you renounce your titles and give the people your pledge, or will you give me your head?"

Pandaran smoothed a sleeve. "I'll give my pledge."

Arawn spat. "I'd rather go to my grave than witness the ruin you will bring upon my beloved nation."

"So be it." Cadarn turned his eyes to Weylin.

Weylin glared at him. "I'll pledge," he said, but Cadarn could tell it was a pledge he didn't intend to keep.

Cadarn turned to Baron Gwawl and pulled his gag from his mouth. "My loyalty is to the queen. Do with me as you will," Gwawl said.

"I expected as much." Cadarn nodded.

He turned to the baroness and had her ungagged. She drew herself up to her full, impressive height. "I am ready to travel Beyond the Far Mountain and will be welcomed by the Holy Mother's arms."

She did have spirit. Cadarn shook his head in mock sadness. "I'm sorry, my dear, but you have a shorter distance to travel at the moment. You will take a message to the former queen. You will tell her she will abdicate and present herself in the city square for execution within six weeks' time, or I will execute her daughter in her place."

The baroness put a hand over her heart. "You can't be such a monster you would murder a baby!"

"Tyranny is monstrous, not the ending of it."

The baroness hugged herself and seemed to be struggling for a response. "I..." she started but trailed off without adding more.

Cadarn nodded to the group. "If there's nothing else, until this afternoon then."

"There is," Father Eadoin said. "I have seen to the false high priest's arrest. I seek to bring Father Hafghan and his supporters to trial."

"As you wish," Cadarn said. Who the fanatic excommunicated was the least of his worries.

* * *

Holding a silk baby dress, Gerard stood in the small dwelling. The palace footman shifted from foot to foot in front of him. "Her Highness definitely was here," the servant protested. "I told you the truth about Vaughan."

Gerard surveyed the mess. The way belongings were strewn about, the entire family had left in a hurry. "She isn't here now." He ordered his men to search the neighborhood, drew his dagger, and cleaned dirt out from under his nails with it. He nodded to one of his men who took hold of the servant. "Where would he have taken her?"

As Gerard approached with the dagger, the servant started gibbering. "Look here. I don't know anything else. The king's squire wasn't in the habit of gossiping with me, was he? Please, I've told you everything I know."

"Get out!"

After the man bolted, Gerard took a seat at the table, and his men began to bring in the neighbors for questioning.

The first was a middle-aged woman. "Mistress Maella," his men announced.

"Have a seat," he instructed the woman. She was trembling and looking around, as if for an escape route.

"As long as you tell me the truth, there is no reason to be afraid," he assured her. "I just have a few questions about the residents of this dwelling."

"What's Gawladys done?" The woman's face collapsed into a scowl. The lines around her mouth and eyes suggested this was her habitual expression. "I always knew she'd come to no good end. She isn't as good as she thinks she is, I can tell you that."

"Go on," he prodded.

Her face became even more unpleasant. "She always seemed to think she was better than the rest of us, but it got worse when that son of hers became the king's squire. You'd have thought she'd been made queen herself the way she tried to lord it over the entire neighborhood."

"It is the whereabouts of that son of hers I am most interested in."

"I can tell you he don't come to visit his mother as much as a lad his age should, I can."

"We found indications he's been here recently, but the entire family seems to have left. What can you tell me about that?"

"I haven't seen them since yesterday. Not even one of the little brats. Rhonda heard some commotion last night, but I sleep pretty heavy."

"Any idea where they might have gone? Family in the city? Or elsewhere?"

The woman shook her head. "Not that she ever talked about."

Gerard asked a few more questions but became convinced the woman knew nothing useful. Neither did any of the other neighbors.

Some had heard sounds the night the family left, but no one knew where they might have fled.

Wanting to hurt someone, he stepped outside. His men had found nothing of interest in any of the neighbors' homes. "Widen your search," he commanded. "The gates have been locked up tight. The boy and his family must still be inside the city."

"I bet they aren't," a boy of approximately twelve said. "There's ways out other than the gates."

Gerard turned on the boy. "What ways?"

"For a drachma, I'll show you."

Mistress Rhonda, who appeared to be the boy's mother, slapped him. "You'll show him for nothing, boy. Don't bring any trouble on us."

He grabbed hold of the boy's arm himself. "I'll give you the same deal I gave the man who brought me here. Show me, and you can keep your eye."

Frequently putting a hand over an eye as if to protect it, the boy led them to a drainage ditch that ran underneath the city wall. Hopping into the ditch, he pushed aside a couple of bushes and revealed an opening large enough for an adult to get through on hands and knees. Gerard swore, let the boy go, and ordered his best tracker through the opening.

When the man returned, he reported tracks of several individuals leading away from the opening, and a sizable group containing mostly children heading south toward Buil.

Gerard ordered one of his men to take a message back to the palace, and he and the rest brought their horses around to pursue the princess.

* * *

Cadarn frowned. All these years he'd thought the throne was made of wood, which considering its size would have made it a bit awkward to move to the city square, but movable all the same. However, when his men had tried, they hadn't budged it an inch. They'd finally pried loose some of the wood to find the wood and velvet had been merely a facade, hiding an enormous solid block of white marble.

With his hands on his hips, Nisse frowned at the throne. "Even if you can figure out how to get it to the city square, it won't burn."

"Yes, I know," Cadarn snapped. "But people are already gathering. I can't tell them, Sorry, we can't burn the throne. It's made of marble and probably weighs about five tons."

Nisse shrugged. "I don't know what else you're going to do. Whoever put that throne there never wanted it moved."

"Excuse me, Milord."

Cadarn sighed and turned to find a soldier behind him. "As I have said, the noble class is no more. That would include me."

The soldier reddened. "I'm sorry, sir, but I bear a message from Captain Gerard."

"Considering how my day is going, it had better be good news."

When the soldier told him Gerard was on the trail of the princess, he clenched his fists. He'd wanted word that the princess had been recaptured, but he'd have to satisfy himself with this. "I don't suppose you have any ideas about moving the throne." Not expecting a response, he turned his back on the man.

"You couldn't move it in a normal cart, that's for sure, sir. It would crush the axles or the wheels or both, right away. But if you got a stone mason cart, like they use at the quarry, you could probably back it up to the dais here and use oxen to pull the throne into the cart."

Cadarn turned and raised an eyebrow at the man.

"My father's a master stone mason, sir. I think his cart would be just about level with the dais here and should be strong enough to support the throne's weight, and he has oxen strong enough to pull it in."

Cadarn laughed. "The goddess is with me, after all. Please, fetch your father and his cart. Tell him he will be well paid."

The man ran off to do his bidding, but Nisse was still frowning at him. Cadarn's mouth stretched into a grin. "Shattering it will probably be more satisfying anyway."

* * *

Carrying a large sledgehammer, Cadarn arrived in the packed city square. He'd asked Father Eadoin to fill the square with as many of his fanatics as possible. The queen had been popular with the ignorant masses, and Cadarn didn't want the spectacle spoiled with boos or catcalls, much less outright violence. Cadarn couldn't be sure how many of those in the square were the priest's, but most seemed in a festive mood. The commoners did love a spectacle. Men were putting up ramps for the cart, but he had to keep the crowd entertained until the throne arrived.

In addition to the Royal Council, Nisse's men had rounded up about fifty nobles—men, women, and children. There were more than that in the city, but some had gone into hiding. They would be found eventually, and he had more than enough to make his point.

Smiling, he mounted the platform that held the city's flower garden. The flowers were in full bloom, surely demonstrating Sulis's blessings on his cause. He held up his hand for quiet. When he got it, he delivered the speech he'd been writing and rewriting for the last ten years. "Today is a historic day in Korthlundia. Yesterday we brought down the monarchy. Too long, my people, our land has suffered under the tyranny of a system that judges a man's worth by the blood in his veins rather than his character. A twenty-year-old girl ascended to this throne for no other reason than she was born to the king. Although I was born a member of the noble class and placed on the Royal Council, I have witnessed the evils of the class system from my childhood. My own father brutalized the peasants who occupied his land. But today we end the system that allowed such corruption to fester. Today, we destroy the royal throne that has crushed this people for centuries and declare the end of the joined kingdoms and establish the Protectorate of Korthlundia. Today, we establish a new government of the people."

The crowd's response was a confused mass of noise. Most seemed to be cheering in approval, but some seemed angry. Spectacle and pageantry were what charmed the ignorant masses. He held up his hand again. "To symbolize the people's assumption of power, we had planned to burn the ancient throne today. This will not be possible. Under the facade of wood, the throne is made of marble. The throne itself is a symbol of deception of the monarchy it represents, having a soft facade that pretends concern for the people but conceals the hardness of tyranny underneath. Since marble doesn't burn, today we will shatter the hidden hardness at the core of the monarchy." He lifted the sledgehammer over his head with both hands, and the crowd roared approvingly.

"The throne will arrive shortly. Until it arrives, let us celebrate an end to tyranny and the destruction of the class that has for so long preyed upon the people." He signaled the musicians he'd had hastily assembled, and the trumpets and lutes on the platform behind him struck up a merry tune. Cadarn danced an impulsive jig, which was soon picked up by members of the crowd. Cadarn ran down the ramp, grabbed the hand of an attractive young woman, and pulled her after him. When they reached the platform, he led her in an improvised Black Nag. He nodded to Weylin and Pandaran, who ran down the ramp and returned with partners of their own. Before long, nearly every member of the crowd had joined in and started a circle dance around the community garden. The commoners could never resist a party.

Cadarn was starting to run out of breath and began wondering again how to keep the crowd from growing restless when a cheer went up from the edge of the square. Pulled by six oxen, the cart bearing the throne had arrived. He bowed to his partner and released her to rejoin the crowd.

Cadarn wiped the sweat from his brow and held the sledgehammer again. "Shatter the throne!" he started to chant. At first, he could barely be heard over the noise of the crowd, but those close to him took up the chant, which then rippled through the crowd, and soon became deafening. The cart made its way slowly across the square.

The dancing had put the crowd in a merry mood, and they continued the chant while the oxen started up the ramp. When the cart reached the top, a ramp was let down from the rear of the sledge. The oxen had to be unharnessed from the cart and moved to the other side of the platform and hitched to the throne itself. Finally, the throne hit the platform with a resounding thud. The oxen were quickly unhitched, and the now empty cart wheeled away.

With the huge marble monstrosity behind him, Cadarn turned to the crowd and led them in a few more rounds of "Shatter the throne!"

He then held up his hand for silence. When he got it, he dropped to his knees and held a hand in the direction of the Far Mountain. "Today I renounce my noble title forever and always, both for myself and my heirs. By Sulis and on my mother's grave, I pledge my loyalty to the new order and the will of the people. Today I take upon myself the title of Lord Protector of the people of the Protectorate of Korthlundia but will hold it only as long as the people will me to do so. To the Protectorate!" He stood to renewed cheers, picked up the sledgehammer, and approached the throne. With all his might, he swung the sledgehammer into the marble, and a few chips flew in a disappointedly anti-climactic manner. It seemed shattering wouldn't be an easy affair. He struck again and inflicted little more damage.

After a third strike, he turned back to the crowd. "When planning to free this people, I hoped that all the nobles in the joined kingdoms would recognize Sulis's will and vow as I have done. Happily, many of those here in the city have agreed to do so. Count Weylin, will you please come forward?" He stepped aside for the count.

Weylin went down on his knees and repeated Cadarn's vow, although with far less enthusiasm. When he rose, he took the sledgehammer and swung it at the throne. His blows caused cracks to appear. Cadarn stiffened. How was it that a coward like Weylin had more upper body strength than he did? After three strikes, Weylin stepped away, and Pandaran took his place. He too made his vow and swung at the throne.

One by one the gathered nobles knelt, renounced their titles, and took their turn striking the throne. Parents made the vows on the behalf of their children. With each blow the crowd cheered. After the early blows weakened the integrity of the marble, it began crumbling so quickly Cadarn feared it wouldn't remain intact long enough for everyone to have a turn. The sun began to set, and Cadarn had torches lit around the platform. The edges of the square contained oil lamps that he had lit as well.

After a fat count made his vow and struck ineffectively at the one remaining arm of the throne, no one else came forward. Cadarn gestured. "Next."

One of his men whispered to him. "The rest have refused to take the vow."

Two dozen? I thought to execute only a handful. Sulis, I can't make the square run with blood as Dritan was said to have done.

Nisse touched his shoulder and whispered. "I know it's more than you anticipated, but if you back down now, you might as well give up your dream."

Cadarn set his jaw and faced the crowd again. "While the brave men and women who vowed to the Protectorate here today have recognize Sulis's will and have accepted rule by the people, others have chosen to cling to greed and evil. It saddens my heart, but such cannot be allowed to live to threaten the new order and the people's will. As your Lord Protector, I have no choice but to execute them here today. We will begin with the queen's chancellor."

Baron Gwawl shook off the hands that reached for him and walked forward with his head held high. He knelt before the executioner's block with so much dignity that Cadarn feared he'd win sympathy from the crowd.

To his relief, someone yelled, "Off with his head!" And the entire crowd picked up the chant.

The baron tried to speak over the noise, but he couldn't be heard. The huge executioner looked to Cadarn. With a hand on his stomach, he nodded. Gwawl's head was forced into position, and the executioner raised his ax. When the baron's head rolled free, the crowd broke into their loudest cheers yet. Blood sprayed the faces of those at the front of the crowd and splattered Cadarn's legs. Cadarn stepped back as Baron Arawn approached the executioner's block with dignity to equal Gwawl's, and the crowd renewed its chant. Cadarn's chest tightened, and he tried to breathe deeply to loosen it. He'd given Arawn and all the others a chance to join the new order. He nodded to the executioner, who swung again. He still wasn't far enough away to avoid the blood splatter, but as Baroness Glynnis came forward on her own power, he grasped his sword tightly to steady himself; moving farther away would signal reluctance. He thought the crowd would greet a woman's death less enthusiastically, but he was wrong. "Off with her head!" rang out just as loudly.

To avoid seeing the baroness's head roll free, Cadarn glanced back at those awaiting execution and froze. Where he'd originally stood, he'd been unable to see the five children, the oldest about twelve, the youngest a mere babe in its mother's arms. *Holy Sulis, no! How did I not see this coming! I can't behead babies!*

Scrambling to think of a solution that didn't make him look weak, Cadarn tried to block out the exuberant cheer that greeted the baroness's death. His brain refused to function as head after head parted with its body and his legs became increasingly bloody. The oldest child walking toward the block with his head held high spurred Cadarn out of his stupor. He stepped forward and put a hand on the boy's shoulder. "Save the children for last."

Fixing Cadarn in a glare that pierced his soul, the woman with the baby handed the infant to the older boy and took her place at the executioner's feet.

"Momma!" the boy screamed as the woman's head was chopped off. But the cheers rang out just as loudly. *How can they be so callous to a child's anguish?* Cadarn shuddered as he looked at the boy. It was his hand on the boy's shoulder, after all.

By the time all the adults had been executed, the city platform was slick with blood. Struggling to keep his breathing steady, Cadarn pictured Annagret and Dritan's statues in the Fribourg city square and imagined ones of him and Nisse being constructed where the people now lost their heads.

When only the five children remained, Cadarn, with his hand still on the boy's shoulder, maneuvered him to the front of the platform. He had the other children brought forward. He held up his hand for silence. "My people, as we begin a new age in the history of our great land, we recognize that children are the future. Therefore, we can certainly spare the lives of those too young to understand the significance of the vows their parents refused to take in their name."

Someone yelled from the crowd, "No! Kill them all!"

And the crowd renewed the chant, "Off with their heads! Off with their heads!"

"My people!" As Cadarn tried to yell over the noise, hands reached out and grabbed the legs of the boy. By tightening his grip, he was able to prevent the boy from being dragged off the platform, but fighting for balance caused the boy to lose his grip on the baby, which tumbled into the crowd below. Before Cadarn could make any move to stop it, someone picked up the infant and bashed its head into the platform. "No!" Cadarn screamed, as the crowd turned into a mob and dragged the rest of the children into their midst.

* * *

Later, Cadarn came to himself in his own chambers in the palace. He was sitting in a warm bath, and Nisse was washing the blood from his body. He couldn't remember how he'd gotten there or what had happened in the city square after the death of the baby.

Nisse was making soothing sounds as he scrubbed the blood from his legs. "Liridona, my love, it will be all right. Everything is fine."

The water surrounding him was pink with blood, and Cadarn bolted from the tub. Nisse took a towel and began drying him off. Cadarn stood rigid, allowing him to do so. Then, staring at nothing, he sat naked on the bed. "What happened?"

Nisse sat beside him and blew out a breath. "I've rarely seen a riot quite like that. They tore the children to pieces, and I think they killed all the nobles on the platform."

"Those that had sworn?"

Nisse nodded. "My men and I were barely able to get you out of there safely. Maybe a few others escaped, but Weylin is definitely dead. I watched him being torn apart. After the carnage in the square, the mob went rampaging elsewhere. There's no way to stop a mob like that. You just have to let it run its course."

Cadarn stared at the wall, saying nothing. *So many dead. This wasn't how things were supposed to be. Why would people act like that? Who would kill a baby?* His tone was flat. "I guess you were right about Master Altherr. The Svizran revolution was surely as bloody as the worst stories depicted it to be. Dritan probably did personally smash an infant's brains out on the scaffolding where its parents hanged."

Nisse kissed his shoulder and trailed kisses down his arm. "I won't say I told you so."

Still staring at the wall, Cadarn asked, "What do I do now?"

"You do what Annagret did. I know you always considered Annagret the true hero of our revolution. But you never wanted to accept that Annagret turned a blind eye to Dritan's atrocities. He gave high-minded speeches about freedom and honor, set up what would one day be just laws and a new system of government, but he let Dritan butcher anyone who objected. Annagret was never the angel you wanted to make him. He made a deal with a demon and lived with the results."

"Are you suggesting Dritan was a demon?"

"Straight from the deepest of your seven hells. History books tend to gloss over the extent of his butchery. He didn't merely commit violence. He reveled in it."

"What a horrible thing to say. If you believe this about your country's hero, why didn't you object when I asked you to be my Dritan?"

"You know I love you as I have never loved another, but you've never been able to face the truth about me, either. I am Dritan born anew. Liridona, have you never wondered why I am the captain of a company of mercenaries?"

"I thought when your father's business interests collapsed, you had no other choice."

Nisse rubbed his check against the smooth skin of Cadarn's back. "I forgot I told you that. My father is as wealthy as he's always been. He wanted me to follow him into the family business, as my older brother did, but instead, I convinced him to front me the money to build my own company of mercenaries. I didn't turn to a life of violence because I had to but because I wanted to. There is nothing like the rush one feels in battle. There is something glorious in having another's life in your hands and taking it. Like Dritan before me, I am a demon. And if you want to succeed in what you've started, you must make a deal with me."

Cadarn stared at the wall for a moment more. His friend was right. He no longer had any choice. He turned, took Nisse's chin in hand, and gently lifted it on level with his own. "All of these deaths cannot be in vain. We must succeed. Guide me, and I will follow into the deepest of the seven hells if I have to." He brushed his lips against Nisse's, and when Nisse deepened the kiss, he didn't resist.

CHAPTER 16

With Nisse standing beside him, Cadarn listened to the reports of looting, vandalism, arson, rape, and murder committed following the ceremony. In the noble section of the city, many who'd hid from Nisse's forces had been found, dragged into the street, and hanged from lampposts. Even their servants hadn't been spared. The same had happened among the foreign population near the docks. When little more damage could be inflicted on the nobles and foreigners, the rioters had moved on to the wealthy merchant district. The rioting hadn't dissipated until the wee hours of the morning.

A sour taste rose from Cadarn's belly, but what was done was done. He just had to make sure something wonderful rose out of the ash and spilled blood. "How many dead?" he asked.

"Bodies are still being found," Ruadh, Gerard's second in command, reported. "But the estimates are between one and two hundred men, women, and children,"

"But order is now restored?"

"Yes, sir."

After Ruadh left, Nisse blew out a breath. "I hope our sweet little plum hasn't been spoiled." When Cadarn looked at him blankly, he said, "The Jeweled Plum Tree is on the border between the noble and merchant districts, is it not?"

He felt like he'd been punched in the gut as he realized Purple Leaf's well-being hadn't entered his mind. *She's only a whore. The fate of all of Korthlundia rests on me.* "Advise me."

Nisse raised an eyebrow at him but didn't comment further on the whore's fate. "The city must be put under martial law with a strict curfew. All remaining resistance must be ruthlessly crushed. There's still a pocket of the Royal Guard holding out in one of the city magistrates' barracks. Everyone should be subjected to search, and carrying weapons forbidden to any except members of your newly formed Protectorate Guard. Many of the city's magistrates retreated or surrendered rather than fight. Get them to join the Guard, if you can. Make sure they're disarmed, if you can't. But most importantly, your priest must call for calm and urge everyone to accept and cooperate with the new Protectorate. To make sure you have his continued support, give him whatever he wants."

"See that it is done. I'll talk to Father Eadoin." As Nisse headed for the door, Cadarn called him back. "And have someone to check on The Jeweled Plum Tree."

* * *

As the sun rose, Baroness Eithne rode out the palace gates escorted by a company of foreign mercenaries as well as two footmen Cadarn had allowed to accompany her. She wanted to close her eyes and block out the damage, but she forced herself to pay attention so she could report to the queen. She stifled a sob as they rode through the city square where so many had lost their lives, including her dear friend Glynnis. The pieces of the shattered throne made the scene seem unreal. The monarchy of her beloved land couldn't be brought down by merely the destruction of a symbol.

In any case, she had to be able to give the queen a full report as quickly as possible. The mercenary guard left them at the city gates, and she and her footmen rode through alone. She was an adequate horsewomen, but her footman Donall was an expert, which was the reason she'd chosen him to accompany her. When they were out of sight of the city gates, she turned to him and handed him the purse containing most of the money and jewels she'd been able to smuggle out of the palace. "As we discussed, ride fast for the queen. Use the money to replace your mounts as necessary. Tell the queen what has happened. Eghan and I will follow as rapidly as we're able."

With a bow of his head, Donall took the purse and spurred his horse into a gallop. As he disappeared over a rise, Eithne looked to her remaining footman. Eghan nodded. "We'll be all right, Milady." She prayed they would. Eghan was huge, which had been her reason for selecting him. Cadarn had confiscated all his weapons. Hopefully, his size would be enough to protect them both.

* * *

Cadarn rode to the Temple of the Mother's Love, which Eadoin had ludicrously renamed the Temple of the Father's love. He kept his eyes straight forward, in order not to see his people being stopped and searched by Nisse's mercenaries. What further demonic deals must he make to get Father Eadoin's cooperation? Korthlundia had never been a theocracy, and history provided no examples of regimes more barbarous than those who thought they ruled in the name of some god.

Cadarn picked his way around the debris that still littered the streets. Somehow, he'd have to get these streets cleaned up. Hadn't the city employed men for this purpose? It was one of a growing list of practical matters he hadn't considered in planning the coup. After visiting the priest, he'd summon the city's mayor.

When Cadarn reached the temple, he found it packed and the high priest in the middle of a service. Rather than interrupting, he took one of the few remaining seats in the back. As he listened to the sermon, he was tempted to skewer the high priest rather than make any concessions to him. The high priest apparently didn't have a problem with his followers rampaging through the streets killing and raping because Father Eadoin wasn't preaching calm or Sulis's forgiveness and gentle love. Instead, he was yammering on about doctrinal purity and how the destruction of heresy was necessary to retain Sulis's blessing, repeatedly pounding the podium as he did so. The sermon ended with what seemed to be a call for more violence: "Only when all of Sulis's children honor him in the proper way can we be free from his wrath. All we whose blood is pure should not hesitate to work for the god's glory. What may seem vile in the eyes of the worldly and impure is pure and holy in the Father's eyes."

As soon as the high priest dismissed the congregation, Cadarn pushed his way through the crowd toward the door behind the altar through which the high priest had exited. When he reached it, two priests stood in his way. "His Holiness is communing with Sulis and is not to be disturbed," one of them said.

Cadarn gaped at him. "Do you know who I am?"

The priest nodded. "Yes, Lord Protector."

"Then inform the high priest I am here and have business with him." He narrowed his eyes at the priests.

The priests hesitated a moment longer and then one of them left the room. The other continued standing in front of Cadarn with folded arms.

The priest took so long to return that Cadarn almost decided to force his way past the remaining one, but before he acted, the door opened. "His Holiness will see you now."

Reminding himself what Nisse'd said about needing the high priest, Cadarn entered an empty room that contained an altar. They passed through this room, down a corridor, and into an office. Eadoin was sitting behind a desk, and he didn't rise at Cadarn's arrival. Eadoin's tendency not to focus directly on anyone seemed to have intensified, and a fire that seemed not quite sane burned in his eyes. Fantasizing about the priest's untimely death, Cadarn sat without waiting to be invited. "Father, over one hundred men, women, and children died in yesterday's violence. Others were raped, and the amount of property destroyed hasn't even been estimated yet."

With a sad expression that teased toward becoming a smile, Eadoin nodded his head. "The god's judgments can be harsh at times."

Cadarn gestured toward the streets. "You call yesterday's violence Sulis's judgment?"

Eadoin drew himself up. "Indeed, it was. Sulis has chosen me to rid his people of contamination and bring them to honor the god without adulteration. Only then can the true power of the priesthood be restored. While some may have gone a little too far in yesterday's disturbance, Sulis was pleased with the overall results."

"Pleased with destruction and carnage? Sulis could not be pleased! Sulis is the Father of us all!"

Eadoin's face reddened, and the large vein in his left temple throbbed. "The absurdity that Sulis cares for all people equally is another heresy of the old religion. Sulis loves and protects those who worship at his feet in the proper manner. He delights in his people being purified from the taint of heretics and infidels! Neither I nor Sulis's true children will stop until Sulis's land is pure. We will do as the god requires."

Cadarn barely restrained himself from grabbing the high priest by the front of his robes and shaking him. This priest was a far worse demon than Nisse. But he thought of the numbers of fanatical followers who'd rampaged through the streets and filled the church earlier. If he opposed the high priest, he'd never defeat the queen. Nisse was right: he had to take one issue at a time.

Instead of attacking Eadoin, he nodded gravely. "I understand the need for purity, but you must see how chaos in the city now plays to the queen's advantage. Surely the queen is the biggest threat to the triumph of Sulis's will. Can further purifying not wait until the queen's defeat? When the joined kingdoms are truly ours, Sulis's will can be followed without restraint. If the queen regains the throne, she will again outlaw Sulis's word."

The fire in Eadoin's eyes seemed to cool, and the high priest leaned back in his chair. "There are a few so tainted that Sulis cannot abide their continued existence, but I agree that further violence doesn't serve the god's interests at this time. If you give me your solemn vow that you will fully support Sulis's purity now and always, I will command my people to remain calm and await the death of the heretical queen."

Cadarn's throat went dry. "I, Cadarn, Lord Protector of Korthlundia, do vow on the god and my father's grave to fully support his servant Father Eadoin in purifying the land of heresy." Sulis surely would forgive his temporary accommodation of evil as well as his false oath in the service of the freedom and prosperity he planned to bring her children. Besides, he tried to tell himself, since he swore on the god rather than the goddess, he had truly forsworn himself.

* * *

While he waited for the mayor, Cadarn paced in front of the dais of what had been the throne room but was now... he wasn't sure what he should call it now, but it was a good place to demonstrate the importance of the Lord Protector to the common people. He'd had a desk and a chair placed in front of the dais, but he was too agitated to sit.

He heard the stomp of boot steps and looked toward the door, but instead of Lieutenant Ruadh with the mayor, Nisse stalked into the room. When he got close, Cadarn could see his uniform was covered with blood. "What happened?" he asked.

Nisse scowled. "The remains of the Royal Guard fought like demons possessed, and some of the city's magistrates were none too pleased either. I lost five men in the fight. The city magistrates have either been won over or subdued, but somewhere between thirty and fifty members of the Royal Guard were able to fight their way free and escape the city. The captain of the Royal Guard was among those killed."

Cadarn nodded. "Any wounded?"

"Mine are being tended to."

"I meant of the Royal Guard."

Nisse smiled fiercely. "None who survived." He sobered. "The Jeweled Plum Tree was a grizzly sight. It had been completely ransacked, and there were several bodies lying about. You don't need to know what was done to them. But most of the whores seemed to have escaped into the tunnels."

Cadarn collapsed into a chair. "Purple Leaf?"

Nisse patted his shoulder. "No sign of her, but I checked the bodies myself. She wasn't one of them."

As Cadarn breathed a sigh of relief, Lieutenant Ruadh arrived with the mayor. Before telling Ruadh to bring him in, Cadarn told him, "I'm placing you in temporary charge of the city magistrates. Find out which ones we can rely on to help keep order. Recruit likely men into their ranks. We can't have criminals thinking they have free reign in the city."

When Mayor Barris entered, he was so white Cadarn feared he'd faint. He had a chair brought and invited Barris to be seated.

The mayor refused the seat and drew himself up to his full height. "I am loyal to the queen. Do with me as you will."

Cadarn sat across from him. "Do you intend to fight for your queen?"

The mayor ran a hand through his hair. "Well... er... I'm not much of a fighter, but I won't work against Her Majesty."

"I wasn't going to ask you to. Because of the riot, the city streets are a mess. Would it be against the queen's interest to have them cleaned up and order restored?"

The mayor looked at him as if searching for a trap. "No, I can't say that it would be."

"All I'm asking of you is to see to the clean-up and exercise the other duties of your office to help maintain order so the people don't suffer unduly." The mayor agreed to continue in his position as long as he wasn't asked to act against the queen.

While so much else had gone wrong, something finally went right. *Damn it, Gerard! Bring me the princess!*

* * *

Gawladys hurried the children along. They were all tired, especially the younger ones. They'd traveled all night and all the next day after Vaughan had foolishly brought the princess to her home. She'd only allowed a few hours' rest. They'd entered Buil, and Baile Margaidh, where her brother lived, was only a half day away. They'd reach it by noon. She only prayed he hadn't moved in the years since he'd disowned her for marrying a blacksmith. Trefor hadn't thought Vernon was good enough for the sister of a wealthy merchant. But she'd loved Vernon, and her only regret in marrying him was how young he'd died. She'd written her brother afterward. Before Vaughan had gotten the job in the palace stables, she hadn't known how she was going to keep all of her children fed. He hadn't answered her letter. She prayed family feeling was still strong enough for him to take them in and hide them now.

She tried not to think of the child who wasn't there. *Sulis bless him. Why wouldn't he see sense?* Vaughan refusing to leave the crown princess would probably get them all killed if she didn't reach her brother's in time. She grabbed up Skye, the youngest, and hurried the others along.

She heard hoof beats behind them, but before she could think to get the children to hide, the horsemen appeared. If they tried to run now, they'd look like they had a reason to. Maybe they weren't looking for them. She slowed the children down and tried to walk as if she had all the time in the world.

Her hopes were dashed as the horsemen surrounded them. *Vaughan, what have you done to us?*

Several of the men dismounted. The one who appeared to be in charge didn't look happy. "Mistress Gawladys, you've led us on quite a chase. I'm Captain Gerard of the Protectorate Guard." She tried for a blank stare and considered denying her name, but he seemed to know what she was thinking. "Don't even try lying. Just tell us where to find your oldest son and the crown princess, and the rest of your children will be unhurt."

She pushed her children behind her, but Wynne stepped up next to her. She guessed that was proper for her next oldest child. "I don't want no trouble. I told Vaughan to leave the baby and come with us, but he wouldn't listen. He never did know what's good for him. He planned to take Her Highness to the queen. I don't know where he is now."

The man drew his sword and placed it under her chin. "You expect me to believe that?"

She closed her eyes and prayed to Sulis to watch over her children if she had to travel Beyond the Far Mountain. "I swear it's the truth. Kill me if you must, but leave my little ones be. They don't know nothing."

* * *

Gerard swore inwardly. The count wouldn't like him resorting to such measures, but he answered to a higher authority. "It's your children that concern you?"

He nodded to one of his men, who grabbed the youngest, a girl of about six. As he brought her forward, the child screamed and kicked her heels wildly against the man who held her. Gerard slapped her across the face. She stopped fighting and broke into desperate sobs.

"Please, don't hurt her!" the mother cried. "Skye don't know nothing about her brother."

Sheathing his sword, he took the child's chin in his hand. He drew his dagger and put the point under her chin. "I never thought she did, but if I slit this one's throat, how many of the others would I have to kill before you give me the information I need?"

"No, please! I swear I told you everything I know!"

"I don't believe you." Father Eadoin said that nothing was evil if done in Sulis's name, but Gerard wondered if he could actually bring himself to kill a child. He reminded himself of the oath he'd taken to Sulis and pricked the girl's neck, bringing a trickle of blood.

"Don't hurt her!" the boy who bravely stood beside his mother cried out. "I know where he went."

With a silent prayer of gratitude to Sulis, Gerard removed his dagger from the child's neck and turned to the boy, who he judged to be about twelve. "And where is that?"

"Vaughan was going to take the princess to her grandfather, the king's father."

You Sulis cursed fool! Why didn't you think of that? He could have sent men in that direction as well. Everyone knew the king had a peasant father, but the man had never been to court. He hadn't even attended the king's wedding. "If you value your sister's life, you better be telling the truth."

"I am. I swear I am. Please, don't hurt her."

He told his man to release the child. She ran to her mother and buried her face in her mother's skirt. "If you lied to me, I'll be back."

* * *

Angus stood in the village square and listened as the herald unrolled a scroll, cleared his throat, and began:

"People of Korthlundia, join us in celebration as the yokes of our oppression are broken, and we breathe as one—free and equal. For far too long, Sulis's children have suffered under the oppression of those who claimed to be their betters but were truly nothing more than ravening wolves feeding on the people as if they were sheep. But all men and women are children of the same God, and Sulis has blessed all with the right of liberty and happiness."

There was a collective gasp, as Sulis was referred as a God rather than the Goddess everyone knew her to be. The herald waited until the noise died down, then continued reading:

"As of this day, the monarchy is no more, and the noble class has been dissolved. Murtaghan and the rest of the land now belong to the people. A new government has been formed with Cadarn having been blessed by Sulis and the consent of the people to serve as Lord Protector of Korthlundia. Representatives will be chosen by the people to come to Murtaghan and advise the Lord Protector on the desires and needs of the people. More information will be forthcoming. For now, join with the Lord Protector in overthrowing those that have oppressed us and celebrate the freedom Sulis has given us."

Wanting to strangle the herald, Angus stepped back further into the crowd. He couldn't gauge the mood of his neighbors. They'd always considered Robbie a demon child. Most hadn't been happy when he became king. Would they be willing to turn against the queen because of it?

But as he turned away from the crowd, he had a more urgent concern. His granddaughter hadn't been with the queen when she'd ridden north. His granddaughter must be in the hands of this Lord Protector. That is, if she was still alive. *Have I lost the last of my blood? Why didn't I go see the princess as I promised?*

* * *

Vaughan crept through the huge trees of the Setenta Forest with Brianna on his back, keeping the road in sight so he didn't get lost. Whenever he heard someone coming, he hid behind one of the trees and urged Brianna to be quiet. She complied every time. Despite her being far too young, Vaughan was now convinced the princess understood him. When they weren't hiding, she made a racket. She seemed excited to be out in the forest because she was bouncing up and down on his back and talking to everything. She became especially animated when she saw a bird or a squirrel or some other little animal. Vaughan prayed there was nothing bigger in the forest. Although he wore his sword underneath his mother's dress, how could he fight with a baby on his back?

Why did anyone ever have babies anyway? Sure, they were cute, but they were so gross. He had to chew Brianna's food up for her and then spit it out and let her eat it out of his hand, and she was always pooping and peeing. Every time they passed a stream, he'd had to stop and wash her, himself, their clothes, everything. Taking that many baths couldn't be healthy, but Brianna loved to splash in the water. Also, he knew babies were supposed to have milk, and he didn't have any to give her. Would she get sick without it?

He'd been traveling for two days now, so he thought he had to be getting close to the king's father's farm. It had seemed much closer when he'd gone with the king, but he'd been riding a horse then, and they hadn't had to stop every Sulis-cursed minute to take care of a baby.

But can that disgusting drunk even help us? Still, he couldn't think of anywhere else to go. Vaughan was pretty sure the king's father had beaten him when he was a child. If the old man tried to hurt Brianna, Vaughan would skewer him.

The trees were starting to thin, and soon he came to an open meadow at the edge of the forest. They had to be almost there. They better be because without the trees he didn't see anywhere to hide from passersby. He'd die of embarrassment if anyone found out he was wearing his mother's dress.

CHAPTER 17

Riding at the head of the column and clad in her armor, Samantha saw Sheen's walls ahead. She gripped her reins tightly. How dare Sheen proclaim himself king of Korth! For fifty years Korthlundia had been at peace, and now he was trying to divide the joined kingdoms again. People would die because of him.

Darhour and Brigitta rode side by side behind her. She wasn't sure Darhour would forgive her if he lost Brigitta, but after that night near Nios Mo, they'd stopped bickering. This morning Darhour had told her that Brigitta was ready should her mission prove necessary. Samantha stopped the column before they got within arrow range. She kept her eyes facing forward as Darhour and Brigitta dismounted. Darhour hugged Brigitta and said something to her in her own language. She kissed him and responded in the same. Then she remounted and rode off with Lord Devyn. She would wait by the entrance to the secret tunnel for the signal to enter it.

Darhour remounted and joined her at the head of the column. When she tried to speak, he held up a hand. "It is done. Let's not speak of it."

Please Sulis, don't let her die! But she had no faith the Holy Mother would watch over Brigitta any better than she had watched over Robbie. She nodded to Baron Teague. "It's unlikely Sheen will simply surrender, but asking him to submit is a formality we must observe. Accompany me."

As they rode forward, Bearach carried the flag of truce. Conroy carried her colors. Darhour and the rest of her bodyguards accompanied them.

When she got within hailing distance of the walls, she called up, "Where is the traitor who calls himself king? Come forward, Sheen. Surrender to your rightful queen and spare the lives of your men."

Wearing what looked like a replica of the ancient crown of Korth, the duke appeared on the parapet. In a symbolic gesture of unity, the original crown had been melted down with the crown of Lundia, and the two were forged to form the crown of the joined kingdoms. Sheen's second son, Lord Cedric was on his right side.

Cedric yelled, "My father, King Sheen III of Korth, refuses to demean himself by addressing a bastard who has tricked her way onto a throne to which she has no right. He orders you to withdraw your army into Lundia immediately or face the consequences."

A man dressed in what appeared to be an officer's uniform stepped closer to Sheen and seemed to whisper something. Without warning, the officer grabbed Sheen and pitched him headfirst from the parapet, yelling, "No traitor will rule over us." Before Samantha could credit what she'd seen, Cedric had drawn his sword, and a fight erupted on the walls.

Samantha's heart lightened at the loyalty the officer and those who fought beside him had shown. She looked at Darhour. "We have to make certain the right side wins." Without waiting for a response, she turned to Bearach and nodded. Bearach lit an arrow and fired it into the sky, the signal for Brigitta to enter the tunnel and open the gate. Then holding her breath, she waited to learn if her decision had cost Darhour his love.

* * *

Holding his reins tightly, Darhour stared straight ahead and tried to empty his mind. He focused on the furious sounds of battle and the sight of men falling from the walls as the gate stayed closed. Devyn had said that getting through the tunnel would only be a matter of minutes, but then Brigitta had to make it to the gate house through the battle that raged within. *Sulis, Mother of us all, keep her safe.* But the knowledge he didn't deserve happiness prevented him from trusting the goddess to do so.

Minutes ticked by, and Lord Devyn rejoined them. The lord reported to the queen, but Darhour didn't listen to his words. Devyn could know nothing of Brigitta's fate once she entered the tunnel. If Brigitta died, Darhour decided he would slit Devyn's throat for revealing the existence of a tunnel too narrow for him to use himself.

The battle continued to rage on the castle walls, and sweat ran down Darhour's neck as he stared at the gate that remained stubbornly closed. His daughter rode close to him, but he didn't acknowledge her. He knew she'd had to make the decision to send Brigitta, but what his head knew, his heart did not. *Shut up, you fool! You don't deserve either of them!*

When his nerves grew tight enough to snap, he heard a grinding sound and the gates began to open. He drew his sword and held it high. When the gates had opened enough, he dropped his arm and yelled, "Charge!" He spurred his horse through the gates with the queen's army behind him and was enveloped in chaos. Men, all wearing Sheen's colors, fought each other, making it impossible to tell who fought for and against the queen. Then he saw Cedric.

He wanted to spur his horse directly for the gatehouse, but he knew his duty: not until the battle was won could he look for his wife. "To me!" he shouted and led the charge. Letting go with his mind, he fought with one purpose: to kill the duke's son. Surely, when Cedric was dead, the rest would surrender. As was usual when Darhour fought, the world went silent. He heard nothing as men died at the end of his sword. With the addition of the queen's army, the forces loyal to Sheen were vastly outnumbered, so it wasn't long before there was only one man between Darhour and the would-be prince. That man fell with an arrow in his chest, and Darhour swung his sword, taking off Cedric's head.

With the loss of their leader, the remainder quickly threw down their arms and surrendered. When Darhour was certain the battle was ended, he turned and galloped for the gatehouse. Vaulting off his horse, he ran inside. Brigitta lay on the ground covered in blood, an arrow lodged in her gut. "No!" he screamed and hurried to her. When he touched her, she stirred but didn't open her eyes. He turned to see one of his men in the doorway. "Fetch Oriana now!"

He tried to staunch the blood flow, but he daren't remove the arrow before the healer arrived. His heart thudding in his chest, he watched as Brigitta's breath grew shallower and slower. At last Oriana burst into the room, and he moved aside for the young healer. She put her hands over the wound and closed her eyes, as healers always did.

When she opened them, she focused on someone behind Darhour. He turned to find his daughter standing behind them. Oriana said, "She's losing blood quickly. If I don't stop it, she'll die. But stopping it will take all the energy I have."

Without hesitation, his daughter gave his wife back her life. "Do so," she commanded.

Blocking out all thought of the others who might die in order for Brigitta to live, he obeyed Oriana's command, broke the shaft of the arrow, and shoved what remained out his wife's back. Then he could do nothing but watch as Oriana closed her eyes and grew still.

After an eternity, Oriana fell beside Brigitta. She briefly opened her eyes. "I did it." She smiled, slipping into unconsciousness.

* * *

Holding her breath, Samantha tried not to see the panic on Darhour's face. She'd never seen him this vulnerable. *How could I have been so cold as to send my father's wife into danger? But what else could I have done?*

When Oriana announced success, Samantha's knees buckled and she grabbed the wall for support. *Thank you, Sulis!* She left the gatehouse and joined Baron Teague and Lord Devyn in the castle courtyard.

Lord Devyn was staring down at his brother's head. "We were never close," he said, as Samantha approached. "But how will I live with this haunting my dreams?" He pointed down at the severed head.

She had no answer to give him and was prevented offering platitudes, as the officer who'd killed Sheen and two other men were brought to her under escort. Lord Devyn identified them as Malvyn, his father's marshal, Calvagh, his steward, and Fiacre, the Master of the Horse. They went down on their knees before her. Malvyn spoke for the group, "Your Majesty, our lord was a traitor to the crown, but we are not. Our lord may have forgotten how the Dead Lands crept ever closer, and if your consort had not stopped the Ancient Evil, the Soul Stone would have devoured our lives as it did those of

Leighaltys. We remember and will not be led by one who defies the goddess's chosen and our savior."

"We will not!" the two others said in unison.

Malvyn continued, "Because of his treason, our lord deserved to die, a feat we accomplished in Your Majesty's presence and in Your Majesty's name. We now surrender this castle to Your Majesty and ask Your Majesty's mercy for ever having served a traitor to the crown and the goddess."

"Your loyalty will be rewarded," she said. "You may rise."

* * *

With his brother's severed head still before his eyes, Lord Devyn knelt before the queen in his father's hall. The queen was seated in his father's chair, which had always looked too much like a throne for Devyn's comfort. He'd knelt here many times in the past, waiting for his father to humiliate him before the rest of the household. He'd once thought there could be nothing worse than that humiliation, which frequently was either preceded or followed by one of the beatings that left scars on his back. Now, he had to question whether he preferred that humiliation to the honor the queen was about to bestow on him.

The queen looked down at him. Although she was several years younger, in wisdom she seemed decades older. "Lord Devyn, your father and brother were traitors to the crown and have paid for their treachery. You have always demonstrated a loyalty to me that your father never did. Can I count on your loyalty as I always have?"

Not wanting to look weak in front of his father's household, which was now his own, Devyn straightened and was proud he kept his voice from shaking. "Your Majesty, I swear by the goddess and on my mother's grave that my allegiance will always remain with you and your heir." He drew Sulis's star. The goddess had a wicked sense of humor in restoring him to the position he'd lost but never wanted. Devyn had never been popular with his father's men at arms. His pathetic display at arms had earned their contempt. Would that change now?

The queen stood and drew her sword. She touched him on both shoulders. "Arise, Devyn, duke of Gnos, and take possession of your lands. Sit beside me in judgment over your father's household."

Devyn stood and sat beside the queen. *Holy Sulis, Mother of us all, how can the queen be so strong after everything she's been through? Can you not grant me a small portion of her strength?*

* * *

Wondering if Darhour would ever forgive her for putting Brigitta's life in danger, Samantha sat in Sheen's seat while the members of Sheen's household came forward to offer her their oaths of loyalty. She didn't regret allowing Oriana to save Brigitta's life, even though it made the novice unavailable to care for any of the other wounded. How had Solar made these decisions for nearly seventy years without being crushed under their weight? How had he still possessed love in his heart to fill her childhood after a lifetime of weighing life against life? But as always, she had duties to attend, so she shoved such questions aside. Using her ability to ascertain their sincerity, she accepted the oaths of Duke Sheen's former men.

* * *

After seeing to the queen's comfort, Lord Devyn called Malvyn, Calvagh, and Fiacre to what had been his father's study, where he'd conducted all the important business of the estate. As he poured himself a drink from the decanter on the sideboard, he knew using his father's office was a mistake. Each of these men had watched his father thrash him in this very room dozens of times. Devyn clutched at the sideboard. *Holy Sulis, no! I can't be Duke.* The men would never respect him when they'd stood by and watched the blood run down his legs.

The image of his brother's head still burning in his mind, he gulped the drink and felt the fire warm his belly. Despite knowing that so much alcohol on an empty stomach was a bad idea, he poured himself another and offered drinks to his father's men. Malvyn refused, but Calvagh and Fiacre accepted. Trying to prevent his hands trembling, he sat in his father's chair and offered them seats before his father's desk. The chair behind the desk was appallingly uncomfortable and was probably older than Devyn himself. Why had his father never replaced it?

He took a sip of his drink. "We all know there's never been love lost among us, but I am now duke."

Malvyn snorted. "You were always spineless and weak, but we'd rather be led by a coward than a traitor. Do you know how many refugees from the Dead Lands we had overrunning these estates last winter? How fast the Dead Lands were spreading? Every servant of the Holy Mother in all of Korth gave her life to stop the advance." Spittle flew from his lips as Malvyn continued, "After the king had given his life to save us all, Father Faolan threatened the life of his child! When I found out your father had taken that scum in, I wanted to kill him myself. I celebrated when his body was found minus his head." He didn't try to conceal his disgust, and the other two men nodded their agreement.

Devyn emptied his glass. "I never wanted to be duke. I'm not fit for the position. I never was."

Malvyn spat on the floor. "True, but you are loyal to our queen and our goddess, Your Grace. Perhaps we can amend the rest of your deficiencies if you're willing to heed our advice."

Devyn lifted his eyes and steadied his voice. "Very well. Advise me."

CHAPTER 18

With Nisse noisily eating breakfast at the table, Cadarn stared at the portraits of Annagret and Dritan on the wall behind him. Snowflake jumped into his lap, and he scratched between the cat's ears.

Nisse snorted. "Starving yourself won't find the princess any faster."

Cadarn's eyes darted to his friend. "I'm not starving myself. I'm just not hungry."

Nisse resumed eating and muttered under his breath, "You never are these days."

Cadarn jumped to his feet, causing Snowflake to dash off with a hiss. He leaned over the table. "Don't you understand? Without the princess, all of this death may have been for nothing."

Before Nisse could respond, a knock sounded at the door. "Come in!" Cadarn snapped.

Ruadh, the man he'd put in charge of the city magistrates, entered. "Sir, Father Eadoin has put up stakes in the square in front of the Temple of the Father's Love, and there's a huge crowd of people spilling out of the temple and into the square. Rumor has it that he intends to burn Father Hafghan and other heretics. What would you have me do?"

Cadarn's mouth dropped open. "Stop it, of course!"

Ruadh wiped his hands on his trousers. "The crowd's really large, sir, and they might turn hostile if we interfere. Also, I think some of my men are in sympathy with Eadoin. A couple even have stars tattooed on their right hands. I can't depend on them. If I'm going to stop it, I'll need more men."

Cadarn turned to Nisse. "Lend Ruadh some of your mercenaries."

Nisse addressed Ruadh. "Give us a moment, please."

When they were alone, Cadarn crossed his arms. "You aren't seriously going to argue that I should allow this barbarism to go forward?"

Nisse laughed without humor. "I wish I didn't have to. But the mad priest has thousands of fanatics at his command. You try to fight him before the queen surrenders, and you might as well cut off your own head before your queen does it for you."

Cadarn poured himself a whiskey and sank into his chair. "I know you said I had to make a deal with demons. But burning people alive? That's far more barbarous than anything the queen would allow."

Nisse met his eyes. "You said you were willing to go as far as necessary to see your people free. This is part of that necessary."

Cadarn wanted to say "to hell with necessary." Instead, he threw the whiskey to the back of his throat. Nisse was right. He'd come too far and too many people had died for him to fail now.

* * *

Wearing the Soul Stone medallion, Father Eadoin sat on the dais in what was now the Temple of the Father's Love. Before him in chains were Father Hafghan, the heretical high priest, and a dozen priests who'd refused to bow before their God. These would be the sacrifices the ritual required. He rested his hand on the precious book on the table beside him. "You have been accused of heresy," he screeched at Father Hafghan. "How do you plead?"

The heretic raised his chained hands. "What is the meaning of this farce? Your predecessor excommunicated me as I excommunicated him. Your 'church' has no further legal authority."

"That was unfortunately true under the corrupt king and his would-be daughter, but with the new order, things have changed. The vile sin of heresy will no longer be allowed in the Protectorate. How do you plead?"

"I am a true servant of the Holy Mother and no heretic."

Eadoin touched the stone that would soon glow with Sulis's power. "It is blasphemy to claim that divine power could inhabit a weak female vessel. Thanks to the God Sulis, the unnatural order has been overthrown, and His truth can at last flourish. Therefore, Father Hafghan, Father Cameron"—he listed a dozen more—"for heresy you are to be burned at the stake so that all may see that Sulis's enemies no longer have a place in the God's lands. Sentence will be carried out immediately. Guards, take the heretics to the square and tie them to the stakes."

"You can't do that!" Father Hafghan cried. "Sulis would never approve such barbarism!"

Father Eadoin ignored the screeches of the heretic and addressed the crowd gathered to see Sulis's justice. They filled the sanctuary and overflowed in the square that fronted the temple. "Let it be known that I alone speak for Sulis, and Sulis himself demands we purify the land. Anyone who will not bow down before the God will suffer the same fate as these men."

Picking up his precious book, Eadoin strolled out of the back of the hall as the protesting priests were dragged out the front. When he was alone, he allowed a smile to spread over his face. They deserved to die in the agony of fire, but the ritual demanded their heart's blood, so they would already be dead when the flames consumed them. One couldn't regret what the god demanded. He touched the alabaster statue of Sulis on his altar, a statue that had belonged first to Father Shylah and then Father Faolan. Now it was his. "Holy Father, it begins! Thank you, Sulis, it begins!"

* * *

Telling himself it had to be a horrible nightmare, Father Hafghan struggled ineffectively. While the sanctuary had been crowded to bursting, even more people filled the square, spitting and throwing rotten fruit at the condemned. He and the other condemned priests were tied to stakes that formed a circle. In the middle of the circle was a huge cauldron bubbling over a fire. *May Sulis damn Their Majesties forever!* It was the king who had insisted that magic was only possible for those of mixed blood. This hadn't been a popular position among the clergy, but he'd proclaimed it because the king had convinced him it was true. Now the queen had left Murtaghan in the hands of lunatics, and he would die an agonizing death before she could return to set things right.

He tried to shout his innocence. But no one could hear him over the roar of the crowd. The crowd parted to allow Father Eadoin to enter the circle. He carried his Sulis-damned book, which he sat on a table beside the cauldron. Then he removed a medallion from his neck and dropped it in the boiling liquid. The madman took a silver knife and chalice from an assistant and approached Father Hafghan.

Over the noise of the crowd, Hafghan said, "You can't do this, Eadoin. It's barbaric."

With eyes that focused into the far distance, the priest slit his robes open in the front. "You give your blood for the god's glory." As Eadoin raised the knife, a horrifying realization came over Hafghan. Eadoin was performing the same type of blood magic Father Shylah had used when he'd sacrificed the children, but on a much larger scale. While Father Hafghan knew little of the forbidden magic, he did know it always resulted in evil. Something greater than his own life was at stake.

Hafghan screamed. "Sulis, do not allow this! Stop this madman!" But it seemed the goddess couldn't hear him either. He struggled against the ropes to no avail. Eadoin plunged the knife into his chest, and Hafghan watched as his life began to drain into the mad priest's chalice. Soon everything went dark.

* * *

With the air fragrant with the aroma of burning flesh, Eadoin made another cut on his badly scarred arm, filled the chalice with his blood, and poured it in to join that of the burning priests. Then he opened the precious book and began to read the words of the prayer that would seal Sulis's power. While he prayed, the potion alternately sparkled and frothed.

But as he spoke the final words, the potion went still rather than exploding with light as the book said that it should. *No! What have I done wrong?* He grabbed the book and carefully reread the instructions to find the error that had prevented the ritual from achieving its purpose, but he had made no error. He had the cauldron dumped out and, using a pair of tongs, picked up the medallion. The jewel in the center glowed no more than it had before it entered the brew. *Is Sulis angry with me because I allowed Father Faolan to die?*

:Thou foolish man!: Eadoin heard a voice from above and looked toward the Far Mountain. *:Did you think the blood of a mere dozen would sate my thirst?:*

Eadoin fell to his knees. He had been stingy with the god. He wouldn't make the same mistake again.

* * *

When Artan heard of the burning of the priests, his mouth went dry. If they'd burn a pure blood like Father Hafghan, just what would they do to him? He grabbed the chest containing the king's letter, put it under his robes, and ran before they came to get him.

When he arrived in the merchant district, his heart sank. The streets were a mess, and many of the houses had been burned to the ground. All showed damage. That is, until he came to the address Father Leigh had given him. Though a burned-out husk stood on either side of it, the fanciest house Artan had ever seen was untouched. It was pure white and covered with elaborate gold and silver designs. The windows, not a one of which was broken, were of stained glass in every shade of the rainbow. As he crept among the undamaged gold statues and marble fountains, Artan worried he'd gotten the address wrong. Father Leigh had always said his father's house was "horrendously ugly." This house was beautiful.

Not daring to go back to the shrine, he knocked on the front door. "What do you want?" a servant said in a voice that made Artan worry he smelled bad. He didn't think he did. He'd bathed just last week.

Hardly daring to speak, he whispered, "Is this the house of Fergal Taranstamm, Father's Leigh's father?"

"It is."

"Father Leigh said I should come here if there was any trouble."

"I will speak with the master." The servant closed the door in Artan's face.

Moments later the door was opened by a large man covered with gold, fur, and other fancy things. He grinned down at Artan in a much friendlier fashion than the servant had. "Is this the novice of my fool son, the priest?"

Artan didn't like Father Leigh being called a fool, but he nodded.

"And do you have any magic?"

"Yes, sir," he mumbled.

"Speak up, boy!"

Artan tried to speak more loudly, but his voice still came out as a squeak. "Yes, sir."

The man threw the door wide open. "Then come in."

Making sure to wipe any dirt off his feet, Artan stepped inside, which was every bit as fancy as the outside. Artan tried to make himself small so he didn't break anything. Still, he had to know. "How is it that your house is the only one that's not damaged?"

The big man laughed. "When Ennis here"—he gestured toward the servant who'd answered the door and was now holding a tray of food—"told me a mob was coming, I wasn't about to cower like a mouse and be robbed and vandalized. No, not me. My sons and I, except the oh-so-pious Father Leigh, of course, grabbed a supply of paipin leaves and hurried out front. We offered the leaves to the mob if they'd just move on and leave us alone. It worked like a charm. It cost me a fortune in product, but you see the results."

The servant cleared his throat. "You took quite a risk, sir. The mob murdered many of your neighbors. They might have just taken the leaves from you and killed you anyway."

Father Leigh's father laughed more loudly. "Ah, but they didn't, did they, Ennis?" While the man's voice was jolly, Artan felt his insides squirming.

Ennis set down his tray on a table. "They did not, sir."

Fergal put his hand on Artan's shoulder. "Have a seat, boy. Eat something, and we'll see how you can help around here."

* * *

Angus sat at his kitchen table with a jug of homebrew in front of him. The stuff couldn't get him drunk enough to stop the visions anymore. He saw his youngest burnt beyond recognition, as rumor said he'd been while destroying the Ancient Evil. He saw his oldest as he'd looked in the dirt on the day he'd thrown him off the farm for trying to kill his brother. Those visions had haunted him for over a year. But to those visions was now added that of the granddaughter he'd never met. What was happening to her now? Was she even still alive?

Cara put a plate of food in front of him. "If you're going to drink that stuff, at least put some food in your belly," she said for the dozenth time.

Angus ignored the food and took another swig from the jug.

She sat down next to him. "Master Angus, I'm sure it's all rumors. You know how people exaggerate. Nobody would hurt an innocent little baby."

Angus wished he could take comfort in those words. But how could his little granddaughter fare well in the hands of the queen's enemies?

There was a knock on the door, and Cara went to answer it. A voice asked, "Is the king's father here? I have to talk to him."

Angus glanced over, and a very dirty young woman holding an equally dirty baby entered the dining room. When the young woman saw him, she pushed past Cara. "Master Angus, I need your help." She pulled off her bonnet, and Angus recognized her as a young man who had accompanied his son when he'd visited the farm after arresting his brother. The baby turned to face him, and Angus gasped. The baby had Donella's green eyes! He stumbled to his feet. "Is that...? Could it be...? No, she's far too old to be the princess. That baby is at least six months old."

As he looked at the baby, the boy's eyes widened as if he never noticed how big she was before. "Her magic's making her to grow faster than normal. But I swear to you, this is the princess. She's your granddaughter," the boy said, as if he might be ignorant of that fact. "I saved her from the palace, but I need help to get her to the queen. I don't have any money or a horse or anything really."

Tears began streaming down Angus's cheeks, and he held out his arms. "Can I... Can I hold her?"

The boy hugged Brianna tighter. "You won't hurt her, will you?"

"Of course not! What kind of monster do you think I am?"

The boy must have thought he was the worst kind of monster because he surrendered the princess reluctantly, and as soon as he did, he tucked up the side of the dress to reveal a sword. "I swore to a sacred oath I'd protect her, and I won't hesitate to kill for her if necessary."

The boy's voice shook, and his eyes darted around nervously. But Angus's attention was fully on the child in his arms. "No... no... no... no," the child babbled and wiped at his tears with her tiny hands. The tenderness of the gesture tore sobs from his throat. His granddaughter was alive, and for the moment, she was safe.

The boy shifted uncomfortably. "They're looking for us, sir, and I need to know if you're going to help us."

Angus hugged the baby to him and kissed the top of her sweet head. "How could you doubt it? We'll get the princess to the queen."

"We?" the boy asked.

"You don't think I'd desert my only grandchild."

The boy's whole body sagged as if he'd suddenly been relieved of a crushing burden. "Thank Sulis, the Mother of us all. It wasn't supposed to be me that saved her. She had all these fierce guards and a nurse and everything. I don't know how to take care of a baby. I know she needs milk and everything, and I haven't got any, and I haven't got any money or a horse or anything." The boy repeated his list of missing resources.

Suddenly sobered by the needs of the child in his arms, he turned to Cara, who was lingering in the doorway. "Send someone to fetch some goat's milk." He then turned to the boy. "Sit down, and tell me everything you know."

The boy complied and told of the harrowing fight to save the princess and how the others had sacrificed their lives to help get the child to safety. "And they're looking for us. My mum says they would have tortured Cece so much that she would have told her I had the princess. I don't think she's right. Cece would never betray the princess." The boy hesitated. "But maybe she would if they hurt her bad enough. And I think—I think they might think to look here, so I don't think we should stay very long at all."

Angus's chest tightened at the thought of this precious child being stripped from his arms. "You're right. We need to leave as soon as possible." He handed his granddaughter back to the boy and set things in motion: getting men to prepare horses for him and the boy, having a goat readied to accompanying them, fetching all the coin he had, having Cara pack supplies. He even sent a man to keep watch on the road. He turned to ask the boy a question, suddenly realizing he didn't even know the lad's name. But the boy's head was tilted back in his chair, and both he and Brianna were fast asleep.

* * *

"Everything's ready, sir," Dillion, his foreman, reported to Angus as Angus was tying up his own bundle in his bedroom.

He tucked a purse with all the ready coin he had under his shirt. "The goat? The pack mule and riding horses for both me and the boy?"

"Yes, sir."

Angus nodded, swung his bundle over his back and walked into the dining room where both his granddaughter and her young hero still slept. They looked so peaceful he wanted to let them sleep a bit longer. He gently touched his granddaughter's head. She was the last of his blood, his only remaining tie to Donella, the woman he'd loved and lost. He would see her safely to her mother, an act that would surely redeem him in the eyes of the queen and allow him to be the grandfather he'd promised Robbie he'd be.

Reluctantly, he shook the boy's shoulder. The boy bolted to his feet, clutching Brianna to him, and fumbling for his sword.

"It's all right, lad. You're safe for now."

The boy looked around wildly for a moment before the panic left his face. "I vowed a sacred vow. I shouldn't have fallen asleep."

Angus chuckled. "Even a sacred vow can't keep you awake forever. But everything's ready. We should go." He held out some of Robbie's old trousers. "You might want to put these on under the skirt. I don't have a side saddle."

The boy nodded and handed him his granddaughter again. While the boy pulled on the trousers, Angus hugged her precious warmth.

As the lad was lowering his filthy skirt, Turi, the man who had been sent to watch the road, burst in. "Someone's... someone's... coming," he panted. "Soldiers, about a dozen of them."

The blood drained from Vaughan's face, and Angus felt ice form in the pit of his stomach. If he tried to flee with the boy now, the soldiers would guess what had happened and pursue them. As he realized what he had to do, a strange calmness settled over him. He took his purse out from under his shirt and handed it to the boy. "Take it and run, lad. Get my granddaughter to the queen." He kissed Brianna on the head and handed her over as well. "Go, lad." He pushed the boy out into the yard, then told Dillion, "Everyone else scatter. I fired you days ago."

As he watched Vaughan mount the horse with Brianna, and his servants and farmhands run off, Angus untied his bundle and scattered its contents about the house. He took the jug of homebrew from the table and staggered out to the horse that had been saddled for him. He adjusted the saddle so that it appeared to have been done clumsily, took a swig from the jug, and waited for the sound of hooves.

CHAPTER 19

Cadarn stiffened as he listened to Gerard's report. "We didn't find the crown princess at the king's father's farm, as Vaughan's younger brother said we should. The man, I believe his name is Angus, said he had seen nothing of the boy or the crown princes."

Cadarn swallowed before asking the question he knew he must. "Did you take measures to make sure he was telling the truth?"

Gerard scowled. "I would have if he'd lived long enough. When we got there, he was dead drunk. He claimed he fired his servants and farmhands some time ago and was trying to drink himself to death. The place was an unholy mess. I believe he was telling the truth and hadn't seen the princess. But in case he wasn't, I drew my sword and pointed it at his throat. When I told him I didn't like liars, he got offended and tried to come after me. I'm afraid he impaled himself on my sword."

Cadarn pursed his lips. "So, he's dead, and you still don't have the princess?"

Gerard looked pained as he answered. "I do not. But the boy was on foot, so it's likely he hadn't made it that far yet. I left men there to wait for him, and I sent men on ahead to search for him in case the sot had lied. One way or another, Sulis will ensure the abomination is caught."

Not the least reassured by the pious statement, Cadarn poured himself a whiskey and threw it to the back of his throat. "We need the princess. Find her."

* * *

Vaughan wanted to stop on the side of the road and dissolve into tears. He was lost and had no idea which direction was north. He'd thought they'd be most likely to look for him on the main road, so when he'd come to a crossroad, he took the smaller road, and he'd done the same thing at the crossroad after that, and the one after that, and who knew how many others? Now he didn't have any idea where he was or how to get to the queen.

He knew people could tell direction from the sun, but he'd never worried about learning how. In Murtaghan, he always knew where he was. When he fled the king's father's farm, his only aim was to get as far away as possible. He'd only come across one small village since leaving the farm, but he hadn't wanted to draw more attention by asking directions.

He tried to not to let his body get tense because Brianna always knew when he was upset, and it made her cranky. It was starting to get dark. A sign awhile back said that Ait Eigin was ahead. It didn't say how far, and Vaughan had never heard of Ait Eigin. He hoped the place was big enough to have an inn and he could find someone he dared ask for directions. He wanted a warm bed and a decent meal. He was sick of sleeping on the hard ground, and although the king's father had provided plenty of supplies, a lot of them required cooking, and Vaughan had never cooked anything in his life. "Sulis was pretty foolish when she trusted me with you, little squirt." He'd taken to always calling the princess "little squirt" so he wouldn't mess up and reveal who she was by accident to the wrong person.

Brianna just bounced on the saddle in front of him and made happy noises. She seemed to love riding on horseback.

When Vaughan finally reached Ait Eigin, it was dark, and Brianna had fallen asleep. He could barely keep his eyes open himself. The village was dinky, but it did have an inn. He carefully adjusted his stupid bonnet so people would think he was a woman.

A stable boy came out. "Traveling alone, ma'am?" He looked around for someone else.

Why is he being so Sulis cursed nosy? Vaughan answered him, imitating the voice of a lady, "Take good care of them." Careful not to wake Brianna, Vaughan dismounted, smoothed his stupid skirt, and gave the boy a big enough tip that he'd stop asking questions.

When Vaughan entered the inn's common room, it was about half full, local farmers probably. As Vaughan took a seat at a table next to the far wall, he counted ten men. He sat the sleeping baby on the bench next to him.

Smiling, the innkeeper's wife hurried over to him. "The little one's all tuckered out, is he? What a sweet baby you have." She leaned down and softly touched the auburn fuzz that covered Brianna's head. Vaughan decided not to correct her on the baby's gender. "How old is he?"

"Three months," Vaughan said in the lady voice again.

The woman straightened, putting her hands on her hips. "No way! That baby's far too big for being three months. He has to be at least six or seven."

Vaughan cursed himself for telling the truth. He knew Brianna didn't look or act her age. "I meant to say it's been three months since her father died." Using the first name that came to his head, he continued, "Iachus be seven months old." He straightened Brianna's blankets.

The woman gasped, sat down next to him, and put her hand on his arm. "What happened to your man?"

Vaughan pretended to wipe away a tear. "He died of the flux. Iachus and me be alone now. I'm taking him to me mum's."

The woman patted his shoulder. "You poor, poor dear. And where does your mum live?"

"To the north," he said.

"Be that Duthchas?"

Assuming that was a city or a village to the north, Vaughan nodded.

The woman patted his shoulder again. "Poor, poor dear. I'm sure your mum will help put things to right for you. Let me get you some warm stew and a mug of ale."

Vaughan moved to get out a coin, but the woman patted his hand. "I'll not take a coin for a poor woman in your condition. The stew's on the house, as is a bed for you and the little one tonight."

Since Master Angus had given him plenty of coin, Vaughan squirmed inside at taking advantage of the woman, but when he tried to press the money on her, she simply turned away, saying, "I'm a mother myself, you know."

While the woman went to fetch the food, Brianna started to stir. He picked her up so she wouldn't roll off the bench. She opened her eyes and immediately broke into tears. Vaughan had learned that babies went from just fine to starving to death in a manner of seconds. He got out the canteen of goat's milk he carried with him. After he'd shown her how it was done, Brianna learned how to drink from it just fine. When he put the canteen to her lips, she quieted and gulped it down. The woman scurried back all smiles, carrying his food. "Little Iachus has woken up, has he?" She sat the food down and took a closer look at Brianna. The smile faded from her face. She stepped back and drew Sulis's star. "The child has green eyes. That ain't natural."

At her words, the inn went silent, and everyone turned to look. One of the rougher looking farmers got to his feet. "Have you brought a demon among us?"

Vaughan's eyes darted around. He realized he'd chosen his table stupidly; he was much too far from an exit. "No, he's just a baby." Brianna looked around with her emerald green eyes.

The farmer jabbed a finger toward him. "There's only two creatures that have green eyes: demons and the king. That is, if the king ain't a demon himself." He pointed a trembling finger at Brianna. "So that thing is either a demon or you've kidnapped the crown princess. Either way, we'll be taking it." All the men in the room stood and formed ranks with the farmer.

Even if they were only farmers, Vaughan was badly outnumbered. Sitting Brianna on the bench, he rose, tore off the skirt and bonnet, and drew his sword. "You'll not lay a hand on her. I'll die before I let you have her."

The rough farmer curled his lip at Vaughan. "A boy pretending to be a woman? I knew there was something funny going on. We're not going to let a demon free among us, are we, boys?" The other men murmured their agreement.

As they spread out to attack, Vaughan panicked. "Yes, she is a demon all right! You leave us alone, or she'll send out more demons to eat your souls!"

Brianna burst into loud wails, and the men turned white. "Holy Sulis, Mother of us all, they're rising out of the seven hells," one of them said, backing away.

Vaughan's mouth dropped open. He hadn't expected his words to work that well. "Skedaddle, or they'll do more than rise."

Several of the men screamed, and they tripped over themselves in their hurry to reach the door. Vaughan blinked at the now empty room. *When did I get so good at lying, or are country folk just stupid?* Vaughan sheathed his sword and picked up Brianna to soothe her, but his hands were still shaking. "It's all right, Little Squirt. I won't let anyone hurt you."

The innkeeper's wife came out of the kitchen, holding a five-pointed star of Sulis carved from wood. "Leave this inn, and take that unholy child with you! The demons may be gone now, but I'll not be waiting for that thing to call them back!"

Vaughan stared at the woman. "What are you talking about? I just made up the demons to get those men to leave her alone."

The star shook in the woman's hands. "Do you think I'm blind? I saw those demons with my own two eyes! Leave now, or those men will come back with more to deal with you both!"

Figuring that was likely to happen, Vaughan gathered up their things and bolted. As he ran to fetch their animals, he hugged Brianna. "I'm glad you're safe, Little Squirt, but what happened in there?"

Brianna just yawned and burrowed against his chest. Vaughan mounted his horse. Leading the pack mule and goat, he left the village quickly. He guessed they'd have to sleep on the hard ground again.

* * *

Samantha couldn't sleep. *Could I have done something else? Should I have?* She decided that maybe if she assured herself that Brigitta would be all right, she'd be able to force the nightmare image of Brigitta lying bleeding in Darhour's arms out of her mind. She pulled her robes around herself and exited the rooms that had been Sheen's just the night before.

Guthrie and Marcan sprang to attention. "Is something the matter, Your Majesty?" Guthrie asked.

She shook her head. "I just can't sleep."

They followed her as she went to the dining hall that had been turned into an infirmary. It was crowded with cots holding the wounded. Both Oriana and Father Leigh had collapsed on cots of their own. A couple of servants milled about, caring for the wounded. They bowed to her, and she instructed them to carry on. In the most easily defensible corner of the hall, she found Brigitta, with Darhour asleep in a chair beside her. *How would I feel if he'd sent Robbie into a situation that had almost killed him?*

She tried to approach quietly, but her guards' noisy armor woke Darhour, his hand going to his sword. When he saw her, he let his hand fall back by his side. He stood and bowed to her. "Your Majesty." His badly scarred features gave her no hint to how he was feeling.

"Please sit," she said. When he complied, she put her hand on his shoulder. "How is she?"

Darhour caressed her arm so tenderly, it almost tore sobs from her own throat. "She hasn't awakened yet, but Oriana assures me she'll recover fully."

Marcan brought her a chair, and she sat beside Darhour. "Can you forgive me for sending her into danger?"

Darhour reached out to touch her but noticing her guards watching, put his hand back on his wife's arm. "There's nothing to forgive. I would have done the same in your position. Any leader worthy of the position would have." When he squeezed Brigitta's arm, his eyes shone with a love that seemed out of place on his stern features. "It was her idea in the first place." He laughed ruefully. "Why has Sulis cursed me with stubborn women?"

Samantha smiled. "A weak woman would never interest you."

Darhour raised an eyebrow at her, then chuckled. "I hadn't thought of it that way, but you're right. I rescued her when I believed her to be a weak victim, but it was her inner steel I fell in love with."

Comforted by finding both Brigitta on the road to recovery and Darhour at peace, Samantha found she had difficulty keeping her eyes open.

"Go back to bed, Your Majesty," Darhour said. "You've done nothing but make the difficult decisions every leader must. Any father would be proud to call you daughter."

Blinking tears out of her eyes, she rose and squeezed his shoulder again. "Thank you, Darhour."

Before she headed back to Sheen's quarters, she made the rounds of the other wounded. When she found any awake, she stopped and offered words of comfort and her gratitude for what they had suffered on her behalf. But seeing the wounded made her think of those who hadn't been so lucky, the ones whose funeral pyres she would light the next day. *How many of them would have lived if Oriana hadn't exhausted herself healing Brigitta?* She stiffened her back. Solar had raised her to make such decisions. She could only do what she thought was best at the moment. It did no one any good to second guess herself.

On her way out, she passed Oriana again. This time the young novice stirred and opened her eyes. Seeing Samantha, she abruptly sat up. "Your Majesty, is it morning already?"

"No, child, you can sleep for some hours yet. I know you have yet to take your vows, but since we have no priestess or priest on hand, at tomorrow's ceremony, I'd like you to lead the blessing of those who have traveled Beyond the Far Mountain."

All the color left Oriana's face and her hand went to her short hair, which had only recently been done in the hundreds of small braids of the priestesshood. "I can't, Your Majesty. I…"

Samantha cursed herself for not recognizing earlier the significance of Oriana's haircut. "That's okay, child. I'll do it myself."

* * *

The next morning Samantha stood in the castle courtyard where those who'd fallen in her service were laid out on funeral pyres. The bodies of those who died fighting for Sheen had been buried in a mass grave; traitors didn't deserve the honor of being sent to the Holy Mother in the flames. The courtyard was packed with the survivors, and Darhour stood at her side. Since Brigitta hadn't yet awakened, she told him his presence wasn't necessary, but he said no commander would fail to honor those who died under his command.

As Samantha was about to give a speech in honor of the fallen, there was a commotion near the gates. The crowd parted, and a man appeared who looked like he'd ridden hard and hadn't slept in a week. He fell at her feet. "Your Majesty, I am Donall, and I serve the Baroness Eithne. She follows behind me. I've ridden ahead at her request with a message. The palace and Murtaghan itself have fallen. The crown princess is a hostage."

Samantha's entire insides screamed, *No! Sulis, not my daughter!* Samantha wanted to dissolve into screams of rage and grief, but the eyes of her army were on her. She had a hard time forcing the words past the panic in her chest. She bid the exhausted man to rise. "We will honor those who have given their lives in my service, and then you will provide a full report."

* * *

Samantha wasn't sure how she made it through the ceremony, and she had few memories of it, but Blaine assured her that she'd acquitted herself as befits a queen. Now she sat in Duke's Sheen's council room with Baron Teague, Duke Devyn, Darhour, and the other officers from her army. Baroness Eithne's messenger told her of the Count Cadarn's coup and its bloody aftermath. When he was finished, she asked, "But the baroness can verify that my daughter was alive and well when she left the palace?"

Donall shook his head. "No, Your Majesty, the count refused to allow her to see the child."

No, Sulis, no! You've taken everything I love! You cannot take my daughter! She hid all her emotions behind a court mask, and when she spoke, she did so with a calm that belied her inner turmoil. "So Murtaghan has fallen, and the crown princess is a prisoner."

Darhour's face was so twisted with rage, she almost scouted away from him. "Since he refused to show her to the baroness, he might not have her. Perhaps her guards were able to get her out of the palace."

Baron Teague said, "Or she could be dead." When Darhour looked at the baron like he wanted to tear out his throat, Teague blanched. "I'm sorry, Your Majesty, but it is possible."

Looking like he was about to dissolve into pieces, Lord Devyn asked the message. "Forgive me, but do you have any news of the Lady Aislinn?"

When Donall reported that he knew nothing of the lady's fate, Samantha dismissed him to get some rest. Teague leaned toward her. "Your Majesty, you will always have my loyalty. We will ride south tomorrow and make the traitor pay for his crimes against you."

With a vein pounded in his temple, Darhour spat, "I won't wait until morning. As soon as we are finished here, I'll head to Murtaghan. Do not worry, Your Majesty. I will find the crown princess and bring her back."

Blinking back tears of gratitude, she turned to Darhour. "If there was another choice, I wouldn't ask this of you."

Darhour gripped his sword hilt so tightly his knuckles turned white. "No one else can do what I can do."

Remembering what Darhour had done to the last man who'd threatened her throne, she said, "We will make Cadarn pay for what he has done, but first you bring my daughter back to me. You are to rescue Brianna and gather information, nothing more. We won't act until my daughter is safe."

Darhour bowed his head. "I won't fail you, Your Majesty."

After they planned to leave tomorrow at first light, she dismissed them. They left her alone with Darhour, and only then did her iron control break and her chin begin to quiver. "It's my baby, Darhour! Sulis couldn't be cruel enough to take her from me, too." Sobs tore from her throat.

Darhour opened his arms, and she fell against his chest. "I have more faith in my own sword than in the Holy Mother. I'll bring her back to you." He held her for far too short a time before releasing her. "I will make one last check on Brigitta, and then I'll be off."

"Thank you," she said, but that thanks felt completely inadequate. The goddess couldn't be trusted, but Darhour wouldn't fail her.

* * *

Before going to bed where she knew she'd get no rest, Samantha went to the makeshift infirmary to check on Brigitta and the other wounded. Oriana and Father Leigh were sitting at a table speaking quietly. Leigh rose and bowed to her. Oriana rushed forward and grabbed her hand. "Your Majesty, I know you're worried about little Brianna, but you don't need to be. Vaughan would never let anything bad happen to her. He'll show up with her any day now."

Samantha paused while she fought back sobs. "I'm sure he will have done everything in his power."

Oriana nodded her head vigorously. "You'll see, he will come with her."

"We can pray to Sulis that he might. How are the wounded?" she asked.

Looking hurt by Samantha's lack of faith in Vaughan, Oriana let Father Leigh answer. "Brigitta is still unconscious, but all her life signs are stable, Your Majesty. The rest are recovering nicely."

"Will they be all right if you two leave them and come with the army in the morning?"

Leigh nodded but avoided meeting her eyes. "Yes, Your Majesty. They can be left in the care of others."

"Then what is wrong?"

Leigh rubbed his hands against his robes, as if they were covered in sweat. "It's nothing to bother Your Majesty with, but I worry for Artan. It was a mistake to leave him behind."

Samantha squeezed the priest's arm, but she could think of no words of comfort. "We all make mistakes."

She made the rounds, speaking to those of the wounded who were awake. At last, she sat beside Brigitta, the woman who had looked past Darhour's scars. She started to thank the goddess for preserving her, but the goddess had taken her daughter. Surely, she wasn't responsible for Brigitta's survival. She touched the woman's shoulder, and Brigitta's eyes sprang open.

Brigitta glanced around as if in a panic and tried to rise. "The battle? What happened?"

Samantha held Brigitta down. "It is won. There's no need to concern yourself. Just rest and get well."

Brigitta collapsed back on the cot. "My Darhour, where is he?"

Samantha stared into nothingness, as she told her mother-in-law of the fall of Murtaghan and what Darhour had done in response. When she was done, she looked down to see tears running down Brigitta's cheeks. Brigitta grabbed her hand. "Oh, you poor thing, I thought I'd never able to bear losing my children. My mother's heart breaks for you." She put her other hand over her chest.

Samantha's mouth fell open. Although she'd known about Brigitta's children, she had always seen her as Darhour's fierce wife, not as a mother. She squeezed the other woman's hand. "I'm sorry we will need to leave you behind to recover. Don't worry. You will be well cared for."

Brigitta wiped at her tears, but her Korthlundian was worse than Samantha had ever heard it when she answered. "Don't worry me. I be fine. My Darhour not fail you. He bring your precious baby back."

Wishing she could have the other woman's faith, Samantha cursed the goddess. *Sulis, if she dies, I'll come Beyond the Far Mountain and bring her back!*

CHAPTER 20

The walls of Cathrach loomed ahead of Vaughan. A sign awhile back had announced the city. Since Brianna had been accused of being a demon baby, he'd avoided people. But now he had to face facts. He had no idea where he was or how to get to the queen. Sure, Cathrach was ahead, but he'd never heard of Cathrach. *Damn me to the seven hells, why didn't I pay more attention in school?*

Food was an even more pressing problem. Beside a handful of dried fruit, they had nothing fit to eat. The king's father had packed all kinds of supplies like dried beans, flour, and oats, and he'd tried cooking some of the beans over the fire last night, but they had turned into a burnt mess even harder than the raw beans were. Maybe he should have cooked them with water. He'd ended up mixing some of the flour with goat's milk. Brianna had eaten it without complaint, but Vaughan had hardly been able to choke it down.

He stopped his horse and looked ahead. "We have no choice, Little Squirt. We're going to have to risk going into the city. If you only had blue eyes like mine, we wouldn't have to worry so much."

Brianna let out a sob. "It's okay, Little Squirt. Your eyes are beautiful. It's just that some people don't understand about green eyes." Brianna stopped sobbing and began bouncing on his back instead. "You understand everything. Don't you, Little Squirt?"

He had an idea. He got down from the horse and picketed the animals. Then he crawled around in the grass and played with her to tire her out. When she stopped laughing and started making cranky tired cries, he tied her on his back and remounted. Before he reached the city gates, he heard her soft snore and prayed she'd sleep long enough for him to finish their business.

As he rode through the city gates, his eyes darted around looking for trouble, but no one paid much attention to them. He bought the supplies first, so he and Brianna wouldn't starve in case he needed to get out of town in a hurry.

Brianna didn't do anything other than snore until he stepped into a shop that advertised "compasses, maps, astrolabes, and other traveler aids." The shopkeeper was waiting on a group of six people who were arguing over whether they really needed a map that cost an entire gold drachma. Wondering if all maps were so expensive, Vaughan gulped. He did have a single drachma among the silver tetras and copper drams the king's father had given him, but he'd hoped to save that for an emergency.

The princess chose that moment to wake up with a cry. He grabbed the baby off his back and held her close to comfort her and so that no one would see her eyes. He drew her into the corner and whispered. "Little Squirt, we can't let people see your eyes are green, so could you pretend to be asleep for a while longer?"

To his intense relief, Brianna closed her eyes. *Praise Sulis!* He stood rocking her until the other group left without the map. The shopkeeper, who had the same vivid auburn hair as the queen, turned to him. "What can I get for you and the little one?" she asked, smiling fondly at Brianna.

"We need—" Vaughan started to say in his fake woman voice, but Brianna's eyes popped open, and she giggled at the shopkeeper. Vaughan cursed silently and prepared to run.

"What an adorable baby," the woman said. "She must be quite the joy to have around."

Vaughan's mouth dropped. The woman hadn't seemed to notice Brianna's eyes, which shone like two bright emeralds out of her face. Brianna reached out to the woman. "Momma! Momma!" she said.

The woman laughed. "The little ones do tend to think every woman is a mother, don't they?" But Vaughan knew Brianna had noticed the woman's hair. The woman reached for the princess. "May I? Just for a moment?"

Vaughan clutched the baby tighter, but Brianna was leaning even harder toward the woman and saying, "Momma," with increasing urgency. She was going to have a fit in a moment.

"Just for a minute. You know how protective we mothers can be." As he released Brianna into the woman's arms, he put his hand on his sword hilt under his skirt just in case.

Brianna squealed and began fingering her face, sticking her fingers in the woman's mouth and up her nose. The woman took hold of Brianna's hand but didn't seem to mind. "What can I get for you?" the woman asked again.

Vaughan told her what he needed. "Do you have something like that?"

The woman nodded and moved toward a shelf on the other side of the room. Vaughan hurried after her, not wanting to let Brianna out of arm's reach. "I believe I do." She took a scroll from the shelf.

Brianna said, "Momma," again. But this time it was more of a question. Then she let out a wail and held out her arms for Vaughan. As Vaughan reached for the princess, the pain in the little girl's voice felt like a hot poker to his gut. He had to get her to the queen.

The woman handed Brianna over. "The little ones do so like their mommas."

Relieved to have her back in his arms, Vaughan held her close. She stopped wailing, but she whimpered against his chest. The woman spread out the map on the counter and pointed at Cathrach on the map. "We're here."

As Vaughan examined the map, he could scarcely prevent himself from letting out a "Yippee" and jumping in the air. The map showed roads twisting throughout the joined kingdoms, including ones leading from Cathrach to Gnos, where the queen was. "How much?"

The woman shook her head sadly. "Quality like this doesn't come cheaply, I'm afraid. I can't let it go for less than eight tetra."

Vaughan scratched his head. That was less than a drachma but not much. He stared at the map trying to memorize the route, but he knew he'd never remember, and he'd probably wander around lost for the rest of his life. "Five tetra?" he asked.

The woman shook her head. "I'll knock the price done a bit on behalf of your little one, but I have children of my own to feed. Seven."

After more bargaining failed to knock the price down any further, Vaughan shifted Brianna around trying to get out his coin purse hidden under his skirt. He'd lived in Murtaghan all his life, so he knew wearing a purse where everyone could see it was just asking to have it stolen. He finally managed to fish out the coins and handed them to the woman.

The woman rolled up the map but didn't hand it immediately over. Instead, she smiled at Brianna, who was still whimpering against his chest. "She has such lovely blue eyes."

"Blue?" Vaughan blurted, and stared at Brianna's emerald eyes.

"Yes, such a lovely shade, just exactly like her momma." She met his eyes, as she handed over the map.

Is she mad? How can she think Brianna's eyes were the same color as mine? Before the woman could come to her senses, Vaughan grabbed the map and hurried out of the store. He stowed the map safely, climbed onto the horse, and grabbed the leads for the pack horse and goat. Brianna let out a sob and looked up at him with tears in her baby eyes. "Momma?"

Vaughan hugged her and kissed her on the top of her head. "Don't worry, Little Squirt. I'll get you to your Momma." He rode for a moment. "Just how did that woman think your eyes were blue?" he asked.

To his shock, Brianna said, "Squirt," and snuggled against his chest, evidently exhausted. As he thought of the woman's mistake and the reaction at the inn, he remembered the king's ability to make people see things differently than they were. He hugged Brianna and whispered, "Holy Sulis, Little Squirt, you can do magic, can't you?" He laughed. He'd known Brianna was bigger and smarter than a normal baby, but magic when she was so little?

* * *

After Darhour had carefully disguised his features, he approached the gates of Murtaghan. The countryside was in such chaos that it had taken him longer to reach the city than he'd liked. Nobles and priests had been slaughtered. Bandits were everywhere, and ordinary people were killing each other over slight disagreements. With the number of dead and the amount of property destroyed, it would take decades to make things right.

But at last he was close to his granddaughter. There were ways into the city under the walls, but they wouldn't allow him to take his horse with him, so he joined a line of people waiting to be allowed through. On the gatepost a flyer was posted. Apparently, the city magistrates were in need of more men. The guards asked a lot of questions, including how much money each person possessed, and demanded to see purses. Based on the contents of the purse, they charged a fee for entrance. They also performed a cursory search. They seemed to be looking mostly for hidden coin, but there was no way his sword would escape notice. He rode toward a copse of trees nearby, dismounted and, pretending a need to relieve himself, entered the copse. He quickly removed his sword and hid it under some leaves. He thought about stowing his knives as well, but there was too big a chance he would need a weapon, so he decided he'd better risk bringing them. He emptied his purse of most coin and concocted a story. Then he left the copse and led his horse back to the line.

When he finally reached the front of the line, the guards looked him up and down and began asking him questions. "Where are you from?"

"Coan." Darhour named a small village on the other side of the Setenta Forest, which hosted an annual horse fair, the fair at which Samantha had met the sorcerer.

"Purpose for visiting the capital?"

Darhour pointed to the flier. "I heard the city magistrates were hiring."

The guards examined him more closely at that news. Darhour guessed they liked what they saw well enough. "They are, but the recruiting office is closed for the night. You'll have to wait until tomorrow."

"I figured as much." He asked for a recommendation of a cheap inn where he could spend the night.

The guard laughed. "No inn in Murtaghan is cheap anymore. You'll have to sleep on the streets in front of the recruitment office." They explained to him how to find it, asked the rest of their questions, and exacted their bribe, which seemed to have been reduced because of his stated interest in joining the magistrates. They didn't even bother to search him as they had the others.

Telling himself that if these men worked for him, they would be immediately fired for incompetence, Darhour led his horse through the gates. *Damn it to the seven hells, I could have brought my sword!*

He rode toward the palace, found a place to leave his horse, and then waited in the shadows near the entrance to the drainage ditch that led under the palace.

* * *

Darhour's heart thudded in his chest as he neared the royal nursery. After entering through the drainage ditches, he'd found the livery of a palace servant in the laundry and grabbed a pile of linens as an excuse for his presence in the corridors. Even for the late hours, they were eerily quiet and empty. In some parts of the palace the torches weren't even lit. Because of his magically enhanced eyesight, this presented no problem, but it was odd.

The corridor near the nursery, though, was brightly lit, and four guards played dice in front of the nursery door. They glanced up as they heard him, but upon seeing the livery, went back to their game. More incompetents he'd fire if he were in charge. Still, he needed to do this quickly. As he approached, he drew two knives and threw them, catching two of the guards in the throat. As the men he hit fell, he palmed a third knife, stabbed a third guard in the back, and drew that man's sword. However, before he could slice the remaining guard's throat, he let out a yell, "Intruder!"

Damn it to the seven hells! He hadn't been quite fast enough. Sure that more company would soon arrive, Darhour quickly killed the guard, retrieved his knives, picked the nursery door's lock, and burst inside. He found only darkness. There had clearly been a fight in the main room. Furniture was broken, and rugs were stained with dried blood. He ran through the nursery, but the place was deserted, a fine coating of dust covering everything. Hearing the clang of armor, Darhour exited the nursery and caught the guard rounding the corner with another knife. He took off running in the opposite direction. Knowing the palace as well as he did, he entered the servants' corridors, which too were bathed in darkness. Because he could see and those pursuing him couldn't, he quickly outdistanced them, found his way to the palace laundry, and back out through the drainage ditch.

He collapsed in the shadows on the banks of the ditch and dug his fingers into the earth. There was only one reason Cadarn could be guarding an empty room. The count wanted to convince someone that the princess was inside, but did that mean that the princess had escaped or…? *No, Sulis, Mother of us all, don't let her be dead. It's all my fault if she's dead.* After all he'd done in his life, he deserved to suffer the goddess's judgment, but Samantha didn't.

* * *

Loud knocking woke Cadarn in the early hours of the morning. Nisse, who lay next to him, groaned, "Would you quiet that?"

One of Cadarn's servants poked his head in the bedroom and informed Cadarn that Captain Gerard was in his reception room, asking to see him. Cadarn stifled a groan, wrapped a robe around himself, and went out to see what the man wanted.

When Cadarn entered his reception room, Gerard was pacing. He stopped abruptly and turned to Cadarn. "We are in serious trouble. The guards outside the princess's nursery have been found dead. It's a complete bloody mess up there. Nearby guards heard the noise, but the intruder escaped them."

"Intruder?" Cadarn questioned. "There were four guards on the nursery."

"I know, but the survivor insists there was only one man. It has to have been Darhour, the queen's pet assassin. Nobody else could have killed so many so quickly."

Cadarn punched his right fist into his other hand. "Make sure the palace is locked up tight. We can't let him escape to tell the queen."

Gerard threw up his hands. "Didn't you hear what I said? The intruder was Darhour. No one knows how he got into the palace to kill Duke Argblutal, either. Either he's already gone, or he's skulking about waiting for an opportunity to take out the Lord Protector. I've put extra guards on you. Not that they'll do any good if he's coming for you."

Cadarn laughed. He hadn't been on the council when Darhour had led the then princess's guard, but people seemed to think him capable of magical powers. "Surely, you exaggerate. Besides, this Darhour went with the queen."

Gerard glared. "You don't understand how dangerous this man is. We are fucked!"

"Really now!" Cadarn raised his eyebrow about Gerard's use of profanity. "You're being hysterical. Give me a moment to dress, and I'll examine the scene."

When Cadarn went back into his bedroom, Nisse was pulling on his trousers. Despite Cadarn's words to Gerard, cold fear set in his belly. "You heard?" he asked.

Nisse nodded. "Yes, it is troubling but not fatal to our plans. As long as the boy doesn't get the princess to the queen, you can insist you are holding her elsewhere."

CHAPTER 21

As Vaughan headed down the mountain pass into Korth, he put one fist into the air and yelled, "Yippee!"

On his back, Brianna took up the cheer. "Yip! Yip! Yip!"

"We'll make it now, Little Squirt. We're are on our way!" With the aid of the map, he'd been able to figure out how far he'd gone in the wrong direction, but now he could see the Toraidhean Highway below, the wide road that led in a nearly straight line from the bottom of the pass to Duke Sheen's estate and the queen.

At the bottom of the pass, he found a stream and some good grass for grazing, so he decided to water the animals and let them rest and feed while he fed Brianna. As he dismounted holding Brianna, she leaned forward and kissed the horse. "Whisk." Vaughan had named the horse Whiskers because it had longer hair around its mouth, making it look almost like it had a beard.

After she kissed the horse, she reached toward the gray mule he'd named Pepper. "Pep." Vaughan carried her to it, and she leaned over and kissed it, too. She then insisted on kissing the goat. Brianna had named the goat Milk.

He tied Brianna to his back with a scarf and led the animals to the stream. When they'd drunk their fill, he picketed them to graze. Then he spread a blanket on the ground and got out bread, cheese, and dried fruit. He set the food on the blanket and then untied Brianna and swung her high in the air. She laughed as she always did when he did that. He sat down on the blanket and set the princess in his lap.

He tore some of the bread and broke some of the cheese into small pieces and put them on the blanket in front of Brianna. He'd learned that she could eat soft things without him chewing them first, and she liked to feed herself.

She was still growing fast, and she was much bigger then when they'd left the palace. She seemed strong, and her cheeks glowed with health. "I'm taking good care of you, aren't I, Little Squirt?"

Brianna giggled, picked up a piece of cheese, and plopped it in her mouth. The queen would have nothing to complain about when they reached her in what couldn't be more than a few days now that he'd entered Korth.

After he ate a piece of bread and cheese himself, he took a mouthful of dried apricots, chewed them, and spit them out in his hand for Brianna. It didn't even seem gross anymore. Sometimes, it seemed like he'd always had a baby to care for. He caressed the auburn fuzz on her head as she ate the apricots out of his hand and thought how happy the queen would be when they showed up.

He'd hand her over…

A completely unexpected pain ripped through his heart. How could he bear not to have her with him all the time? She was *his* little squirt now.

"It's not like we'll never see each other," he assured Brianna. "I can visit you in the nursery every day. It wouldn't be that different, Little Squirt. Really, it won't."

Brianna looked up in alarm, trying to decide if she needed to cry or not. *Sulis curse me. There's no reason to get her all upset.* He smiled and tickled her. She giggled. Reassured, she went back to eating.

* * *

Cadarn sat with Nisse in his reception room, listening to Ruadh's report on the city magistrates. "We have a problem, sir. I discovered a protection racket of sorts among the magistrates. They've been extorting money from shops and businesses. If someone fails to pay, the shop tends to get broken into, smashed apart, or even burned to the ground."

Cadarn's mouth dropped open. "How many are involved?"

Ruadh had difficulty meeting Cadarn's eyes. "I'm just beginning the investigation, but quite a few, it appears, sir."

Before Cadarn could respond further, a woman's scream came from the corridor. He jumped to his feet and ran into the hallway. Two of the Protectorate Guardsmen were tussling with a woman. Her dress was ripped open to the bodice and blood was pouring from her nose. "What in the seven hells is going on out here?" he bellowed.

His guards came to attention. The woman drew her dress together with one hand and covered her nose with the other, blood streaming through her fingers.

One of the guards, Cadarn believed his name was Irven, pointed to the woman. "We found this woman creeping through the deserted part of the palace. She was evidently looking for something to steal."

"So you decided to assault her?" Cadarn said

"No, sir, she assaulted us," the other claimed. A rather significant bruise was forming on the guard's cheek. "We questioned her to determine what business she had in that part of the palace. When she couldn't give satisfactory answers, we tried to arrest her."

"They tried to rape me," the woman choked out through the blood and her broken nose.

As Cadarn's eyes swept over her, taking in her torn dress, he clenched his jaw to stop himself from yelling. He spotted a nearby guard and instructed him to take the woman to the infirmary. When he turned back to the guards, Irven threw up his hands. "Are we supposed to allow intruders to skulk about the palace?"

"Of course not but rape is beneath the forces of the Protectorate Guard." He summoned guards and ordered the first two arrested and taken to the dungeon.

Cadarn stomped back into his quarters, where Nisse and Ruadh still waited. He snapped at Ruadh. "You find all involved in this protection racket, and you arrest them now!" He pointed to the door.

"Yes, sir. I'll do my best, sir."

When Ruadh exited, Cadarn slammed the door behind him. He went to the sideboard, poured himself a whiskey, drank it in a single gulp, and poured himself another. He turned to Nisse. "What have I done wrong? How is it that shops are being burned down by the city magistrates and guards are raping women in the palace corridors?"

"It's not entirely your fault, Liridona. Chaos attracts opportunists who think to use the lack of order to fulfill all of their base desires."

Cadarn growled. "How do I stop them from running amok?"

"To put an end to this, harsh measures are necessary. These two who attacked the woman in the corridor? Castrate them in the city square with as much blood as possible. There's something about seeing another man's balls cut off that reminds other men how much they value their own. Those involved in the protection racket? Cut their hands off. If someone is guilty of assault, beat him to death. When someone—"

"That's barbaric! Not even the queen would sanction such cruelty! Punishments like those would never happen in Svizra."

Nisse shrugged. "Not now they wouldn't. But according to the history books, Dritan and Annagret did much worse. As I told you before, if you want to win this thing, you have to make a deal with demons."

Cadarn whirled away and punched the wall. He would not become known as Cadarn the butcher!

Nisse touched his shoulder, and his voice was gentle. "Liridona, at this point, you have a choice between chaos and tyranny. Freedom can arise from tyranny, but never from chaos."

Cadarn took off down the corridor toward his own rooms. When he reached them, he drew his sword and slashed the portrait of Dritan, then he did the same to Annagret. But it didn't make him feel any better, so he kept slashing at the paintings until he'd reduced them to ribbons. That wasn't enough, either, so he picked up the fire poker and attacked the frames. When he'd reduced them to splinters, he dropped the poker and stood there, breathing heavily.

Nisse watched without saying a word.

When he'd caught his breath, he turned his eyes to Nisse. What choice did he have? Order had to be restored before the queen arrived. "I will have these men castrated and their still beating hearts torn from their chests and cast into the fire before their dying eyes. I will do the same to any of my forces guilty of rape. I will treat similarly any of those under my command who abuse their power."

Nisse nodded in approval.

Bile rose in his throat, as he spat out the words. "You will stop me if I go too far."

* * *

As Samantha passed through Korth, rumors of chaos spreading through Lundia reached her, and peasants flocked to join her army, swelling its size and slowing her progress. Despite that, by the time they camped near Nios Mo, there was still no sign of Darhour with her daughter. *Sulis, if you have let her die, I will never forgive you.*

As she waited for her tent to be set up, Blaine told her that Baroness Eithne had been spotted, and Samantha told him to bring her to report as soon as she arrived. When the baroness arrived, she looked like she'd aged a decade. Her clothes were torn and dirty, and exhaustion lined her face. She was accompanied by a large man whose head was wrapped with a filthy bandage and who leaned on a staff for support.

Seeing the baroness's exhaustion and the man's wounds, Samantha rose and sent Blaine to fetch Oriana or Father Leigh. "Baroness, please sit." She led the baroness to her seat and called for two more. She made sure the injured man was seated and informed them that she had called for a healer to see to them. Then she sat next to the baroness. "What happened?"

The baroness sagged in the chair. "Your Majesty, let me introduce my footman, Eghan. Without him, I would have never made it through. He deserves great honor for his bravery and devotion."

Father Leigh arrived and began examining the injured man.

Samantha nodded toward him. "Then he will receive it."

"Your Majesty, Lundia is in chaos, a chaos that grows worse with each passing day. The clergy are killing or being killed. No noble is safe from his own peasants. The law is ignored, and bandits are everywhere."

Samantha stiffened. "Why would the peasants act this way over Cadarn declaring himself king?"

The baroness shook her head. "He hasn't made himself king. He's abolished the noble class and is calling himself the Lord Protector. He seeks to establish a government similar to that of Svizra, where he went to university." The baroness handed her a torn broadsheet. "Notices like this have been posted everywhere. As the notices go up, the chaos spreads."

Samantha took the broadsheet and read it:

"As of this day, the monarchy is no more, and the noble class has been dissolved. Murtaghan and the rest of the land now belong to the people. A new government has been formed with Cadarn having been blessed by Sulis and the consent of the people to serve as Lord Protector of Korthlundia. Representatives will be chosen by the people to come to Murtaghan and advise the Lord Protector on the desires and needs of the people. More on this will be forthcoming. For now, join with the Lord Protector in overthrowing those that have oppressed us and celebrate the freedom Sulis has given us."

Samantha looked up after reading. The baroness nodded sadly. "The people have taken this as an invitation to violence."

Samantha put a hand on her stomach. "The people are in favor of the monarchy's end?"

The baroness made a noise of disgust. "Some are. Others have merely taken it as an opportunity to redress grievances or profit themselves. Most, however, are afraid. They are holed up in their homes, waiting for Your Majesty to ride south and restore order. Never have your people needed you more."

Samantha told Blaine to summon the members of her council and officers to hear the baroness's report. When they arrived, she had the baroness repeat what she'd told her.

Baron Teague snorted. "I always knew Cadarn was a little off, but this is absurd. What is this Svizran system of government?"

Samantha knew little, but apparently Blaine knew more because he spoke up without being asked. "Milord, they run the government of the country in much the same way as our guild halls run their affairs. Rather than inherited positions of power, all citizens vote on who will be the Lord Protector, and each region elects representatives to advise the Lord Protector. The land of the king's uncle runs much the same way."

Teague looked like he wanted to spit. "Such a system could never work. The ignorant masses don't know where their best interests lie."

"Forgive me, Milord, but the people usually know their interests better than the noble class does, and if the people aren't happy with how they're being led, they can always vote in someone different at the next election. In their system a bad ruler can be replaced without violence."

Samantha remembered how Solar had always taught her that a queen must rule with the people's interests at heart, but history showed how often that didn't happen. The people suffered terribly under a bad ruler, and only violence could rid a nation of a tyrant.

As she went to bed that night, Samantha tried not to think of Darhour traveling through the chaos the baroness described with her infant daughter. She started a prayer to Sulis for their safety but decided the goddess had allowed far too much to happen to trust her with Brianna's safety.

* * *

Just past the Reidhlean plains, Darhour saw dust in the distance that indicated the approach of a large group of people. He'd finally reached his daughter's army, but he didn't know how he'd break the news to her. After his failure to find Brianna in the nursery, he'd entered the palace twice more to make sure she wasn't being kept elsewhere. He spoke with as many of his contacts that he could locate, and while they passed on a variety of rumors about the princess's fate, most believed her to be a captive in the palace. When he could think of no other course of action that would be helpful in locating his granddaughter, he'd left the city. Soon he'd face his daughter with the terrible news.

He arrived at the outskirts of the army as they were setting up camp and was immediately taken through. Samantha awaited him in her tent. He stepped inside. Finding her alone, he enclosed her in an embrace and whispered into her hair, "I'm so sorry, Samantha. Brianna isn't at the palace." He told her what he'd found. "Cadarn wants everyone to believe the princess is safely within the nursery, but there was dust over everything. She hadn't been there in some time." He reported the additional steps he'd taken to locate her. "I could find no news of her."

Samantha shook his arms, clearly struggling not to break. "Tell me the truth, Darhour. Is my daughter dead?"

Darhour shook his head. "I don't know. But if someone did sneak Brianna out of the city, he's left no sign of where he went."

Samantha looked about as if she were trying to pull the pieces of herself back together. "What of Murtaghan?"

Darhour nodded. "It's a nightmare inside those walls." He told her of destruction and death. "Very few nobles in the city are still alive, and there is no telling how many commoners have lost their lives. The clergy are also in disarray. The True Church of Sulis has been given the power of the state to enforce its doctrine. They are burning heretics at the stake."

Samantha looked as if she were struggling not to vomit. "This can't continue. Will we be able to retake the city?"

"While in the end I'm certain we will succeed, it will be bloody. The actions of the common people are an unknown that could make things either better or worse."

"Darhour, do I have any choice?"

Darhour shook his head. "Not unless you can get Cadarn to surrender to you. You cannot surrender to him. He is unfit to rule."

Darhour watched as the regal presence of the queen replaced his daughter. She sent for Baroness Eithne. When the baroness arrived, Samantha asked her to be seated. "Eithne, I hate to ask this of you without giving you more time to rest, but I need you to deliver a message to Count Cadarn. I will send you with a guard sufficient to ensure you have no difficulties getting through."

The baroness's spine straightened, and her eyes cleared. "I'm ready to serve Your Majesty. It is an honor to be needed by my queen."

"Tell him that I and my army will be at the base on Gloine Torr in one week. Order him to meet me there to discuss the terms of his surrender."

CHAPTER 22

With a naked Brianna playing in the dirt beside him, Vaughan crouched in front of the blacksmith shop and counted his few remaining coins. He'd had to toss the rags she'd been wearing because she'd grown so much they bit into her skin, which made her very cranky. Vaughan didn't blame her. Still, if she kept growing at this rate, she'd end up a giant by the time she was five, which didn't make any sense. Both the king and queen were short.

A naked baby wasn't his only problem. The horse had thrown a shoe, and they were almost out of food. He thought he'd make Duke Sheen's estate by this evening, which meant he didn't need much food, but Whiskers needed to be reshoed, and he wasn't going bring the princess back to the queen naked. He surely wouldn't be able to find something princessly in the small town, but he wanted Brianna wearing something halfway decent when they arrived. Vaughan scowled at his skirt. There was no way in the seven hells he was going to show up dressed like a girl, either.

In the beginning, it had seemed like Master Angus had given him so much money. Where had it all gone? It was like it had fallen through a hole in his purse or something, except the purse didn't have any holes. He glanced over at the pack mule. Since they were so close, they could do without most of the supplies she carried, but Brianna wouldn't like leaving the mule behind. Could he make it work with the remaining coins?

A man approached the blacksmith shop, and the blacksmith came out to greet him. "Good morning, Makan."

"Oskar." The man removed his hat and wiped the sweat from this brow. "Weather's sure turned hot."

"My weather's always hot." The blacksmith nodded toward his forge, and the two men shared a laugh.

"Suppose it is. Suppose it is. Well, at least there won't be any rain to make it hard for the queen to cross the mountains back into Lundia, so she can put those bastards to right."

Vaughan went still at the mention of the queen. The blacksmith nodded in agreement. "She should be getting there right about now."

"What?" Vaughan jumped to his feet. "The queen's not in Gnos?"

The blacksmith snorted in disgust. "'Course she's not. Just what kind of queen do you think we have? Our queen is going to hold up and cry while some bastard smashes her throne, kidnaps her child, and turns all of Lundia into a bandit free-for-all?"

Vaughan stared at him aghast. If the queen was heading back to Murtaghan, it could be at least a week before he caught up with her.

Misinterpreting Vaughan's expression, Makan put his hands on his hips. "Now listen hear, Miss. Don't you go judging our queen because she's not acting like a lady! What Sulis cursed good would a lady do on the throne? No, sirree, King Solar raised his daughter right. She'll show those bastards who are trying to say Sulis is a man the what-for and the when-for, she will."

Vaughan turned his back on the men, crouched back down, and slammed his fist in the dirt. *You Sulis cursed fool! You're an idiot from the seven hells for thinking the queen would just stay put and let you come to her.* Vaughan called himself a litany of bad names. Well, he had no choice now. He'd have to sell the mule and make do with the supplies the horse could carry.

He glanced over at Brianna. She wasn't going to like it.

* * *

After putting the supplies he saved into Whisker's saddlebags, Vaughan secured Brianna to his back, mounted the horse, and took Milk's lead rope. Reshoeing Whiskers had cost far more than he'd anticipated, and he hadn't been able to get much from the sale of Pepper, but he had been able to get clothes for the two of them and what he thought would be enough food to last until they caught up with the queen. As soon as he started moving, Brianna twisted around on his back and let out a cry, "Pepper!"

Vaughan hoped if he didn't say anything, the crown princess would soon forget about the mule. But she began frantically wailing and twisting about on his back as if trying to get back to the mule.

In a moment of horror, he felt the baby slip. He dropped the reins and twisted, catching Brianna just before she went plummeting to the ground. He hugged her to him as she continued to wail as if her world were coming to an end.

"I'm sorry, Little Squirt, but we had to sell Pepper to get to Momma."

"Momma!" Brianna paused in her crying and looked around. When she didn't see the queen, her wails became louder than ever.

* * *

Cadarn scowled at his breakfast plate while Nisse sat across from him, eating noisily. Nothing seemed to interfere with his friend's appetite. The fragments of the frames that had once held the pictures of his heroes still clung to the wall.

Nisse picked up a piece of fruit. "It's working, Liridona, as I told you it would."

Although order had been restored to the capital, Cadarn took little comfort in it. In addition to the tyranny he himself had imposed, Father Eadoin had turned the basement of The Temple of the Father's Love into a prison of sorts and crammed it full of "heretics." Even so, Cadarn's success was limited. "The country outside the capital is still in chaos, and my men still haven't found the crown princess. The deadline I gave for the queen for surrender is in two days, and we've heard no word from her. What if she calls my bluff?"

Nisse shrugged off the carnage in the countryside. "You're sure she doesn't have the baby herself?"

Cadarn nodded. "I've had the routes to her well watched. My men will prevent the princess reaching the queen."

"Then you have options. You'll find an orphan baby and cut off a limb or something. Let the queen know you're serious. All babies look alike, after all."

Cadarn put down his roll and pushed his plate away. "I couldn't do that. You said I had options."

Nisse raised an eyebrow. "You could issue empty threats about killing a baby you don't have and let them eat you alive."

Not knowing how to answer, Cadarn got up from his chair and went to the window. He stood there shaking his head. He'd authorized horrible things, butchery that made him ill to think of it. Those deaths had to mean something. But dismembering a baby? *Holy Sulis, that's evil.*

Captain Gerard knocked and entered. "Baroness Eithne has returned, escorted by a contingent of the Royal Guard. We made the soldiers wait outside the city, but the baroness will arrive at the palace shortly."

A smile began to spread over his face, and Nisse joined him at the window. "You think she comes to offer the queen's surrender?"

Cadarn dug his fingernails into the window frame and breathed out, "Sulis bless that she is."

* * *

Before he received the queen's messenger, Cadarn had his chair moved onto the dais in the throne room and had all the other chairs removed from the room. He had Nisse stand beside him.

The baroness made her way across the throne room with her head held high. When she reached the dais, she nodded slightly. "I bring a message from the queen. She will arrive in two days' time and commands you meet her at the base of Gloine Torr to parley. She guarantees your safety."

Even with the dais, she almost met his eyes. Why had he chosen a messenger so Sulis-cursed tall? He did his best to look at her as if she were no more significant than the dust on his feet. "I think not. Tell her I will accept her surrender in the city square."

The baroness lifted an eyebrow. "The queen has no intention of surrendering, and the only way she'll enter the city is with her army at her back. This, she is more than capable of doing. But the queen loves her people and would regret such an unnecessary loss of life. If you fail to appear, the next you will see of her will be the point of her sword." She turned and walked toward the door.

Cadarn was so taken aback by the queen's boldness that he gaped after Eithne for a stupidly long moment. He finally had the presence of mind to shout, "I didn't dismiss you." Two of his guards stepped into the baroness's path. When she turned toward him, he stood. "You may tell the queen that if she fails to arrive at the city square as ordered, I will execute her daughter in her place."

"You can't execute someone you don't have." She turned her back on him and waited for the guards to move out of her way.

"The queen will regret this rash move."

The baroness didn't respond, and eventually he waved the guards out of her path.

* * *

Only moments after Cadarn and Nisse retired to a private room to discuss the queen's demands, Father Eadoin was announced. Not wanting to deal with the high priest, Cadarn sighed and looked to Nisse. But Nisse nodded, so Cadarn told the page to allow the high priest in.

When Father Eadoin entered with an underling, Cadarn gestured toward an empty seat. Eadoin didn't move, and his underling cleared his throat. "His Holiness, the Mouth of the God, and High Priest of the Mighty Sulis, Father Eadoin. You will rise in his presence."

Cadarn's jaw dropped, and he stuttered, "We will not! Just who do you think you're speaking to, Father? I am the Lord Protector of Korthlundia and rise for no one."

Eadoin's eyes narrowed, but it was the underling who spoke. "Sulis's servant outranks any worldly authority. All must rise in the presence of the Mouth of God!"

Before Cadarn could respond further, Nisse stood and drew his sword. "We don't have time for your silly games, priest. Either sit"— he waved his sword toward the empty seat—"or leave"—he waved it toward the door.

The underling looked at the sword aghast. "You dare draw steel on Sulis's representative on earth? We will leave, and you shall rot in the seven hells." He turned toward the door.

Eadoin put up a hand and spoke for the first time. "They will pay for the insolence when the time is right. But for now, we must discuss the queen's messenger." He sat. Cadarn wasn't surprised the priest knew of the baroness's arrival. He was certain Eadoin had spies everywhere. After Nisse sheathed his sword and retook his seat, Eadoin continued, "When will the queen arrive for her execution?"

Cadarn wanted to refuse to answer, but without the crown princess, he couldn't afford to alienate him yet. "The queen has refused to surrender and requests a parley at the base of Gloine Torr."

Eadoin made a noise in his throat. "A bastard and a heretic can have no true mother's love. I will preside over the sacrifice of the demon child on the morrow." He rose as if to leave.

Cadarn clenched his fists. "We can't kill the crown princess."

"We both can and will. The queen's offspring is an abomination. Sulis demands that the land be cleansed of its presence."

"If Sulis demands it, he had better find the princess. I lied when I said she'd been recaptured. We don't know where she is, and we can't kill what we don't have."

The high priest stood. "Sulis is displeased with your folly, but I will make sure Sulis still brings us victory."

CHAPTER 23

Vaughan gaped at the mayor of Nios Mo. "You have to be joking!"

"Why would I joke about such a thing? The queen has gone to put an end to that traitorous fool. She's probably camping at the base of Gloine Torr as we speak."

"Camping at Gloine Torr?"

"Torr! Torr!" Brianna added, not helping anything.

The mayor chuckled. "What a precocious thing! Mimicking language so young!"

Vaughan muttered foul words under his breath. His stomach rumbled. They had run out of money and had few supplies left. Vaughan had been giving most of the food to Brianna. He laughed hollowly. He'd spent weeks chasing after the queen, traveled further and farther than he'd ever thought he would in a lifetime, only to learn the queen was right back where he started. Sulis had one hell of a sense of humor. If the queen wasn't at Gloine Torr when he got there, maybe he'd just give up looking for her and become a farmer or something.

* * *

As the sun set, Samantha's army spread out across the plain at the base of Gloine Torr. The queen stared at the city walls. A battle to retake the city would cost hundreds if not thousands of lives. She'd sent Darhour ahead of the slow-moving army to scout the city. He was to rejoin them when darkness had fallen. But there was still no word on Brianna.

When the army was settled, Samantha stared in the direction of the Far Mountain. *What does the goddess expect from me? Why has she deserted me?* Abruptly, Samantha decided it was high time to ask the goddess herself, and she would do so at the goddess's holiest shrine: on top of Gloine Torr. Surrounded by her personal guard, Samantha began the long trek up the hundreds of steps.

Samantha had only visited the shrine once before, when she'd been confined there by the king during a bout of madness caused by Father Shylah's blood magic. That was the time when Robbie, on his magical horses, had managed to climb the steep sides of the pyramid shaped monument to become her consort. The goddess had sent Robbie those holy horses, but somehow the goddess had changed. Sulis had sent Samantha only heartache and chaos.

Samantha's legs and lungs burned as she neared the top. Bearach and Conroy led the group. As they reached the top, Bearach gasped and spoke to someone Samantha couldn't see. "Holy Sulis, Milady, what happened to you?"

A voice answered that Samantha had heard before. "You are welcome, but this is a holy place and your weapons are not. Leave them here."

Shocked that Bearach and Conroy began to remove their swords without consulting her, Samantha topped the rise. Facing her men was the same priestess who had spoken to her on the island in what now seemed like another lifetime. When doubts had assailed her about her right to the throne, the woman who stood before her now had assured her that she was the goddess's choice. Although it was undoubtedly the same woman, she appeared to have aged fifty years. Her hair that had been blond streaked with gray was now as white as snow. Her smooth face was now pitted with deep lines and wrinkles. Her sparkling white robes were dull and tattered. Only her eyes were unchanged. It still seemed as if all the ages of the earth looked through them and her voice was still strong and clear. "Welcome, my daughter, I have been awaiting your arrival."

Samantha had once suspected this priestess was the goddess herself. Now she was certain of it. She fell to her knees. "Sulis, Mother of us all, your children suffer and die. Why have you abandoned us?"

The goddess's eyes fell. "My child, I have not abandoned my children. They have abandoned me. Please rise and come into my temple, and I will give you what guidance I can still offer." She stretched out her hand to take Samantha's, and Samantha felt a jolt of power that sang of pure unconditional love. But the power paled in comparison to that she'd felt when the goddess had touched her on the island. That touch had rendered Samantha unconscious.

As Samantha rose and followed the goddess, she heard her guards whispering behind her and the clank as their weapons hit the ground. Entering the goddess's shrine, Samantha removed her shoes as she had that long-ago day on the island. Sulis knelt at the altar, and Samantha knelt beside her. Behind her, her men entered and went down on their knees. The goddess was quiet for a moment, as if in meditation. When she spoke, her voice sounded tired. "My child, you charge me with neglect, but it is not so. Do you know where we goddesses and gods derive our power?"

As shocked as Samantha was to hear the goddess talk of multiple divine beings, she was even more shocked by the question. "I don't understand, Holy Mother. Does not your power come from yourself?"

Sulis shook her head. "No, my daughter, we grow strong on the prayers of our true worshipers. As Lundia's church wandered from the path I had revealed, I have been growing slowly weaker for decades. The recent schism in the church and the insistence that I am a man aged me even more rapidly. But the age and the weakness you see in me this day was completed by the death of my priesthood. Their sacrifices in fighting the Soul Stone dealt me a devastating blow. I had little power left to aid your consort in the destruction of the Ancient Evil. Now I can barely manifest myself outside of this shrine, the heart of my power." The goddess turned sad eyes toward Samantha. "Pure evil now corrupts the temples in my capital. False worshipers fill them, and my true children are frightened into silence. If you do not bring my people back to me, I fear I will soon fade away completely, becoming nothing more than a shadow."

Samantha had difficulty breathing. "But I too lost faith. I blamed you. I…"

Sulis smoothed Samantha's hair and again she felt the goddess's love. "My child, you have served my people well, and I harbor nothing but love for you. A mother can understand her children's doubts."

Samantha trembled as a horrible thought hit her. "Holy Mother, if worship gives a deity power, are the false worshipers giving power to another?"

Sulis shook her head. "As yet, they are not. The god they worship does not yet exist to receive their homage, but some shadows of faded gods have begun to sniff this unclaimed power. If it grows much stronger, one of the evil gods of times long past will awaken and claim it, becoming the one they worship. I shudder to think of my children under the power of such a god. It isn't fair to ask anything of you, but this time the mother needs her child. There is little time to waste. The false priest plots a great evil that may sever me from my children forever and lead to the ascendance of my rival. I feel sick with fear of what will happen to my people if this happens. Bring my children back to me, Samantha."

With those words, the goddess faded from her sight. As tears streamed down Samantha's cheeks, she realized she had failed to ask the goddess about Brianna. A hole tore in her insides; as much as it pained her, her own child couldn't matter. No matter how much it cost her, she had to save her people and the goddess herself. She rose to her feet and turned to find her men looking at her with fear and awe. "You have heard the Holy Mother speak. See that her words spread among the army below. Tomorrow, we fight not merely for ourselves, but for Sulis."

* * *

When Samantha returned to the base of Gloine Torr, she gathered the nobles and her officers into her tent to relate her encounter with the goddess. Darhour, who had returned from his mission, joined them. After she finished, everyone stared at her with wide eyes, and silence filled the tent so thick she could almost touch it.

At last Baroness Eithne drew the star of Sulis. "We will fail neither Your Majesty nor our goddess, even it costs us everything."

Darhour caressed his facial scars. "The baroness is right, but the cost will indeed be high. I have found a way for a force to sneak into the city before sunrise to open the gates for us, and there are many within the city who will likely rise up in Your Majesty's support. But Cadarn's forces are more numerous than they had been when I was last in the city, and discipline has improved markedly. We already knew Cadarn's mercenary army numbered close to five hundred, and that as many as thirty members of the Royal Guard had betrayed our queen to join forces with him. But now many of the lower sort have joined the count's forces. They aren't well trained or armed, and likely won't be reliable if it looks like the tide is turning against them. But they are a significant number. But worst of all is the huge number who have joined the True Church of Sulis. They are fanatics and number in the hundreds, if not a thousand. They will fight to the last drop of blood."

Samantha put a hand over her heart. "It is the high priest, not Cadarn, who will rule if we fail, isn't it?"

Darhour nodded. "Yes, Cadarn won't be able to pay the mercenaries forever, and without them, there will be nothing to stop Father Eadoin from taking the throne."

To Samantha's shock, Devyn stood and, with a shaking hand, rolled up his sleeve and drew a small dagger. His voice was steady as he spoke. "This isn't a fight we can lose. Victory must be had even if we all lose our lives in the attempt. I, for one, swear to the goddess and my mother's grave that I, Devyn, Duke of Gnos, will fight until all the blood is drained from my veins to restore our great queen Samantha I to her throne and Sulis to her proper place in our hearts. I will seal this oath with my blood." He made a quick slash on his forearm and held out the blood tinged dagger. "Who will join me?"

Samantha's heart beat faster as everyone assembled rose. Eithne took the dagger. "We all will." She repeated Devyn's words and cut her forearm.

The dagger made its way around the table, and without any apparent hesitation, all gathered did likewise. At last, the dagger reached Samantha. She repeated the oath, rolled up her sleeve, and cut her arm. She placed her bleeding arm in the middle of the table, and all present laid their arms over hers. She felt a jolt of power nearly equal to that she'd felt the first time the goddess touched her, as all gathered spoke in chorus, "With our blood we seal this oath."

* * *

In the early morning light, Samantha, clad in her armor, stood on the stairs of Gloine Torr. After the meeting in her tent, Darhour had sent men into the city to open the gates for them. Now she needed to make sure her army understood what was at stake: that the cause they would fight and perhaps die for was worth the sacrifice. While it was impossible for her voice to reach everyone, she pitched it as loudly as possible to make sure most would hear her and spread her words.

"My people, I speak to you today not of myself or my throne. These things pale compared to the evil that threatens us. You have all heard how the goddess herself met me on the top of Gloine Torr. I had lost faith in Sulis and blamed her for deserting me and my people in our time of need, but the truth is far more horrible. We have deserted her. Without our prayers and our worship, the Holy Mother has grown weak and has begun to fade, and another god, one who will revel in the blood of this people, threatens to take her place. To prevent this, we must retake Murtaghan today and restore Sulis to her proper place in our hearts and our prayers. I will attempt to obtain Count Cadarn's surrender, but if he proves obstinate, we must be prepared for an immediate assault on the city. Some of you will travel Beyond the Far Mountain today, but the Holy Mother will welcome you in her arms because by giving your lives, you will have served the goddess well and saved this people from a terrible evil. Prepare your weapons and armor, and ready yourself to ride to Murtaghan at a moment's notice. Know that today, you don't fight merely for your queen, but for Sulis herself!" To the roars of the army below her, Samantha raised a gauntleted fist into the air.

Brimming with power such as she'd never felt, the queen descended the steps, and with Darhour beside her, she approached the awning that had been set up for her meeting with Cadarn. Despite what he had done, his aura had told her that at heart he wasn't a bad man, so maybe the bloodshed she feared could be avoided.

As she neared the awning, Cadarn approached from the opposite direction. He had brought fifty soldiers with him from the city, but like her, he approached with only one man, a foreigner. They reached the tent at the same time. She inclined her head slightly. "Cadarn."

Cadarn returned the gesture. "Let us stop this farce! I have left word that if I don't give the signal of your surrender within the hour, the crown princess will be skewered on a pike and hanged from the city wall."

Samantha sat in the chair. "There is more at stake than my daughter's life. Besides, you don't have her." Her whole body tensed, waiting for his answer and praying her daughter was indeed not in his hands.

Laughing easily, he sat across her. "I know the person you sent didn't find her in the palace nursery, but do you really think I'd leave her where she could so easily be found? I assure you I patted her bald head only moments ago. You are a mother before you are a queen. You won't risk her life."

She called forth his aura. The bright orange and yellow that had dominated it had dulled in color, and the jagged black lines had widened and grown in number. He'd committed horrible deeds that haunted him, but a flash of purple also announced he was lying about Brianna. *He doesn't have her. Where is my baby?* Knowing what was at stake, Samantha shoved her love for Brianna into the hole in her heart. "We have no time to waste on this game. I am an aurora. Your aura announces your lies. You don't have my daughter."

Cadarn gaped and blinked. He looked at the foreigner with him, who nodded. A look of resolve crossed Cadarn's face, and he leaned forward. "I had hoped to avoid bloodshed, but this people have been in chains long enough. While I still breathe, you and what remains of the nobility will never usurp their freedom. Victory has cost too much to let it slip through my hands now."

His aura went mad with activity. She wasn't certain what it all meant, but she could see some justice to his beliefs. "I do not argue that the nobility are sometimes corrupt and act in a manner that is detrimental to the common good. Compromises less than ideal have been made to avoid war. But I and my father before me have always ruled with the people's best interests at heart. As my father taught me, it is always the common people who suffer most when those at the top fight for power. You have destabilized the joined kingdoms, and how many have died as a result? A few, you may say, were guilty and deserved their deaths, but most were innocent commoners just trying to live out their lives. You have also let an evil flourish at the core of the realm that is a threat to the goddess herself. This so-called True Church of Sulis attacks the very heart of our people and spreads evil among them. Father Eadoin has burned those he calls heretics. How can you call that freedom? You aren't a bad man. How can your conscience live with this barbarism?"

A shadow crossed Cadarn's face, and his aura flashed red as with anger. "What is truly barbarous is a system that judges a person's worth by the blood in their veins rather than their actions and character. I will not allow the chains of monarchy to hold this people down again, but once you surrender or are defeated, I will deal with the priest's excesses."

Samantha leaned toward him. "You aren't strong enough to control Eadoin and never will be. If I did as you asked, Father Eadoin would soon rule this people, and their chains would become far stronger than any you hoped to break. You have wrought devastation with your folly. In some ways, Svizra's system of government may be superior to our own. With the death of so many of the nobility, we may be able to implement some of your designs for this people. If you surrender now, I will allow you to keep your life and perhaps advise me from your dungeon cell, but the True Church of Sulis must be destroyed, and Father Eadoin must be made to answer for his crimes against this people and against the goddess herself."

Cadarn stood. "He will answer, but not to you. If you refuse to surrender, we have nothing more to say to each other." Followed by the foreigner, he stalked back to his horse.

As Cadarn and his men rode back toward the city walls, an eerie calm stole over Samantha. She glanced at Darhour. "Ready the army. We take back our city."

* * *

As soon as the city gates closed behind them, Cadarn turned to Nisse. "Her army is bigger than we anticipated, and she will attack. Will we win?"

Nisse shrugged one shoulder. "The city walls negate a lot of her power. Backed by the Protectorate Guard and the city magistrates, we should be able to hold them. As long as the gates remain unbreeched, we'll be fine."

He and Nisse climbed the stairs to the top of wall where Captain Gerard awaited them. As Cadarn surveyed the number of archers waiting to pepper the queen's army, as well as the boulders and boiling pitch they would employ against anyone who tried to breach the gates, he pasted on a smile. *Nisse knows how to protect a city! We will win! This people must be free!*

Attempting to calm his rapidly beating heart, Cadarn joined Nisse at the front of the battlement. As they watched the queen's army preparing to attack, Nisse rubbed the back of his neck. Then a smile spread over Nisse's face, and he let a sudden high-pitched laugh that emptied out Cadarn's insides. "What's wrong?" Cadarn asked.

Still smiling, Nisse shook his head. "Your queen is more clever than I gave her credit for, but not as clever as she thinks. She's given away her secret. Look at that army! She is preparing no siege engines, no catapults, no battering rams. This is an army that expects the gates to be open when they get here. I would bet my life she has a force inside the city already, just waiting to seize the gatehouse and open the gates."

Thinking of how easily the queen's man had sneaked in and out of the palace, Cadarn's eyes widened. "Then we have to protect the gatehouse."

Chuckling, Nisse nodded. "That we do. But if I withdraw men from the walls to do so, there wouldn't be enough to protect them, in case she is truly clever and has another trick up her sleeves. She may be trying to fool us into emptying the walls."

Cadarn shook his head. "You worry too much. The queen has never commanded an army. Surely she can't have out-thought you."

Nisse smiled down at the army like a master admiring the work of a precocious apprentice. "Your queen? No. She is little more than a girl. But the man that accompanied her to the parley, the one you call Darhour. I met his eyes as you spoke with the queen. That man is both deadly and very, very clever. We need more men. It's time for your priest to do his part. Even if his zealots have little skill, they should be able to hold off an attack on the gatehouse long enough for us to join them. The queen's force inside the walls can't be that large, or it wouldn't have been able to hide itself."

"Yes, of course." Cadarn released the tension from his shoulders and sent a message to Father Eadoin to gather as many of his followers as he could and send them to protect the gatehouse.

The Temple of the Father's Love was in the middle of city, and Cadarn fidgeted while awaiting his messenger's return. *Sulis, I've come so far. Holy Mother, give me victory. Free your people from bondage.*

The messenger returned more quickly than he'd anticipated. Out of breath, he had to pant for a moment before he could speak. "Sir, the high priest refused. He said all of Sulis's pure children must gather round the temple square to ensure the ritual isn't interrupted. He said after the ritual is completed, Sulis will protect the city." The messenger put a hand to his stomach. "Sir, he's emptying out his dungeon and tying people to stakes. Close to a hundred of them, I think. Some of them are children."

Cadarn's chest tightened, but before he could respond, a priest joined them on the city wall. "His Holiness instructs all to gather round the temple square. It is Sulis's will."

Spittle flying with every word, Cadarn jabbed a finger at the priest. "You remind Father Eadoin who's in charge and tell him to get men here now."

But the priest ignored Cadarn and looked at Gerard. "You disappoint His Holiness and Sulis by keeping the secret of the abomination's escape. Will you continue to defy god now?"

Gerard bowed humbly. "I will not. We will come at once."

As Cadarn turned to Gerard, his vision narrowed. "We will not. You answer to me, not this priest."

Gerard drew Sulis's star. "I only answer to Sulis. I have never served you, only the god. I forswore myself because I didn't want to admit to the mouth of Sulis that I allowed the princess to escape, but I will not defy the god again. Who do you think has brought us this far? Your mercenary friend?" He gestured contemptuously at Nisse. "Sulis will grant us victory today."

As Gerard started for the stairs, Cadarn grabbed his arm. "Don't be a fool. If the queen gets the gates open, we could lose everything."

Gerard's lips curled, and his eyes went cold. "You have already lost. I'm not alone in placing God's will above man's will." He gestured to the walls. Men were trickling off and heading in the direction of the temple. "Father Eadoin has called, and Sulis's true children answer his call. His Holiness speaks for Sulis, and he will rule."

"No, he will not! Eadoin is mad." Without thinking, Cadarn drew his sword and shoved it through the captain's throat. Gerard's eyes widened as he gurgled out his last breath.

Holding his bloody sword, Cadarn whirled on the priest who'd brought the message. But Nisse grabbed his arm. "Liridona, killing this man won't change anything."

Cadarn dropped his sword arm and backed away. As the priest fled, he said, "His Holiness will hear of this. He will not be pleased."

Cadarn watched as his forces guarding the walls became sparse. Nisse lay a warm hand on his shoulder, shocking him out of his stupor. Cadarn met his friend's eyes. "The queen was right, wasn't she? If we win today, freedom loses. Eadoin will unleash a reign of terror, and I won't be able to stop him."

Nisse caressed his arm and spoke in the soft voice of a lover. "Ah, Liridona, my friend, I'm so sorry. It was a bold vision. I love you as I will never love another, but I can't ask my men to give their lives in a lost cause." He drew his sword, held it high in the air, and whirled it in a circle four times. As the signal spread, the walls began to empty. "I told you few things go as planned, and knowing this, I arranged to have ships standing ready to see my men safely out of the country in case things went badly. Come with me, Liridona. I could use a commander I can trust."

Cadarn could only stare at the man who'd planned for their defeat as fully than he'd planned for their victory. He released the bloody sword he was still holding and allowed it to fall to the battlement.

Nisse looked desperately between Cadarn and his men fleeing toward the harbor. "I'm sorry, my love. Your gods, be with you." Nisse drew him close and kissed him in the center of the forehead. Then the friend of his heart deserted him, leaving him alone on the city wall. For decades he'd planned for victory. He'd never planned for defeat.

* * *

As Darhour prepared what he called a turtle, men with shields over their head to protect them from the archers on the wall, to precede the main army, Samantha watched those very archers disappearing from view.

"Darhour," she called, pointing to the wall. "What is happening?"

Darhour shook his head. But the gates of the city swung open, and the men Darhour had sneaked inside for this purpose appeared. "Wait here, Your Majesty. It could be a trap." He rode forward with the bulk of her army following. She remained behind with her personal guards.

After speaking to the men at the gate, Darhour dispatched a rider to her. He reported, "Your Majesty, Cadarn's mercenaries are fleeing to the harbor, but a large force has gathered around the Temple of the Mother's Love. We ride to confront it. The captain says for Your Majesty to wait here until he determines it's safe." The man spurred his horse back to the body of the army.

Watching her army ride into the city unopposed, Samantha whispered, "Sulis, what is happening? You said you need me to save you."

She touched her heels to Roberta's sides and rode slowly forward. As she did so, colors rose from the center of the city—an aura that was a violent mixture of the darkest black and deepest crimson swirled through the air above the Temple of the Mother's Love. Nausea cramped her stomach, and terror clawed at her heart. "Holy Sulis, Mother of us all, what is that?"

Her guards stared at her blankly, and the goddess provided no answer. Knowing whatever was happening had to be stopped, she spurred Roberta into a gallop. "Your Majesty, no!" Conroy called. She ignored him, but they soon surrounded her.

By the time she caught up with the main body of her army, they were involved in a pitched battle against mostly crudely armed peasants who blocked the way to the Temple. No match for the Royal Guard, they fell by the dozens. But they were numerous, and their bodies slowed her men's progress toward the square almost as effectively as they had when they still breathed. Seeing the colors rise even higher above her city, Samantha spurred her own horse into the fray.

Her guards fought beside her, and her sword became wet with blood. Time slowed as she slashed about her, trying to fight her way into the temple square. The aura over the temple continued to grow, forming a bubble that seemed to be pressing against an invisible force restraining it. Somehow, Samantha knew that if the bubble burst, they'd be too late.

Seeing Darhour before her, she screamed, "For Sulis!" Ignoring the blood splattering her armor, she pressed forward until she and her father fought side by side. She didn't know how many lives she took as she battled to save both her goddess and her people. But the ground became slick with the blood of the fallen.

Smoke rose over the square, and she caught the scent of roasting flesh. The aura continued to grow.

After an eternity, or a second, the last resistance fell beneath her sword and those of her men, and with Darhour beside her, she burst into the temple square.

Her mind almost refused to process the horror. Nearly a hundred people were tied to stakes, and fire consumed their flesh. Although they seemed already to be dead, that did little to lessen the horror. In the midst of them, Father Eadoin stood over a cauldron. His hands were raised in the direction of the Far Mountain as he prayed. The aura she'd seen arose not from the temple as she'd thought but from the priest himself. He couldn't be allowed to finish his prayer. She whirled toward Darhour. "Stop this! Kill him now!"

Without hesitation, Darhour spurred his horse toward the priest, and worshipers fell beneath his onslaught. When he reached the cauldron, he slammed his horse into it. As the cauldron's contents spilled onto the cobblestones, Darhour vaulted from his horse and plunged his sword straight into the priest's heart.

The entire world seemed to explode. Darhour flew across the square, and then a shockwave hit her, her body flew into the putrid air, and everything went dark.

* * *

Riding toward the Temple of the Mother's Love beside Father Leigh, Oriana put a hand on the headband Vaughan had given her and traced one of its stars. The Holy Mother was in danger. How much had her failure to return to Balley Beg contributed to the goddess's deterioration? The air in front of her seemed to grow thick with evil. It felt as if she were pressing against an invisible force trying to hold her back. Then an explosion erupted from across the city. Waves of evil washed over her, so strong that she barely clung to her horse. When the waves had passed, she looked toward Father Leigh.

He'd gone white. "Holy Sulis, Mother of us!" He traced Sulis's star before him, and they rode toward the source of the explosion. Bloody corpses filled the street, making their passage difficult, but at last they reached the temple square. The first thing they saw was the queen unconscious on the ground amid a host of others in similar condition. Both she and Father Leigh vaulted from their horses and ran to her. Father Leigh reached her first. As soon as he touched her, she groaned and began to stir.

As the queen opened her eyes, others began to stir and waken. Father Leigh leaned over her, searching for injuries. "Thank the goddess, you're alive. Your Majesty, what happened?"

The queen sat up abruptly, her eyes darting about the square. Then she smiled. "It's all right. We were in time." She caught sight of

Darhour, who unlike the others hadn't begun to move. "Father," she whispered.

Responding to the queen, Father Leigh hurried toward the fallen man. From this distance, Oriana could merely tell that he was still alive. "He lives," she assured the queen.

Father Leigh touched the scarred man and closed his eyes. After a moment, he opened his eyes and gestured to Oriana. "Oriana, I need your help to save him. Quick."

She ran over and placed her hands beside Father Leigh's. Darhour's insides had been shattered, and he was bleeding internally. She joined her power to Father Leigh's and together they closed the leaking vessels.

* * *

His head bursting with pain, Devyn rose from where he'd fallen. He staggered as exhaustion sapped all strength from his muscles. The last thing he remembered was the thunder of hoof beats as they approached the temple square. But the blood on his sword and splattered on his armor told him that in this moment of crisis, he hadn't failed as he'd always believed he would. He'd comported himself as the duke he'd become.

The sight of the temple square was more horrifying than anything he'd experienced in his worst nightmare, even more than his brother's severed head. Blood, charred bodies, smoke! Maybe if he didn't look at it too closely, it wouldn't be forever burned in his memory. He saw the queen, giving orders for the care of the wounded and for the arrest of those of their enemy who'd survived. He stumbled toward her.

"Devyn! Devyn!" he heard the scream behind him and turned to see Aislinn dressed in leather and holding a long pole that had been sharpened into a makeshift spear. Her hair was matted to her head, and her face dirty and blood stained, but she was alive. Her maid Zinerva was beside her, similarly clad and armed.

"Aislinn!" he cried. She ran to greet him. With tears streaming down his cheeks, he threw his arms around her and held her. "Aislinn! You're alive! I was certain I'd never see you again!" He stepped back and felt her to make sure she was real, taking in the bloodstained spear she'd dropped at her feet. "How did you survive? How are you here like this?"

Aislinn laughed through her tears. "Zinerva saved my life. I've been hiding among the palace servants, and we've all been preparing to help the queen when she arrived."

Devyn gave out a yelp of pure joy and twirled her in a circle. Then exhaustion hit him, and he stumbled. As he held her tight, he realized nothing was stopping him now. He released her and went down on one knee. "Aislinn, my love, will you marry me? Will you become my duchess?"

Aislinn took his face in her hands. "Yes, with all my heart!"

* * *

Standing in the city square, Cadarn stared at the pieces of the shattered throne that remained on the dais. The city's flower garden surrounding it was dead and brown. Why hadn't he noticed that before? Surely it's been an omen if he'd only been paying attention. Mounting the steps, he remembered the last time he stood here and again saw the baby tumbling into the crowd. Someone had picked it up and bashed out its brains, an act of brutality he'd been helpless to stop. To achieve victory, Nisse had told him that he needed to make a deal with demons, and he'd done so.

The queen's words echoed in his ears. "You have wrought nothing but devastation with your folly."

She was right. It didn't matter that he'd intended something far different. He was responsible for unleashing evil among the people he thought to save. He was no longer worthy of the goddess's love and would soon be suffering in the seven hells where he belonged.

He sat on the largest piece of the throne that remained. He bowed his head and offered a brief prayer for the goddess's forgiveness of others but not for himself. Then he drew his sword, took it in both hands, and placed the point over his heart.

"For the queen!" he shouted and plunged it through his breast.

* * *

Unable to block the horror of the temple square out of her sight, Samantha rode beside a litter carrying her father. She stayed at the temple until all the wounded had been seen to. Fortunately, Father Leigh and Oriana hadn't been fully exhausted in healing Darhour and had been able to lend a hand. But after the wounded, came the dead.

She left her men piling the bodies of the fallen into carts. She wanted to feel joy that she'd saved the goddess and prevented the rise of a dark god, but the cost had been crushing. Even now she saw the stacks and stacks of bloody corpses.

Passing through the city square, she saw a man with a sword through his heart lying on a bed of rocks.

"He took his own life, so I guess you won't have to kill him," Bearach said.

Only then did she recognize Cadarn. She realized the rubble was the remains of her father's throne. She'd have to have a new one constructed. Blood pounded in her ears. A cold voice ripped the words from her throat. "Have his body hung from the palace battlements. Let his folly be displayed until the flesh rots from his bones."

Bearach lifted an eyebrow at her. Yes, she had become hard, but hard she needed to be so that there was no softness that her enemies could exploit to the detriment of the people who she'd been raised to protect.

CHAPTER 24

Vaughan gaped at the mayor of Nios Mo. "You have to be joking!"

"Why would I joke about such a thing? The queen has gone to put an end to that traitorous fool. She's probably camping at the base of Gloine Torr as we speak."

"Camping at Gloine Torr?"

"Torr! Torr!" Brianna added, not helping anything.

The mayor chuckled. "What a precocious thing! Mimicking language so young!"

Vaughan muttered foul words under his breath. His stomach rumbled. They had run out of money and had few supplies left. Vaughan had been giving most of the food to Brianna. He laughed hollowly. He'd spent weeks chasing after the queen, traveled further and farther than he'd ever thought he would in a lifetime, only to learn the queen was right back where he started. Sulis had one hell of a sense of humor. If the queen wasn't at Gloine Torr when he got there, maybe he'd just give up looking for her and become a farmer or something.

* * *

As the sun set, Samantha's army spread out across the plain at the base of Gloine Torr. The queen stared at the city walls. A battle to retake the city would cost hundreds if not thousands of lives. She'd sent Darhour ahead of the slow-moving army to scout the city. He was to rejoin them when darkness had fallen. But there was still no word on Brianna.

When the army was settled, Samantha stared in the direction of the Far Mountain. *What does the goddess expect from me? Why has she deserted me?* Abruptly, Samantha decided it was high time to ask the goddess herself, and she would do so at the goddess's holiest shrine: on top of Gloine Torr. Surrounded by her personal guard, Samantha began the long trek up the hundreds of steps.

Samantha had only visited the shrine once before, when she'd been confined there by the king during a bout of madness caused by Father Shylah's blood magic. That was the time when Robbie, on his magical horses, had managed to climb the steep sides of the pyramid shaped monument to become her consort. The goddess had sent Robbie those holy horses, but somehow the goddess had changed. Sulis had sent Samantha only heartache and chaos.

Samantha's legs and lungs burned as she neared the top. Bearach and Conroy led the group. As they reached the top, Bearach gasped and spoke to someone Samantha couldn't see. "Holy Sulis, Milady, what happened to you?"

A voice answered that Samantha had heard before. "You are welcome, but this is a holy place and your weapons are not. Leave them here."

Shocked that Bearach and Conroy began to remove their swords without consulting her, Samantha topped the rise. Facing her men was the same priestess who had spoken to her on the island in what now seemed like another lifetime. When doubts had assailed her about her right to the throne, the woman who stood before her now had assured her that she was the goddess's choice. Although it was undoubtedly the same woman, she appeared to have aged fifty years. Her hair that had been blond streaked with gray was now as white as snow. Her smooth face was now pitted with deep lines and wrinkles. Her sparkling white robes were dull and tattered. Only her eyes were unchanged. It still seemed as if all the ages of the earth looked through them and her voice was still strong and clear. "Welcome, my daughter, I have been awaiting your arrival."

Samantha had once suspected this priestess was the goddess herself. Now she was certain of it. She fell to her knees. "Sulis, Mother of us all, your children suffer and die. Why have you abandoned us?"

The goddess's eyes fell. "My child, I have not abandoned my children. They have abandoned me. Please rise and come into my temple, and I will give you what guidance I can still offer." She stretched out her hand to take Samantha's, and Samantha felt a jolt of power that sang of pure unconditional love. But the power paled in comparison to that she'd felt when the goddess had touched her on the island. That touch had rendered Samantha unconscious.

As Samantha rose and followed the goddess, she heard her guards whispering behind her and the clank as their weapons hit the ground. Entering the goddess's shrine, Samantha removed her shoes as she had that long-ago day on the island. Sulis knelt at the altar, and Samantha knelt beside her. Behind her, her men entered and went down on their knees. The goddess was quiet for a moment, as if in meditation. When she spoke, her voice sounded tired. "My child, you charge me with neglect, but it is not so. Do you know where we goddesses and gods derive our power?"

As shocked as Samantha was to hear the goddess talk of multiple divine beings, she was even more shocked by the question. "I don't understand, Holy Mother. Does not your power come from yourself?"

Sulis shook her head. "No, my daughter, we grow strong on the prayers of our true worshipers. As Lundia's church wandered from the path I had revealed, I have been growing slowly weaker for decades. The recent schism in the church and the insistence that I am a man aged me even more rapidly. But the age and the weakness you see in me this day was completed by the death of my priesthood. Their sacrifices in fighting the Soul Stone dealt me a devastating blow. I had little power left to aid your consort in the destruction of the Ancient Evil. Now I can barely manifest myself outside of this shrine, the heart of my power." The goddess turned sad eyes toward Samantha. "Pure evil now corrupts the temples in my capital. False worshipers fill them, and my true children are frightened into silence. If you do not bring my people back to me, I fear I will soon fade away completely, becoming nothing more than a shadow."

Samantha had difficulty breathing. "But I too lost faith. I blamed you. I…"

Sulis smoothed Samantha's hair and again she felt the goddess's love. "My child, you have served my people well, and I harbor nothing but love for you. A mother can understand her children's doubts."

Samantha trembled as a horrible thought hit her. "Holy Mother, if worship gives a deity power, are the false worshipers giving power to another?"

Sulis shook her head. "As yet, they are not. The god they worship does not yet exist to receive their homage, but some shadows of faded gods have begun to sniff this unclaimed power. If it grows much stronger, one of the evil gods of times long past will awaken and claim it, becoming the one they worship. I shudder to think of my children under the power of such a god. It isn't fair to ask anything of you, but this time the mother needs her child. There is little time to waste. The false priest plots a great evil that may sever me from my children forever and lead to the ascendance of my rival. I feel sick with fear of what will happen to my people if this happens. Bring my children back to me, Samantha."

With those words, the goddess faded from her sight. As tears streamed down Samantha's cheeks, she realized she had failed to ask the goddess about Brianna. A hole tore in her insides; as much as it pained her, her own child couldn't matter. No matter how much it cost her, she had to save her people and the goddess herself. She rose to her feet and turned to find her men looking at her with fear and awe. "You have heard the Holy Mother speak. See that her words spread among the army below. Tomorrow, we fight not merely for ourselves, but for Sulis."

* * *

When Samantha returned to the base of Gloine Torr, she gathered the nobles and her officers into her tent to relate her encounter with the goddess. Darhour, who had returned from his mission, joined them. After she finished, everyone stared at her with wide eyes, and silence filled the tent so thick she could almost touch it.

At last Baroness Eithne drew the star of Sulis. "We will fail neither Your Majesty nor our goddess, even it costs us everything."

Darhour caressed his facial scars. "The baroness is right, but the cost will indeed be high. I have found a way for a force to sneak into the city before sunrise to open the gates for us, and there are many within the city who will likely rise up in Your Majesty's support. But Cadarn's forces are more numerous than they had been when I was last in the city, and discipline has improved markedly. We already knew Cadarn's mercenary army numbered close to five hundred, and that as many as thirty members of the Royal Guard had betrayed our queen to join forces with him. But now many of the lower sort have joined the count's forces. They aren't well trained or armed, and likely won't be reliable if it looks like the tide is turning against them. But they are a significant number. But worst of all is the huge number who have joined the True Church of Sulis. They are fanatics and number in the hundreds, if not a thousand. They will fight to the last drop of blood."

Samantha put a hand over her heart. "It is the high priest, not Cadarn, who will rule if we fail, isn't it?"

Darhour nodded. "Yes, Cadarn won't be able to pay the mercenaries forever, and without them, there will be nothing to stop Father Eadoin from taking the throne."

To Samantha's shock, Devyn stood and, with a shaking hand, rolled up his sleeve and drew a small dagger. His voice was steady as he spoke. "This isn't a fight we can lose. Victory must be had even if we all lose our lives in the attempt. I, for one, swear to the goddess and my mother's grave that I, Devyn, Duke of Gnos, will fight until all the blood is drained from my veins to restore our great queen Samantha I to her throne and Sulis to her proper place in our hearts. I will seal this oath with my blood." He made a quick slash on his forearm and held out the blood tinged dagger. "Who will join me?"

Samantha's heart beat faster as everyone assembled rose. Eithne took the dagger. "We all will." She repeated Devyn's words and cut her forearm.

The dagger made its way around the table, and without any apparent hesitation, all gathered did likewise. At last, the dagger reached Samantha. She repeated the oath, rolled up her sleeve, and cut her arm. She placed her bleeding arm in the middle of the table, and all present laid their arms over hers. She felt a jolt of power nearly equal to that she'd felt the first time the goddess touched her, as all gathered spoke in chorus, "With our blood we seal this oath."

* * *

In the early morning light, Samantha, clad in her armor, stood on the stairs of Gloine Torr. After the meeting in her tent, Darhour had sent men into the city to open the gates for them. Now she needed to make sure her army understood what was at stake: that the cause they would fight and perhaps die for was worth the sacrifice. While it was impossible for her voice to reach everyone, she pitched it as loudly as possible to make sure most would hear her and spread her words.

"My people, I speak to you today not of myself or my throne. These things pale compared to the evil that threatens us. You have all heard how the goddess herself met me on the top of Gloine Torr. I had lost faith in Sulis and blamed her for deserting me and my people in our time of need, but the truth is far more horrible. We have deserted her. Without our prayers and our worship, the Holy Mother has grown weak and has begun to fade, and another god, one who will revel in the blood of this people, threatens to take her place. To prevent this, we must retake Murtaghan today and restore Sulis to her proper place in our hearts and our prayers. I will attempt to obtain Count Cadarn's surrender, but if he proves obstinate, we must be prepared for an immediate assault on the city. Some of you will travel Beyond the Far Mountain today, but the Holy Mother will welcome you in her arms because by giving your lives, you will have served the goddess well and saved this people from a terrible evil. Prepare your weapons and armor, and ready yourself to ride to Murtaghan at a moment's notice. Know that today, you don't fight merely for your queen, but for Sulis herself!" To the roars of the army below her, Samantha raised a gauntleted fist into the air.

Brimming with power such as she'd never felt, the queen descended the steps, and with Darhour beside her, she approached the awning that had been set up for her meeting with Cadarn. Despite what he had done, his aura had told her that at heart he wasn't a bad man, so maybe the bloodshed she feared could be avoided.

As she neared the awning, Cadarn approached from the opposite direction. He had brought fifty soldiers with him from the city, but like her, he approached with only one man, a foreigner. They reached the tent at the same time. She inclined her head slightly. "Cadarn."

Cadarn returned the gesture. "Let us stop this farce! I have left word that if I don't give the signal of your surrender within the hour, the crown princess will be skewered on a pike and hanged from the city wall."

Samantha sat in the chair. "There is more at stake than my daughter's life. Besides, you don't have her." Her whole body tensed, waiting for his answer and praying her daughter was indeed not in his hands.

Laughing easily, he sat across her. "I know the person you sent didn't find her in the palace nursery, but do you really think I'd leave her where she could so easily be found? I assure you I patted her bald head only moments ago. You are a mother before you are a queen. You won't risk her life."

She called forth his aura. The bright orange and yellow that had dominated it had dulled in color, and the jagged black lines had widened and grown in number. He'd committed horrible deeds that haunted him, but a flash of purple also announced he was lying about Brianna. *He doesn't have her. Where is my baby?* Knowing what was at stake, Samantha shoved her love for Brianna into the hole in her heart. "We have no time to waste on this game. I am an aurora. Your aura announces your lies. You don't have my daughter."

Cadarn gaped and blinked. He looked at the foreigner with him, who nodded. A look of resolve crossed Cadarn's face, and he leaned forward. "I had hoped to avoid bloodshed, but this people have been in chains long enough. While I still breathe, you and what remains of the nobility will never usurp their freedom. Victory has cost too much to let it slip through my hands now."

His aura went mad with activity. She wasn't certain what it all meant, but she could see some justice to his beliefs. "I do not argue that the nobility are sometimes corrupt and act in a manner that is detrimental to the common good. Compromises less than ideal have been made to avoid war. But I and my father before me have always ruled with the people's best interests at heart. As my father taught me, it is always the common people who suffer most when those at the top fight for power. You have destabilized the joined kingdoms, and how many have died as a result? A few, you may say, were guilty and deserved their deaths, but most were innocent commoners just trying to live out their lives. You have also let an evil flourish at the core of the realm that is a threat to the goddess herself. This so-called True Church of Sulis attacks the very heart of our people and spreads evil among them. Father Eadoin has burned those he calls heretics. How can you call that freedom? You aren't a bad man. How can your conscience live with this barbarism?"

A shadow crossed Cadarn's face, and his aura flashed red as with anger. "What is truly barbarous is a system that judges a person's worth by the blood in their veins rather than their actions and character. I will not allow the chains of monarchy to hold this people down again, but once you surrender or are defeated, I will deal with the priest's excesses."

Samantha leaned toward him. "You aren't strong enough to control Eadoin and never will be. If I did as you asked, Father Eadoin would soon rule this people, and their chains would become far stronger than any you hoped to break. You have wrought devastation with your folly. In some ways, Svizra's system of government may be superior to our own. With the death of so many of the nobility, we may be able to implement some of your designs for this people. If you surrender now, I will allow you to keep your life and perhaps advise me from your dungeon cell, but the True Church of Sulis must be destroyed, and Father Eadoin must be made to answer for his crimes against this people and against the goddess herself."

Cadarn stood. "He will answer, but not to you. If you refuse to surrender, we have nothing more to say to each other." Followed by the foreigner, he stalked back to his horse.

As Cadarn and his men rode back toward the city walls, an eerie calm stole over Samantha. She glanced at Darhour. "Ready the army. We take back our city."

* * *

As soon as the city gates closed behind them, Cadarn turned to Nisse. "Her army is bigger than we anticipated, and she will attack. Will we win?"

Nisse shrugged one shoulder. "The city walls negate a lot of her power. Backed by the Protectorate Guard and the city magistrates, we should be able to hold them. As long as the gates remain unbreeched, we'll be fine."

He and Nisse climbed the stairs to the top of wall where Captain Gerard awaited them. As Cadarn surveyed the number of archers waiting to pepper the queen's army, as well as the boulders and boiling pitch they would employ against anyone who tried to breach the gates, he pasted on a smile. *Nisse knows how to protect a city! We will win! This people must be free!*

Attempting to calm his rapidly beating heart, Cadarn joined Nisse at the front of the battlement. As they watched the queen's army preparing to attack, Nisse rubbed the back of his neck. Then a smile spread over Nisse's face, and he let a sudden high-pitched laugh that emptied out Cadarn's insides. "What's wrong?" Cadarn asked.

Still smiling, Nisse shook his head. "Your queen is more clever than I gave her credit for, but not as clever as she thinks. She's given away her secret. Look at that army! She is preparing no siege engines, no catapults, no battering rams. This is an army that expects the gates to be open when they get here. I would bet my life she has a force inside the city already, just waiting to seize the gatehouse and open the gates."

Thinking of how easily the queen's man had sneaked in and out of the palace, Cadarn's eyes widened. "Then we have to protect the gatehouse."

Chuckling, Nisse nodded. "That we do. But if I withdraw men from the walls to do so, there wouldn't be enough to protect them, in case she is truly clever and has another trick up her sleeves. She may be trying to fool us into emptying the walls."

Cadarn shook his head. "You worry too much. The queen has never commanded an army. Surely she can't have out-thought you."

Nisse smiled down at the army like a master admiring the work of a precocious apprentice. "Your queen? No. She is little more than a girl. But the man that accompanied her to the parley, the one you call Darhour. I met his eyes as you spoke with the queen. That man is both deadly and very, very clever. We need more men. It's time for your priest to do his part. Even if his zealots have little skill, they should be able to hold off an attack on the gatehouse long enough for us to join them. The queen's force inside the walls can't be that large, or it wouldn't have been able to hide itself."

"Yes, of course." Cadarn released the tension from his shoulders and sent a message to Father Eadoin to gather as many of his followers as he could and send them to protect the gatehouse.

The Temple of the Father's Love was in the middle of city, and Cadarn fidgeted while awaiting his messenger's return. *Sulis, I've come so far. Holy Mother, give me victory. Free your people from bondage.*

The messenger returned more quickly than he'd anticipated. Out of breath, he had to pant for a moment before he could speak. "Sir, the high priest refused. He said all of Sulis's pure children must gather round the temple square to ensure the ritual isn't interrupted. He said after the ritual is completed, Sulis will protect the city." The messenger put a hand to his stomach. "Sir, he's emptying out his dungeon and tying people to stakes. Close to a hundred of them, I think. Some of them are children."

Cadarn's chest tightened, but before he could respond, a priest joined them on the city wall. "His Holiness instructs all to gather round the temple square. It is Sulis's will."

Spittle flying with every word, Cadarn jabbed a finger at the priest. "You remind Father Eadoin who's in charge and tell him to get men here now."

But the priest ignored Cadarn and looked at Gerard. "You disappoint His Holiness and Sulis by keeping the secret of the abomination's escape. Will you continue to defy god now?"

Gerard bowed humbly. "I will not. We will come at once."

As Cadarn turned to Gerard, his vision narrowed. "We will not. You answer to me, not this priest."

Gerard drew Sulis's star. "I only answer to Sulis. I have never served you, only the god. I forswore myself because I didn't want to admit to the mouth of Sulis that I allowed the princess to escape, but I will not defy the god again. Who do you think has brought us this far? Your mercenary friend?" He gestured contemptuously at Nisse. "Sulis will grant us victory today."

As Gerard started for the stairs, Cadarn grabbed his arm. "Don't be a fool. If the queen gets the gates open, we could lose everything."

Gerard's lips curled, and his eyes went cold. "You have already lost. I'm not alone in placing God's will above man's will." He gestured to the walls. Men were trickling off and heading in the direction of the temple. "Father Eadoin has called, and Sulis's true children answer his call. His Holiness speaks for Sulis, and he will rule."

"No, he will not! Eadoin is mad." Without thinking, Cadarn drew his sword and shoved it through the captain's throat. Gerard's eyes widened as he gurgled out his last breath.

Holding his bloody sword, Cadarn whirled on the priest who'd brought the message. But Nisse grabbed his arm. "Liridona, killing this man won't change anything."

Cadarn dropped his sword arm and backed away. As the priest fled, he said, "His Holiness will hear of this. He will not be pleased."

Cadarn watched as his forces guarding the walls became sparse. Nisse lay a warm hand on his shoulder, shocking him out of his stupor. Cadarn met his friend's eyes. "The queen was right, wasn't she? If we win today, freedom loses. Eadoin will unleash a reign of terror, and I won't be able to stop him."

Nisse caressed his arm and spoke in the soft voice of a lover. "Ah, Liridona, my friend, I'm so sorry. It was a bold vision. I love you as I will never love another, but I can't ask my men to give their lives in a lost cause." He drew his sword, held it high in the air, and whirled it in a circle four times. As the signal spread, the walls began to empty. "I told you few things go as planned, and knowing this, I arranged to have ships standing ready to see my men safely out of the country in case things went badly. Come with me, Liridona. I could use a commander I can trust."

Cadarn could only stare at the man who'd planned for their defeat as fully than he'd planned for their victory. He released the bloody sword he was still holding and allowed it to fall to the battlement.

Nisse looked desperately between Cadarn and his men fleeing toward the harbor. "I'm sorry, my love. Your gods, be with you." Nisse drew him close and kissed him in the center of the forehead. Then the friend of his heart deserted him, leaving him alone on the city wall. For decades he'd planned for victory. He'd never planned for defeat.

* * *

As Darhour prepared what he called a turtle, men with shields over their head to protect them from the archers on the wall, to precede the main army, Samantha watched those very archers disappearing from view.

"Darhour," she called, pointing to the wall. "What is happening?"

Darhour shook his head. But the gates of the city swung open, and the men Darhour had sneaked inside for this purpose appeared. "Wait here, Your Majesty. It could be a trap." He rode forward with the bulk of her army following. She remained behind with her personal guards.

After speaking to the men at the gate, Darhour dispatched a rider to her. He reported, "Your Majesty, Cadarn's mercenaries are fleeing to the harbor, but a large force has gathered around the Temple of the Mother's Love. We ride to confront it. The captain says for Your Majesty to wait here until he determines it's safe." The man spurred his horse back to the body of the army.

Watching her army ride into the city unopposed, Samantha whispered, "Sulis, what is happening? You said you need me to save you."

She touched her heels to Roberta's sides and rode slowly forward. As she did so, colors rose from the center of the city—an aura that was a violent mixture of the darkest black and deepest crimson swirled through the air above the Temple of the Mother's Love. Nausea cramped her stomach, and terror clawed at her heart. "Holy Sulis, Mother of us all, what is that?"

Her guards stared at her blankly, and the goddess provided no answer. Knowing whatever was happening had to be stopped, she spurred Roberta into a gallop. "Your Majesty, no!" Conroy called. She ignored him, but they soon surrounded her.

By the time she caught up with the main body of her army, they were involved in a pitched battle against mostly crudely armed peasants who blocked the way to the Temple. No match for the Royal Guard, they fell by the dozens. But they were numerous, and their bodies slowed her men's progress toward the square almost as effectively as they had when they still breathed. Seeing the colors rise even higher above her city, Samantha spurred her own horse into the fray.

Her guards fought beside her, and her sword became wet with blood. Time slowed as she slashed about her, trying to fight her way into the temple square. The aura over the temple continued to grow, forming a bubble that seemed to be pressing against an invisible force restraining it. Somehow, Samantha knew that if the bubble burst, they'd be too late.

Seeing Darhour before her, she screamed, "For Sulis!" Ignoring the blood splattering her armor, she pressed forward until she and her father fought side by side. She didn't know how many lives she took as she battled to save both her goddess and her people. But the ground became slick with the blood of the fallen.

Smoke rose over the square, and she caught the scent of roasting flesh. The aura continued to grow.

After an eternity, or a second, the last resistance fell beneath her sword and those of her men, and with Darhour beside her, she burst into the temple square.

Her mind almost refused to process the horror. Nearly a hundred people were tied to stakes, and fire consumed their flesh. Although they seemed already to be dead, that did little to lessen the horror. In the midst of them, Father Eadoin stood over a cauldron. His hands were raised in the direction of the Far Mountain as he prayed. The aura she'd seen arose not from the temple as she'd thought but from the priest himself. He couldn't be allowed to finish his prayer. She whirled toward Darhour. "Stop this! Kill him now!"

Without hesitation, Darhour spurred his horse toward the priest, and worshipers fell beneath his onslaught. When he reached the cauldron, he slammed his horse into it. As the cauldron's contents spilled onto the cobblestones, Darhour vaulted from his horse and plunged his sword straight into the priest's heart.

The entire world seemed to explode. Darhour flew across the square, and then a shockwave hit her, her body flew into the putrid air, and everything went dark.

* * *

Riding toward the Temple of the Mother's Love beside Father Leigh, Oriana put a hand on the headband Vaughan had given her and traced one of its stars. The Holy Mother was in danger. How much had her failure to return to Balley Beg contributed to the goddess's deterioration? The air in front of her seemed to grow thick with evil. It felt as if she were pressing against an invisible force trying to hold her back. Then an explosion erupted from across the city. Waves of evil washed over her, so strong that she barely clung to her horse. When the waves had passed, she looked toward Father Leigh.

He'd gone white. "Holy Sulis, Mother of us!" He traced Sulis's star before him, and they rode toward the source of the explosion. Bloody corpses filled the street, making their passage difficult, but at last they reached the temple square. The first thing they saw was the queen unconscious on the ground amid a host of others in similar condition. Both she and Father Leigh vaulted from their horses and ran to her. Father Leigh reached her first. As soon as he touched her, she groaned and began to stir.

As the queen opened her eyes, others began to stir and waken. Father Leigh leaned over her, searching for injuries. "Thank the goddess, you're alive. Your Majesty, what happened?"

The queen sat up abruptly, her eyes darting about the square. Then she smiled. "It's all right. We were in time." She caught sight of

Darhour, who unlike the others hadn't begun to move. "Father," she whispered.

Responding to the queen, Father Leigh hurried toward the fallen man. From this distance, Oriana could merely tell that he was still alive. "He lives," she assured the queen.

Father Leigh touched the scarred man and closed his eyes. After a moment, he opened his eyes and gestured to Oriana. "Oriana, I need your help to save him. Quick."

She ran over and placed her hands beside Father Leigh's. Darhour's insides had been shattered, and he was bleeding internally. She joined her power to Father Leigh's and together they closed the leaking vessels.

* * *

His head bursting with pain, Devyn rose from where he'd fallen. He staggered as exhaustion sapped all strength from his muscles. The last thing he remembered was the thunder of hoof beats as they approached the temple square. But the blood on his sword and splattered on his armor told him that in this moment of crisis, he hadn't failed as he'd always believed he would. He'd comported himself as the duke he'd become.

The sight of the temple square was more horrifying than anything he'd experienced in his worst nightmare, even more than his brother's severed head. Blood, charred bodies, smoke! Maybe if he didn't look at it too closely, it wouldn't be forever burned in his memory. He saw the queen, giving orders for the care of the wounded and for the arrest of those of their enemy who'd survived. He stumbled toward her.

"Devyn! Devyn!" he heard the scream behind him and turned to see Aislinn dressed in leather and holding a long pole that had been sharpened into a makeshift spear. Her hair was matted to her head, and her face dirty and blood stained, but she was alive. Her maid Zinerva was beside her, similarly clad and armed.

"Aislinn!" he cried. She ran to greet him. With tears streaming down his cheeks, he threw his arms around her and held her. "Aislinn! You're alive! I was certain I'd never see you again!" He stepped back and felt her to make sure she was real, taking in the bloodstained spear she'd dropped at her feet. "How did you survive? How are you here like this?"

Aislinn laughed through her tears. "Zinerva saved my life. I've been hiding among the palace servants, and we've all been preparing to help the queen when she arrived."

Devyn gave out a yelp of pure joy and twirled her in a circle. Then exhaustion hit him, and he stumbled. As he held her tight, he realized nothing was stopping him now. He released her and went down on one knee. "Aislinn, my love, will you marry me? Will you become my duchess?"

Aislinn took his face in her hands. "Yes, with all my heart!"

* * *

Standing in the city square, Cadarn stared at the pieces of the shattered throne that remained on the dais. The city's flower garden surrounding it was dead and brown. Why hadn't he noticed that before? Surely it's been an omen if he'd only been paying attention. Mounting the steps, he remembered the last time he stood here and again saw the baby tumbling into the crowd. Someone had picked it up and bashed out its brains, an act of brutality he'd been helpless to stop. To achieve victory, Nisse had told him that he needed to make a deal with demons, and he'd done so.

The queen's words echoed in his ears. "You have wrought nothing but devastation with your folly."

She was right. It didn't matter that he'd intended something far different. He was responsible for unleashing evil among the people he thought to save. He was no longer worthy of the goddess's love and would soon be suffering in the seven hells where he belonged.

He sat on the largest piece of the throne that remained. He bowed his head and offered a brief prayer for the goddess's forgiveness of others but not for himself. Then he drew his sword, took it in both hands, and placed the point over his heart.

"For the queen!" he shouted and plunged it through his breast.

* * *

Unable to block the horror of the temple square out of her sight, Samantha rode beside a litter carrying her father. She stayed at the temple until all the wounded had been seen to. Fortunately, Father Leigh and Oriana hadn't been fully exhausted in healing Darhour and had been able to lend a hand. But after the wounded, came the dead.

She left her men piling the bodies of the fallen into carts. She wanted to feel joy that she'd saved the goddess and prevented the rise of a dark god, but the cost had been crushing. Even now she saw the stacks and stacks of bloody corpses.

Passing through the city square, she saw a man with a sword through his heart lying on a bed of rocks.

"He took his own life, so I guess you won't have to kill him," Bearach said.

Only then did she recognize Cadarn. She realized the rubble was the remains of her father's throne. She'd have to have a new one constructed. Blood pounded in her ears. A cold voice ripped the words from her throat. "Have his body hung from the palace battlements. Let his folly be displayed until the flesh rots from his bones."

Bearach lifted an eyebrow at her. Yes, she had become hard, but hard she needed to be so that there was no softness that her enemies could exploit to the detriment of the people who she'd been raised to protect.

EPILOGUE

Previously

The passenger awoke to something rough licking the scarred half of his face. He opened his one good eye to see the gray-striped cat that had been with him on the ship. The sun was shining overhead, and he lay on wet sand. As he sat up, he remembered the great storm that had arisen, and the great wave that had swept over the ship, taking him with it. He remembered nothing after that and had no idea how he'd made it to shore. The beach as far as he could see was littered with debris. The ship must have broken apart, and this increasingly hot sand had to be his new place in the seven hells.

If you enjoyed the novel, please leave a review on Amazon or Goodreads.

To learn where Darhour has been, check out *The Ghost in Exile*. An excerpt follows.

Also, subscribe to my mailing list to
get monthly updates on my writing, specials,
and advanced news on upcoming releases.
You will also received a free ecopy of my short story collection,
Blood Cursed and Other Tales of the Fantastic.
http://jamie-marchant.com/newsletter/

THE GHOST IN EXILE (EXCERPT)

A Korthlundian Kronicle

By Jamie Marchant

CHAPTER 1

The Ghost sat in the temple district of Argos staring at the Temple of Ares, the god of war and of killers. Due to the disguise he now wore, people passed without exhibiting the fear that his own features usually invoked. With the aid of wax and cosmetics, he'd hidden his numerous scars and remade his face in the image of a Saloynan mercenary, a persona he'd never thought to assume again. He pulled his cloak more tightly around him to protect against the chill. It was mild for mid-winter, but still the cold was biting. Ares's temple looming in front of him deepened the cold. It was constructed of black marble and decorated in blood-red stone with sharp lines and geometric shapes, conjuring images of the horrors of the battlefield. He looked from the red and black temple to his fingernails. During the three-month crossing from Korthlundia to Saloyna—the rough winter sea making the crossing take longer than usual—he'd succeeded in scrubbing the blood out from under his nails, but it hadn't been easy. When he'd been the world's most notorious assassin, he'd owned a brush specifically for that purpose. But after he'd knelt at Sulis's holy altar and made the vow never to kill again, he'd thrown that brush away. He guessed he'd need to find a new one.

The Ghost rose abruptly. There was no point in delaying any longer. He'd broken his vow, and it was past time to admit that making it had been foolish to begin with, as if such a small act could cleanse his blood-drenched soul. He'd long ago earned his place in the seven hells. Now, he must embrace the fact that he had one skill and one purpose—to kill those who needed to die. For a brief time he'd tried to forget that, and because he hesitated to kill a monster, the man had nearly destroyed his homeland and his daughter. Some people's deaths were a thing to be celebrated rather than mourned, and because he was forever tainted, forever a killer, he should be the one to kill them. He hoped the high priest had an appropriate target for him. Zotico was a ghoul, but he'd always been reliable in ferreting out the fiends whose deaths were most needed.

As The Ghost entered Ares's temple, an oppressive presence settled over him. He seemed to be alone in the huge sanctuary, but he knew the acolytes of Ares watched through hidden panels. Rumors claimed they waited for someone with signs of weakness to enter. Then they would pour forth, seize the unfortunate, and sacrifice him to their god. The Ghost had found no evidence to support such rumors, but he knew that animals and criminals were regularly sacrificed on Ares's altar, bleeding out their lives into the bowl at the foot of his statue. It was a hard death, both the blood and the pain feeding the magic of Ares's priests.

The Ghost knelt at Ares's feet, where the stench of blood was nearly overpowering. The altar was stained with it, and the bowl at the god's feet was full from a fresh sacrifice. The power present in this place was undeniable—dark and forbidding, far from the peace and serenity in Sulis's temples. But he was no longer worthy of Sulis's blessing. The Ghost drew his dagger, held his left forearm over the sacrificial bowl, and sliced a new cut alongside his numerous scars. As he bled into the bowl, he felt the magic of the place coalesce around him. His blood sizzled as it hit the bowl, and the wound on his arm healed instantly, signaling that The Ghost truly belonged to the Saloynan god.

A door opened behind him; he stood and faced the high priest. Zotico was completely bald and looked no older than he had when The Ghost had first met him ten long years ago. He had small, beady eyes and a typical Saloynan narrow nose. "Pandaros! How wonderful!" the priest beamed, calling The Ghost a name he'd decided he must take up again. He could no longer be either "Ahearn" or "Darhour"; they were both dead. "Rumors said you were no longer among the living. Come in, come in." Zotico gestured toward the doorway. "I can't tell you how happy I am to see you."

Zotico's enthusiasm seemed excessive even for him. Warily, The Ghost followed Zotico down the corridor to the high priest's office.

It was large, the walls covered with instruments of war—swords, shields, battle axes, and plaques ornamented with what looked suspiciously like human ears. The ears were new. Zotico caught The Ghost looking at them and swept his hand over a plaque that contained five ears nailed side by side. "Do you like the new decor? Sacrifices, all of them. I had them moved from our private sanctuary so I could better remember the devotion demanded by the god I serve."

Zotico may not appear to age, but his ghoulishness grew with each passing year. The Ghost carefully schooled his features to avoid betraying any sign of revulsion.

In the center of the office was a large desk with one chair behind it and two large, comfortable chairs facing it. Zotico gestured The Ghost into one of the facing chairs. The Ghost sat, and the high priest offered him a glass of oenomel, a sweet mixture of honey and wine. Zotico poured himself a glass from the same pitcher and sat behind the desk. "Pandaros, my friend. Why have you neglected your obligations to Ares?"

The Ghost waited for Zotico to take a sip of his drink, then took one of his own. It was cloying in its sweetness. "I've been distracted."

Zotico smiled sadly. "A true tragedy. There's no one better with a blade." The priest mimed drawing a knife across his own throat. "I've had acolytes scouring the city more than once looking for you, but I gave up years ago when not the slightest sign of your whereabouts could be found. Tell me, my son, where have you been?"

"Away." The Ghost had no intention of ever letting Zotico learn anything about Samantha, who was both his daughter and his queen. Because of his careful disguise, Zotico believed The Ghost was a Saloynan.

Zotico laughed. "Long have I wished for the power of Delphi to penetrate your secrets. Is there a person in the world who knows even half of them?" Zotico looked expectantly at him, but The Ghost didn't answer. "I see my curiosity shall have to be contained. Ares is a harsh master and not attentive to trifles. Still, I can't tell you how happy I am that you have now returned to his fold. His temple has truly felt your absence."

The Ghost grunted, "Do you have a job for me?"

Zotico's eyes gleamed. "Do I ever! I'd nearly despaired of finding a capable assassin, but your fortunate arrival proves that Ares will never fail those who serve his name."

"Who do you want dead?"

"I think it would be best explained by the one in need of Ares's assistance, but I assure you it is your sort of kill. May I tell the client you'll meet?"

The Ghost nodded.

Zotico's entire body relaxed. "Good, good. The client would prefer not to be seen here. I've an arrangement with the high priestess of Aphrodite. The two gods were lovers, after all. Enter the goddess's temple tomorrow morning and choose the acolyte wearing the pendant of a vulture." Zotico smiled broadly. "Pandaros, my friend, it is a great day for you to have returned."

"You are not my friend." The Ghost left with Zotico's laughter ringing in his ears.

* * *

Desperately needing the distraction, The Ghost went for a walk after his supper at the Green Sandpiper, an inn that catered to mercenaries and other unsavory types. The falling of night deepened the cold, but he didn't cut short his walk. He wandered the filthy streets of the poorer section of the city, thinking about past kills—those in the distant past, not those connected with his daughter. He couldn't think of her ever again. The few short years he'd spent with her had been the best in his life, but he hadn't deserved them. The only thing he deserved was to rot in the seven hells. He wondered how many had died at his hands. Two hundred? Three? More? He'd never kept count.

Few of the street lights were lit in this part of town, but that was no hindrance to The Ghost. When he'd been the Saloynan king's personal assassin, he'd had an enchantment performed on his eyes, giving him the ability to see in the dark, even the complete darkness of a cave.

Passing an alley, he heard a commotion. He turned to see a young woman pleading with two men. "Don't make me go with him," she begged. "He hurts me." The Ghost recoiled when he heard her Massossinan accent. He hated Massossinans.

The first man slapped her across the face, and The Ghost saw the iron slave collar around the woman's neck. Her red hair confirmed her nationality. She wore a low-cut, red bodice trimmed with black lace and an extremely short red skirt. She had to be freezing in this weather. "You'll do as you're told and like it, or . . ." He drew a knife and ran it across her right breast, drawing a thin line of blood.

The second man grabbed the woman. "You know you like it rough." He too drew a knife. "Maybe I'll slice you open when I'm through with you."

"That will cost you extra," the first man warned.

The second man shrugged. "I'm good for it."

He imagined his daughter being similarly assaulted. He stepped into the alley. "Let her go."

The man pulled the woman closer to him. "You can have a turn when I'm done with her." He grabbed the woman's breast, and she tried to squirm away. She looked older than he'd thought at first, nearly thirty—old for a whore. Most didn't live that long.

The Ghost drew his sword and stepped forward. "I said let her go."

The woman's master stepped between The Ghost and the other man. "Mister, you have no right to interfere with lawful commerce. She's mine, and I'll do with her as I see fit."

"Not tonight you won't. Move aside."

It must have been too dark for the man to see the menace in The Ghost's eyes. Few men dared stand up to him after they'd gotten a good look at the coldness he held there. The slave owner, however, crossed his arms. "Go away."

The Ghost raised his sword and struck the man on the head with the flat of his blade. He went down, and The Ghost stepped over him and addressed the customer. "I said let her go."

The man placed his knife at the woman's throat. "She's mine, or she's no one's."

The Ghost surreptitiously palmed a knife with his left hand while he continued holding his sword with his right. Even more than he hated Massossinans, he hated those who preyed on women's flesh. He looked at the woman. "Your choice. Does he live or die?"

* * *

For an instant, Brigitta was too shocked by the stranger's actions to answer. Saloynans were nothing but godless barbarians. She'd once been raped in the street, and not a single Saloynan had done anything to help her. The few men who had even deigned to notice merely did so to applaud her rapist and to vilify her homeland. Still, if he was offering help, she wasn't about to turn him down.

"Kill him," she hissed. Antero would not use her again.

She never saw the stranger move, but Antero toppled over, taking her down with him. He rolled off her, screaming and clutching at his face. She barely had time to notice the knife in his eye socket before the stranger had moved again and plunged his sword through Antero's throat. *Frigg preserve me!*

Fearfully, she scrambled to her feet and glanced in her rescuer's direction, but she was too late to call out a warning before her master hit the stranger from behind with a rusty pipe. She cried out as the stranger fell to his knees, dropping his sword. After Damien killed the stranger, he would punish her horribly. She looked around for a place to run, but she knew it was useless. There was nowhere in this savage land that her master couldn't find her.

To her relief, the stranger survived the blow, and he somehow had another knife in his hand. He twisted, and before she'd realized what was happening, Damien was on the ground as well, his entrails exposed to the night air. The stranger's sword was next to her foot. She grabbed the heavy sword with both hands and rushed the man who'd made her life a living hell. Her rescuer rolled aside and allowed her access to the ogre. She raised the sword over her head.

Damien flung up an arm. "No, please!"

"You kidnapped me!" she screamed, as she rammed the sword into his heart. She raised the sword and plunged it over and over again. "You raped me! You made me a whore! You left my children motherless!"

The stranger grabbed her arm. "Enough. He's dead." He took the sword from her and wiped it on her dead master's clothes.

He stumbled as he slid it into its scabbard and put his hand to the back of his head where Damien had hit him with a pipe. His fingers came away bloody. He tore off Damien's shirt and pressed it against his scalp. "Damned fool!" he muttered, seemingly to himself.

Brigitta thought she should offer her rescuer assistance, but she looked down and saw her master's blood covering her legs. Her legs buckled, and she sank to the alley floor. Slaves who killed their masters were subjected to the cruelest deaths. "I killed him," she whispered. "I killed the bastard. Dear gods, what will they do to me?"

Her rescuer threw her master's shirt aside and held out his hand. "Come with me."

She scrambled away from him and grabbed the knife from Antero's eye. She pointed it at the stranger. "Stay away from me. Before you people made me a whore, I was an honorable wife and mother. I'll die before being used again."

The stranger dropped his arm. "I don't intend to use you."

But Brigitta knew better. Saloynans were worse than the trolls that peopled the bard's tales of her land. She got to her feet, her trembling hand holding the knife. "I'm leaving now. Going home to my little ones. Move out of the way."

She knew the situation was hopeless. She'd tried to fight when Damien's squad had invaded her hut, but it had done nothing to stop them from raping her in front of her children. She was certain that this stranger could disarm her without even trying.

"I can't do that," he hissed through his teeth as if trying to convince himself of something. "You're covered in blood. You're collared. You're dressed like a whore. You'll never make it out of the city on your own, probably not even out of this neighborhood. They'll capture you and torture you to death. I can't let that happen. I'll find a way to get you home, and I won't touch you without your permission. I give you my word."

Brigitta laughed. "And a Saloynan's word is worth ever so much."

Brigitta's mouth dropped open as the stranger switched from Saloynan to her own language. "I'm not Saloynan." The light was poor, and the stranger was wearing a large hood. Was it possible that one of her countrymen was here in the heart of the enemy's capital? Was there hope for her after all?

Her entire body trembled as she lowered the knife and answered him in the language she'd despaired of ever speaking again. "Do you swear on Frigg that you'll do as you promised?"

"You have my word. I'll get you home."

"May Frigg curse you with barrenness if you lie."

The stranger took off his cloak and draped it around her shoulders. She wrapped it tightly around her, grateful for the added warmth.

* * *

The Ghost looked down at the Massossinan woman sleeping in his bed. *What in Sulis's name have I gotten myself into it?* He'd been able to break into a blacksmith shop and use his tools to remove the slave collar from the woman's neck. He'd sneaked her up the rear staircase of the Green Sandpiper, but she'd hardly stayed awake long enough to wash off her master's blood. She was still dressed as a whore and unmistakably Massossinan. For Sulis's sake, the very sound of a Massossinan accent made his stomach heave. Without provocation, he'd come close to stabbing the Massossinan prince who had courted his daughter. He rubbed his arms. They felt as if insects swarmed over them. While he served in the Saloynan army, a Massossinan officer had tortured The Ghost, coated him in honey, and staked him over an ant hill. That same officer had eaten Phelix's heart.

And he'd promised this woman to take her home to her husband? Had he lost his mind? He'd come to Saloyna to be a killer again because it was the only thing he'd ever really been good at. He'd barely set foot in the country, and he was already acting like a knight in shining armor from the worst of the bards' tales, rescuing damsels in distress. Just how was he going to keep his promise to both Zotico and this woman? He should know better than to get involved in things like this. He was not a good man.

He groaned and collapsed on the chair in front of the mirror. He picked up a poultice of crushed cabbage leaves and parsley he'd made in the inn's kitchen and held it to the back of his head. Phelix would probably have had better advice on what to use to treat the ridiculous injury. No, Phelix would have cursed him for being a brainless twit for allowing an enemy to get behind him. He'd lost his edge.

He threw down the poultice and turned to the mirror to remove the wax and cosmetics from his face. As he did so, he revealed the extent of his facial scarring, horizontal lines carved every inch from his forehead to his chin. The scars gave him a fearsome look, one that Samantha said could make men piss themselves if he so much as glanced in their direction. They also made him look far older than forty as did his gray hair and beard. He wondered what the woman would do when she saw the scars. Perhaps she'd run screaming from the room and relieve him of his responsibility to her.

When he'd cleaned his face, he looked back at the bed. The woman slept exactly in the middle, leaving no room for him on either side, and he was sure the woman wouldn't welcome his company. He arranged his weapons and settled down on the floor in front of the door with the poultice. He stared at the wall for a long time, holding the poultice to his head and reminding himself that he was a killer, not some knight errant hero.

* * *

Brigitta woke in a panic, at first not remembering where she was. The weak light of early dawn streamed through the window, and a male voice muttered in his sleep in a language she'd never heard. She sat up and noticed that the weight of her slave collar was missing. She put her hand to her neck, and the entire horrible memory came back to her. She'd killed her master. If she was found, she'd be tortured to death. Her children would grow up without a mother's love, and she knew how little they could count on their father's. Worse yet, the man who rescued her seemed to have lied to her about being a countryman. She couldn't see him well in the thin light, but the language he was speaking was certainly not Massossinan. If he'd lied to her about that, what else had he lied about? She heard her husband's voice telling her how stupid she was, and it was true. Only a true idiot would have gone with a man that had proven himself to be as good at killing as the stranger obviously was.

To make things worse, he was sleeping in front of the door, evidently to stop her escaping, but his sword rested on the floor near his hand. If she could get his weapon, maybe she could force him to let her go. If not, well, she'd already killed one man. She'd kill another if that's what it took to get back to her children.

She slipped silently from the bed, trying to move across the floor without sound, but the boards creaked under her weight. She froze, but the stranger continued to mutter without waking. She crept forward more carefully. The stranger stopped muttering, but he remained still and didn't seem to be awake. Not even daring to breathe, she took the last few steps and put her hands on the sword. She tried to draw it from its sheath, but she'd forgotten how heavy it was. Before she'd cleared it more than an inch, the stranger's hands grabbed hers. How had he moved so fast?

"Let's put that away before someone gets hurt," the stranger said.

As she pulled her hands free from the stranger's grasp, Brigitta wanted to cry. She was certainly no match for this barbarian. The sun's light streamed more brightly though the window, and she gasped at the sight of the stranger's face. Someone had carved it into mincemeat. She backed away from the nightmare. "You're not Massossinan. What kind of monster are you?"

Brigitta expected the stranger to sneer at her stupidity in believing him, but instead, he stretched, as if shaking off the last of his sleep. "The worst kind of monster." He got up from the floor and towered over her. She'd always been small, and this man was huge. "I'm also Korthlundian."

She wondered if this were some kind of demon she'd never heard of. "What's that supposed to mean?"

The stranger leaned against the wall, keeping his distance from her. "Korthlundia's a small country, a great distance from here."

Brigitta decided that where he was from didn't matter. What mattered was that he was standing between her and the door.

"I won't hurt you," he said in a gentle voice completely at odds with his appearance. "I haven't even tried to touch you."

Brigitta had to admit this was true. If he was going to do something to her, why had he slept on the floor? Still, she shuddered at the horrible scarring. "Let me go." She was ashamed that her voice trembled.

For a moment, the stranger looked like he was considering stepping aside, but then he shook his head. "You don't need to be afraid of me. Despite how I look, I'm a man of my word. If you trust me, I'll get you home." He left his place by the door and sat at the vanity in front of the mirror. He picked up some wax and began spreading it over his scars. She inched her way toward the door, not believing he would truly let her go. But he ignored her movements and continued to work on his face.

She opened the door, and he still did nothing to stop her. She heard male voices speaking Saloynan coming from the common room below. She closed her eyes and imagined what would happen if she walked into that room alone, dressed as she was. She closed the door and looked back at the stranger, who was applying cosmetics. He didn't look quite as frightening now, but how could she trust a man who killed so easily?

"Who are you?"

He shrugged. "It doesn't matter." He said nothing more as he continued his transformation. She stared as the scarred monster became a normal looking Saloynan man, just like the hundreds who had used her against her will.

The stranger stood, got out his purse, and handed her some coins. Her eyes widened as she saw the glint of gold among them. It would take half a year on her back to earn this much for her master. If the man had this much money, what was he doing staying in a dive like this?

"I have an appointment to keep. If you truly think you're better off on your own, leave when I'm gone. But if you have any sense, you'll still be here when I get back. I'll bring you some new clothes, and we can make plans." He buckled on his sword and stowed his knives all over his body. She couldn't see a one of them when he was finished.

When he was gone, she sank onto the bed. *Please, Frigg, what should I do?* she prayed. *My children need me.* She thought of the huge smile that had appeared on Elva's face every morning when she woke and caught sight of her mother. That smile had brightened Brigitta's entire world. But Elva had run to her and hid her face in Brigitta's skirts when her father came home drunk. *Dear Frigg, protect Elva and little Vigi until I can get back to them.* She curled up in a ball, clutching the coins in her fist and hugging the pillow to her. She was so tired of trying to be strong.

* * *

The Ghost rubbed the back of his head as he went down the back steps of the Green Sandpiper. It still hurt, but not too badly, making it clear that he'd suffered no serious injury. Still, what had he gotten himself into with the woman? *I tried to reform; it didn't work. I'm a murderer. Nothing more.* He had no idea what he would tell Zotico about the job they'd discussed. If it truly was his type of kill, should he turn it down to help a woman whose name he didn't even know? He saw Samantha's face. He knew what his daughter would expect, but she'd never known the murderous depth of his soul.

He blocked her out of his mind and focused on his surroundings instead. Five years had dulled his memory of the horrors of the Saloynan capital. Beggars were everywhere—young children and old men and women, emaciated and covered in running sores. In the poorer sections of the city, sewage ran down the middle of the streets. Whores, far younger than his daughter, plied their trade, and a few bodies of those who'd frozen in the night hadn't yet been gathered up. The capital of Korthlundia was not without problems, but poverty was nowhere near this widespread or abject. In Saloyna, King Salome, like his father before him, cared nothing about his people. They starved while he lived in luxury that would empty the Korthlundian treasury.

The Ghost was relieved to reach the temple complex, which was kept clean and free of beggars. In sharp contrast to Ares's temple, Aphrodite's shone a brilliant white with carvings of lovers frolicking in every imaginable position. While The Ghost had seen Aphrodite's temple every time he visited Ares's, he had never been inside. The only thing a woman's love had ever done for him was ruin his life and send him into exile when he had been only eighteen years old.

When he entered the temple, he was greeted by soft music and delicate perfume. Young women and men—acolytes of Aphrodite—in sheer robes that concealed nothing, danced in celebration of the goddess. Worshipers watched the dance until they found an acolyte to their liking. They gave the priestess the proper donation and disappeared with the acolyte into one of the private rooms that lined one wall of the temple, where they worshiped the goddess in a more intimate manner. Some of the acolytes danced near him. He examined their necks until he saw the one wearing a vulture pendant. He took the young woman's arm and led her to the priestess. "I'll take this one," he told her.

The priestess looked him over and nodded. "Chrysante, make sure this gentleman receives our special treatment."

Chrysante led him toward the rear of the temple. She opened a door, and they entered a room with nothing other than an altar. Climbing onto the altar, Chrysante purred, "Would you like to take your pleasure on Aphrodite's altar before meeting your guests? Ares's high priest said you might, and it will bring you luck with the young woman who accompanies him." Chrysante arched her back, making her breasts stand out beneath the sheer fabric.

Embarrassed, The Ghost felt himself harden. "I would not," he snapped.

The acolyte paled and jumped off the altar. *Sulis curse it! It isn't her fault the Saloynan gods are twisted.*

"Right this way, sir." She scrambled to the door on the opposite side of the altar and opened it. Following her, The Ghost entered a corridor. She took him to the end of the corridor and stopped before another door. "They await you in there. I'll leave you now." She fled back down the corridor. He must have sounded even harsher than he thought.

When the acolyte had disappeared, The Ghost knocked on the door, and Zotico's voice bid him enter. Zotico luxuriated on a sofa decorated with nymphs doing things The Ghost would rather not imagine. Two easy chairs flanked the sofa, and a table in the middle of the room was covered in breakfast food. A woman stood on the opposite side of the room with her back to him. She was studying a tapestry. "Do you think this is even possible?" she asked of the act the tapestry depicted.

Zotico waved his hand dismissively. "I'm sure it is. Those who worship Aphrodite are quite talented." The priest looked at The Ghost. "But considering how quickly you arrived, I take it you didn't avail yourself of their expertise. I assure you, young Chrysante can—"

"I didn't come here to 'avail' myself," he snarled. "I came to tell you I may not be able to take the job after all."

"You what?" The young woman whirled around. The Ghost gasped and hurriedly bowed. Last time The Ghost had seen her, Princess Acantha had been a gangly girl of fourteen with a fondness for horses. Now, she'd filled in her womanly shape. She was tall, with dark hair flowing around her head, deep set eyes, and an extremely narrow nose. "You would refuse to do a service for your queen?"

The Ghost blinked. "I hadn't heard of your father's death."

"He's not dead yet," Zotico answered for her. "But I'm sure shortly you will help spread the good news. The monster has ruled for far too long, and at the rate he's going, he soon won't have any heirs left. He had the last of his sons executed just last month."

The princess glared at The Ghost. "How long before he decides I, too, am a threat?"

"A true lover of his country wouldn't let such atrocities continue," Zotico said. "Besides our land will be plunged into chaos if he dies without an heir. We'd be completely vulnerable to those heart-eating fiends."

The Ghost sickened as he remembered the sound of the Massossinan officer taking a bite out of Phelix's heart. But it wasn't the thought of the Massossinan menace that moved him. He thought of the children starving in the streets and of the Salome he'd known when he worked as his father's assassin.

You could tell a lot about a person by the way they treated animals. When The Ghost had been the king's assassin, his cover was as assistant master of the horse. Salome had been brutal to his horses. The Ghost had spent countless hours doctoring the injuries the prince inflicted on his beasts and in calming their agitation after he'd ridden them. But his most vivid memory of Salome involved the young stable boy, Paulos.

Paulos hadn't been quite right in the head. He was slow catching onto things and needed any order explained slowly and carefully before he was sure what to do. But once he understood, he was reliable, and he was always smiling. The Ghost had never known how the lad had gotten a place in the king's stables, but he assumed he was the bastard of someone important.

The Ghost had been on an errand for the king and had just finished cleaning the blood from under his fingernails. As he was returning to the stables, Prince Salome and some of his hanger-ons—Salome didn't have any true friends—were leaving. Salome had laughed. "That will teach him to obey his lord and master."

The Ghost had assumed the prince was referring to his stallion, who had developed an intense fear of Salome and resisted all of Salome's attempts to control him. But when The Ghost entered the stables, it wasn't Aquafire the others were gathered around. The Ghost pushed through the stable hands to find Paulos staring sightlessly at the ceiling with bloody stumps where his hands and feet used to be. Blood dripped onto Paulos's face, and The Ghost looked up. The missing appendages hung above him.

"Dear Gods, what happened?" he asked.

One of the stable hands lifted his head from the carnage. His face was white, and his entire body shook. "You know Paulos. He didn't get the prince's horse saddled fast enough."

The Ghost had wanted to kill Salome then and there, and he should have. Frare had been a horrible tyrant, but Salome made his father look like a saint. He clenched his fists. *Damn all of Massossina to the seven hells! I don't owe her anything.*

He berated himself for his initial hesitation to take the job. He'd hesitated when he should have killed his daughter's enemy, and he couldn't bear to think of the pain that had caused. He wouldn't fail another young woman who should be sitting on a throne. He'd keep his promise to the Massossinan woman, but she could wait a day or so. And who knew, maybe he'd be lucky, and she wouldn't be there when he got back.

"When do you want it done?"

"As soon as possible."

"Tell me your father's habits, as thoroughly as you can."

Zotico gestured to the table. "Please, let us do this over breakfast."

The Ghost and Acantha seated themselves in the easy chairs on opposite sides of the breakfast table. Princess Acantha poured herself a glass of wine and sipped it as she detailed her father's routine. She ate nothing. "He has everything tasted before he eats or drinks. He wears amulets protecting him for all kinds of magic, and he has guards with him constantly, except at night when he sleeps with two large boarhounds. They'd tear a man to shreds at the slightest provocation."

Excitement built in The Ghost as he continued to ask questions and a plan formed in his mind. "I'll need the livery of a palace servant," he said. He closed his eyes and savored the rush. If he was destined to be a killer, he might as well enjoy it.

* * *

After leaving the temple district, The Ghost went to a nearby apothecary. The man behind the counter looked at his weapons warily. "Can I help you?"

The Ghost nodded and rattled off a list of ingredients.

The man frowned. "There's only one thing you could be making with that lot—Uttvos serum." Uttvos serum was a powerful sleeping potion, one The Ghost had made frequent use of. He preferred to kill no one but the target.

The Ghost put menace in his eyes. "Is that any concern of yours?"

The man shrugged. "No, but I could save you the trouble. I have some already made up." The man took out a vial containing a thick liquid. "First class quality. Knock out your strongest stallion so you can castrate it without the least fuss."

The Ghost nodded in acknowledgment. "I prefer to make my own." Only in that way could he ensure the proper strength.

The man shrugged and assembled the ingredients.

Next, The Ghost went to a second-hand clothier and bought two gowns for Brigitta. He thought he could guess her size, but he was unsure what colors and style to choose. Just what class had Brigitta been in before she'd been enslaved? He settled on two wool dresses—one a midnight blue and the other an emerald green, both with minimal embroidery. He also bought a black cloak with a large hood and a veil like those worn by all respectable women in Saloyna. He hoped Brigitta liked his choices. He'd never purchased clothing for a woman before.

When he returned to the Green Sandpiper, the Massossinan woman was asleep in the bed. He set the package containing his purchases beside her and quietly began making the serum over the fireplace. He made it extra strong on account of the boarhounds. As he stirred, he played over in his mind his intended trek through the palace and King Salome's death at his hand. Part of him thrilled at the idea of Salome's life in his hands. The rest of him knew his excitement meant his soul was forever lost.

He'd come back to Saloyna to take up his former profession because it was the country that had turned a simple stable groom into an assassin whose reputation spanned the world. Still, he wondered, *Holy Sulis, Mother of us all, could Ahearn have taken a path that didn't leave a pile of corpses in his wake? Or was the choice taken from him when a naïve young queen chose him as her lover?*

ABOUT THE AUTHOR

Jamie began writing stories about the man from Mars when she was six, and she never remembers wanting to be anything other than a writer. Everyone told her she needed a back-up plan, so she pursued a Ph.D. in American literature, which she received in 1998. She started teaching writing and literature at Auburn University. One day in the midst of writing a piece of literary criticism, she realized she'd put her true passion on the backburner and neglected her muse. The literary article went into the trash, and she began the book that was to become *The Goddess's Choice,* which was published in April 2012. Her other novels include *The Soul Stone, The Ghost in Exile, The Shattered Throne,* and *The Bull Riding Witch.* In addition, she has published a novella, *Demons in the Big Easy,* and a collection of short stories, *Blood Cursed and Other Tales of the Fantastic.* Her short fiction has also appeared in the anthologies--*Urban Fantasy* and *Of Dragons & Magic: Tales of the Lost Worlds*—and in *Bards & Sages, The World of Myth, A Writer's Haven,* and *Short-story.me.* She claims she writes about the fantastic… and the tortured soul. Her poor characters have hard lives. She lives in Auburn, Alabama, with her husband and three cats. She still teaches writing and literature at Auburn University. She is the mother of a grown son, who is a fantastic young man.

OTHER BOOKS BY JAMIE MARCHANT

The Kronicles of Korthlundia

    The Goddess's Choice, original edition (2012)
    The Soul Stone (2015)
    The Ghost in Exile (2016)

The Bull Riding Witch (2017)
Blood Cursed and Other Tales of the Fantastic (2016)--short story collection
Demons in the Big Easy: A Novella (2013)

Story Collections including her work
    Waiting for a Kiss: A Princess Fairy Tale Anthology (2017)
    Of Dragons & Magic: Tales of Lost Worlds (2014)
    Urban Fantasy (2013)
    Best Genre Short Stories Anthology #2: Short-Story.Me!
    (Volume 2) (2010)

www.ingramcontent.com/pod-product-compliance
Lightning Source LLC
Chambersburg PA
CBHW020213260626
47156CB00002B/357